To Jerry, my patie[illegible] and friend,

To the faithful hiking buddies who encouraged me up the infamous Chilkoot Trail: Suzi, Karma, Chris, (author), Karen, Joan, Natalie.

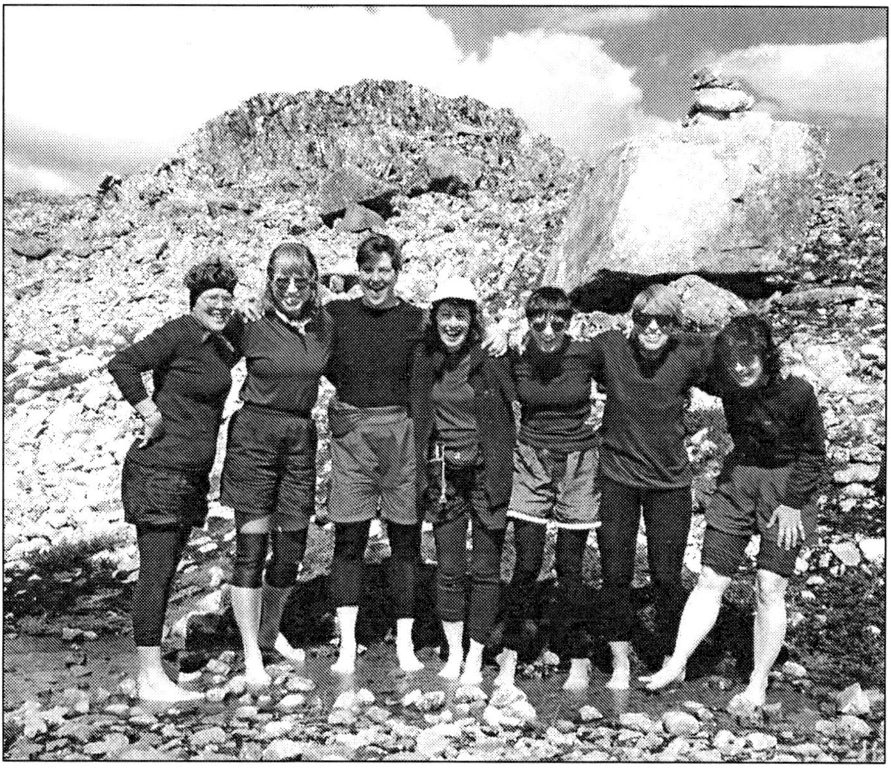

And especially to Linda B and Linda M who proofed and encouraged . . .

Thank you from the bottom of my heart!

Grace comes into the soul, as the morning sun into the world.

Thomas Adams

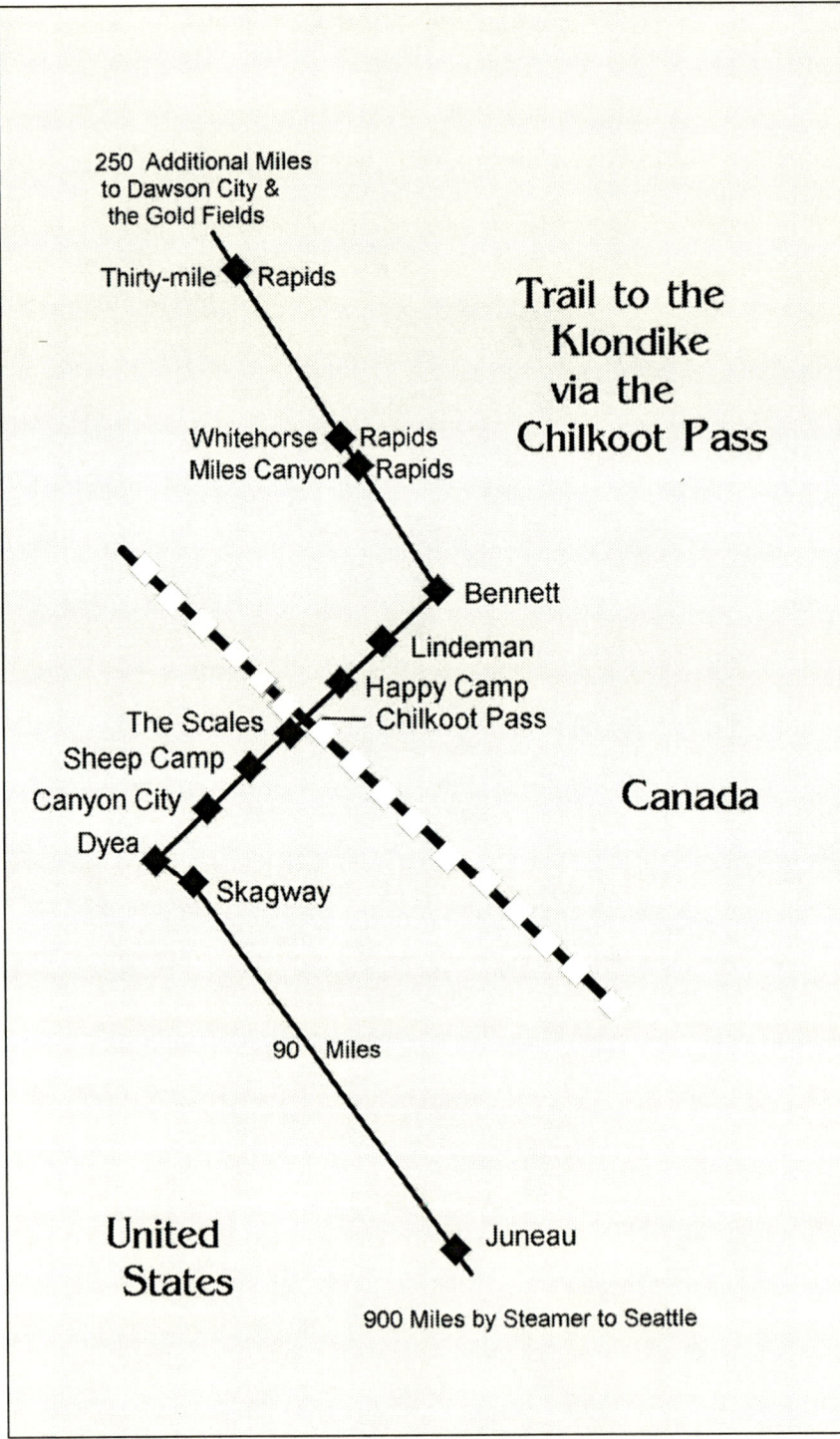

The Promise

Part One

Prologue

Benton, Wyoming, December 22, 1897

Her gown perfect, her dark hair lustrous in its upward sweep with antique pearl-edged combs, she was a picture of calm beauty that belied any emotion other than happiness, but Abigail Colton knew her stomach lay in a tangle of knots as she stepped into the warm room and her husband-to-be turned with a slow, seductive smile.

Listen to me carefully. Whatever you do now, you will have to live with this decision for the rest of your life. Do you understand?

Abby swallowed. Her mother's stern warning minutes before was hardly a comforting declaration. But then, it was to be expected since neither her mum or papa had demonstrated any enthusiasm for her and Dundee's request.

It could have been worse, she imagined. Her father could have said "no" and then what would she have done? Run off with Dundee as she had threatened?

"Here we are," Reverend Anderson declared as she stepped forward. "My, what a lovely bride we have this evening. Please," he added, "come right up beside your betrothed, my dear, and you may take his hand."

Abby did as she was told, at once feeling the warmth of Dundee's fingers as well as the intensity of his gaze. Her heart fluttered. His smile and the look of hunger in his eyes had a way of weakening her knees, and it was an uncommon thing for Abigail to feel this way.

Her twin, Jonathan, called her his tyrant, while her older brother Sam often referred to her as *that stubborn little critter*, although to her delight, her chubby little brother Taddy lovingly dubbed her Missy. They were a handful, the four of them, and perhaps that was why she and Jonathan were so determined to go.

They had to.

The ranch was about to go under and they all knew it.

She heard the exchange between Dundee and the Reverend, the repetition of his vows as he held her steady beside him. She sensed the coarse texture of Dundee's jacket sleeve against her arm and wondered at the smooth feel of his hand wrapped about her own. It wasn't the touch of a rancher. Her father's hands, by comparison, were hard and calloused.

Abby glanced to her right, just beyond Dundee to where her mother and father stood, one blond and fair, the other dark and impassive—side by side as she'd seen them countless times. It was the look of two who shouldered life as a team.

She turned her focus back to the brown eyes beside her, twinkling and almost mischievous as he looked at her.

She and Dundee would be like that, wouldn't they?

Dundee had verve, an excitement about him, money. He would help her rescue the ranch with his plan. They, too, would be a team.

"Repeat after me, Abigail."

She nodded. "Yes."

"I, Abigail, take thee Dundee Andrews to be my wedded husband . . ."

Abby repeated the words offered, phrase upon phrase, her voice sounding somewhat odd in its huskier-than-normal tone as she repeated the continuing vows.

". . . till death do us part."

". . . till death do us part."

"So help me God."

"So help me God."

Oh, Lord, please let it be so.

Chapter One

Abby wiped her mouth on a towel and moaned. Taking a deep breath, she steadied her body as she clung with shaky hands to the edge of the dressing table. When at last her legs stopped trembling, she wiped her mouth then tossed the cloth over the basin filled with the remnants of breakfast and stepped back. The moment her hips eased onto the rumpled bedcovers, she heard a light knock on the door.

Dundee? Could it possibly be?

She looked up with a start. "Who is it?"

"It's me, Abby. Are you all right?"

"Yes, Jon. I'll be fine."

"Abby, we need to talk. May I come in?"

She wiped her hands along the folds of her dress and gazed thoughtfully at the door. "If you must," she said weakly. "Come in."

The moment he stepped inside, a frown firmly planted on his face, she looked down to the flowered rug at her feet. They didn't need to talk. She knew what he was going to say, but she also knew what her response would be. "No. I'm not going back."

"Be reasonable, Abby. You're sick!"

"I'm not dying from some strange illness, Jon. I'm simply to be a mother."

"You're certain of it?"

"Fairly so."

"Then all the more reason you should go back to Wyoming. The North Country at this time of year is not good for a woman, not even one like you, and now . . ."

"How long can we wait?"

Jon shrugged as he walked closer and sat in the chair near her bed.

"Lord but it smells in here," he muttered with a shake of his head. "But before I call for a chambermaid, I need to tell you some bad news."

She glared at him. "So the disappearance of one's husband is good news then I take it?"

Jon blinked. "You know I didn't mean that."

Abby sighed and closed her eyes. She wanted to tell him to get out, wanted to scream out her anger, but what good would it do? Fighting to keep her frustration under control, she opened her eyes and studied the serious look on her brother's face.

"What have you heard?"

When her twin brother removed his hat and fingered its brim a moment, Abigail felt a twinge of sorrow surge through her. It wasn't easy for him to sit around and wonder what happened, either. After all, it was Dundee who had contacted Jon long before they'd arrived at the ranch. It was friends of Dundee's family who had commissioned them to find an uncle's cache of gold. It was even Dundee who had made the plans to go to Seattle and then to the Yukon by way of Skagway. And now, Dundee had simply disappeared.

"Well," Jon said slowly, "I've done a little more leg work and think it best to tell you what I know. First of all, I found out that Dundee's been gambling. And to make matters worse, I'm afraid he made some foul enemies along the way. Everyone I talked to was pretty tight-lipped, but it appears that he still owes money to one very onerous gambler in town."

Abby felt a tight knot forming in her stomach. She stared at her brother. "You're certain?" she whispered. "Who told you this?"

"I was showing a photo around, the one from your marriage but with you cut out of it, when a bartender at a fancy eatery told me I ought not to do that. He was certain Dundee had been gambling in the upstairs room above his establishment a few days ago and whispered to me that there had been some trouble." Jon gave her a long thoughtful look.

"I didn't mention this to you earlier, but yesterday I discovered that near a third of our money is gone."

As a deep ache filled her chest, Abby reached for the edge of the bedside table. She felt dizzy. Her stomach roiled. "Oh, Dundee," she moaned. "What have you done?"

"Listen, I hate having to tell you this. It's been hard enough for me to wait around myself, wondering where he is and all. But Abby, if he owes people of influence, then we may have to leave this hotel, and soon. Should they find out that you're in town, and that Dundee has some funds in the bank, then all our finances may very well disappear—or worse."

Abby closed her eyes. Her head pounded. She envisioned her husband's slow smile and wondered. How could he take such chances? How could he fritter away their money when they barely had enough and leave them in such a strait?

He wouldn't. Would he?

Yet hadn't she known that something was amiss. Hadn't she heard that small voice inside her mind? The looks he'd given her, the nights out, the passion and then the rejection when she'd been ill.

Oh Lord, what now? Abby could barely breathe.

"Jon, I . . ."

Jon rose to his feet and placed a broad hand on her shoulder. "I'm sorry," he said. "You're as white as a sheet, Abby. Do you want me to find a chambermaid and give you a few minutes?"

Abby leaned her head against his arm and shook her head. "No . . . no, I'll be all right. Just give me a moment." She gulped in a breath of air and released it slowly before looking up at him. "What are we to do now?"

He gave her shoulder a slight squeeze then dropped his hand and stepped back. "For starters," he said, "I've made arrangements to board elsewhere. I want to get out of this establishment as soon as possible. I checked for an earlier steamer to Skagway, but they're booked up full, so unfortunately, our March fifteenth passage is still the earliest opportunity to leave."

He paused, looking at her intently. "I'm figuring the best thing for us to do is withdraw that money from the bank then lay low while we wait for the steamer. I'll keep my eyes and ears open and see if I can find out more about Dundee. Meantime, we'll continue to purchase our supplies and be ready. He'll be back."

"But how will he find us?"

"He knows when we planned to depart, and so I listed us as Mr. and Mrs. Jon Colton. If he asks about me, he'll find us."

"So does that mean you'll agree to let me go?"

"Can I stop you? Would you consider returning to Wyoming?"

"No."

Jon sighed. "Listen, you might think you're conditioned by the years of hard work on the ranch, but this is different. You're not riding herd over some cattle this time. You're walking miles, and it'll be spring thaw. You know what that's like in the mountains. Besides, from all the information I gathered, the weather from Alaska's coast through the pass is wet and cold, not to mention the fact that the trail will hold unsavory characters and there will be hundreds of miles to float on the Yukon waterways. You understand?"

"How long have you known me, Jonathan?"

She faced him squarely, watching as he studied her with that familiar, serious gaze. At last, he looked away, but she knew he was speaking truthfully. She would need to be steady on her feet and able to work. She would be worthless to him sick like this.

"I don't think the sickness will last," she mumbled. "We won't leave until March fifteenth?"

"With the look of that crowded steamship dock, that's the earliest."

"I'll be better by then, Jon. I promise."

He frowned. "We'll see. But for now, you need to start packing while I find a maid for you." Jon started for the door then turned back. "One more thing," he said. "I'm being extra conservative with what money we have left, and so the room I secured for us is modest at best. With the horde of humanity in this city, I was lucky to even find one. I listed us as Abigail and Jon Colton, as I did on the steamer, and figured you can have the bed. I'll throw some gear on the floor." He hesitated. "You certain you want to do this?"

Abby tried to keep the quiver from her voice. "Yes."

"All right. Can you be ready to leave within the hour? The sooner the better. Don't want anyone coming after you or what money we have left."

Though numb with worry, Abigail managed to nod. "I'll hurry," she said.

After Jon left the room, Abby rose slowly to her feet. With a sigh, she reached for her hairbrush and started to place it in her small travel bag when her eyes came to rest on a few coins lying on the dresser. A shiver ran up her spine when she recalled Dundee removing them from his pocket a mere three night's ago. In frustration, she reached out and scooped them into her hand, but at the cold, hard feel of their surface against her palm, tears began to form beneath her eyelids.

With a sob, Abigail spun around and heaved the coins across the room. Like hail in a sudden storm, they skittered across the floorboards and pounded against the wall, and as they came to rest, Abby buried her face in her hands.

He couldn't love her and do this! Not really. She wondered if he ever loved her or just *lusted* for her. And with the thought, hot tears rushed down her cheeks.

Was Jon right? Should she admit defeat and go home? Maybe this time she should listen to his advice instead of being that same young and willful Abigail. The one her mother had tried to warn—the one who refused to listen.

Sucking in a deep breath, Abby swiftly wiped the moisture from her cheeks and started for her trunk against the far wall. In her mind, she had little choice.

She couldn't go back to Wyoming. Not now.

Not yet.

Not this way.

Chapter Two

He shivered and drew the blanket against him tighter. Though fully clothed and in dry garments, there seemed to forever be a damp chill in air. He was tired of the damp and cold. But he was alive. Somehow, Lady Luck still remained at his side. But this time, if not for those two fisherman rowing away from the dock, for their willingness to take him to the Hampton, then things might have been altogether different.

His father despised his luck. *Luck is for the no account*, he had sternly warned. The successful man, his father, always accusing—he had never lived up to the old man's expectations. Would he ever?

With a grunt, Dundee rolled to his side. It had been a close one. Had the thugs been a bit faster, a little braver, he'd have been done for. But he was a fair swimmer, and he had not hesitated. For a moment or two, he had wondered if he should have remained on the dock and simply fought it out. The slap of the water's hard, frigid surface had left him breathless for what seemed like an eternity, until instinct kicked in, and then in the shadows of the pier, he'd somehow managed to slip away from them.

Dundee tried to clear his mind. It did little good to think on it again.

As he drew his legs up and adjusted his body into the stiff mat beneath him, he considered what lay ahead. The captain of this miserable wreck of a ship was nearly hijacking him for every cent he had, but at least the prospects didn't appear to be as bleak as they might have been. He'd be untouchable now, considering the distance of their destination, and though he wasn't sure what would come next, somehow he'd find a way.

He thought of Abby and Jon. If he was any judge of character and need—and for the most part he was, given that he was a winner at the tables—then he was certain they would go on. Whether or not he would be able to catch up to them, or whether or not he even wanted to, was the critical question. And for right now, he didn't have an answer.

For the most part, he didn't have a choice.

Hawaii.

It had been a rather tantalizing surprise when the captain had spoken of their destination. The sugar plantations of Kauai. He'd heard about them.

Most likely he'd be able to find work, certainly enough to earn steerage to Seattle and on to Skagway, if that's what he wanted. He thought of Clarence and Margaret Smythe and their generous proposal. Half of their inherited gold had the potential to be a lot of money, if it could even be found. There was always that big *if.* He was a gambler, but only if his instincts told him something would pay out.

And things had changed.

For now, he'd have to simply go with the tides of life. Experience had taught him that it did little good to swim upstream anyhow.

Hawaii. The more Dundee thought about it, the more relaxed he became.

Chapter Three

Carson Stuart stood looking at the pile of goods bundled at his feet, and then counted the number of bags filled with food, clothing, and assorted gear once again. Satisfied everything was all there, he turned his attention to the press of humanity gathered about him. At the far end of the dock, shipmates were busy hauling baggage of all sizes and shapes aboard the steamer where several other men stood shouting orders. Behind him, a crowd pressed ever forward, lugging their goods toward that perceived gangplank of opportunity. To his observing eye, every man, woman and child appeared to be scrambling for a place to claim as his own.

They would soon be on their way, he and thousands more, whether on this steamer, the *Willamette*, or others to follow, and all with high hopes for what awaited their destiny.

Would it be riches as so many headlines promised or merely a life of harsh endurance on a hellish adventure? Only time would tell.

Carson studied the faces of those around him, some stoic, some impatient, others filled with an obvious eagerness. As he watched them, he breathed in the aroma of brisk salt air and listened to the clamor of voices, from deep to high. He was being paid to be an observer. Paid, of all things, to do what he enjoyed most in life. To be given the opportunity to write about this stirring rush to the Klondike was excitement enough, but when he considered the opportunity ahead for his own future, he knew the pounding of his heart beat in rhythm to the action around him, that his emotion was tuned to that same, hopeful longing. It was a pitched emotion, touching him right to his very core.

As his eyes scanned the crowded dock, he began to wonder about James. He hoped his friend wouldn't be so foolish as to return too late. Without a doubt, if Jimmy was there, he would see him. Jimmy was as tall and broad-shouldered a man as any he'd ever known. He'd be hard to miss, but for the moment, Carson couldn't spot him. He shook his head, remembering the look on Jimmy's face when, not more than ten minutes ago, they had dragged their luggage as far forward as possible and then Jimmy had paused, wiped his brow, and stared out at the steamer with a slack-jawed groan.

I'm a big man, he'd quipped. *A fella could starve on an itty-bitty ship like this, what with it packed plumb full of humanity!* And with that, James had headed back toward shore, muttering something about a food vendor beyond.

Deep inside, Carson was grateful that Jimmy had agreed to come along. They shared a friendship that went to their early days as young boys, but the past few years had been a long haul for them. After Carson had entered college, James had remained in their small town working at the Stuart Flour and Grist. They continued to have good times when he came back and they worked together summers and holidays, that is, until his father's business had floundered. That had changed everything. He grimaced at the thought. It still angered him that a man with his father's reputation could not find a single bank to help carry them through.

Gold.

The whole country needed more of it.

And yet, in some uncanny way, the very need for it—and the very lack of it—had given him new opportunity as well as a chance to trek into a land that intrigued every fiber of his being. And, if he could make good on this adventure, if he could capture the feel of this gold rush on paper—offer a glimpse of history in the making—it might very well embolden a tenuous new career. One he very much wanted to have.

As he continued to search for Jimmy, Carson's eyes were drawn to a young couple moving closer to him. The young man, strong in his movements, heaved two bags toward the feet of a square-backed woman who came to a standstill within reach of him. When she dropped her two bags and then stood staring at them as if they might come alive any minute, Carson found his curiosity rising. Her face, somewhat pale and stark against the depth of color in her hair, held a troubled expression as she looked up and gazed across the water to the city beyond. Like he, she appeared to be looking for someone. The gentleman beside her continued to shuffle two more crates forward, and then removed a pack from his back and glanced around.

Carson smiled. "You think our goods will be sufficient for the madness?"

The young fellow gave him a brief but intense appraisal, carefully measuring the stranger who'd spoken, then offered a slow smile and a quick nod. "Madness would be a good word. Never been in such a mess like this before."

Carson noted the traveler's tanned and hardy appearance and recognized a fellow outdoorsman. Although he lived in an area not far from a bustling California city, Carson's family prized their long treks into the mountains, and if looks could determine it, he was certain that this young adventurer would be as comfortable on the edges of civilization as he was.

"You from around here?"

"Nope. From Wyoming."

"Well, Mister Wyoming, my name's Carson Stuart. I'm from a small town between San Francisco and the Sierras. Nice to meet you." Carson extended his hand, pleased to feel the energy and firmness of the responding grip. He liked meeting people, especially ones that held an intelligent and healthy look about them.

"Pleasure's mine. My name's Jon Colton."

When the woman standing alongside turned to face him, Carson was struck by the intensity of her sky-blue eyes. Judging from the cold stare she gave him, however, he doubted she approved of their chance meeting. Jon seemed to hesitate and then waved a hand her direction.

"This is my, uh . . . Abigail. Abigail Colton."

If looks could kill, Carson figured Jon was in trouble, but then the look passed and she offered Carson a small, polite nod. He found his hand reaching for the fedora on his head in one swift motion. *My Abigail*, whatever that meant, was beautiful in a most uncommon way.

"I'm pleased to meet you," he said.

With her dark hair and high cheekbones, she held a noble appearance and yet her face, like Jon's, carried a hint of the outdoors as well. Her complexion, though somewhat pale about the eyes, was not pasty white like that of the city ladies he'd known. In that manner, she reminded him of Josie, his sister.

"Are you a part of this adventure, or are you too wise for such things?" Carson asked. He was suddenly curious if she was coming aboard or merely waiting to see Jon off. He gave her an encouraging smile, but to his surprise, there was little change in her countenance.

She blinked. "I suppose it may not be the wisest decision I've ever made, but yes, I am to be a part of the madness as well." After eyeing him carefully, she turned away, cutting off any other questions he might have, and once more gazed toward Seattle's skyline.

Carson shrugged off her unfriendly gesture but was surprised to note how the young man's face was reddening. He was curious about the subtle messages of misgivings he saw between them. Were they in disagreement about taking the journey?

No. He thought it was probably something more. He could sense it. He wondered what it was, the death of a child or the loss of a farm and home, like so many were enduring these days?

Carson cleared his throat then pointed at Jimmy who was hurrying forward through the throng. "Here comes my friend, James Patten," he said, "the man who is always hungry. I think he felt a near panic when he saw the *Willamette* so loaded with folks. It sent him scurrying for more vittles."

Jon smiled, his deep brown eyes twinkling with amusement. "Had an uncle like that," he said. "Happiest fellow alive, as long as you kept him well fed."

"That's it," Carson nodded. "And what with nearly eight hundred boarding this old girl, I hope he's brought enough to share."

"Eight hundred? Is that right? I hadn't heard the numbers." Jon released a low whistle before turning to appraise the ship. "I hope there's enough room for us all. I'm not the best swimmer."

Carson laughed. "Wouldn't do much good in this ocean anyhow. We'll be plowing through frigid water while heading north, although the Archipelago passage is protected by islands and the going shouldn't be too rough. In fact, I've heard it can be a grand trip, providing we don't have any storms."

"Well, then," Jon said slowly, "let's hope for fair skies."

After Jimmy strode up and Carson introduced him, several shipmates reached for their gear, and the four of them, along with the swelling crowd nearby, began shuffling up the gang plank and into the mass of folks already aboard. Once on deck, Jimmy grabbed Carson's arm and pointed to the stern of the boat.

"Let's watch," he said.

Following a quick nod, he and Jimmy slipped into a small opening between shoulders near the deck railing. For several minutes, Carson drank in the look of the packed docks jammed full with men and women, watching with curiosity as the shipmen began to cast off the heavy lines. When the steamer at last sounded a long whistle and the throng of wellwishers started to wave and shout, Carson heard the sound of a female voice in the melee repeating a phrase he'd heard often in Seattle.

"Bring me a stocking full of gold!" she screamed. "Bring me a stocking full of gold!"

After making their way down the narrow hallway, Jon and Abby pushed open a door and stepped into a tiny, dark room. Jon tossed their luggage on the bottom bunk of a two-berth cabin while she stood in silence and looked around their cramped space.

To her dismay, it smelled of rotting timbers and old men. She would stay here only if she were sleeping or ill. Fighting back her tears, Abby swallowed.

"You feeling sick?"

"No," she said, "not at the moment, but just in case, let's find some fresh air."

Jon nodded and turned for the door. As they reached the aft deck and began to push through the crowd, Abby grabbed Jon's arm. They were packed into the area like cattle in a rail car at loading time. Feeling the press of bodies around her, Abby's stomach began to churn. It was with complete relief when Jon managed to find a small clearing near a pile of crates and drew her in front of him. Though she'd been feeling much better this week, she imagined the tension of the day had done little to help the nausea.

In an effort to keep her mind in a positive state, she gazed out into the harbor where two large cargo ships and a small fishing trawler passed by. After several minutes, a group of men in front of them walked off, and in spite of all good intentions, she found herself at the rail and looking back to Seattle. As Abby studied the disappearing buildings and docks, she gripped the cold iron railing tight within her hands.

Dundee! Oh, dear God.

She'd been terribly angry and worried over the last few weeks, helpless to do anything but pray that he was still alive. Abby began to tremble. Was there a chance that he'd merely run away? Or was he in truth dead, as Jon had decided was a distinct possibility. At the thought of it, her legs grew weak.

No. She wouldn't believe it. She couldn't. Dundee had such verve. He was funny and charming, a man with a zest for living. If anyone could make it, he could. Taking a deep breath, Abby closed her eyes against the rising fear.

At the feel of Jon's arm slipping around her shoulders, Abby looked up. Seeing the concern in her brother's eyes, she forced her lips into a tight, brave smile. But when she turned her gaze once again to the distant city, hot drops of moisture rolled from her eyes as if they had a will all their own.

Chapter Four

"You seem content enough," Carson laughed.

"Couldn't be happier. Eggs and flapjacks? I never expected it."

"And two helpings, no less. I would hope you've left enough food for those still waiting." Carson nodded to the long line of people waiting to be fed, though as far as he could tell, there appeared to be ample breakfast for everyone. As he glanced along the line of waiting customers, he saw the young couple he'd met yesterday entering the dining hall.

"You about finished?" he asked quickly.

"Who? Me?" Jimmy blinked, his hazel eyes filling with concern.

"Yes, you. I see that Jon and Abigail Colton have just walked in. Maybe we should offer them our seats."

Jimmy turned. "Handsome couple."

Carson nodded, all the while remembering the scene he'd witnessed while the ship steamed out of the harbor yesterday. He'd been strolling along the deck when he noted the two of them standing by the rail. He'd thought to speak when he saw her look up into Jon's face. He'd been struck by the sadness he saw there, by the tears. Indeed, something was amiss in their lives.

"How do you do that?"

"Do what?" Carson glanced at him, puzzled.

"How do you remember the names of people like that? You only talked to them a few minutes, right? I think you have a gift."

Carson shrugged off Jimmy's comment and raised his hand, waving to them. He saw Jon bend to Abigail's ear, pointing, but she simply shook her head, said something briefly to him, and then turned for the door. As Jon smiled and stepped toward them, Carson found his immediate sense of disappointment to be a bit surprising. It wasn't like him to feel any interest in an attached woman, though as he thought about it, he wondered if they were married or not. Jon had not introduced her as his wife.

"Hello again." Carson said as Jon walked up. "Are you hungry? You can sit here if you'd like. I'm finished." He rose from his seat and then motioned to the door with a jerk of his head. "Is she coming back? I think Jimmy's just about done here."

With a resigned look, Jon shook his head. "Don't think so. She's feeling poorly."

"Oh. Sorry to hear that. Well, grab a seat." Carson waved to Jimmy to remain seated while he stepped to one side and leaned against the ship's sidewall. "Appears we're well on our way into the Inside Passage," he said. "You still excited about the adventure?"

Jon nodded. "Some, though I hear that it will be a jumble of commotion and confusion when we get to Skagway. Not looking forward to that."

Carson gave him a wry smile. "I've heard that said as well. Think you'll head out as soon as we arrive?"

"Not sure. I was told to look for a certain packer when we get there. Have a map that was in a Seattle newspaper last year. It shows two trails to Bennett. Abby's in . . . uh . . . in a bit of a health condition, but since she's a good horsewoman, I thought we'd pack up the Skagway Trail. How about you?"

"Actually, I've been hired by the *Seattle Post-Intelligencer* to stay on the Chilkoot Trail out of Dyea. The newspaper did an earlier piece on the Chilkoot back in early ninety-seven, so I'm following up, plus writing about the current progress of the stampede all the way to Dawson City." He shrugged. "In my effort to research the situation, I was told on good authority that the White Pass out of Skagway, or the Skagway Trail as you call it, will be the route of the future. It's already reported that a railroad may have backing and will soon create a new way into Canada."

Jon's eyebrows rose. "You don't say? Now that's a piece of news."

"Well, not quite. I don't believe the dust has settled yet on who's to do it."

Jimmy drank down the last of his coffee and stood. "Well, guess I best be giving up my chair for someone else. Good to see you again, Jon."

Jon nodded with a smile.

Jimmy patted his stomach as he turned to Carson. "You coming? I think I'll get some fresh air."

"Be right along." Carson had more questions he wanted to ask Jon, but knowing there was a long line of diners, he instead offered a light salute and pushed off from the wall. "You have a nice day, Jon. Am sure we'll be seeing you around."

Jon started to say something in return, but just then a waiter brought over a platter of food and Carson saw Jon's words slip away as he reached for a plate of pancakes. With a knowing smile, he walked on. Maybe later he would ask this young Mr. Colton a few more questions. He was curious about what Jon knew regarding the trails into the Yukon. It never hurt to gain information and insights from whomever he could.

Carson stepped outside and looked around for Jimmy, but instead of spotting his red-headed friend's large frame, he saw Abigail Colton standing alone at the rail not far from the door. He hesitated, giving her slender form a quick scrutiny. He wondered if talking to her a bit would be prudent, and then quickly dismissed it when he considered her aloofness, her beauty, and the fact that Jon was occupied and he very well knew it.

Turning, he caught sight of Jimmy farther down the walkway. He was resting his shoulders against the outside wall of the dining room, lingering in the sunshine as he gazed off at the scenery. Thinking it best, Carson started for his friend.

Without a word, he leaned back against the wall alongside Jimmy and began to study the passing hillsides while the steamer moved slowly through a narrow channel of water between the mainland on the east and a large island on the west. Dense shrubbery hugged the island's rocky shore and mingled with the tall evergreens covering the hillsides. The landscape around them, he decided, held a richer tone of green than any he'd ever seen.

Though the ship had slowed for this narrow passage, Carson figured they were steaming north, for the most part, much faster than he'd anticipated. He remembered that it was near to a thousand miles from the Puget Sound to Skagway, which meant at least four more days of travel, and yet even knowing that there was plenty of time to formulate final plans, the recent talk with Jon started him to thinking.

Though he and Jimmy would be taking the Chilkoot Trail out of Dyea, he also needed to interview shop owners and various people in the infamous town of Skagway, the gateway town for the White Pass Trail. While there, it might be a good time to secure more gear and food, as well inquire about a packer to help carry his supplies to the pass. He wondered if finding one would present more problems than he originally figured, especially when he considered how many steamers jammed with people were leaving the docks of Seattle these days.

As required by Canadian customs, he'd have to make certain that he and Jimmy each had two thousand pounds of supplies. And all this effort was just a start. Once they made it off the pass and down into the Yukon River system, they'd have even more issues since floating the Yukon to Dawson was another matter entirely.

He hoped to arrive at Lake Bennett at least a month before the thaw, giving them time to build a boat for their passage into the goldfields, but he also wanted to be there long enough to get a sense of what it was like to winter in such an area. It was his goal to give a thorough report on any aspect of the story he'd been hired to tell.

He sighed.

Jimmy looked over at him and smiled. "Mighty big sigh."

Carson chuckled. "Just thinking, I guess."

"About your plans?"

Carson nodded. "Wish I had a few more facts. Not too many folks, except those who've lost everything or turned tail, came out this winter. Most of the information I was able to glean isn't too current, especially about the status of the camps in Canada's high country."

"Well," Jimmy shrugged, "guess we'll know soon enough."

Carson bent the brim of his hat down low over his eyes and nodded. "Yes, soon enough."

"It's a strange land," Jimmy murmured. "Nice and green, but looks fairly wild and overgrown with every plant imaginable."

"Yeah, I was noticing that."

Carson scanned the mountains that loomed up high in the north horizon and realized that not all of their adventure would be fun and games, in fact, maybe not much of it at all, especially if he couldn't find a packer. Still, he felt drawn to the beauty and wildness of it. He knew from the information he did have in his guide sheets that the terrain between Dyea and the Yukon River would compete with any peaks and valleys in the Sierras.

"James, my friend," Carson drawled. "This is going to be the adventure of a lifetime." Indeed, he could feel the truth of his words in his bones.

Abby stood quietly, breathing in the freshness of the ocean air. Though she'd become somewhat chilled by the breeze, watching the lush green forests pass by was far preferable to being trapped in the dining hall with its nauseating aromas. She'd never realized how much everything, from food to people and even the walls of a room, could have such strong odors as they did now. No doubt, her sensitivity was a result of being with child, for by now, she'd become certain of her condition.

Abby was struck by the thought. *A baby. Her and Dundee's baby.* And as near as she could estimate, it would be born sometime in September.

With a shiver, Abby drew her coat around her more closely as she tried to envision the days ahead. Dundee had planned for the three of them to take no more than a year to find the whereabouts of Dan Fogherty's cache, secure it, and then return south to give it to the Smythe family and collect their half. With any luck, she and Jon could do the same, but how would she ever manage those last few months of awkwardness, not to mention the birth of a child? She could barely even remember Taddy being born. She'd been young, perhaps only ten at the time. With so very little experience or information, she could only pray that some medical knowledge would be available in Dawson, or at the very least, a woman to help her.

"Are you still out here? Aren't you cold?"

At the sound of Jon's voice, Abby turned to see her twin walk up beside her. She shrugged. "A little perhaps, but anything's better than the smells in that room."

"You need to eat, Abby."

"Yes, I know, but I couldn't stand being in there. I felt like I was one of our steers going off to slaughter."

"How about I go back and ask for a plate for you. I'm certain they'll let you eat out here, especially if I tell them about your condition."

Abby smiled. *Her condition.* What was she, not quite three months along now? Talking about her condition seemed so far removed from reality that she could barely believe it.

"Abby?"

"Yes. Yes, I suppose that's best. I'll wait here."

Within minutes, Jon returned with food and a young boy carrying a chair as well. She offered her thanks as she reached for the plate.

"Find a better place for breakfast, did you?"

Abby looked up to see the two men they'd met on the dock before boarding yesterday.

"Hello," her brother said brightly. "Abby, you remember Carson Stewart and James Patten. We met them at the dock."

"Yes, I do." Abby nodded before taking a small bite of her food.

"Took some talking to get her to eat," Jon said, as if to explain her eating on the deck, "but she needs to take care of herself."

The man called Carson examined her with a quick, appraising glance before he offered a warm smile. His deep hazel eyes held a gentleness and intelligence, she decided. As her gaze turned to the man beside him, she was struck again by his height and stout frame. He looked as if he could carry the weight of three men. Abby gave them a feeble smile and turned back to her food.

Though the two gentlemen seemed friendly enough, she'd had her fill of men ogling her recently, what with all the youthful, masculine companions aboard ship. Most likely, she'd have to take that kind of thing all in stride over the months ahead. What she preferred to see standing above her was a friendly female, not two more of this gender.

"Looks like we may be approaching a small storm," Carson said.

"I noticed that," Jon answered. "Not too surprising. According to the youngster helping me with Abby's food, it's misty or raining most of the time in these parts, especially in March. In fact, he said it was still snowing some in Skagway. Are you planning to get to Lake Bennett before the thaw?"

"That's the idea," Carson said with a smile. "It's why I brought Jimmy here. He can do the work of two men, though he eats his way through any cash reserves one might have."

Jimmy seemed oblivious to his friend's comment and grinned at Jon. "You expecting to build a boat in Bennett like us?"

"We had originally planned to build one," Jon said, "but I may have to make some adjustments. I was told that I could likely find some help when I get there. Maybe I can pay a boat builder or hire a worker or two."

"Shoot, we'd be glad to help ya'."

As Abby watched the men above her, she thought she saw a flicker of surprise move through the hazel eyes of the man named Carson.

"Maybe it would work fine if we joined forces," Jimmy continued. "Do you plan to locate at Bennett or Lake Lindeman?"

"If we can get there soon enough and find a place to camp, I'm hoping Bennett." Jon responded. Abby heard the slight hesitation in her brother's voice. "I've heard there are some rough rapids out of Lindeman, so I'd prefer to build a boat farther downstream. Don't want to take any more risks than necessary with Abby and all."

"Sounds like a wise plan," Carson agreed, "though I've been told there will be hundreds of stampeders converging on Bennett for the thaw, and all of them eager to be the first down the river and into Dawson. I'm hoping the area won't be too chaotic." Carson shifted his weight, glancing first at Jimmy and back to Jon. "But," he said carefully, "if we can find one another, as Jimmy said, we could join forces to build a couple boats."

"Well, I sure do thank you for your offer. It just might be helpful."

As the steamship rounded an island and moved into open waters, Abby felt the cool breeze bearing down on them bringing with it a few drops of moisture. With a shiver, she reached out to touch Jon's arm. "I've eaten enough. I'm going inside since it's beginning to rain."

"Fine. I'll be right along. You want me to take your plate to the kitchen?"

"No, I'll do it. You might return the chair for me."

Jon nodded. "I'll take care of it."

Abby stood, offering a small smile. "Good-day, gentlemen," she said. But as she stepped forward, a rolling wave shifted the deck beneath her. When she reached out for support, she found a large arm directly in front of her.

"Here, ma'am, let me help you," Jimmy said. "It's a bit rocky at the moment." As Abigail took hold of his arm, the tall man continued. "I hope you don't mind me, Jon," he said, "just thought I'd help your pretty wife a bit." He gave her a broad smile.

Abby glanced back to her brother, wondering what to say.

Jon returned her glance with a questioning look of his own.

"Wife?" he said hesitantly. "I imagine I could be honest about it now, Abby."

She frowned. That was like Jon, too goodhearted to hold any dishonesty in his thinking, but what would it hurt to let them think she was his wife? They didn't owe these men anything, did they?

Peeved at the thought, Abby quickly found her balance and released Jimmy's arm, but as she headed for the door, she was dismayed to hear Jon's voice behind her.

"Actually," Jon said, "Abby isn't my wife. She's my sister."

Abby could feel the gape of the two strangers without even bothering to look back.

Chapter Five

*For I am persuaded, that neither death, nor life, nor angels, nor principalities,
nor powers, nor things present, nor things to come,
Nor height, nor depth, nor any other creature,
shall be able to separate us from the love of God, which is in Christ Jesus,
our Lord.*
Romans 8:38-39

Abby closed her grandmother's soft leather-bound Bible and gently rubbed its worn cover. She thought about another verse in this same chapter of Romans, one she'd been given to memorize during confirmation, and one she'd been clinging to since she'd become certain that she was to have a baby. *And we know that all things work together for good to them that love God, to them who are the called according to his purpose.*

She sighed.

In her heart, she was certain that God had granted her the good sense to know that he offered grace and forgiveness, but beyond that, her life appeared to be simply growing in its complications. How would she handle the challenges ahead? If sorrow would be her lot, how would she deal with it, especially if her problems were a result of her own foolishness?

After all, she had chosen to marry Dundee and now to follow Jon. Was that His will? At this point, she was not as convinced of it as she'd been a mere month ago.

Abby stared at the Bible a moment longer then reached for her satchel and slid it inside. Her mum had given the Bible to her to take on the journey. Long ago, it had been a gift from her grandmother to her mother and then carried on a long journey from Missouri to Wyoming. *It had been a lifesaver*, her mother had said. Abby could only hope it would bring some sort of peace to her as well. And yet, until the past few weeks, it had remained in her luggage, unopened.

Abby stood and looked around. Though the room held few creature comforts, at least it had been shelter against the storms that had raged outside for the past four days, a place to rest after her retching had returned. Until this morning, she'd been certain that she would be worthless by the time they arrived in Skagway, but by the grace of God, today the skies had cleared, and now, after resting and bathing as best she could with a small basin of water, she felt her spirit somewhat restored. Thinking it time, Abby tied on her cape and reached for the door.

As she stepped out into the light of a cloudy but calm day, Abby was surprised to see Jon directly ahead. He was talking with a well-dressed young woman and the man named Carson Stuart. Jon turned as she approached.

"Well, well, if it isn't Abby. And looking much better, I might add." Jon smiled. "Abby, I'd like you to meet Miss Georgia Mulroy. Miss Mulroy, this is my twin, Abigail Colton."

"Very nice to meet you, Abigail." The woman, who looked to be about ten years her senior, gave Abby a surprisingly strong handshake.

"The pleasure is mine," Abby said.

Georgia looked to Jon. "A twin, you say? I'd never have guessed it."

"Strangers seldom do," Jon said. "Our mother is quite fair while our father is near to the opposite. I guess we're sort of a mix, Abby having the blue eyes and dark hair and me with the dark eyes and light hair."

He turned to Abby. "Miss Mulroy is a business woman in Dawson. She's on her way back to the Yukon after purchasing merchandise for her grand new hotel there."

Abby raised an eyebrow. "A grand hotel in Dawson?"

"Perhaps not as spectacular as some," Georgia said with a coy smile. "Still, I believe it will be an elegant place with the finest dining possible." She shrugged. "Of course, there are a variety of other establishments in the area, but it's my hope that nothing will compete with my new enterprise. I'm calling it the Grandview since it's located along the Yukon River."

Abby's eyes widened. "Goodness, that's wonderful news. I'm afraid I had a much, shall we say, harsher picture of the town of Dawson than you're giving me now." She looked at Jon. "If all goes well for us, perhaps we might even have a celebration at Miss Mulroy's before we leave Dawson."

Jon shrugged.

"That would please me very much," Georgia Mulroy added quickly, "and even if your adventures don't prove as prosperous as you'd hope, I want you to come by and let me give you a personal tour."

Abby smiled. "I would truly like that."

"Then, it's decided." Georgia gave Abby a decisive nod then turned to Carson. "When do you hope to have your story finished?"

"My plan is to send my editor several stories, do the report in stages, so to speak. I'll start by describing Alaska's coastal area as well as the hopes of the men and women along the Chilkoot Trail. The second submission will cover the river passage from Lake Bennett to Dawson. Then," he smiled, "hopefully, the third portion will cover the stories of a prospector's life in and around the Klondike."

"Only the prospector?" Georgia asked. Her voice held a soft, slight drawl.

"My assignment was such, but I'm confident, by the sound of your descriptions, certain people like yourself will add great interest to the Klondike tales. In fact, might I have an interview with you when I arrive in Dawson?"

"That would be my delight! Come see me when you arrive. Most everyone knows that my original lodge is located in Grand Forks, though most likely I won't be there since I'm working on the new place in Dawson. Either way, you can always find information on my whereabouts from the Bonanza mining office." She smiled. "Not wishing to brag, of course, but the year has been very good to me."

"So it seems. When did you decide Dawson was the place to be?" Carson asked.

"I had a business in Juneau, a rather interesting place in itself for a single woman," she said. "But early in ninety-seven, when news spread among the miners about strikes along the Yukon, I was certain that a fortune might be had as much in supplies and lodging as in the gold itself. So I set about it, moving goods into the area and building a hotel and some cabins. On the side, I also pursued some mining interests. So far, it has all proven to be well worth my effort."

Jon spoke up. "I've heard a rumor that at least a fourth of the people aboard this steamer are entrepreneurs like yourself rather than miners. Have you found that to be so?"

"Actually, I would guess that is true. I was completely surprised when I came out from Dawson a month ago. Since so many men and women are beginning to head for the interior of Canada, there has been a great increase in establishments all along the routes. And yet, I fear there are far too many hopefuls, merchants as well as the novice stampeder."

Thinking of the letter in her possession, Abby was suddenly curious. "Were there many miners in Dawson when you first arrived?"

"Mm," she said slowly, her dark eyes rolling a bit as she paused to consider. "Maybe only a hundred or so last spring, but by fall, I would guess they numbered in the thousands. When I left Juneau in the spring of ninety-seven, opportunities were plentiful. Many gold nuggets were being bandied about, some pokes better than others, of course, but when I built my first lodge in Grand Forks, land for a claim was still available on both Bonanza and Eldorado Creeks. Now, they have mostly been taken and land prices everywhere are proving to be dear. One building lot in Dawson recently sold for as high as twelve thousand dollars."

Jon whistled. Abby glanced at the stunned faces of Jon and Carson before shifting her attention back to the spirited woman who wore a stylish wool cap over chestnut-colored hair. Georgia Mulroy leaned forward a bit, as if to share the latest gossip.

"Though I believe potential mining opportunities are still waiting," she said, "what with the masses arriving constantly, I suspect that even claims above the creeks will soon be purchased at steep prices. So, if you want any land, you must check into circumstances quickly." She lightly pursed her lips then straightened. "Still and all, who knows where gold will be found. Nothing truly surprises me anymore."

With warmth radiating from her dark brown eyes, Georgia turned directly to Abby. "What are your plans, Abigail? Is it your desire to be a Cheechako gold seeker or an entrepreneur?"

"A Cheechako?" Abby stumbled over the word as she spoke.

Georgia laughed. "Yes, that's a newcomer, one who's not yet seen a winter."

Abby heard the shift in Georgia's voice, as if to issue a warning.

"To tell you the truth," Abby said, "I'm not sure how long we will stay. Jon has his plans and my hope is merely to support him." She smiled at her brother who held, in her estimation, the handsome and even features of their mother. "I'll simply do my best to help him recover what we can."

Georgia gave Jon a quizzical look. "Recover? That's an interesting choice of words. Well, I wish you luck."

Abby decided to take a chance and inquire further. "Miss Mulroy, have you ever heard of any miners by the name of either Dan Fogherty or C. R. Thorne?"

"No. I can't say that I have. But then, I know a few people who might know them. Are you looking for these men?"

"In a way, yes. Perhaps when Jon and I arrive in Dawson, I will come by and we can talk again. It's important that we locate Mr. Thorne or a lawyer named Arthur Gray. Have you heard of Mr. Gray?"

"Actually, I have heard that name," Georgia said carefully. "Sounds like you're involved in a bit of a mystery?"

Abby smiled. "You might say that."

Jon shuffled his stance, and though the movement was subtle, Abby knew he was concerned and said no more. Yet when the conversation ended with the arrival of Georgia's acquaintance coming to take her for dinner, Abby knew Miss Georgia had given her hope. Perhaps Dawson would be a bit more civilized than she'd envisioned, especially if the town had shops and fine eating establishments as well as other women about. And though Miss Mulroy's information certainly did not sound promising for incoming miners, they were, after all, not going to the Yukon for that reason.

With a sense of relief, Abigail took her brother's arm and followed Miss Georgia to the dining hall.

The last rays of sun gave a soft pink hue to the skyline as the *Willamette* edged against Skagway's long dock. With the equinox at hand, the days would soon lengthen rapidly here in the north, but for now, Carson knew that he and Jimmy would have little daylight left for unloading their gear and finding the hotel.

With the cacophony of voices and harbor activity swirling about him, Carson peered between the ship masts and smokestacks to where the beginnings of a small town stood in a narrow valley dwarfed by snowcapped mountains. Though the landscape appeared to be somewhat ominous in bearing, to his experienced eye, it at least held a hint of spring thaw to come.

He recalled his departure from San Francisco not more than a year before with the roundedness of the hills, the green, and the grand ships. And though this Skagway port held the familiar odors and sounds, he found the frenzy of the people milling about, as well as the chaotic assembly of tents, shacks and various city buildings in the distance, an altogether different experience. It was a far cry from any port town in his memory.

For the first time since he'd left Seattle, Carson decided that the harsh reality of this adventure was beginning to show its face. He wondered if his assignment might be more challenging than he imagined.

"In case we happen to find ourselves separated," Jimmy said beside him, "you say we're to stay at the *Grand Pacific* on Broadway?"

Carson shook his head. "No. You're thinking of the hotel in Dyea. Our rooms in Skagway are at the *Skagway Grand*, that's providing you can trust any hotel to hold a reservation in such conditions. I'd suggest that once we find our baggage, one of us heads for the hotel to make certain of our rooms before we haul anything to town."

"I'll stay with the goods," Jimmy said. "You go on, and here's hoping we've a room. Finding a bed at this hour might be trying."

Carson smiled. "We'll manage. Besides, we're only in Skagway two nights. Hopefully, just long enough to secure the rest of our supplies and give me time for an interview or two."

"Still thinking about interviewing that Soapy character?"

"That's my plan."

Jimmy shrugged. "Watch your backside."

Noting the scowl on his friend's face, Carson grinned. "When you hear so much good and bad about a person, you might as well go to the source and take a spin at finding the truth yourself."

Jimmy snorted. "Let him tell you all about his *good* life? Is that it?"

Carson shrugged. "I'll judge that later. First thing I have to do is meet him."

"You want me to keep a listening ear for some good stories?"

Carson nodded then stepped forward to the gangplank. "Might be a good idea. If something truly interesting comes along, it won't hurt to pursue it a bit before we leave for Dyea."

The two of them had barely found a place to stand near the mounds of luggage when Carson spotted a large contingent of men marching down the dock toward them. By the soured expressions and determined gait, the group had the look of trouble, he was certain of it. But the moment two shots rang out, their echoes reverberating loudly over the water, he was stunned.

"What the . . ." Startled, Carson stood dead in his tracks.

A booming voice rang out behind him. "Halt, gentlemen!"

Carson turned. A tight knot of four or five seamen stood together near the top of the gangplank at the port side of the ship. A tall, stately man stepped out from among them and into full view. It was the captain. Carson quickly noted that at least three of the seamen nearby held revolvers, and each was aimed at the mob of men heading toward them.

Though the ragtag group on the dock hesitated, the air was filled with threatening mutterings as a slim, rather handsomely dressed man with a bulbous nose and a bushy beard stepped forward. The gang quieted immediately.

"We've come to speak to Inspector Wood," the man called out. "Let us on board."

"I'm Captain Reese," the captain's voice rang back. "This is my ship, and I will say who will and who won't board her. You do not have permission to come aboard."

"Sir," the bearded man sneered back, "are you telling me that you plan to protect the rascal that robs our American citizens of their hard earned cash? A foreigner who's taking fees off a land that belongs to us? Listen," he shouted even more forcibly, "he'll come to no harm, I swear. Just let us take what rightly belongs to our people and we'll have no trouble here."

"We'll have no trouble here either way, Mr. Smith. I've been hired by Inspector Wood to take him to his destination, and take him I will.

And if you and your men don't disperse immediately, I will do what must be done. It will not profit you, I guarantee it."

As the mutterings ran through the mob, Carson caught the look in Jimmy's eyes and raised an eyebrow. "Appears we have a standoff," he whispered. "We might want to get ready to duck."

Jimmy nodded. "Maybe, but I'm betting on the captain."

After a long tense moment, the mob's spokesman bellowed into the night once again. "Have it your way for now, Captain. But if I were you, I'd watch my backside the next time I was in town."

For several more heartbeats, his words hung in the still evening air, and then slowly Mr. Smith and his cohorts turned and began their swagger back toward town. For close to a minute, every onlooker stood silent, simply watching, until suddenly as if the timekeeper at a local fight had rung the bell, they all started talking and the shuffling about their luggage once more.

"Well, well," Carson crooned in the same drawl of the infamous Mr. Smith, "might we have already met the Soapy Smith gang?"

Jimmy shook his head. "And if I know you, you'll be interviewing him by tomorrow's nightfall."

Carson shrugged then moved toward a familiar piece of baggage. "It's all a part of the wonder of it, Jimmy. All a part."

Chapter Six

Abby released a long sigh as she looked down the cluttered street filled with so many vendor signs and jostling men that she could barely see beyond the next few buildings. Jon had left near to an hour ago to find a professional packer to haul their goods to Lake Bennett, but soon after he'd left the hotel, she'd spoken with the proprietor and discovered that the reputation of one of the packers in Skagway was far from reputable.

For a moment, she stood at the doorway, debating the wisdom of trying to find Jon. He wouldn't like her interference, but then again, shouldn't she at least try to warn him? With an eye on the busy street, Abby at last started forward.

Taking cautious steps, she worked her way along the narrow boards strewn alongside Skagway's muddy thoroughfare. She had picked her way along plenty of sloppy streets over the years, and that was no issue for her. Of more concern was the image of the men on the dock last evening. Men that she knew resided in this cramped town.

Over breakfast this morning, she and Jon had learned that many in the area were angry about Canada's mounted police taking fees from American stampeders at the pass, on what was purported to be American soil, but no matter the reasons, the mob's hostility still left her skin crawling. And yet, if she could believe the proprietor's comment that Soapy Smith, though a person one ought not to cross, was gentleman enough, she imagined she'd be safe enough to look for Jon. It was, after all, broad daylight.

After passing nearly a dozen side streets, Abby spotted a grassy knoll covered with a patch of snow. Having been directed to this small hill, Abby lifted her skirts, crossed the street, and then climbed the rise and looked around. She immediately spotted a corral not more than a few hundred feet ahead, but as she stared at the sight, she was filled with dread.

The poled enclosure was quite small and the horses within it were near to knee deep in mud. More, the poor creatures appeared about as worn and thin as any she had ever seen. Even from where she stood, she could tell they were very near to starving.

Abby stared at the place. Surely Jon would not be dealing with such a packer as this, would he? With a tense feeling inside her chest, she started for the shabby structure off to the side of the corral.

As she neared the ramshackle building, she heard a man shouting curses at the top of his voice, and though she winced at the ugliness of his words, it was another sound that brought her feet to a standstill. Abby's anger rose in her throat as she recognized the pitiful whinny of a creature in pain.

With hands balled into fists, Abby marched through the shack's entryway, rounded a front stall, and came to a sudden halt. Beyond, a pinto reared back trying to keep away from a man with a whip, but the poor thing was tied up and couldn't get away. While she watched in horror, the tip of the whip snapped forward with an earsplitting crack, slapping hard against a rear flank. When the mare went into a near frenzy, the man struggled to regain his footing and then raised his arm to strike again. Abby thought of Molly, her prized mare, and ran forward.

"Stop! What in heaven's name are you doing?" she shouted.

The hand hesitated in midair as a man with a scraggly beard turned to face her. For a moment, he just stared at her with a half-toothless gape. Then the look of alarm quickly faded into one of pure rage. With a face flushed to near red and darkening eyes, the bully lowered his whip and took a menacing step toward her. "Well, well. What have we here?" he hissed.

Coming to a halt not more than a few feet from the scruffy old man, Abby swallowed as she considered what she was doing. And though a voice inside warned of imminent danger, she found her old habits returning and instead of turning and running, she instead squared her feet and placed her hands on her hips, as if in full authority.

"I am here with my brother and seeking a packer, that's what you have here," she shot back, her voice strong with passion. "And if you wish for any employment from us, I would suggest that you put the whip down immediately!"

The man's gaze moved beyond her a moment, as if to seek the brother. While he stood trying to grasp his situation, his hand reached out for a nearby gate to gain his balance. As if in a drunken stupor, he stared at the doorway, but when no such brother appeared, he turned back to her with a snarl.

"A brother 'tis it? Har! You've no such brother, you wicked wretch."

"I wouldn't be so sure of that."

With a swift intake of air, Abby spun at the sound of the voice, shocked to see Carson Stuart standing just inside the doorway.

"I believe the lady asked you to put down the whip," he said slowly. "Is it your intention to follow her instructions or should I come a little closer and help you?"

Seeing the stony look in Carson's darkened eyes, Abby glanced back to the menacing face behind her. She saw a slow, crooked smile slip across the ruffian's lips as he lifted his whip. By the look on his face, she was certain he would use his weapon. Then in a fit of sudden rage, the man lunged forward.

Abby felt his body brush past her as he charged Carson. Instinctively, she kicked out her right foot with all her might. With a yelp, he went down on one knee. At that same instant, Carson grabbed his arm and yanked the whip from his hand. Grasping the man by the collar, Carson pulled him to his feet and shoved him back against the side of the building.

"You own this horse?" he said in a low growl.

The man gasped as he struggled to stand. "So what's it to ya?"

Carson released him and stepped back. "I'll say it again, do you own this horse?"

"Yesss . . ." The drunk nearly hissed out his words.

Carson leaned forward. "What do you want for it?"

Wordless, the frizzy-haired man gathered his feet beneath him and wiped his mouth. Carson dropped the whip to his side.

"I'll say it one more time, my friend. If you give me a halfway decent price, I'll buy this horse from you." Though Carson's body language had softened, Abby could hear the low, steel-edged tone to his voice and was surprised by it.

"That fool horse?" the old drunk snorted. "Why, it's not worth a tinker's damn, mister." He waved his hand about like a madman. "But even at that, every critter in this hellhole is worth a'plenty, let me tell you! Two hundred dollars," he slurred.

"You own this place?"

"Yup. Me and my brother Joe, we owes it all." He laughed then. "And in case yer thinkin' you can hire ol' Joe Tulley, you got another thought comin'. Even now, he's out taking some men to Bennett while half the town is still waitin' in line to go next." He snickered and rubbed his scrubby face. "Two hundred dollars."

"Seventy-five and not a dime more," Carson said. He patted the palm of his left hand with the butt end of the whip then shoved his hat back and eyed the man carefully.

"By the way," he added, "as a reporter, I had a rather interesting conversation with a group of men in town this morning. Seems many of the good folks of Skagway are looking to bring some law and order to their fair city and have formed a rather large committee to do so. They told me they plan to lock a few of their lawbreakers away to cool them off a bit. Perhaps a slow walk back into town might be a better idea?" Carson motioned toward town with his head. "Can't imagine what they might do to a man who threatens a pretty lady with a whip, can you?"

"I ain't goin' to town, mister. I'm drunk and I sleeps it off right here, just like me brother Joe says, and ye best not be crossin' ol' Joe either. So you take this critter and give me a hundred dollars and that's that."

"I'll take the critter and put your seventy-five dollars on deposit at the Skagway bank, in Joe's name for good measure. You can explain it to your brother later. It's either that or I'm dragging your nasty hide down the street."

Abby's heart was still racing as the scoundrel swore thickly then slumped to the dirt. As he tucked his chin to his chest in surrender, Carson began to move slowly for the pinto. But the mare had no mind to cooperate, and instead, she snorted and pulled back, wild-eyed as he tried to untie it. Abby knew Carson would have his hands full if he tried to lead her away.

"Wait," she said. Without giving him a chance to respond, Abby stepped forward. "Slow, girl. Slow now. It's all right. Here, watch me. Watch my hands, little Patches."

Talking in a soothing voice, Abby kept her eyes directed to those of the pinto as she moved carefully forward. When she drew up within touching distance, the pinto nickered and stepped back. For a moment, Abby wondered if the mare would bolt and all would be lost, but when Abby held out her hand and simply stood in silence, reassuring the horse in her mind, she was delighted to see the mare respond in kind. Speaking again in soft tones, Abby reached out and ran her fingers gently down the pinto's nose.

The poor creature trembled as she drew her hand tenderly down its neck and over its front shoulder. While she soothed the pinto, Carson untied the rope from the post. Seeing that the mare had settled down, Abby took the rope from Carson's hands and tugged her forward.

"Come on, girl. Let's see if we can't find you a better place," she whispered. Abby moved past the drunk and out through the shabby barn door, mare in tow. Outside, she waited for Carson to catch up.

"How did you manage to get yourself in that mess?" Carson asked when he finally emerged and moved alongside.

Abby shrugged. "And how, may I ask, did you happen to come along at the right moment?" She turned her gaze to the road ahead. "Or maybe more importantly, where do you want to take your mare?"

Carson scratched the back of his neck thoughtfully. "Now there's a good question," he said. "You have any suggestions?"

"I believe there's another packing outfit up the road. I was told that there are two of them in the area, and that's why I'm here. I was afraid that Jon might be dealing with the wrong one."

Carson reached for the rope. "I'd say that didn't happen," he said, "so maybe we'd better keep looking." Carson started to step away, pulling the horse behind him, but the pinto suddenly dug in her hooves and wasn't about to move. After tugging on the rope several times, he stared at his newly purchased mare and sighed. "Can you believe this ungrateful bag of bones?"

With a light chuckle, Abby took hold of the halter and clicked her tongue. "Come on, Patches. Let's get away from here."

Carson looked sideways at her as he caught up. "I think you've got yourself a skinny little mare. She doesn't much cater to men, I'd say. So what's your plan?"

"Jon came up here to find someone to pack us over the trail," she said. "Like you said, we'll look for him." She smiled. "And, of course, also find a place to keep *your* horse."

"Fine," he muttered.

They turned up a trail and walked a few feet when Carson spoke up. "I'm not sure I got a complete answer earlier," he said. "How'd you get in a tangle with that brute?"

"I don't know. I wasn't thinking. I heard him yelling and this poor thing scream, and then I just got angry and went inside the stable. I've heard enough horse talk to know when a creature needs help. Guess I simply ran into a bad situation." Abby walked in silence a moment and then glanced over at the man beside her. "Now it's my turn. Why were you there?"

He shrugged. "I went out for a walk. I was trying to get the layout of the town clearer in my mind. Then I heard the shouting and a young woman's voice, so I stopped to listen. That's when I decided I'd better show my face." He looked at her a moment.

"I don't doubt that walking on the main streets with plenty of folks about is safe enough, but heading off to the outskirts of a town like Skagway, and especially going alone into a place like that . . . well, you should be more careful."

"Maybe so, but I'm not entirely helpless."

"Perhaps not," he said, chuckling. "That was a splendid kick. It seemed to take the steam right out of him, but what if he wouldn't have been a drunken old codger? What if you had run into that shack and found two men, and maybe two from that same crowd we saw on the dock?"

Abby remained silent for a moment. "Did anyone ever tell you that you ask too many questions, Mr. Stuart?"

"On occasion."

"I would appreciate it if you wouldn't tell Jon," she said quietly. "He's unhappy enough that I've come along, and in truth, I need to start proving my worth, not making things more difficult for him."

Carson studied her face a moment. "I'm surprised that someone like you is even taking this adventure."

"I thought I could be of some help," she said. "I can cook, sew, and I'm an excellent horsewoman. All my life I've had to keep up with three brothers, and with my past experiences and all, I thought I could manage. Maybe I'm no match in physical strength, but it isn't always physical strength that accomplishes the final goal, now is it?"

He smiled. "You may have a point."

"I want to help Jon. Our family needs it," she continued. "And God willing, I will." She looked at him directly. "You won't tell him, will you, Mr. Stuart?"

"Carson, call me Carson," he said. He hesitated and then nodded. "All right, Abigail, I won't say anything about this incident to your brother, but promise me that you will be more careful in the future. Is that a deal?"

Abby gave him a quick perusal and then turned away without comment. She pointed ahead. "It looks like we've found another barn and some horses. Hopefully, we'll find a more accommodating business this time."

Silent now, they walked up a narrow lane that led to a small wood-framed home. As they approached, a young girl barely old enough for school opened the door and gave them a long quizzical look.

"Are you looking for my mommy?" she said.

"Does she own some horses?" Smiling, Carson nodded toward the barn and a set of corrals.

"Oh, yes," the little child offered. Her bright brown eyes smiled up at Carson. "She's talking with a man at the corral now. You can go down there if you'd like."

"Thanks, I appreciate that," Carson said.

Abby saw him give the little girl a broad smile and felt a sudden lump forming in her throat. *Another charmer*, she thought dolefully.

Without warning, a tight, hot sensation spread across her chest. She thought she'd been able to tuck away those thoughts, to keep the memories of Dundee locked away, but the pain inside was a searing reminder that no matter how hard she tried, she was not able to do so.

Jimmy laughed. "So, you're telling me that you paid seventy-five dollars for a beat-up horse and then tried to warn Jon about the old drunk down the road?" He chuckled. "Not sure who got taken with that deal."

Carson noted Abigail's frown while Jon sat smiling beside her. "Besides that," Jon added, "I'd already been forewarned about the Tulley place and could have saved them both time and money." He looked at Carson. "So what are you going to do with your mare?"

Leaning back from the table, Carson swallowed his bite of food and smiled back at him. "I may live to regret this, but after thinking about it, I decided that she'd come in handy to help Jimmy and I pack our goods up the Chilkoot for as far as she can go. Trail's too steep at the pass for horses, but I understand a new tramway has been built to carry goods from The Scales up to the top. So if she can help us get our goods even near The Scales, it will be enough. After that, I'm sure I can sell her."

Carson watched as Abigail dug her fork into another bite of meat. She looked unhappy, but for his part, he was certain that the day had been quite a success. Not only had he rescued, more or less, a damsel in distress, but he'd managed a good interview with several in Skagway, purchased a packing horse and a temporary place to board it, and now as a bonus, he was having good company for dinner. In addition, Jimmy had even found a man with a small barge who could take their goods to Dyea tomorrow. Indeed, everything proved to be coming along even better than he'd expected.

"Well, I'm glad it's working out for you two," Jon said. "I'm afraid we're going to have to sit it out awhile. Though the Thames family looked to be pretty decent packers for hire, the Missus told me that her husband is off to Bennett for the week, and as soon as he returns, he has plans to pack in another two groups." Jon frowned. "So with them busy and this Joe Tulley out of the picture, at this rate, it'll be three weeks before we can even start."

Jon shook his head. "Not too inclined to spend that much time in Skagway. It's expensive and we're losing precious time."

"Come with us on the Chilkoot," Jimmy said.

Carson and two other pairs of eyes turned to the voice that had so far spoken few words. Jimmy lightly ducked his head as he faced Carson with a shrug.

"Why not? With three of us and a horse and sled, we'd be able to move supplies quite handily up the Dyea valley. And if Abigail would be willing to cook for us, it might come in handy to have someone watch over our remaining goods and fix a little supper while we shuffle our stuff up the trail. For my part, I sure wouldn't mind coming back from a day's work to find a good hot meal." He gave Abby a shy grin. "You can cook, can't you?"

Abby stared at him a moment as if to consider his words. "I might be able to keep up with your appetite, James, but I'm not sure if you'd really want us along." She stole a quick glance across the table to Jon.

"Abby's right," Jon said. "We could be holding you back, I'm afraid."

Carson studied the faces across the table. At first he'd been startled by his friend's suggestion, but the more the idea lingered in his mind, the more it made good sense to him. It would be good to have extra manpower for moving the supplies, and if warm food was waiting when they returned, that wouldn't be so bad, either.

"I'm not in any hurry, Jon. My job is to be looking for stories, not gold. Besides, without Abby's help, I'm not sure we can get that little mare to cooperate."

Jon stared at him. "You mean it? You really want us to join you?"

"I do. Maybe working together would benefit all of us." He offered a sincere smile. Without a doubt, he would welcome their company. Another trail-smart helper, and especially one with a comely sister to cook for them, sounded fine with him.

Jon searched Abigail's face. "What do you think, Abby? They might be a big help to us."

Abby looked down with a thoughtful, quiet countenance. As Carson watched her, he wondered about the unexplained sadness that lingered there. Maybe Jimmy had sensed it as well, for it wasn't like him to jump ahead of Carson and make such a suggestion.

With a solemn look still in her eyes, Abigail offered a light shrug. "It's up to you, Jon."

Jon nodded. "We'll have to work things out fairly, the supplies and sharing the workload and all, but . . ." He hesitated. "But I like the thought of it."

After several minutes of talking about supplies, the timing to leave Skagway and other such details, Abigail cleared her throat. In the same somber manner that she'd been listening to their conversations, she asked Jon if she was needed, and seeing him shake his head, she rose quickly and slipped away.

At the sound of another man's voice through the thin partition, Abby rolled to her side. Filled with disgust, she grabbed her pillow and threw it over her head. She had known little privacy in all their boarding rooms, but this was beyond what she could endure. She had heard the door opening and closing, the voices, and the moaning for several hours now, and the more she thought about what was happening on the other side of the paper-thin walls, the angrier she became.

Men. They sickened her. She hated how they could want you for your flesh and then disappear. How could a woman fall for such a life?

Indeed, how could have she fallen for it?

At the moment, she hated Dundee with all her heart.

It would be a miracle if she could help Jon find the gold, a miracle if she could help rescue the ranch, let alone raise a baby. She needed miracles.

Hot tears stung her eyes. Her nosed burned. She felt the deep sobs filling in her chest. Covering her mouth with her hand, she tried to stop the sound of them from rising to her throat. She seemed to be shaking to her very core.

Though she felt sickened by the things men could do, deep inside a voice seemed to challenge her—who was it who paraded their beauty and tempted a man? Who was it, after all, who sashayed about many towns in low necklines and tightly drawn corsets? Women were not innocent. And though she did not parade herself like those she'd seen in Skagway and Dyea, she knew in her very soul that she was as much a temptress as any.

Had she not flirted wholeheartedly and then swiftly jumped into a man's arms, eager to give him what he desired, though her mother and father had warned against it? And even now, if she was honest, was she not filled with a mix of emotions? Hadn't she even been thinking of another man earlier this evening?

Lord help her, she couldn't deny it. It was true.

She'd been drawn tonight to the smiling eyes of the man across the table. They had radiated such warmth. It was the first time she had considered him, his dark hair neatly trimmed, his ruddy complexion, the deep dimples. She'd been thankful for his appearance at the foul Tulley barns, but if they were to travel together, what would she do?

Until she knew for certain whether Dundee was alive or dead, she was still married. How could she be noticing someone else? She was with child for heaven's sake! Filled with anger toward Dundee and disgust at her own weakness, Abby sniffed aloud and wiped her cheeks.

"Abby, are you all right?"

She heard Jon's voice and released a deep breath. After pulling the pillow from her head, she looked over to where Jon slept on a mat by the wall. "I'm sorry I disturbed you," she groaned.

"It's all right. I know you're hurting."

She rolled to her back and looked up at the ceiling. "I don't know. Maybe I should have gone home. I want to help you, but I'm afraid I'll be more effort than I'm worth by tagging along. I can't believe Dundee isn't here. Do you think there's a chance he's alive, that he'll follow us?"

"Not sure, Abby." Jon's voice trailed off.

"I wish I knew," she whispered. "And though I tell myself to be patient, I would give anything to know whether to grieve or to hang on and hope for the best."

"Abby, listen, I would guess that if he can, he'll come and find us. He knew our plans. You'll have to wait and see, but then again . . ."

"You think he's dead, don't you."

In the silence of the room, Abby took a deep breath and swallowed away the hurt as best she could. "Should I have written his father?"

"No, I don't think you should yet. Give it some time, just in case."

She considered Jon's advice for a few moments before her thoughts turned again to their dinner tonight. "Do you think this will work to accompany Carson and James?"

"I think so. I believe we'll have a much better chance of getting to the Klondike in one piece now. I've been worried about you."

"I know, Jon. And I'll buck up. I'll be a help, I promise."

She heard Jon's long sigh. "I suppose."

It was silent for several heartbeats before Abigail spoke again. "So, you don't regret my decision?"

"Go to sleep, Ab. Just go to sleep."

With a sniff, Abby rolled to her side and drew the blankets over her shoulder. With all her heart she wished that she *could* just go to sleep, *could* rid her mind of those worrisome thoughts. She closed her eyes.

To be of any use at all tomorrow, she had to try. If only her chest didn't feel like some large fist was pressed tight against it.

Chapter Seven

Abby stood in amazement as she gazed at the sea of goods stored in sacks or crates and lying in heaps along Dyea's long beach. Like bees humming about their hive, men, women and even a few children scurried about gathering their freight from the flat-bottomed barges and scows. While the ocean waters slipped forward, they rushed to put all they owned far up on shore, to where the sea grasses met a rutted trail leading to town. As their boatman had described it, Dyea's inlet, a shallow area with a great extreme in tides, was a far cry from the deep waters of Skagway.

After dropping her final load near a growing mound of supplies, Abby turned to watch as Jon and Jimmy jumped in haste from the barge, the last of their goods in hand. Meanwhile, Carson was still trying to get his newly purchased mare to follow him off the deck, but it appeared that she was not too eager to do so. Abby stepped forward, thinking to help Carson harness the mare to their recently purchased sled when her attention was drawn to Jimmy's flat cart with large wheels. He had loaded it with several bags and was panting as he pulled it to a stop beside her.

"How do you like my special handcart," he called out. "Kind of a mixed contraption that a builder in Skagway helped me put together." He gave her a broad grin and pointed. "See, it's a cart for dry ground, but in two swift moves, you can remove the wheels, put on skids, and then we've got ourselves a grand sled. What do you think of it?"

Abby smiled. "It appears to be a marvelous invention. And you told me that Carson was the smart one."

Jimmy cocked his head and winked at her. "So now you know, eh?"

She laughed. "Genius is your middle name, James."

He grinned at her. "And here I thought you might never notice, Miss Abigail."

"You can call me Abby if you'd like."

"That I would, Miss Abby, and please, I'd like you to call me Jimmy. About the only one that doesn't is Carson's momma. She's kind of old world, she is."

Jon walked up and tossed down a sack on Jimmy's cart. "It's amazing," he said. "That ocean is coming in like a herd of spooked cattle. Never imagined how fast it could move."

"Where's Carson?" Jimmy said.

"He's bringing the mare."

Jimmy looked surprised. "Carson?"

Jon picked up another bag and threw it on the cart before he looked around. "He said he could."

Jimmy looked back to the barge. "I think this might be your first lesson about Carson, Jon. He can sometimes be a bit more confident of his ability than is useful."

Jon and Abby turned to see Carson fastening a harness line from their sled to the pinto, but the moment he released his hands and stepped forward to guide Patches up the beach, she flicked her tail straight up and started off on a dead run. Carson shouted and waved his hands, but the mare ran on, narrowly missing several stashes.

Speechless, Abby watched as Patches streaked off to their left, the half-filled sled behind her skimming along the damp coastal surface as slick as you please, until it hit a bump in the rutted trail. At once, the sled flew into the air, bounced twice, and then very nearly yanked the horse off its feet as it landed on its side and dumped off all its goods. But the little mare took it all in stride and merely dug in with all four hooves as she turned and headed up the trail to Dyea.

Abby found her feet and started running. "Patches!" she screamed. "Patches, no!"

The mare ignored her call and, instead, moved off at a fast gait until she neared another cart with two men standing alongside. When the men turned and saw the horse speeding toward them, they began to wave and shout. Immediately, the little pinto shifted to her left, came about, and then started on a dead run back the way she'd come. As Patches now raced back to her, Abby waved her hands, trying to slow her down, but by now the poor thing was wild-eyed with fear and completely confused.

Seeing the mare's frenzy, Abby stopped in her tracks and lowered her hands to her mouth. Holding her fingers to her lips, she whistled as loud as she could.

"Patches! Whoa!"

For a moment, she thought the mare would run her over, but instead, the small pinto swerved past her and veered north, prancing up a grassy slope a short distance before she slowed her pace and came to a dead stop. As if in abject sorrow, Patches lowered her head, and with heaving sides, stood completely still.

Abby started for her, but before she could move more than two steps, the mare suddenly reached for a mouthful of grass and began to eat as peaceable as you please. Struck by the mare's antics, a small chuckle rose up in Abby's throat, and the more she watched Carson's calm little pony eating away, the more she began to laugh. Finally, a full gale of laughter came rushing out. Unable to move, she held her sides and giggled until Jon walked past her with a frown, grabbed the lead rein, and then started back for their dumped pile of supplies.

With every effort to stifle her smile, Abigail pushed her fingers against her lips, but even that didn't seem to help. She was still chuckling when she approached Jon and Jimmy, who by now were loading the sled. As Carson came up the beach muttering, it was all she and Jimmy could do to keep from laughing all over again.

For several hours, they'd been pushing and pulling up the trail heading north out of Dyea. To Carson, it felt good to finally be on their way.

The night before, they'd made camp in a small clearing between tents next to the Taiya River. Knowing it would take at least two and maybe three days to move all their goods from the area called Finnegan's Point to Sheep Camp, they sat up both sleeping tents and also erected a third tent for cooking, eating, and storing food. But since darkness had come on them quickly, it wasn't until morning before they were able to ready both the handcart and the sled for a first haul.

"All right," Jimmy called out. "Does anyone else want to take a break from this?"

Jon, who was leading Patches through the mud and broken snow, looked over his shoulder. It had been Jimmy and Carson's task to alternately pull the handcart along, but it was getting increasingly difficult in this particular area of the river drainage.

"Think we're fast approaching the time to turn this cart into another sled," Jimmy groaned as he pulled off to the side of the trail. "What with this muck and all it might be easier with sled runners."

Carson nodded as he took a deep breath and removed the cumbersome backpack from his back. "True, but we were told that the trail was frozen solid only a week ago, and that would have made all the difference in the world."

"Frozen sounds better."

Carson opened his pack and pulled out three sandwiches from inside. After handing one to each of them, he reached for his canteen and found a stump for sitting. Jon sat on another cut log lying nearby.

"After our break," Jon said, "I'd be happy to help you turn that thing into a sled, Jimmy, and then the both of us could work it. You can pull and I'll push. Carson, you can take a turn with Patches if you'd like. She seems to be agreeable enough now that we're following others up the trail."

Carson smiled as he reached for his leather pouch and pulled out his journal. "So you're saying it's only a matter of time and trust? Then that pony will come around?"

Jimmy gave Carson a curious look. "You're going to write, not eat?"

"I'll eat, but first I need to jot down some thoughts. Can't let too much time and space go by, lest I forget all these wonders around us."

Jimmy shook his head and frowned. "Each to his own."

After opening his journal, Carson found his last entry and scanned through it before he began to scribble down the thoughts that had been circling in his mind.

The great biodiversity beyond the trail, he scribbled quickly, *makes this wilderness not only impassable and lush, but also filled with an ample supply of rich edible offerings—berries, salmon, mountain goats, moose, deer and grouse—though few are at hand due to the time of year and the crush of humanity along the trail. I did find it refreshing, however, to hike about the forest last evening and be serenaded by the hooting of one such blue grouse. In addition, though it is early in the season, I also spotted a few bear tracks among the great boulders and rich, dark soil along the Taiya River. I'm told there are daily sightings of other mammals such as the porcupine, snowshoe hare, and river otter, but the mink and marten of the furbearing kind are few and far between. For my part, I've spotted only the weasel.*

Most enthralling of all creatures, however, are those found in flight. These are the ones that give me the greatest sense of American destiny: the great bald eagle. To see their broad wings soaring high on the coastal breeze is alone worth the journey. There are thousands of them along the north Pacific, especially in the area called the Inside Passage, the southern tip of Alaska, nearly a thousand miles from Seattle. And it leaves me wondering if they, like the countryside they represent, will someday be a grand prize to this ever expanding nation.

Carson held his hand still a moment, trying to recall more of his recent experiences. He knew he needed to write more about Dyea, and though he'd composed some notes a night ago, most of them had only been a factual and brief description of the land.

He wrote on: *Notes on Dyea, the town:*

Though less raucous than crime-ridden Skagway, Dyea is by no means tame. A mushroom of a town, it appears to be growing even as one pauses on the street to look around. With a wave of humanity flowing from the sea and up to the range of mountains that divide Alaska from the Northwest Territory, many an entrepreneur awaits those seeking the Klondike gold. Snuggled against a wide inlet, Dyea is filled with narrow streets that hold commotion from day to night, such that the air is never still from cries of human and animal alike.

Within a short walk from this hastily erected village, each and every stampeder and entrepreneur, whether equipped with a boat, a native packer, a horse, sled, or even a mere pack on a back, all begin their first experience on this, the Chilkoot Trail, at the edge of the Taiya River. Heading north through thickets of cottonwood and alder, men, women and even children trudge up a narrow canyon to such camps as Finnegan's Point, Canyon City, Pleasant Camp and finally, Sheep Camp, where the trail emerges from the canyon and winds toward a great rise—the Chilkoot Pass.

It is wet and cold here. A place dense with biodiversity: willow, devil's club, moss, fern, spruce and hemlock to mention a few. But they plod on through it all. Hoping for gold. Seeking the promise. Testing the spirit of adventure.

Will it be of profit to them?

Only time will tell, and yet for each who has taken his first steps on the infamous Chilkoot, one immediately hears of their sense of pride, of excitement—if for no other reason than the experience itself. To the last man (or woman), each stampeder seems to believe that this event is history in the making, and that they, most remarkably, are a part in it.

He studied his words. Were they adequate to describe the mountains surrounding them, the mud beneath their feet, the buildings lining the streets of Skagway and Dyea—the dance halls, fine hotels, flimsy lodges, the trading posts and every tool, trade and gimmick in between? Was he telling it accurately enough?

With a sigh, Carson began to fold up his journal. He could only hope.

For now, all he could do was record as much detail as possible. Later, he would have to sift through it all to create a shorter, more precise piece. It wouldn't be easy, but then, nothing of late had been easy.

In his younger years, he'd felt full of promise what with college, his father's mill, and honing his skills by writing advertisements for the local press. On the side, he'd even been privileged to write several other articles for the local *Sentinel*. But then life had taken an abrupt turn. The mill had failed.

Strange how adversity had brought him opportunity. Until then, he'd never thought that his future could be anything more than eventually running his father's business. He never dreamed he would become a newspaper man—not until, in desperation, he'd quit his studies and signed on with a newspaper first in San Francisco and then in Seattle. Now, at twenty-five, he had an opportunity to secure an even better future, a chance to write for one of the most prestigious presses in the country, and to record for posterity one of the most incredible events of the decade.

"Hey, Carson, I'd say there's not much eating and a whole lot of pencil pushing going on." Jimmy pointed at his journal. "What are you writing about?"

"Dyea and the canyon."

"It takes all those words to write about the canyon?"

Carson shrugged. "I'm noting all that comes to mind, though in the end, I imagine most of it will be edited."

Jimmy nodded. "Think we'll be able to get all our gear into Sheep Camp this week?"

Carson offered his friend a weak smile. "Mostly, I think hauling two thousand pounds per man into the high country is more backbreaking than it looks on paper," he said ruefully. "Even with Patches and the sled, a cart, and packs on the back, I have a feeling that it's going to take several trips."

"Just getting organized this morning was peevish enough," Jon said. "It'll be an effort all right, but I'm wondering if we could consider moving our cooking and sleep tents on to Sheep Camp on the next round. If we set up our main camp at Sheep Camp instead of Finnegan's Point, then I think Abby would have more of a community around her. Besides, I'm thinking we should secure a spot up there as soon as we can. Every day there seems to be more and more people coming, and Sheep Camp is where we need to regroup and get organized before we head over the pass."

"That's a good idea," Jimmy said. "Canyon City's too close, and though Pleasant Camp might be fine, if we can settle in Sheep Camp right away, it would be best." He turned to Carson. "Any thoughts?"

"I like your idea, Jon."

Jimmy waved toward three men who sat in a grove of trees about a hundred yards away. "Was talking to those fellas earlier this morning. A couple of them sound like they're straight out of Norway. Man named Hansen said they've two women waiting at Sheep Camp. Hansen was a little envious that we had little Patches here. He said it was slow going since they don't have a horse or packers and have to carry everything they own on their backs and the one small sled they've got."

Jon swallowed his bite of sandwich. "Maybe for Abigail's sake, we could try to locate somewhere near them. I'd like Abby to meet other women since she's alone in camp."

"Good idea," Carson said. To his way of thinking, Abigail was too handsome a woman for her own good. Several times he'd seen men gawking at her. The thought of leaving her alone from dawn to dusk left him a might uncomfortable, especially when he considered the incident in Skagway.

"At least she's feeling pretty good now, considering her condition."

Carson glanced up. He saw the look of concern on Jimmy's face as well. "You said that once before, Jon. Is Abigail sick?"

Jimmy leaned forward. "Is there something we should know?"

Jon glanced from Jimmy to Carson. "Yeah, I'm thinking you should know. Just in case."

Carson stopped eating and stared at his new friend.

"The reason Abby is even here," Jon went on, "is that my partner and I decided to stop by the ranch in Wyoming before we went to the Klondike." He hesitated.

"And . . .?"

"And, well, Abby fell in love with my partner Dundee and he with her, and so they got married. Then, Abby insisted she join us."

Carson swallowed. "Abigail's married?"

"Not sure, at this point." Jon shrugged. "It's complicated. Dundee disappeared in Seattle, and meanwhile, she's going to have a baby."

Silence fell between the three of them like a curtain on a Shakespearean tragedy. Carson's mouth gaped open as he stared at Jon.

"Well, I'll be," Jimmy breathed. "Abigail's to have a baby and she's still going to the Klondike?" He shook his head. "That sounds plumb crazy."

Jon looked down to his hands. "I know. I should have been more forceful in trying to get her to go back home, but it isn't easy to force Abigail to do anything. At least she's not far along. I think she'll be all right until we get to Dawson. Hopefully, once there, she can find some help. I was purely relieved to hear Miss Mulroy talk of the different establishments up there."

"A little momma, well I'll be," Jimmy repeated softly, as if saying it again would make it more believable. "Shoot, that will almost make me an uncle or something, won't it?" He beamed.

For the first time since he'd spoken, Jon smiled. "That's right good of you, Jimmy."

"So where's her husband, this Dundee?" Carson asked.

"I don't know. Had no idea that Dundee had problems with gambling until we reached Seattle. I was working for his father, who owns a nice spread in Montana, when one day this son shows up. A week later, Dundee told me about this idea he had to rescue some gold and asked me if I'd go with him. Evidently, some family friend from Chicago stood to inherit a couple Klondike claims as well as a decent poke of gold, and they were willing to give us half of whatever we recovered. Since Dundee was my boss's son and appeared to have all the money we needed for the expedition, I thought it was a good idea. But there were problems in Seattle. Following a night of gambling, he disappeared and . . ." Jon hesitated, as if to find the words, "and, unfortunately, a third of our funds for getting to the Klondike went with him."

"Disappeared?" Jimmy said, his voice sounded disbelieving.

"I'm afraid so. I tried to find out what happened, and it was pretty hush-hush, but from what I gathered, Dundee made it as far as a dock after a disagreement with this gambler. After that, nothing. I don't know if he's alive or dead, though I never told Abby about the dock part. Guess I haven't the heart to tell her right now."

Jon gently rubbed one hand over his knee as he stared off into space. "All I know is that I wanted to keep on with the plans. My own father is struggling to keep his ranch going, and knowing this, Abby decided to come along. She figured she could help me."

Carson felt a strong tension deep in his gut. *Too many businesses, too many farms, lost and gone.* "You think she can handle all the travel?"

Jon nodded. "Actually, she's a pretty fit woman. For some reason, I'm not as worried about getting to Dawson as what might come next. You know, the baby and all." He looked away a moment then rose slowly to his feet. "I'm sorry. I should have told you sooner, but she seemed to be feeling fine, so I kept quiet. But, well, I just didn't feel good about keeping this a secret."

Carson pushed his journal and pencil inside his travel pouch then rose to his feet as well. "I appreciate the honesty," he said. He glanced at Jimmy who still had the look of wonder on his face, and though Carson thought he should say more, he couldn't quite think what it would be. He was surprised. It wasn't like him to be without words.

As the three of them silently readied for the trail, Carson sensed that something was gnawing at his insides. What was it? Did he feel sorry for Abigail's circumstances? Or was it more about discovering she had a husband? And whether that husband was alive or dead, of all things, she was going to have a baby.

Either way he looked at it, he knew that the new information created something of a hole in him.

Chapter Eight

Abby gazed at the maze of tents and supplies piled in the distant encampment. She was still somewhat dazed to find herself in the midst of a veritable city in the wilderness. She had never dreamed the journey would be like this. In her mind's eye, she had thought the trek would be like their excursions into the Wyoming backcountry. Those days in the mountains had been one of the joys of her youth, horseback riding, running through the forest, visiting old Shoshoni friends at their summer encampments. But so far, this outdoor experience was a far cry from any she had ever known.

Instead of forest solitude, this was complete chaos. In fact, they'd been fortunate to even find a flat spot left at Sheep Camp. And as it was, their tents were jammed between tree stumps and backed against dense brush as well as another encampment. She was certain that in the four days they'd been at this camp, she'd counted hundreds of tents lining the various trails as well as dozens upon dozens of assorted establishments tucked into every nook and cranny.

Abby stepped up to the small spring, sat her camp jugs down, and then drew her woolen mackinaw tighter about her shoulders. For a moment, she allowed her gaze to linger beyond the sweeping limbs of a nearby spruce to the mountains and narrow canyon beyond. It was through this northern passage that they had to carry all their goods to an area called The Scales. Here, Carson had said, a tramway would carry their things to the top of the pass. The problem was, it had been snowing. The canyon trek, not to mention the steep rise of the infamous pass, would not be easy.

Turning away, Abby filled her jugs and then began the long descent to the encampment. After filling their drinking canteens, she would later go to the river. For the most part, the river was near to frozen, but men had dug several holes along the shore and enough meager offerings could be had for boiling and washing. Thankfully, her new friend Ingrid had told her of the small spring, and though it was not close at hand, it was worth every step.

As Abby approached their camp, she tried to put away the worry that seemed to plague her these past days, but at least she'd not been sick in the mornings any longer.

"Mornin', Abigail."

Abby turned to find Ingrid Johansen moving toward her. Though wrapped in a hooded coat, Abby could see her broad smile and wondered at it.

"Good morning, Ingrid. How are you this morning? Was your tent better last night?"

"Ya. Not so wet now. I feared da thing would fall down, but Hansen shoveled away the snow from under where Edie and I sleep. Been a miserable mix of rain and snow." She shook her head. "Was a frightful night."

"I'm afraid so, and even now I think it may be snowing at the pass."

Ingrid nodded, her gray-blue eyes wide as she spoke. "Hansen said yust this mornin' that it snowed near two feet at The Scales yesterday. I wish he'd not be makin' such fuss about getting over that pass quick like. I worry about the men being in a storm and all."

"Well, at least it's April and spring thaw is almost here." Abby gave her new friend a thin smile. "Besides, there are many men on the trail, so they will be able to help each other if it storms."

"Ya. Hansen says I shouldn't fuss so much."

Abby shrugged. "Isn't that our role?"

Ingrid gave her a slow smile. "So," she said lyrically, "you coming for the weddin' tonight?"

"I'm not certain, Ingrid. From what I've heard, half the camp is going, but I don't know these people. Do you?"

"Ya. Met her in Canyon City with her Papa." Ingrid spoke with an even greater lilt to her voice than normal. "The papa is an immigrant like me and Hansen. From old Prussia. She's beautiful like you."

Abby laughed. "Beauty, you know, is often skin deep."

"Ya. But she seems to be a nice girl, n' so happy. Hope her man is good for her."

"Who is he?"

"A miner from Montana. Hansen says the miners about do like him."

"Well, that's a good sign. What about you, Ingrid? Are you and Hansen thinking about marriage?"

Ingrid ducked her head and shrugged. "For now, we be only friends."

"He seems like a nice friend."

"Ya."

"Well," Abby sighed, "perhaps I'll be able to go tonight. That is, if I can get all my chores done in time. I need to add some wood to the old Yukon stove and bake a batch of bread plus do a bit of laundry. Hopefully, things will dry inside the cook tent. What are your plans for the day?"

"Oh, vell, me and Edie are to go out walking later. We thinking to visit with the mission folks. They camp up there." Ingrid pointed up the hill. "You come too, Miss Abby?"

"I would love to go with you, providing I can get my baking done first."

"Good. We wait for you. And you come to wedding."

Abby smiled. "We'll see. I'll see you soon, Ingrid."

"Da. Soon."

"You're leaving?" Carson looked up past the kerosene light as Abby stepped into their dining tent attired in a furry hat and her dark warm cape.

"Yes. I think I'll attend the wedding festivities with Ingrid and Edie."

"Are Hansen and the other men going?"

"I'm not certain, but Ingrid wants me to join her, and so I'm on my way. I won't be gone long."

Carson looked at Jon and Jimmy a moment. "You boys going?"

Jon shrugged. "Not me."

"Nope, me neither," Jimmy said. "I'm ready to find my bed."

Carson rubbed his chin, wondering if a wedding might make a good story. "I'm thinking this might be of interest to my readers. Wait for me, would you?"

Though she had turned to leave, he saw her hesitate and look back with a somber gaze. "All right," she said carefully.

Carson grabbed his hat and coat off a peg on the center post and followed her through the exit flap of their cramped tent. As the damp cold air filled his lungs, he coughed.

"You've been coughing lately," Abby said in a flat tone. "Are you under the weather?"

"No, I'm fine. Think it's just the night air."

"I'm not so certain, Carson."

Though Carson thought to question her more, he held back since Abby was two steps ahead of him and had now moved into the small clearing of Hansen's camp. Nearby, Hansen and a friend stood warming themselves by a campfire. As he heard the animated conversations in Norwegian, it brought to mind a young man he'd known in college who'd been from Norway. Like Hansen, he also was a tall gangly fellow and always smiling.

"Howdy, boys," Carson said cheerily. "Miss Abigail tells me that she and Ingrid are about to attend a wedding. I think I'll join them, for the story of it if nothing more. Any of you men interested?"

He heard a few grunts, but no answer. Just then Ingrid stepped out of her tent with a smile and waved. In a rather shy demeanor, she moved to Hansen's side and spoke a few words to him in a soft voice. After he nodded, she turned and walked toward them.

"Edie's feeling poorly," she said. "Guess it's only me coming."

She glanced from Abby's face to his own and paused. "That be good? I . . . I don't wish to bother."

"Bother? Of course not, Ingrid. I'm only going because you wanted me to join you," Abigail pronounced. And then grabbing Ingrid's arm, Abigail turned and the two women started off toward the center of Sheep Camp while he dutifully followed.

As they walked a small trail twisting and turning between tents and gear, Carson began to mentally record the sights around them. It was still amazing to him that this wilderness camp, even in the dark of night, contained enough kerosene lanterns and campfires that they could see to walk the trails without effort. It was remarkable. He listened to the voices and laughter filling the night air and knew that those sounds would be forever sealed in his mind. A sense of community was felt here, and even though the stampeders were eager and competitive on the trail by day, he found it amazing how the mood appeared to change at night.

As the three of them stepped into a crowd of people now gathering in a small clearing, a bagpipe immediately started to wail. Carson, Abigail and Ingrid moved to one side when a young woman began to walk forward. In the glow of several lanterns, he saw that her hand was tucked within an older man's arm and that she was dressed fashionably with a white shawl draped about her shoulders. As everyone circled in behind them, the couple moved slowly to where two men stood in silence, waiting.

"There's the Reverend Garner," Ingrid whispered. "The one Miss Abigail met today."

With surprise, Carson stole a glance to where Abby stood keenly observing the scene. In the shadows, he studied her face. No doubt, Abigail Colton held a greater sense of mystery within her contemplative expression than any woman he'd ever known. She intrigued him. There had been moments over the past week when she had leveled her gaze at him or Jon or Jimmy, and without saying a word, she seemed to communicate her thoughts and feelings more than most. Was it her eyes, her mannerisms? He wasn't sure.

As if she'd heard his very thoughts, Abigail turned and met Carson's gaze. Knowing instantly that she did not approve of his perusal, he looked away and gave his attention to the threesome standing within the circle of gathering stampeders. While the bagpipe groaned to a halt with a low moan, the Reverend stepped forward and began to speak.

Carson listened to his words remembering the last ritual of marriage he'd attended. It had been his sister Josie's wedding, not more than three years before. He never dreamed to be witnessing such an event while going into the Klondike, but then, there had been several unanticipated events—a newfound friendship with Jon and Abigail being one of them.

He watched the round-faced young woman step up to a tall miner. After they repeated their vows and kissed, all the men and women around them began to whoop and shout, and then the bagpipes once more discordantly wheezed into action. With the commotion erupting around them, Carson turned to see Ingrid smile at another tall and husky man who was standing beside her. Hansen had come after all. Carson leaned forward to Abigail's ear.

"Perhaps we should go on and allow Ingrid and Hansen to walk home together?"

Abigail glanced at her friend then spoke to her. After Ingrid nodded, she started off on the trail toward their camp as if she cared little whether he came along or not. For a few minutes, he simply followed along listening to the merry voices of men and women, one group gambling and others singing. Then remembering Ingrid's comment, he picked up his pace and walked beside her.

"Did Ingrid say you met the Reverend earlier today?"

She walked a few more steps before responding. "Yes. There's a group of missionaries camped on a flat, part way up the east hillside. It's more of a permanent campsite since he's trying to establish services both here and in Dyea."

"That so? I hadn't heard about it."

"He hopes to have a church building started soon. Says one of his companions has already established a congregation in Bennett, although Bennett has the advantage of having some families live there all year while Sheep Camp, so far, does not."

Carson was surprised at the amount of information Abigail was often able to gain while staying in Sheep Camp during the day. He imagined Ingrid and the other Norwegian lady named Edie had something to do with it. He thought about her comment regarding year-round dwellings in Bennett.

"Amazing," he muttered. "Cities in the wilderness."

She glanced at him with a face void of expression. "The mission church could use Patches, Carson. I know we will have to leave her behind soon, and so I told them I would talk to you. But they haven't much money."

He hesitated. "How much can they pay?"

"I thought maybe fifty dollars would be fair."

"Fifty?"

"I'll give you the rest of the money you paid for her after we reach Dawson."

Carson scratched the scraggly whiskers that were beginning to form on his chin. He didn't exactly have unlimited funds, but he knew Jon was stretched as well.

"No," he said. "I'll consider it my offering for a good cause."

"It's more than a good cause, Carson. It's for God's purposes."

"All right," he smiled. "If you say so."

She frowned lightly and turned away. In the awkwardness of their silence, they walked several more steps before Abigail came to a halt and faced him squarely. "I'm not certain if this is a good or proper time for me to say something, Carson, but I think the words need to be said. I am more than Jon's sister. I am a married woman."

He nodded. "Jon told us." Carson immediately saw a flicker of surprise in her eyes. "Did he also tell you that I'm to have a baby around September?"

"Yes."

She cocked her head, her eyes sparkling in the dim light. He saw her anger. "So, what else did he tell you?"

Carson shifted his weight from one foot to the other. Though she held a peevish look about her face, for some reason, he couldn't look away. She held a beauty that drew him.

"He said he didn't know for certain what had happened to your husband." When she blinked and swallowed, he hated himself for being so blunt.

"That's right," she said at last. Her voice was low but intense. "Which means, Carson, I am still married. Do you understand me?"

He hesitated. Had she somehow reached inside his mind and nailed his very hide to the wall? "I believe you are making your thoughts quite clear."

"Good," she said tartly.

Without waiting for any response, Abigail turned and started off. Flushed still from her words, he simply followed along in silence. When at last they reached their own encampment, she paused near the flap of her sleeping tent.

"I don't mean to be rude, Carson. Just honest. Please tell Jon that I am retiring now." She started to lift the tent flap and then stopped and looked over her shoulder. "Please also tell Jon that there will be church services tomorrow at the same area where the wedding took place." She paused and then continued. "Would you care to join us?"

Surprised by her invitation, Carson stood in silence, weighing her words. Her recent comments had perhaps been understandable, but somehow he felt wounded, and now she was inviting him to services? Was it in any way an extension of friendship, a small acknowledgment that her words had been cutting? Maybe. He wasn't certain, but knowing that church services had not been his forte for a long time, he shrugged.

"I'll see what the morning brings."

Wordless, Abigail nodded and slipped inside the tent. Feeling an extra chill in the air, Carson turned for the dim light in the dining tent, to where he could hear Jimmy and Jon talking, but as he moved forward, he began to wonder all the more about the days ahead.

Aware that a morning light would do little to warm his body, Carson pulled his coat tight against him and closed his eyes.

"Amen," Abigail whispered softly beside him.

At the sound of her voice, Carson wondered at himself.

Why he had decided to join Jon and Abby, he didn't know. Today was to be a day of rest from the burden of moving supplies, and so he had planned to linger in his bed. Instead, he was sitting on a cold log and breathing in the damp morning air. But when Jon had risen and put on his clothes, he'd found himself wide awake, and at the last minute, threw aside his covers and dressed. Surprisingly, Jimmy had joined them as well.

Carson watched as Reverend Garner rose to his feet and strolled to the center of the circle. He was a short and stoutly built man with a trimmed beard and a dark hat pulled low to his ears. And though he offered a rather weak smile to the crowd, when the portly man began to speak, his words were uttered in a surprisingly deep, baritone voice, a voice that displayed much more strength than it had at the wedding the night before.

"Ye lust," the Reverend said, "and have not. Ye kill, and desire to have, and cannot obtain. Ye fight and war, yet have not, because ye ask not. Ye ask, and receive not, because ye ask amiss, that ye may consume it upon your lusts." At that, the Reverend paused and looked around, his eyes roving from face to face.

"You will find these words, my friends, in the holy Word of God, James, chapter four. Does it ring true? Yea and if it does, let me assure you, it does for me as well. For all men have sinned and fallen short of the glory. All. And only by the grace of God can we raise our heads."

Reverend Garner stood still a moment then brushed his hand up and down his long black jacket as if trying to decide what to say. "Listen, friends, I shall speak more about this sin, but at the present, I am inspired to bring more of the Word to you from the book of James."

After opening his Bible, he thumbed through a few pages and then looked up.

"James, whom most scholars believe was the half brother of Jesus," he said carefully, "speaks here with such authority. Many of you will identify with it, for brothers and sisters, is it not true that within the core of your North Country adventuring, you bear a certain sense of need? But is that *need* what should really carry the day? Or should it be, instead, acts of wisdom and kindness. What, then, prevails in your life?"

He held up the Bible. "If ultimate truth needs to be considered to live well in both this life and the next, then we must take heed of it. Allow me to read verses thirteen to seventeen."

The Reverend adjusted his small pair of spectacles against his nose before he started. "Go to now, ye that say, today or tomorrow we will go into such a city, and continue there a year, and buy and sell, and get gain: Whereas ye know not what *shall be* on the morrow." He paused for emphasis.

"For what *is* your life? It is even a vapor that appeareth for a little time, and then vanisheth away. For that ye *ought* to say, If the Lord will, we shall live, and do this, or that. But now ye rejoice in your boastings: all such rejoicing is evil. Therefore to him that knoweth to do good, and doeth *it* not, to him it is sin."

Though Carson had been listening with some intensity, when the Reverend began to read on in length, he found his mind turning back to his youth and the church his family attended. He could still envision his mother's graying hair and the stern expression in her dark eyes as she told him of the mill being shut down. *'Tis the Lord's will*, she said. *The best laid plans of men that come to naught.*

His mother and father held the notion that *whatever was to be, would be*. But Carson felt differently. Sometimes one had to accept what couldn't be changed, but far too many times, it was easier to blame everything on circumstances rather than search for a way to fix problems. A man had to adapt, but accept defeat? Never.

When at last Reverend Garner finished speaking and everyone rose to their feet to sing, Carson stood listening as the words rolled over him. *What a friend we have in Jesus, all our sins and griefs to bear. What a privilege to carry, everything to God in prayer.*

With a certain longing, Carson thought of the loved ones left behind in California, of family and friends. For the past few years, he'd been seeking his own way, adventuring on and never looking back. He'd lived only for the future, and his only sense of presence was to make it serve his future. But if this struggle did not bring about his desired accomplishments, what then?

With the blending of sonorous and lilting voices around him, Carson looked up.

It was beginning to snow.

Chapter Nine

"Glory, I don't believe I've seen it snow so hard for years."

"When did you *ever* see it snow like this," Carson growled.

"Well now," Jimmy said thoughtfully, "you might have a point there."

Carson yawned in the dim light and rolled out of bed. He reached for his pants, noting how the bottom of them were still damp as were his boots. He groaned. At least the stockings on his feet had dried overnight under the bedding, but for the most part, everything he touched felt either damp or cold. It had been a long two days and nights of constant snow.

Feeling the grogginess in his head, Carson sat at the edge of his bed and rubbed his hand over his jaw, rough now from a three-day beard. He wondered if he should shave today or let it go until he reached Dawson. Though he'd always kept his jaw clean shaven with a well-trimmed mustache, he was beginning to care less about appearance and more about protection from the elements.

"I figured we'd be past the time of year for big storms like this," Carson mumbled. As he stood and reached for his shirt, he saw Jimmy pull his head back inside the tent and firmly close the flap. "What's it like out there?"

Jimmy frowned. "Maybe not as bad as yesterday, but it's still coming down pretty hard." He sighed. "I'm gettin' cabin fever, and unfortunately, I'm not even lucky enough to be in a cabin. Besides that, I'm as hungry as a bear."

"I think Jon left to start the cook stove a few minutes ago," Carson mumbled. "Why don't you head over to the dining tent and help him. I'll be along shortly."

"All right. Abigail will most likely be up and have things going anyhow, but I'll check on it." He smiled. "She sure does her part, I'd say. As long as we're snowbound for awhile, I'm thinkin' it was real smart of me to invite *her* along."

"We'd have managed."

"Oh? Is that so? Are we a bit grumpy this fine morning?"

"Go help Jon, Jimmy. The only heat I can feel in this place is the hot air rising from your throat."

Jimmy reached for his coat and grinned at him. "Indeed, we are grumpy."

Carson wanted to tell Jimmy that his babble was giving him a headache, but instead, he began to cough. By the time he gained control of his spell, Jimmy had his coat fully buttoned and was watching him from the tent flap. When Carson waved him on, Jimmy stepped outside muttering as he went. "Don't like that cough, friend. No sir, not one bit."

Abby sat her pot of water on the small but sturdy wood-burning stove and began to gather the dirty plates. As she worked, she wondered how long they would be stuck in this snowbound setting. Although Patches had been good help pulling the supply sled from Finnegan's Point to Sheep Camp and then on to the long hill staging area, she was gone now, sold to the Reverend's friend from Dyea. And though she would be of no further use at the pass anyhow, it now meant the men would have to pack all their remaining goods on their backs to the tramway. When they'd sold Patches, the distance of less than two miles seemed minimal, but now with this snow, it was a different matter entirely. In fact, over the last two days, progress had ground to a complete halt.

Abby thought about the tone of the men at breakfast earlier and hoped they would be sensible. She hadn't wanted them to go out this morning, but all three seemed anxious to take another load. With the past two days of being shut inside, even Jon sounded impatient to get on with shuffling supplies to their drop-off point. In her mind, he was far too eager to get over the pass and be done with it, regardless the weather. For the most part, Jon was practical and cautious, surely he wouldn't take chances if the snow was too deep, would he?

Thinking about the pass ahead of them, Abby sighed. From what she'd heard, the last climb to the top was extremely steep and difficult. She was not eager for it, especially in such snowy conditions.

Tense with her worry, Abby lifted the lid on her pot, and seeing that the water had not yet come to a simmer, she reached for more kindling. When she opened the small but heavy steel door to their stove, she wrinkled her nose and turned away, disappointed with her smoldering fire. Unlike the ranch's beautifully dried firewood, the miserable damp fodder they used here seemed to create almost more smoke than heat. She tossed a few of her driest wood pieces into the firebox, blew hard, and then once more shut the door.

After rising to her feet, Abby looked about the tent. Once the fire warmed the water for the dishes, perhaps she would also wash a few other items and hang them near the stove, for though she did her best to keep her clothing dry and somewhat clean, the hem of another skirt and petticoat was discouragingly filthy.

When she at last finished washing the dishes as well as the hems of her skirts, Abby grabbed her pan of dirty water and stepped outside. She tossed it across a bush and then stood quietly to look out toward the canyon. It was a gray day, and though the air was much warmer, the sky held a heavy, almost ominous quality to it.

Abby felt her body shiver. She hoped they would return soon. At least Jon had said that they would check the trail for conditions before they went very far, and if it appeared to be dangerous, they would come back to camp. Carson and Jimmy had agreed, saying that Hansen, Finn and Erickson were heading out to see for themselves as well.

But so far, none of them had returned.

Whispering a quick prayer, Abby turned back to the tent and thought of Ingrid. Perhaps some company would keep her mind off her worries. It was, after all, April and nearing Easter. The thaw was reported to come around the end of May. Surely, this was a minor setback, merely one of those spring storms like all mountains could have. She needed to be patient.

They all did.

After tossing her skirt over a line by the fire, Abigail wiped her hands, found her coat, and then trudged off through the snow to the nearest tent.

"Hello, Ingrid," she called out.

"Do come," a high, singsong voice replied.

As Abby stepped inside, she was greeted by the delightful aroma of good coffee and something spicy and sweet. "Hmm, it smells wonderful in here, Ingrid."

"Da," her friend declared. "So nasty a day, I try to cheer us with dried apple dumplings. They be ready soon. You stay, eat?"

"That sounds wonderful," she said. Finding the familiar rough-hewn log bench empty, Abby sat before her friend with a frown. "I would hate for the men in my camp to know how well you can cook, Ingrid. I might be let out, you know, and they would hire you."

"Ah, Abby. You joke. I smell what you make. 'Tis good, no?"

Abby smiled. "Good enough for those three, I suppose."

"Do you think the men will find the trail passable?"

"I don't know. It's awfully gray out there. I hope they don't take any chances, though I imagine if it was dangerous, they would have turned back by now."

Abby looked around. "Where's Edie?"

"She vant to visit her new friend in the center of camp. Maria. You meet her?"

"No, I don't believe so."

"Maria works in camp with her papa. They are from Dyea and sell food and hot meals to travelers who not so lucky to have womenfolk, eh?" She smiled.

"On the main street?"

"Ya. Her papa is Mr. Riley. Riley's Food. Maria is pretty, like you, her hair is like the raven. She told us how her momma's people have been taking goods over the Chilkoot for long time now."

"She's Tlingit?"

"Her momma, yes, I think so. Papa is a white man, and her brother packs goods for men. He is very handsome. I think Edie has noticed."

"Ah, that's why she visits?"

"Oh, maybe I yust think so. I believe Finn would be jealous if he knew of it."

"I see. So . . ." Abby stopped mid sentence and looked over her shoulder. "Do you hear something?"

Ingrid turned and listened as Abby rose to her feet. "It's shouting," Abby said. "I hear voices in the distance."

Abby lunged for her cape and raced out of the tent, buttoning her coat as she moved. Once outside, she hesitated and looked around. The shouts were coming from the north, from the trail into the canyon. With her heart pounding, Abby began to run.

As she struggled through the deep snow, she realized that many other men had come alongside, breathing heavily as they tramped through the snow and up a small hill. When they came around a turn in the trail and had a view to an open hillside, Abby stopped in her tracks. Her fingers flew to her mouth. Beyond, several men were rushing forward, some pulling a sled, others waving.

"Quick!" one yelled. "Grab your shovels. An avalanche! Hurry, there are men buried!"

Jon! Oh, dear God, let it not be Jon.

As if frozen in her tracks, Abby stood rigid. Her heart thumped wildly in her chest as she watched the men approaching.

"Is someone hurt?" she shouted. She pointed to the sled.

"Yes, ma'am," one said. She heard their panting and puffing as they pulled the sled forward as fast as they could move.

She ran up to them. "What happened? Can I be of any help?"

The men at the sled paused as others gathered around. Between breaths, they explained. "An avalanche hit," one said. "We were working to pull people free. Then more snow came down. From right above us." He breathed in deeply.

Another leaned forward, "Come on, men, put your legs to it. We need to get this poor fella warm and then head back."

"May I . . . may I see him?" Abby asked quickly. At once, the lead man threw the top of a canvas aside.

Carson! Oh, Lord! No!

"He was knocked off his feet and down the mountain. We pulled him out. He's breathin' but there are others."

"No . . ." Abby moaned.

"You know him?"

"Oh, my . . . yes," she stammered. She swallowed. She could barely speak. "Do you know if a Jon Colton was there or . . . or a friend named Jimmy?"

"Sorry, ma'am," one of them said, "we've no names. Lead on, ma'am. We need to go back. Ten or so men are still digging, but we have to hurry or it will be too late."

Abby simply nodded. "Of course. Follow me." Still numb with shock, she whirled about and started off for the tents. A wave of cold fear pressed against her heart as the shouts of men rang out around her.

"Avalanche! Hurry, men! We've little time!"

Chapter Ten

Abby stared at the near lifeless form on the cot beside her. Carson lay bundled in several blankets, his knees drawn up and eyes closed. His breathing was still labored and the gray color of his skin told her that he had gained little progress over the past week.

She reached for his forehead. His brow felt hot beneath her fingers. As her fingers fell away, Jon and Jimmy step inside the tent.

"How's he feeling?"

"He's still very warm. A few minutes ago, he managed to drink some soup broth and a portion of Grammy's medicinal tea, but he took very little of it, I'm afraid." She shook her head. "Earlier today," she sighed, "Ingrid took me to see her friend named Maria, who's part Tlingit. She gave me a root to boil and use the water for medicine, which I did, but I'm not sure what else to do now, except pray and wait."

Jimmy leaned over his friend and patted him on the shoulder. His eyes looked tired as he studied his friend. "He'll make it," he said. "He'd better or I'll kick his hide. You hear me, Carson?"

When Carson only groaned, Jon shook his head. "So what'll we do now? It's been over two weeks since the avalanche, and though we've managed to get past the mess of things and stash some of our supplies at The Scales, we can't go on until we have a plan here. And right now, I don't see a good one."

"If we wait for Carson, I doubt we'll be getting off at the beginning of thaw," Jimmy mumbled. He looked up at Jon. "Is a quick getaway important for you?"

Jon looked at Abby, his eyes filled with silent questions. "It would be helpful, but we can't leave with Carson being so sick."

"Then you two go on," Jimmy said, "and I'll wait it out here."

"No, I have a better plan," Abby said. "When I went with Ingrid for some medicine at Maria's store, I spoke with her about our dilemma. During our conversation, Maria said her brother is a packer and maybe he could give us aid. He just returned from the pass last night. I think we should talk to him."

Jon raised his eyebrows. "A packer, you say? But how will that help Carson?"

"You and Jimmy should go on. I can stay here with Carson. When he's well enough to travel, perhaps we can hire Maria's brother to pack our remaining goods to The Scales. From there, I'll do the same as you're planning to do—use the tram for carrying supplies to the top of the pass and then hire another packer to transport them to Bennett."

She calmly looked from Jon to Jimmy before allowing her eyes to fall on Carson, still motionless on his cot. "Wouldn't it be best for me to keep nursing him while you find a place to set up camp and start building the two boats?"

Jimmy nodded. "Sounds like that might work."

"Where does this Maria live?" Jon asked. "I'd like to talk with her brother."

"I figured you'd say that," Abby said quietly, "and so I already asked Maria if we could speak to him this evening."

Jon studied Carson a moment. "All right," he said. "If you wouldn't mind, Abby, let's see if we can talk to him now."

A few minutes later, Abby and Jon stepped up to the door of the Riley Food Company and entered the small wooden building. Though it held only three long rough-hewn tables and side benches, the shop was filled to the brim with food supplies, and the aroma of freshly baked goods made the overall atmosphere pleasant to the senses. Beyond a handwritten sign that read *meals, 50¢*, a young, dark-haired woman turned and smiled. Abby smiled back.

"Hello, Maria. Would it be possible to have a word with you? This is my brother, Jon, and he has some questions."

Maria gave Jon a shy nod. "How can I help you?"

Jon took a step closer, his fingers rubbing the bottom edge of his jacket as he moved. "Do you have a brother who's a packer?"

"Yes, his name is Arlie. He's staying in the cabin behind our store." She gave Abby a quick smile, as if to say she remembered their conversation. "Do you need his help?"

"I believe so," Abby replied. "I told my brother that I think it's best for me to remain here with Carson while he and another friend go on to

Lake Bennett, but if I stay behind, I'll need help getting our remaining supplies to The Scales later."

Jon nodded. "I'd like to talk to him about it, if possible."

Maria paused as if to gather her thoughts. "He's only seventeen, you understand, yet he is a good and strong lad. But, Abby," she said, her voice filling with concern, "if you stay in a wet tent for long, you might have more problems, so I talked with Papa after you left this morning. He agreed with me that you should bring a few supplies and stay here. Papa says if Arlie is around, he can sleep by the stove in this room, and that way, you and Mr. Stuart can stay with me in the cabin out back. Mr. Stuart can have Arlie's bed and you can sleep with me."

Maria's gaze moved from Abby to Jon, her steady, dark eyes holding a delicate sparkle as she looked at him. "I believe it will be much healthier for Carson and for Abby. Besides, she could help me here at the store now and then, and I would like her company. What do you think?"

Jon hesitated. "You . . . you would do that?"

"My papa and I would be glad to help. We will take good care of your sister and friend, Mr. Colton."

In the awkward silence that followed, Abby studied Jon's face and knew that he was quite taken with Maria. She smiled. She, too, had found Maria to be a pleasant woman with a soft voice and graceful manner. In several ways, she held the look of her mother's dear Shoshoni friend, Nangai. Abby had always imagined that her grandmother on her father's side, a half-blood Shoshoni, would have looked like Nangai, and so Nangai had found a special place in Abby's heart.

Maria turned to Abby. "Is Mr. Stuart any better this evening?"

"No, I'm afraid not. I gave him a sip of the root water as you directed and a little of my grandmother's herbal remedy, but I'm certain he needs more time to shake his illness."

"Time and perhaps a less drafty room," Maria replied. "I think he'd be much more comfortable in Arlie's bed."

"But I don't want to intrude."

"No," Maria said quickly. "It is custom in my family to care for others, especially ones we like." She smiled. "My momma is very good at it, and the Reverend has taught us that we are brothers and sisters, are we not?"

Abby felt her heart going out to this young woman. "Thank you, Maria."

"Well, come now. Let's find Arlie. He and your brother can make arrangements while we make plans of our own." As Maria turned for the exit, Jon stood silent a moment, simply watching her walk away.

With a smile, Abby reached out and touched her brother's arm. "Jon, are you going to follow her?"

Suddenly, Jon shifted his feet and started for the door. Wordless, Abby followed, but as she continued to consider the looks that had passed between Jon and Maria, clear memories returned. She would never forget that first encounter with Dundee.

But it seemed like so long ago.

Chapter Eleven

Carson awoke to the sight of Abby sitting quietly under a dim light. He turned his head and studied her. She was leaning forward reading a letter, a small sheaf of papers lay to one side. He tried to focus. As he looked about, he suddenly realized that they were not in his sleeping tent, but in a log cabin. Did he remember coming here?

The more he thought about it, the more he could vaguely remember walking up a few steps and crawling into a cold bed. *But why was he here?*

With a light grunt, Carson rolled to his back and stretched his legs. He immediately felt his weakness, even the muscles in his calves held an achy tenderness as he settled flat on his back. But he knew he was more fully conscious and alert than he was other times. He could remember sipping some broth, a strange man coming to help him, and of course, Abby.

"Are we at last awake?"

"How long have I been sleeping?" he mumbled.

"How long in hours, or days?"

Carson saw Abigail's look of concern as she rose to her feet. He found her words incredulous. "It's been that long?"

She gave him a tired smile. "Afraid so."

He tugged at the covers around him and started to sit up, but when he saw he wasn't fully dressed, he pulled his blanket back over him and looked at her, startled. "What day is it?"

"Tuesday, April twenty-fourth, and almost dinnertime. Think you can eat?"

He blinked. *April twenty-fourth? It couldn't be!*

"God Almighty, Abigail. What in thunder am I doing in this room, in only a nightshirt, and even more, just now coming alive so late in the month? Where are Jimmy and Jon?"

She frowned. "Carson, first and foremost, please cease your swearing if you want any answers from me." She gave him a dark look.

He felt his head spin as he leaned back against the rough wall behind the bed and tried to think. "I'm sorry, Abigail. But I can't believe this. I've lost so many days!"

With pinched lips, she walked closer and put both hands to her hips. "In my opinion, these so-called lost days have brought good fortune. In spite of your foolishness, you are alive. Perhaps you don't remember, but basically while you, Jon, and Jimmy were out in a snowstorm, which you ought not to have been in, you were swept off a mountain. And then to worsen matters, you proceeded to help dig out several men before you fell down in a faint. After that, you lay in a near stupor, feverish and groaning, for more than two weeks."

Abby sighed and lowered her hands as well as her voice. "Now, I know that's only a beginning for questions and answers, but before I continue, let me feel your head."

When she placed the palm of her hand on his brow with familiarity, Carson stared into her serious blue eyes. How often had she touched him like this in the past few days?

As if she heard his thoughts, she pulled her hand away and walked back to the table across the room. She picked up a towel, tossed it over her shoulder, and then reached for a large pan sitting nearby.

"The fever is gone," she said quietly. "I believe it broke last night." She turned back for his bed, pan in hand. "I think you're stronger now, so this time, I'll let you do the honors and bathe yourself."

He raised an eyebrow. "Am I to understand that you've been doing it?"

"Somewhat, but I can assure you, it wasn't very personal."

With a small smile, he sat up straighter and reached for the pan, but while she found a small chunk of soap, he felt his head begin to spin. He groaned and closed his eyes, taking a deep breath as he tried to regain his senses.

"Light headed?"

"A little." He cleared his throat and looked up. "Where are we?"

We've been staying in a cabin owned by George Riley, a kindly merchant in Sheep Camp. He lives here from spring until fall with his daughter, Maria, and a son, Arlie, but also has a home, wife and two younger children in Dyea. They offer meals and food supplies to stampeders and were extra kind to help you and I while Jon and Jimmy went on."

He blinked. "Went on?"

"Yes, I'm afraid so. We all thought it best that the two of them go to Bennett and start building the boats."

"When did they leave?"

"Ten days ago."

Carson groaned. He'd lost critical time. Not only did he need to get back on his feet, but he needed to do so in a hurry. April twenty-fourth meant it was near the end of the month. Carson felt his panic and looked around.

"Where's my leather pouch? I need my notes."

"They're in another room where I slept. Though Jimmy packed most of your gear with him, he left all of your personal items, I believe."

"Abigail. This is important. Would you look for my pouch?"

"Now?"

"Yes, please. Now."

Abigail walked to the other bedroom and then returned with his leather satchel. "Is this what you're looking for?"

He sighed, thankful to his core to see it. "Thank you. Would you bring it to me? I need to start gathering my thoughts."

Abigail frowned. "At this very moment?" she asked pointedly. With a shake of her head, she plopped the satchel on the table and then faced him, her eyes flashing with anger. "I'm afraid I shall not bring it to you quite yet, Mr. Stuart. You smell like death warmed over, and I *do* have a few sensibilities. Now as soon as you wash and get dressed, then you must eat some supper. After that, if you insist, we can light the lantern and you can look over your notes." Still frowning, she pulled the towel from her shoulder and threw it at him.

"Abigail," he groaned. "Listen, you don't understand. I have to complete my story about Skagway and Dyea and send it off to my editor. He needs it by May first."

"I do understand. Use the soap, Carson, and don't be stingy. I need to help Maria for awhile, so I'm leaving now. There is food in the shop next door. If you're too weak to come eat it, I'll bring some later. Your clothes are on that bureau." She waved a hand, pointing them out, and then turned on her heels. When she reached the drapery hanging over the doorway, Abigail hesitated and looked back.

"I know your work is important to you, Carson, but you will have time. Before you start, however, you might want to look at what I've already written. It's lying on the table. After I discovered that your writing had a deadline and I was uncertain of your recovery, I put a few thoughts together. But then, first things first. Now wash!" And with that, Abigail moved to the other side of the curtain and disappeared.

For a moment, Carson stared across the room to the table. *I've already written? What on earth did she mean by that?*

Abby poured a fresh cup of coffee for an older gentleman sitting at the end of the table as Carson walked into the room. She felt his eyes and turned to catch the long dark look in his face. She offered a slight nod.

Instinctively, she'd known he would be unhappy with her decision, and perhaps for good reason. She would be deeply offended to have someone touch her writing. But what else could she do? In an effort to escape his stare, Abby walked to the counter where Maria stood dishing up a large bowl of soup.

"We have a new customer."

Maria looked up and opened her eyes wide with surprise. "Mr. Stuart?"

"In the flesh, and he is most annoyed with me I might add. May I finish dishing up that soup for you and let you serve him?'

"He's angry with you? But why?"

"Remember the writing I've been doing?" she whispered.

"Yes."

"That was his work to do. He's a reporter for the *Seattle Post-Intelligencer* and his first submission was due the first of May. I was afraid he couldn't meet the date, so I was compiling his notes and creating a story. He just discovered me."

"Oh, Abby," she breathed. "Well, yes, perhaps I should go to him." She nodded toward a man with red hair close by. "The soup belongs to him."

Abby fell to work serving the red-haired customer, though she did manage a glance over her shoulder as Maria walked up to Carson, who was now seated and staring at her.

"Mr. Stuart?" Maria said sweetly. "I'm Maria Riley. It is so good to see you up and about. May I offer you a bowl of soup?"

"That would be good, Miss Riley. Thank you. And thank you as well for your kind hospitality. I am truly impressed by your family's generosity."

"You are most welcome, Mr. Stuart. We're glad that you're back to better health."

For several minutes, Abby kept her distance while Carson ate. But after she finished washing a few dirty utensils, she took a deep breath and started for Carson, coffee in hand.

"Hello again. Would you like your coffee warmed?" she asked politely.

"No. This will do, thank you." He didn't even look up at her.

Wordless, she picked up his empty soup bowl and carried it to her pan of dishwater. Maria came alongside. "I'll finish this," she said. "You've done enough for one night. Perhaps you should try to make amends?"

"For what?" she mumbled. "Giving him three weeks of my life and helping him with his deadline?"

"Abby..."

She released a deep sigh. "Oh, all right. I suppose I must. Perhaps, if I'm fortunate, he'll be too weak to argue anyhow. And even more, I'm certain he shouldn't be up long and needs to return to his room."

"I would agree," Maria said quickly. She gave Abby a soft, demure smile. "And remember, *a word spoken in due season, how good it is.*" Before Abby could respond, Maria waved her away then turned to serve two more customers just entering the store.

Abby removed her apron, and after tossing it on the counter, she slowly ambled over to Carson's table. Though uncertain her heart had followed her feet, she sat down across from him. He looked up and gave her a blank stare.

"I'm truly sorry, Carson. I imagine I stepped over the boundary of helpfulness, but I was afraid you would miss your deadline."

"I read your writing," he said.

She lowered her eyes, unable to meet the disappointment she saw in his.

"It's good," he muttered. "Very colorful, but precise."

She looked up, shocked by his words. "I simply used your own notes, which I might add, were very complete."

"I was quite surprised," he said slowly. "Do you write often?"

"No. Not really."

"So, how did you come to this talent? Or did you merely lift that slender hand and take to it like a duck to water."

"No, not that either. My mother drilled it into me."

"On a Wyoming ranch?"

"She was a teacher, and we don't necessarily have to be ignorant if we herd cattle, do we?"

Carson, who had leaned forward to talk to her, straightened. "No, I suppose not," he said. "Now I'm showing my ignorance. I just never would have guessed it."

"Well, what *would* you have guessed about me, Mr. Stuart? That I am a simple, young, and foolish girl who had nothing better to do than marry the first man she met, one that would bring her to ruin in the process?" Abby heard the hiss in her last word and fell silent.

Why had she struck out in such anger?

The room was filled with an eerie stillness as she released a shaky breath. Tears formed in her eyes. She looked at the far wall and tried to regain her composure but couldn't help wondering if Maria had overheard. She swallowed and turned back to face him.

"It appears I need to apologize again, Mr. Stuart. Maybe we are both a might tired and should go to bed straightaway. Tomorrow, I will remove a few things that I kept in your room and give you all your space. You've been sleeping in Arlie Riley's bed, but it is not a problem since he is still out on the trail packing for someone."

She rose to her feet and started to turn away when she heard his voice beside her.

"You forgot your promise."

Abby glanced back. "What promise?"

"You promised you wouldn't call me Mr. Stuart. My name is Carson, Abigail. And I would like to thank you for your effort to nurse me back to health, and for helping me in every other way as well."

She stared at him, disbelieving. "You're welcome," she finally mumbled.

"Good night, Abigail."

"Good night, Carson."

Chapter Twelve

The next day Carson sat for several hours at the table pouring over his notes and her writing. After editing her narrative here and there, he added a bit more to her story about Skagway, and then stopped to reread the particulars about the avalanche. He found it fascinating to read how the community had set up a morgue and made every effort to identify the nearly fifty men uncovered from the avalanche. At last, he gathered the papers into a neat pile and shoved them into a large manila envelope.

His work might not be as complete as his editor had in mind, especially since they'd progressed only a few miles up the Chilkoot Trail. He could only hope that though his report didn't include the infamous pass and the descent into Bennett, the extra commotion caused by the avalanches would be of equal interest. To his chagrin, he'd incorporated much of Abigail's writing, especially the stories about women that were told with a rather interesting perspective. He particularly enjoyed the way she had pieced together a story about the wedding and the supportive community at Sheep Camp.

As the image of Abby's flashing blue eyes came to his mind, Carson sighed. When she'd come to retrieve her things this morning, they'd spoken but few words. She was a puzzle to him, and yet the more he considered her apology, as well her writing voice, the more he saw an entirely different woman emerging. She was intelligent and observant. Until now, his manly eyes had mostly focused on her beauty and what he thought was her fragility.

Rising to his feet, Carson quickly stuffed the envelope in his satchel and reached for his coat. Now he would need to find the small tent on the main street called the Post.

On his way back from his delivery, Carson began to consider the days ahead. He'd been fortunate that the postal clerk would be taking a bag of letters to Dyea early tomorrow, and if he and Abigail would start for the pass tomorrow as well, then he might have a chance to keep his accounts on a timely track.

Still deep in thought, Carson started up the steps of the Riley cabin when Abigail came out the door. He hesitated at the bottom step as she gave him a curious look and then slowly walked toward him.

"Good morning, Abigail."

"Good morning, Carson."

"I'm just now returning from the Post," he said. He smiled. "It appears the story may reach Seattle in time."

A warm smile spread across Abigail's face as she gave him a light nod. "I hope it will go well for you," she said.

"Thank you." Carson drew in a quick breath. "Listen, Abigail, I seem to be feeling much stronger today. I've hardly coughed at all. I think it's time that we move on. Do you know when Arlie will return?"

"I believe he's coming back in a day or so, but I don't know, Carson."

"Don't know what? Is there a problem?"

She studied his face for a long moment. "I don't believe leaving directly is a wise decision. Although we have Arlie and the tram, you might be too weak to take the pass now. Give yourself a little more time. I don't want you ill again."

Carson smiled. "I'll make it. I might have to rest a bit more often than usual, but it's not far to The Scales. If you recall, I've been there several times before."

"Yes, but I've heard the pass has a harsh, vertical rise," she said. "And with such elevation gain in a short space, you could have a relapse. Besides, Mr. Riley said the summit is windy, the Canadian customs tedious, and furthermore, it's a long distance past the summit to any lodging. Please, don't push too hard. We've time."

He looked at the firm way she set her jaw and sighed. "I can't convince you?"

"No."

"All right, I'll start walking about camp and see what I can do to get myself in condition. But," he added quietly, "I plan to wait no longer than two days."

She raised an eyebrow. "We'll see."

"Yes," he said. "We'll see." He smiled. He couldn't help himself. She had such a serious look on her face and somehow it amused him. When she cocked her head and gave him a peevish glare, he realized that he could watch her for a very long time and would have little inclination to turn away.

"Carson, I believe you're blocking my path."

"Oh? Well then, please excuse me." He stepped back with a light bow.

She gave him a thin smile as she passed by. "Will I see you at supper?" she asked. "I think you will find it especially fine. Maria and I are preparing fresh chicken, potatoes and pie."

"Fresh chicken?" He stood erect. He was impressed. "Goodness, that is something. Are we celebrating?"

"No," she smiled. "Recovering."

Abby moved down the trail several steps before she called back over her shoulder. "I'm off to say goodbye to Ingrid," she said. "She and Hansen will be going over the pass tomorrow. Supper will be ready by five."

"Yes. I know . . . about Hansen that is. I'll see you soon then." Carson was struck by the inept words coming from his lips. He watched her saunter down the trail a moment longer, then shook his head and turned for the cabin. He would find a bite of bread and cheese and then begin his first walk about camp. Two days.

He would get stronger.

He had to.

"So, how is our Mr. Stuart? He is still on the mend?"

"I suppose." Abby released a deep sigh. "But I do fear he is terribly impetuous. He wanted to leave for the pass tomorrow, if you can imagine, and he's barely on his feet. I will have to watch him closely."

Ingrid grinned. "Ya, you do that."

"Please don't give me that smile, Ingrid. I have enough burdens in my life with these plans to the Klondike and a baby coming. I have no interest in any man. You know my circumstances. I'm not even certain if I'm still married or a widow."

Ingrid nodded, her eyes filling with concern. "I'm sorry, Abby. I know. This life, it's hard. Look at me and Hansen up here in all this. I'm nearly frightened out of my mind to go over that pass tomorrow. I don't know what we thinking."

Ingrid stopped stirring her pot and looked up, wide-eyed and fearful. "I saw it today. Went up with Hansen to watch Edie and Finn go over. But I yust hated to go there. All the way up the canyon, I can think of nothing but poor Erickson buried in the snow and all." She shook her head. "I am so scared, Abby."

Abby encircled an arm around Ingrid's thin shoulders. "I know, my friend. I know. We all have our fears to face, but we never know when it's our time. All we can do is trust what strength God can give us and simply go on." She pulled back and offered Ingrid her best smile. "You have a great strength in you, Ingrid. I'm certain of it. You'll do fine. Besides, won't Hansen be with you?"

Ingrid lowered her head, momentarily biting her bottom lip. "Ya, you are right." She heaved a deep sigh. "Besides, I've no love left for this muddy ol' camp, and I hear it is much drier on the other side. Truly, I am ready for something different. It's yust so high up!" Ingrid chuckled nervously.

Abby laughed. "I remember a time when I was a small child and my whole family went to the mountains. When my brother raced up a steep cliff, I wanted to go, but I got halfway up and began to cry. My mother climbed up to me and said, *don't look down the hill, Abigail. You must always keep your eyes facing up.*" She shrugged. "So far it's been good advice. Maybe it can be for you as well."

Ingrid's blue eyes grew thoughtful. "Will I ever see you again?"

Abby had the same question running through her mind earlier. "Who's to say," she replied, "but I believe we need to hold on to the possibility. Don't you?"

"Ya, I will do it."

"As will I."

As they hugged each other, Ingrid spoke into her ear. "Bless you, Abby. Be safe. I vill pray for you."

"And I for you."

Abby's nose burned as she blinked back her tears and stepped back. "I think I best go and help Maria," she said quietly, "but you remember what we talked about while you're climbing that mountain tomorrow, and know that I will be praying for you until we meet again." She turned and started for the trail and then paused and looked back. She felt a deep sadness inside.

"Goodbye, Ingrid."

"Ya. Goodbye, Abby."

Chapter Thirteen

Abby sucked in a deep breath of cool air as her gaze lingered on the great craggy mountain and the line of men that snaked up the steep incline. Over the years, she had ridden horses through her share of mountains, but it had been summertime. Never had she crossed a steep rocky pass by foot, let alone do it in winter. But here she was, the icy pathway called the Golden Stairs rising before her, and in her mind's eye, it appeared to reach up to the clouds.

From descriptions being bandied about in Sheep Camp, Abby knew the pass would be steep, but she hadn't dreamed that the area would have such open and windswept slopes or such grandeur. The Chilkoot Pass! And unimaginably, they would cross it under the brilliance of a rare clear day.

She turned, gazing at the snow-covered mountains that encircled the U-shaped canyon where she stood. As she turned full circle, she saw Carson approaching.

"Those men up there look like ants," she called to him. Is that our trail?" Abby pointed to the long line of stampeders above them.

"That's our pass," he said dryly.

Carson, who had been helping Arlie load their supplies on the tramway and making arrangements for them to be hauled to Bennett, stooped to pick up his daypack. She watched him while he shuffled it over his shoulders.

"Thank heavens for the tramway," she said, "otherwise it would be a very difficult climb, especially if one had a full load like some of these men do."

Carson nodded. "I've heard that some of these men have to take twenty and even thirty trips up that steep trail in order to get all their supplies to the top." He looked back at her. "So, the question is, are you ready?"

She heaved a sigh and nodded. "As much as one can be, I imagine."

He smiled. "Do you want to lead or follow? This appears to be a one-man or one-woman staircase, however you might say it."

Abby considered. "If I should slip, you will promise to stop me from sliding all the way back down, won't you?"

"I take it you're leading?"

Flashing him a thin smile, Abby set out for the line of men, but as they passed various groups of stampeders, tents, and piles of supplies everywhere, she recalled Ingrid's fearful face and felt her own anxiousness rising. When at last it was their turn to start up the icy pathway, she took a deep breath and stepped up, silently steeling herself for whatever effort it would take. *Just move steady and keep looking up.* Surely, she could do this, couldn't she?

Earlier in the day, she had managed their hike just fine, even finding the sights of the mountains around them to be glorious. She'd been especially amazed at one massive blue-tinged glacier that flowed over a cliff and down into a small, high plateau. The only moment that seemed unnerving was when Arlie pointed out the avalanche area. Otherwise, the trek had been more pleasant than she'd expected, especially when she considered that the weight of her pack, unlike Arlie's and Carson's, consisted of a mere loaf of bread, a canteen of water, a few personal toiletries, and one oil-skin slicker. In addition, they had rested often beside the trail's giant boulders, standing and gazing down into the ever disappearing canyon with its deep green forest.

"Never could understand why anyone taking the Chilkoot would come this far and then not climb the stairway." Carson quipped to a man below him.

"For certain," the young man called back. "I tried the Peterson Pass on one climb," he said. "But that trail is nastier than it looks from the bottom."

Abby glanced to her right, to the alternate route called the Peterson Pass. As she paused to catch her breath and glanced down the hill, she was struck by the burden on the back of the man behind Carson, for not only was he carrying a large pack filled to the brim, but in addition, he'd tied a long sled to the top of it all. It looked as if his goods would pull him backward at any minute.

"That so?" Carson said. "Is this your final climb or have you more?"

"Should be my last," the man grunted.

"Congratulations," Carson said. "Now pay the Mounties for your two thousand pounds."

"Y'up."

It grew quiet after that, and as she and Carson bent to the task of taking one step after another, neither spoke. Though the icy staircase held steps notched in the snow, now and then Abby found it difficult to keep from slipping due to the sun's warming affects on the packed snow. Trying to be extra cautious, she concentrated on her feet. They moved steadily upward for several long minutes before Abby felt her lungs crying out. Remembering Carson's illness, she paused, took a deep breath and looked back. Though Carson's cough had all but disappeared over the past few days, she still worried that he was in a weakened state.

Below her, Carson looked up, released a breath and smiled.

"Steep," he said simply.

Still winded, she merely nodded and then opened the top part of her coat. Her heavy wool cape felt far too warm and the high buckram collar of her dress much too tight, and when she considered the lightweight corset digging into her sides, she wondered why she had worn it at all. She should have been more sensible and packed it away with other clothing supplies.

After her heart calmed and normal breathing resumed, Abby turned and continued up the slope. But she had barely taken ten steps when she began to bemoan, more than ever, her cumbersome skirt. Although she had shortened it at Sheep Camp, she had to be careful to keep from stepping on its hem. Moving slow and steady now, she worked her way up the slope for several more minutes until she saw a man rising from a small dugout cave carved in the snow. Immediately, she turned and called over her shoulder.

"Carson, would you like to sit a moment?" She pointed to the resting area.

Seeing his nod, she stepped out of the line and clawed her way to the shelter. Once seated, she leaned back against the snowy wall behind her and released a deep breath. When Carson plopped down beside her, she heard how his breathing was heavy as well.

Abby searched his face, wondering. "Are you feeling up to this?"

Carson released another breath with a whoosh and then smiled a smile that made the edges of his eyes crinkle. "Here's to a break for both of us, eh?"

She nodded. "You may have had an illness to deal with," she gasped "but I do believe I have been sitting in camp far too long." Abby gulped in another breath of air and stared out over the scene below.

"A year ago, I would never have believed I could be in such a place. Who could imagine such a sight?" Abby squinted against the sun as her gaze swept the valley below. A group of men stood by the hut at The Scales, but they looked small and almost insignificant when measured against the mountains rising all around them.

"Is this not incredible?" she breathed. "In all my life, I shall never forget it."

"My thought exactly," Carson declared. He released another ragged intake of air and looked at her. "Are you glad you came then?"

"Oh, yes. Well, at this moment anyhow." Abby nodded at the young fellow who had been following Carson. He had fallen behind but was still moving slowly up the trail. "What a heavy load for that young man," she said quietly. "Our packs are so small compared to his."

Carson nodded. "Unfortunately, the haves and the have-nots progress this trail at a different rate of speed. Hansen and his crew started from Dyea weeks before us, and yet they weren't able to cross the pass until two days ago." He smiled at her. "But then, we had Patches. She was a good investment."

"Perhaps we ladies can be helpful."

"Indeed, not can, but are."

Abby felt the ribs of her undergarment digging into her waist and edged her rump forward to adjust her position. Without thinking, she reached for her stomach protectively as she shifted her weight.

"Are you feeling all right?"

She glanced at Carson, wondering at his comment, and was surprised to find that his smiling eyes had taken on a sudden look of concern. Abby felt a minor shift in her heart's pace.

"I'll be fine," she said. She looked away. "How are you feeling? Are you having any trouble breathing?"

"Not doing too badly," he said quietly.

"Well then," she shrugged, "perhaps we should go on."

Without dropping his gaze, he peered at her ever more keenly. "Are you certain you shouldn't rest a little more? The sun feels most welcome, wouldn't you say?"

She looked up. "It is bright, isn't it? I can't believe how warm I feel, considering what it was like three weeks ago."

Abby heard a vague murmur of agreement before she took a deep breath and pushed shakily to her feet. As she reached out to the slope for balance, Carson stood and grabbed her hand. "Here," he said, "let me help you. I don't want you slipping away. You could end up at the bottom and I'd hate for us to have to start all over again."

Abby thought to pull her hand away, but seeing his smile and sensing the strength of his grip, she instead allowed him to hold her hand as they made their way back to the snowy staircase and into the line of men pulling their great burdens upward.

"What do you mean, we should glissade?" She looked at him in disbelief.

"Just what I said," Carson returned. He pointed a finger to the downward slope ahead and a lake far below. "It's a long way down to Crater Lake, and though we've come a fair distance from the top of the pass already, I see a few folks over there handling this part of the descent in a much better way."

Abby studied the area below the trail, to where a woman was shouting with glee as she swept down the slope on her bottom, her skirts flying.

"I hardly doubt the wisdom of doing that," she mumbled. "How on earth do you keep from tumbling forward on your nose and making quite a scene?"

Seeing the challenge in her eyes, Carson smiled. "Easy," he said. "I thought you were a mountain woman. You've never tried this?"

"I rode horses, Carson. A more sensible way to descend a mountain trail."

He snorted. In his experience, horses meant broken tail bones and a whole pack of trouble, but glissading? Now that was a different matter. His brother had shown him while on a hike in the Sierras and he'd found it incredible. And the more he watched a party of men and women laughing and shouting their way down the mountain, the more his mind turned to the supplies he had in his pack. He had a small tarp he'd brought for sitting, and to boot, he had a rope. Besides, both of them were carrying strong hiking sticks. It could be done. He looked back at her.

"So, are you telling me, Abigail, that you can't handle a little fun in the snow?"

Abby puckered her lips and turned her gaze once again to the last man sliding down the hill. "I didn't necessarily say that," she said crossly. "I simply meant that on a slope like that, one could tumble quite easily."

"Oh, well, I must have heard some other woman talking earlier, I guess. Thought I heard someone say those men looked like they were having fun."

"I had no idea you could keep such small bits of information stored away in that mind of yours, Carson."

He chuckled. "Listen, from my point of view that group appears to be doing fine. Women included. And if you need assurance that you can have a safe landing, I will tell you that I have some things in my pack that will insure it." He paused a moment before giving her a curious look. "Unless you're worried for another reason."

She tossed him a scorching frown. "I'm to have a child, Carson. I'm not an invalid."

"All right." He hesitated, wondering whether to pursue his idea. "So do you want me to show you how or not?"

"You're really eager to do this?"

"Absolutely."

She straightened her shoulders and placed both hands on her hips. "I may regret it, but all right, you win. Lead the way."

After sidestepping fifty yards or more across the snow, to where the other group had begun their descent, Carson saw why they had selected that spot. The slope here appeared to be free of rocks, and the draw where the four men and two women were now moving away, held a slow rise on the back side of it that would naturally halt their descent without any other aid.

"We're in luck," he called back brightly. "Come over and see for yourself."

As Abby approached, he pointed below. "See that slow rise on the back side of the draw? If you make sure you slide that direction, you'll have a nice, slow landing." He studied her skirt, coat and pack.

"If you want something to sit on, I've a tarp in my pack. You'll stay drier that way."

"So, we're sliding down there?" She pointed.

"Yes, ma'am. Step a little to your right and you'll be in line with a nice path down the mountain that someone already made just for you."

She shrugged. "Much to my distaste, I'll have to admit that I have taken a slide or two down a hill, just perhaps not such a *long* hill." She wrinkled her nose at him. "But surely I won't need the tarp." She waved her hand at his pack.

"Whatever you say."

"Well, you're the so-called expert. What do you think?"

Carson slipped his pack from his shoulders and opened it. He reached inside and pulled free a small tarpaulin then stepped up beside her. "I think you should sit on this," he said. "Here, let me help you."

Abby sat on the tarp and looked up with a puzzled frown. "Now what?"

He smiled. "You grab the front of that thing and pull it between your legs. Then you lean back against your pack, raise your legs, and off you go."

She looked up at him and then back to the slope.

He leaned forward and took her walking stick from her hand. "Use it like this," he said. He sat beside her and began to demonstrate. "By tucking the top of your stick into the tarp, you can hold it and the tarp firmly while you use your right hand to hold the base of your stick. Then, if you want to slow down, you drag the base of the stick into the snow. To speed up, you release it. Simple as that."

Abby considered him a moment then did as he said, grasping the folds and the stick tightly in her hands. She looked at him with a smile. "Lead the way."

He grinned at her. "Tell you what. Let's slide together. I'll start out and then you follow on my left. That way we won't run into each other, but if you get in trouble, just yell for my help. I should be able to slow or stop my descent and come help you."

Turning, Carson sat down about ten feet from her. He adjusted the pack behind his back and grabbed his hiking stick. "You ready?"

She shrugged. "I suppose."

He shoved his hat under his jacket, and then leaned back and pushed off with a shout. "Let's go!"

For several minutes, Carson heard nothing but wind and his own groans as he picked up speed and sailed down the mountain faster than he ever imagined. It was steeper than he thought and keeping his speed in check more a challenge than expected. As he bounced along, he realized that he was flailing down the slope in a less than graceful manner.

When he slid to a stop, his buttocks tingling from slapping against the snow, he began to laugh. After a moment, he gathered his strength and rolled to his side just in time to see Abby, legs up in the air, come to a screeching halt beside him.

"Good girl!" he shouted.

Abigail threw her legs down and her arms out then simply lay still, facing up toward the bright sky. He heard the awe in her voice when she finally spoke. "Whoa," she moaned. "Oh, my word!"

He laughed at her expression. No longer the tyrant and boss, instead, she lay sprawled on her back, wide-eyed and youthful, and deep in Carson's heart, he knew he would picture her that way for many years to come.

It was nearly dark when Carson and Abby at last stumbled past a long line of pack mules and edged toward the small lodging accommodations that Arlie had recommended. Though Carson could tell it wasn't much of a hotel ahead of them, at least it looked better than the place where they'd eaten supper. That building had been a miserable-looking structure, half tent and half crude log, in an area called Happy Camp, a misnomer of a name if Carson had ever seen one. Abby had grown somewhat quiet and reserved after their brief rest there and said little as they continued wearily on to Deep Lake camp. In fact, she hadn't spoken for nearly an hour and Carson suspected that she was bone tired, as was he.

To him, one of the most surprising aspects of this journey was the number of woman trekking into the Klondike. And to his surprise, though some were young and ready for adventure in youthful fitness, others were older mothers with a pack of children. He recalled the shabby-looking man and woman who fed them earlier, who for all appearances were barely able to eke out an existence on a barren mountainside. It didn't seem right for a woman to endure such a place. He hoped it wouldn't come to that for Abby.

As they stepped inside the doorway, Carson saw a man in gray suspenders and a blue wool shirt look up. "Hello there, folks," he said with more cheer than necessary.

Carson jostled past a group of men to the small wooden counter and smiled. "Have a friend who recommended that we overnight here," he said. "Have you beds for two?"

"Sorry, sir. We don't. Have you tried the establishment across the way?"

Carson puckered his lips in contemplation. As he recalled the place, it had looked mighty small and even more bedraggled than this establishment. "Well," he said slowly. "I'm sorry to hear it."

The man nodded. "A lot of people going over the pass today."

"That's what our young friend Arlie told us earlier. Now that the avalanche business has been put behind, everyone is heading out. In addition, I heard there are even more people coming up from Dyea this week."

"You know Arlie?"

"Yes. We stayed with Mr. Riley and his daughter Maria while I recuperated from the avalanche."

"Say, did you get caught in that thing?"

"I did for a few minutes anyhow. A terrible tragedy."

"Mister?"

Carson looked over his shoulder to see a young man about half his height staring up at him. "Listen, Arlie's my friend. I can stay at another place where I know people. Why don't you take my quarters down the hall there. Just a small spot with curtains between beds, but you and the Missus can have it."

"Well, that's mighty kind of you." Carson looked over to where Abigail stood by the doorway. She had a tired and drawn look on her face. She needed a bed. He turned back. "You wouldn't possibly have a chair to put in the room with us, now would you?"

"A chair?" The man gave him a curious look. "I suppose I do. I reckon I can bring it by later on."

"All right," Carson said with a hesitant voice. "We'll take the room. How much do I owe you, young man?"

Chapter
Fourteen

Within the tight confines of the bed covers, Abby awoke from her dream with a start. She had a strange vision of water whirling about her as if she and others were caught in the vortex of a huge river plunging over a falls. Taking a quick breath, she took note of the shadowed room and rolled to her back.

She groaned inwardly as she began to stretch her legs. Everything ached—her ankles, legs, back, even her neck. She doubted if she would ever again walk so far, not to mention endure that degree of elevation and descent without aid of horse or wagon. Her feet still ached. The long hike into Deep Lake from the top of the pass had taken far more time than she had expected, not to mention the difficulty she had keeping her footing as they moved down the long trail surrounded by a rocky, treeless terrain in all direction. The way had been bleak to say the least. Releasing a long sigh, she rolled to her side.

During cattle roundups and excursions into Wyoming's mountains, she had often gazed at the rugged peaks and timbered hillsides and known a thrill for it. Long ago, she'd decided that no man held power over such forces but Providence himself. In those days, she'd felt an awareness of God unlike any other time, and without a doubt, yesterday had been filled with those same sensations.

She could still envision the snow, the long climb, the mounds of gear piled nearby while they waited in line at the tent of the North-West Mounted Police. She could almost feel again the power of the wind whipping her coat and hair. She had enjoyed incredible views of distant mountains and valleys, from south to north.

With a wide yawn, Abby turned her head to where Carson sat nearby, his feet tucked under the bottom of their bed quilt, his head and neck scrunched against a chair back for support. He looked miserable.

Neither of them had spoken much last night. She hadn't been pleased with the accommodations he'd agreed to, but at least Carson had found her a bed, though it was merely a large canvas stretched across four logs and lined with a straw shakedown. Still and all, she had rested well, which was more than Carson could probably say.

Abby studied the thin pillow cushioning Carson's head and the awkward bend in his back, and then with a long sigh, she rolled to her side and sat up. Fully dressed except for her boot shoes, she scooted out from beneath the covers and silently moved to Carson's side. He needed to stretch out as well. At the feel of the hard, cold surface beneath her feet, she shivered. It was freezing in this room.

"Carson."

He jumped as she tapped him on the shoulder. "Wha . . .?"

"Sorry, didn't mean to startle you. Go lie down on the bed. I'm not sleepy now."

He struggled to sit up and then rubbed his hand across the back of his neck. With a sigh, he looked from her face to the bed. "You certain?"

"I am. You've been cramped in this chair for most of the night," she whispered, "and it can't be good for you."

She heard him groan as he rose to his feet. Wordless, he shuffled forward then crawled between the covers and sighed again. Abby reached for her coat and sat back on the chair. As she struggled to get comfortable, she did as Carson had done, and stuck her own feet beneath the bottom of the quilt. In the darkness, she listened to the snoring beyond and watched the curtain sway in the night air. Without a doubt, that had to be the thinnest curtain she'd ever seen and it did little to keep out the cold from the freezing hallway. Maria's cabin had been heaven compared to this. Maria, of all things, had even produced a tub for bathing. Wrapping her arms about her, Abby closed her eyes and tried not to dwell on her present circumstances.

"Abigail."

Abby opened her eyes and saw Carson looking up at her. He patted the bed. "Come lay down," he mumbled softly. "I won't touch you. You're tired and cold and I can't let you sit there like that, but my back needs to stretch out."

She looked at him, wondering what to say.

"I mean it, Abigail. Don't be making more of this than it is. We're fully clothed and you know I'm right." With a sigh, he rolled over giving her his backside, as if to say she could do what she wanted but he needed to sleep.

For a long moment, she considered his words, but when she began to feel the ache of her hip bones against the cold wooden chair, she rose to her feet and slipped gingerly into the bed. For a moment, she shuffled her hips, and then lying as close to the edge as possible, she slipped the covers over her shoulders and closed her eyes. He was right about one thing, that chair would make any back feel miserable.

When Abby awoke with a start, she looked around and found the bed beside her empty. With a light groan, she stretched out and thought about the hours ahead. One more day of walking and then they'd find Jon and Jimmy at Bennett. Hopefully, they'd be well into their boat building and with a camp at the ready. She would welcome back her own small cot and quilt.

As she considered the months ahead, Abby slipped her hand below the covers. After running her fingers from hip bone to hip bone, she rested the palm of her hand flat to her stomach. Would the journey ahead be too dangerous for her child? She thought about the many pioneer women in their valley. Several, including her mother, had taken long journeys to far away places and managed to have children along the way. Was it different for them? Did they have more support by husbands and other women?

But even then, some had died, hadn't they?

Abby took a deep breath and released it slowly. Perhaps it didn't matter where you were, or whether you were with family or not. There was always sickness and death. All at once, Abby felt a sudden stretching, a motion beneath her hand. With a gasp, she held completely still, waiting.

Her baby! Had it moved?

At once, she found her confidence for the days ahead fading. From now on, she would need to be careful, to eat well, and above all else, never do anything as foolish as sliding down a long hill in the snow!

With a sigh, Abby sat up. Yesterday had brought her a sense of joy and adventure, like in her youth, but life was changing for her and within her. And everything she did now needed to take another person into consideration. Abby thought about Dundee.

Was he alive? Would he find them? She tried to picture him, to see his smiling face and feel his arms around her, but as she closed her eyes, the only vision that came to mind was of Carson watching her while she adjusted her hips in the snow cave.

With a shaky intake of air, Abby pushed away her covers and rolled from the bed. Though stiff and cold, she quickly laced her boots and then brushed her hands across her skirt as if to free it from its wrinkles before she reached for her toiletry bag. She pulled out her silver brush, and after removing several pins from her tangled hair, she brushed it thoroughly before twisting it into a loose bun. How she longed to once again tie her long and heavy tresses back with a simple leather tie as she'd done years ago. It would be so much simpler. But she was a grown woman now. Life, like her hair, had to be managed in a proper manner.

After dabbing a bit of lotion across her face and hands, Abby carefully placed the jar of cream back in her bag and started for her coat, but as she moved, nearly every muscle in her legs and hips began to argue against it. Groaning, she took a quick breath and then limped on. She had little choice but to continue her effort to find a toilet, some water, and then most assuredly, something to eat.

Carson turned as Abigail stepped inside the meager hotel dining area. For a brief instant, he felt a warm surge in his chest as she walked forward. When she sat across from him, he noted how she'd gathered her dark hair more casually behind her head and was struck by the soft fullness of it against a slim neck.

"Good morning, Abigail. How are you feeling?"

"As if every muscle in my body has been overused," she said with a wan smile. "But other than that, I'm fine. Have you eaten?"

"No. Had some hot coffee, but haven't been up long enough to do more than make myself awake." He smiled back at her. "That pan of cold water they offer a body in the morning is a real eye-opener, isn't it?"

Abby nodded, her eyes twinkling. "Indeed. I do believe it's straight from a glacier."

He chuckled. "I would agree."

"So," she said lightly. "What's on the menu? More cold bread and tinned meat?"

"I hope not." He nodded to the men across the way. "They're having, would you believe, eggs and bacon and hot bread. I imagine we'll have the same."

"It smells wonderful. Why haven't you eaten?"

"I told them that I thought you might be along directly. And, praise be, here comes our food as we speak."

"Are you and your wife ready now, sir?"

Abby gave him a cold stare as Carson looked up to the woman with a platter of food. "We are indeed," he said, smiling. "Thank you for bringing it so promptly. We're hoping to get on our way what with the miles ahead to Bennett."

"You and a thousand others today," she said with a smirk.

"That many?"

The waitress sat her tray before them then handed a plate to Abby. "Well, I might be stretchin' it a bit," she said with a laugh, "but that's what I hear tell. It's near a mob down Bennett way."

"A mob? Are there problems?" Carson asked.

"Oh, no, nothing of that sort," she said quickly. "I reckon it's a fair organized place, just cramped. I lived in Skagway before I came here. Now that's a mob." She snorted with laughter and then looked from Carson to Abby.

"Now, don't you worry, ma'am, the Mounties and the law is in place in Bennett. You'll be fine."

Abby gave her a weak smile. "Thank you," she said.

As the woman turned away for more coffee, Abby closed her eyes. Carson glanced at her, wondering at first, then felt somewhat embarrassed when he realized that she was praying. When she opened her eyes, she reached for a fork.

"The missus?" she said carefully.

"On my honor, Abigail, I merely said I was waiting for someone to join me." As Carson took a bite of his food, he considered her again. "You're not being a little extra sensitive about me, are you?"

Abby looked up. For a brief moment, her eyes held an uncertain, faraway look before she spoke in a low voice. "I don't know, Carson. Maybe I am. All I know is that my only goal is to endure all this for my family and help Jon recover the inheritance. Then, whether Dundee returns or not, I'll need to find a place to call home and raise my little child as best I can. I must concentrate on that and nothing more. I think I've already made myself clear, but perhaps we still need a reminder?"

He studied the calm expression in her blue eyes, the way her gaze never wavered as she spoke to him, and though he heard her words, he knew his mind was recording the look of her smooth, taut skin against high cheekbones, the way her dark hair framed a distinctive narrow face, a straight nose and full lips. And when she finished speaking, though he gave her his practiced smile, he couldn't help but note the quick slant of her eyes as she tilted her head in distrust of him.

"Abigail," he said carefully, "I don't need a reminder of the fact that you are in uncertain times. I don't even need a reminder that you have goals, as I do. I think all I need is a smile or two, and a friend who can relax and call me friend in return. Is it a deal?"

Abigail took a bite of food and chewed it slowly. For a while, she simply studied him as if she were looking right into his very soul, searching for any honesty she might find. He knew he'd been forthright. He thought her beautiful, a good and upright woman, but he knew she was entangled and that losing his heart to her would be a foolish move on his part. And though he would enjoy the sight and presence of her, he had no intentions of taking any steps toward something more.

After a moment, Abby swallowed and gave him a thin smile. "All right, Carson. Friends. But nothing more."

"Good, now that we've settled all that, I can eat in peace."

She shook her head and smiled. "Here? In this place?"

To his chagrin, even as she spoke five men entered the room, and as if they'd heard her very comment, they immediately squeezed in beside them at the table and called for food in raucous voices.

Carson leaned forward. "Well," he said, "at least I'm eating."

After gathering their shoulder packs, Abby stood to one side while he spoke to the owner of a pack train readying to leave. The man was connected to the tramway operation and, to Carson's satisfaction, assured him that their supplies would, as earlier directed, be taken from the top of the tramway to the hotel and part-time church in Bennett. Most likely, the packer added, their goods would arrive in Bennett in a day or two.

With a sense of hope that he and Abby would be able to locate their supplies as well as the minister who would have information on Jon and Jimmy, Carson started for the trail with Abby a step behind. For nearly twenty minutes, they hiked along the narrow canyon with the ground solid beneath their feet, but the more the sun rose overhead, the more the trail became slick with soft pockets of snow and downright nasty mud holes. Now and then, he would pause and look back to see if Abigail needed a hand, but each time he inquired, almost to his amusement, she would answer with an abrupt, "I'll be fine." After several attempts, he no longer offered.

They hiked for more than an hour through a boreal forest when they came to an open area where many trees had been logged for shelter or boat building. Seeing the numerous stumps about them, Carson hesitated and looked around. Not far up the hill he saw a small rivulet tumbling over a stony creek bed. He turned to Abby who had come alongside.

"I believe we may be getting close to Lindeman," he said. "Shall we rest a bit before we go on?"

"Yes, I'd like that." And without further word, Abigail tromped through a melted snowdrift and slumped down on a nearby stump. He walked to another stump not far from her and slipped off his pack.

"Would you care for some water?" He pulled a metal cup from his bag, complete with dents from years of use, and smiled. "Not the prettiest thing in the world, but it retrieves good drink without getting the knees wet. I see a spring just up the hill."

She nodded. "Sounds wonderful but I can get my own water."

"Nope," he said quickly. "Not a problem."

As he scampered up the hill and bent to the spring, he noted a small band of three women and two men approaching Abigail on the trail. He studied them for a moment, thinking he recognized the red-headed woman in the group. He was certain that he'd seen her singing to a crowd of laughing men at Sheep Camp, and by the look of them, he imagined that they were headed for Dawson to mine gold in a rather different manner.

All three of the women wore garments that were bright, unlike the dark colors most of their gender wore on the trail, and two even sported brightly colored hats. The woman with red hair had a cap with a large tassel jostling gaily off to one side, its bold burgundy tone in odd contrast to the hair beneath. The man in the lead smiled at Abigail then hesitated and waved his hands to the remaining stumps downhill from her.

"I say, Miss, are these seats taken?"

Abigail gave him a polite smile. "No. It appears they are quite empty."

"Well, then," he said, his voice deep and jovial, "I believe we have found seating for ourselves, ladies. Shall we rest?"

Carson quickly downed his cup of water and then refilled it and started back down the hill, curious at their sudden company. As he approached, the man who had spoken earlier tapped a finger to the brim of his hat.

"Morning, sir, I do hope we're not disturbing you, but this appears to be a wonderful area to rest the weary body."

Carson smiled as he moved to Abigail and handed her the cup of water. "That it is," he said. He returned to his stump and sat back, curious. "Although I personally have known more comfortable seats, as I'm sure you have as well."

"Indeed," the man said quickly with a large, toothy smile. He then nodded toward the other women who were resting on stumps downhill from them. "Me and the ladies are, in fact, on our way to Dawson where we hope to fill a good many comfortable seats for their talent. Where are you folks headed? Dawson, I assume?"

"Later, yes. At the present, finding Lake Bennett will suffice."

"Yes, yes," the man agreed. He cocked his head and leaned toward them. "You and the lady going to the Klondike? Somehow, you don't quite look the part of a grubstaker."

"Actually, I'm a reporter seeking my fortune in writing about the Klondike, and the woman with me is my partner's sister."

The man offered a rather crooked smile as he reached in his pocket and extended a card to Carson. "Jack Conrad's the name. Theatre manager extraordinaire," he quipped. "Perhaps you might extend my introduction to the lady in your party."

He leaned in closer, dropping his voice to a low whisper. "A real looker, that lassie. If she's any talent a'tol, she'll be able to earn more gold nuggets than any of the rest of us."

Carson felt a slow creep of warmth rising from his neck to his cheeks, the muscle in his right arm twitched. Calmly, he leaned forward and lowered his voice to match his neighbor's. "You have an eye for character and drama I'm certain, my good sir, but look closer. Do you really believe she has the appearance of *entertainment* about her?"

The man sat back rather quickly as Carson kept his eyes glued to Jack Conrad's. It took everything within him to keep from grabbing the man's narrow, pinched face and placing a distinct dent within its fine features.

"No, well, I suppose not," Jack Conrad stuttered. He nodded to the women seated downhill from them. "I imagine I best be seeing to my ladies' needs." He looked up. "I say, did you find a spring up there?"

"Yes. All for the quick taking," Carson said with a smile.

Jack stood. "Well, now, you folks have a nice journey into Bennett," he said. "And if you get the chance, you come see us. The girls are set to sing and dance at the Star Palace," he added with a near puffed-up chest.

Carson nodded. "I might just do that. Always makes for an interesting story."

"Yes. That and more." The stranger's lips drew tightly together in a slow upward turn.

Carson watched as the thin shouldered man strutted off toward the women nearby. With a light shake of his head, he turned to Abigail who sat uphill from him eyeing him carefully.

"So you've declined my part in being an *actress,* have you?"

He shrugged. "They might very well be singers and dancers, but I figured that smile somehow embraced a little something more." He motioned with his head down the hill. "You rested enough?"

She stood. "Yes, but whether I am or not I'm more than happy to be on our way. I'm eager to find Lake Bennett and Jon and Jimmy."

"I agree."

After taking the cup from her hand, he tossed it in his pack and started forward. As they rounded the bend in the trail leaving the small party behind, he heard her voice behind him.

"Do you suppose they make much money as singers and dancers, Carson?"

Carson smiled in spite of himself. "I've read that they do. Before we left Seattle, I had a rather interesting discussion with my editor. Although we had talked earlier about the Chilkoot Trail into Dawson, we also discussed the possibility of securing a room on a steamer and have me travel by way of St. Michaels to Ft. Yukon and Dawson. It was his understanding that a rather colorful group of ladies and gents often took that route and might make for some interesting stories."

"That would have been easier, I imagine."

"Perhaps so, but reports have come back that the ships going north often carry a raucous bunch." He smiled over his shoulder to where she was walking about a step behind him. "Besides," he said, "most ships are cramped and some nearly starve a body. Jimmy wouldn't care for that. I read of one account where a rather well-to-do family lodged a complaint against a steamer and its captain. Guess the carrying on was quite startling not to mention the near-death experience when the ship was caught in the gathering ice."

"That so? My, wouldn't a story like that be right up your alley?"

He laughed. "Might be, Abigail, I guess I don't mind reporting on whatever life brings. It's all a part of the human condition." He turned and grinned at her before resuming his walk.

"Although in all honesty," he continued, "the thought of being cooped up weeks longer on a ship with such noise, smells and commotion wasn't as appealing as hiking the Chilkoot. My family, especially my father and brothers, but even my sister, all spent time exploring the Sierra Mountains not far from my hometown. So, you might say the mountain route was much more compelling to me, although I was told to take a Yukon River steamer to come out of Dawson." He thought about Jon and Abigail and wondered.

"What about you and Jon? What are your plans?"

There was a long pause before she spoke. "I have no idea," she said wistfully. "Even though life was a constant adventure where we lived in Wyoming, Jon and I were taught to be careful and prudent in all our plans. But I fear this journey seems to be different."

They walked in silence for several steps before she continued. "I've been praying over it for weeks now. And as far as I can tell, we will simply have to take one day at a time. Exactly how or when we'll return is too distant to contemplate, though our basic hope is to leave Dawson before winter sets in."

"I'm not sure I fully understand what you and Jon are about, except that you plan to recover gold for another family?"

"For the most part, that is the plan. The confusing issue is not whose gold we're to recover, but where it is. A man by the name of C. R. Thorne wrote a letter to some friends of my husband, the Smythe family. This Mr. Thorne told them that Dan Fogherty had passed in October of ninety-seven and that they should be inheriting Dan's claims and a rather large poke of gold. C. R., a friend and neighboring miner, said he'd witnessed the signing of the will before it was taken from Dan's bedside by a Dawson lawyer. But no lawyer ever made contact with my husband's friends. So they asked Dundee to help recover the gold."

She sighed. "All we have is the lawyer's name, the letter from C. R. Thorne, and a previously written letter by Dan Fogherty himself, explaining that he'd struck it rich and planned to bring out his poke as soon as possible. But Mr. Fogherty must have gotten sick before he was able to leave."

"What relationship did your husband's friends have to this Dan Fogherty?"

"Mrs. Smythe is Mr. Fogherty's sister and she has a husband and two children. It was Mr. Smythe who hired Dundee and Jon," she continued, "but other than the letter from Dan and one from Mr. Thorne, we don't have any specific claim information and have nothing else to go on. It may take some time to sort it all out. Jon fears that someone might be hoarding the nuggets for themselves and will try to keep us from getting any information."

At that, Carson slowed his steps to come alongside Abby. He looked at her, as much curious as worried. "Is this a substantial sum?"

She nodded. "Yes. C. R. wrote that he believed his friend's poke was worth as much as eight hundred thousand dollars, and that didn't even include what could be dug up from the claim if they wished to carry on with the diggings."

Carson whistled. "That's quite an inheritance, Abigail. I agree with Jon that someone with a greedy attitude might not wish you to know anything about this claim."

She glanced at him, and for the first time, he saw the worry in her eyes.

"I know. That's why I didn't want Jon to go it alone. The Smythe family promised Jon and Dundee half of whatever we retrieve, and though Dundee is not around, we knew that the ranch would most certainly go under unless we carried on with plans."

Carson took a few more steps, trying to process all that Abigail had told him. He looked at her. "You'll have to be careful."

She shrugged. "Jon has had his share of battles. I think he can handle himself."

"Abigail, I was talking about you."

She looked away and pointed down the trail. "I believe we're nearing the river, Carson. I can hear it now."

He turned his gaze down the hill. "I think you're right," he said. "Sounds like rough water directly ahead."

Chapter Fifteen

"Look," she called out. "There are so many supplies strewn along the riverbank. Let's check to see if some articles might be of use."

Carson walked closer to where she stood gazing at the river. True to her words, supplies were scattered everywhere, from wooden crates, to various articles of clothing, and even a broken piece of boat lying alongside the river.

"Appears the stories about the rapids between Lindeman and Bennett are true," she murmured.

"It does look as if a few didn't make it," he said. He shook his head. "From what my guide notes said, I've been concerned about a place some fifty miles north of Bennett, not here."

Abby turned to him. "Miles Canyon and the White Horse?"

He nodded. "Wild enough to make any traveler reconsider his goals, one magazine reporter wrote."

She looked back to the river. "That's comforting."

"Come on," he said, "let's scoot down the embankment and have a look."

Abby slid down the slope behind Carson. When they reached the rocky bank, they began to wander along looking through the various boat planks and an odd assortment of goods. After a few minutes, she spotted a pile of soggy materials heaped along a rock and some brush. Curious, she moved closer. As she rounded one bush, movement caught her eye. She came to a sudden halt when a great shaggy head looked up at her. With a light gasp, Abby held her breath as she studied the large, sad eyes of a huge golden dog. But when it rose on all four feet and offered a tender whine, Abby felt her heart go out to it.

"Oh, you poor thing," she whispered. Kneeling immediately, Abby held out her hand, though she recoiled with a start when a second dog moved into view and stared at her almost nose to nose. For a fleeting moment, Abby feared she was in danger, but the longer she looked into the two sets of eyes, the more she began to relax.

"Hello there. Where's your master, hey?" She rose slowly to her feet and reached out, palm up, but as she stepped forward and saw the sole of a large boot, Abby's heart leaped into her throat.

"Carson!" she cried out. "Carson, come quick!"

When Carson came running, she felt her body growing limp. "Look there," she pointed, "beyond the dogs. I do believe there is a man lying there."

"A body?" Carson moved cautiously forward, speaking low to the dogs as he moved into the brush. She heard his low utterance.

"Ugh. I'm afraid you shouldn't come this way, Abigail. It's not pretty. It appears he's been shot or shot himself."

"Oh, my," she breathed. "Oh, goodness, what should we do?"

Carson, slightly flushed, came back around the bush and looked at her. "We're not far from Bennett. The Royal Mounted Police have a station there, so I imagine the first thing we should do is report this."

Abby looked back to the dogs with growing concern. "What about them?" she asked.

"I don't know." He shook his head. "You're not thinking of bringing those creatures along with us, are you?"

"But we can't just leave them here."

"The Mounties will find them a home."

When the smaller dog rose to its feet and walked up to her, Abby couldn't resist. She rubbed its ears and ran her hand along its golden neck ruff. As she patted the dog, it sat back on its haunches and uttered a soft plaintive moan. Abby's heart broke for it.

"Abigail, listen, we'll find someone to take them."

"Carson, please. Let's just take them with us to Bennett. If the Mounties won't find them a home, I will. But I can't leave these dogs here."

Carson shook his head. "What next," he groaned.

"I promise, Carson. They won't be a problem."

With a sigh, Carson turned and started to climb up the riverbank. Wordless, he walked on without waiting for her.

"Come," she said quickly. "Let's go." Abby patted her skirt to call them to her and started off. To her delight, both dogs followed.

While Abby walked along the trail, fifteen or more steps behind Carson, she began to appraise the two creatures now happily running alongside her. They appeared to be happy to find a friend.

Their fur held a rich gold tone and, to her delight, they felt soft and downy to the touch. In general, she thought them altogether beautiful, but they were large animals. She imagined that they'd been bred as sled dogs. The male, being larger in size, appeared to be more dominant in the way he ran back and forth along the trail. His fur held darker streaks and was more reddish in tone about the neck ruff. The female, who was lighter in color, stayed close to Abby, as if she wanted to be in equal stride with her. Abby smiled as she looked down.

"You're a beauty, little lady," she called out. She smiled as the dog beside her looked up with big brown eyes as if to agree. Abby chuckled. "So, we're a beauty and we know it, is that it?" With the sound of the dog panting beside her, Abby recalled the medium-sized hound that had been a part of the Colton ranch for years. It had nearly broken her heart when he died less than a month before Dundee arrived.

She would welcome the idea of having a dog along on their trek, but would Jon allow it? Reaching out, Abby stroked the soft fur between the female's tall, pointed ears. "You're quite a girl," she said gently. "Beauty. Do you like that name? I think it fits you."

The dog's quick glance upward held the look of intelligence and complete acceptance, and Abby knew it would be easy to become this one's mistress. If she did, Abby would call her Beauty.

"If only I could adjust to a new life as well as you," she murmured quietly.

When they finally entered an area of camp where there was an even greater mass of tents and buildings, Carson at last turned and waited for her to catch up. She could tell by the look in his eyes that he still could not believe the three of them were following him. As she walked up and came to a stop, he looked down with a light frown.

"Maybe we should separate," he said. "But first, I want to speak with the shop owner here," he nodded to a nearby large tent that had been secured along the main path of town. Abby was astounded to see apples hanging in netting from the doorway and canned goods stacked beneath. Carson moved inside, spoke to a woman, and then shortly reappeared.

"The Klondike Hotel is about a half mile from here," he said, pointing down the trail. "There you should be able to find this minister, Reverend Morley, who runs the place. On the other hand, the North-West Mounted Police have a cabin just a short distance from here. I'm thinking that while I inform the authorities, you should find the minister and get the location of Jon and Jimmy."

Carson took a deep breath and looked around. He raised his fedora and scratched his head a moment before he turned back to her.

"Somehow, even with the warnings we had, I had no idea we would be in such a spread out city of tents. It will take us a month to find them if Jon hasn't left directions."

Abby nodded. "He said he would, Carson, so I'm sure he has. But how will I find you after I find Reverend Morley?"

He started off down the road, speaking as he walked. "I'll find you at the hotel. Just wait there and then we'll look for Jimmy and Jon together."

With his words lingering in her mind, Abby made her way down the road until she spotted a large building situated on a rise above the street. The sign in front read Klondike Hotel. Abby called to the dogs still following her but wondered if they would continue to keep her commands.

"Come," she said. She motioned with her hand, but as she moved up the steps, Beauty stayed beside her while the male dog she'd previously dubbed Handsome raced on up the steps. Abby lightly shook her head as she spoke to the dog next to her. "So quickly the male and female reveal themselves, do they not?"

At the entry door, Abby raised her hand and commanded Beauty and Handsome to stay. She motioned and pointed, saying, "lay down," at which both dogs hesitated a moment and then slumped to the wooden deck while she reached for the door. Once inside, Abby walked toward a small woman who was working behind a large wooden counter.

"Pardon me, ma'am, but I was told you might know the whereabouts of a Reverend Morley?"

The woman glanced up and offered a friendly smile. "Oh, yes," she said gently, "but I'm afraid he's not here at the moment. I'm not sure when he'll be back. If you want to look for him, I believe he will be finished soon. He's helping with a funeral." The woman's lips moved downward. "It's a sad thing," she added. She turned and pointed to the back of the building. "Just take the trail that goes up the hill behind the building."

"Thank you," she said. At that, Abby turned back for the porch where she found Beauty waiting but not the male dog. Frowning, she looked around.

"Well, that rascal of a brother has escaped us, I'm afraid." Abby shook her head. "I hope it's not his loss."

When Beauty rose to her feet in expectation, Abby gave the dog a warm pat, and then moved down the steps. She looked up the hillside where she'd been directed and started walking along the side path that led around the building. At the back of the hotel, she found a larger pathway that rose in a slow, curving manner up a steep rise.

Abby walked the trail for some distance and then stopped to look down on the tents and buildings below. From her perch on the hillside, she surveyed the multitude of dwellings scattered along trails that paralleled the long lake. She had never dreamed to find so many people camped here and wondered if they would find Jon and Jimmy as easy as she'd expected.

While she and Beauty stood in silence, she heard the sound of voices and turned to see a group of people descending the trail toward them. A man and woman led the group, discussing matters in low voices. Behind the first couple, a second woman leaned heavily into a man beside her. She watched them as they drew near, all silent and with downcast eyes. She was immediately drawn to the tear-stained face of the second woman.

Oh, Lord, she breathed.

Abby felt her body stiffening. The woman had lost a child, she was certain of it.

Pulling her gaze from the woman's face, Abby saw a third man slowly descending the pathway behind the two couples. He was dressed in simple black pants with a clean white shirt and a Bible clasped in his hands.

A cold feeling swept over her as she stepped to one side and let them pass. Swallowing back her sudden emotion, she looked away, unable to bear the sight of the crying woman. As she stared down the hill, a vision of a woman with red and swollen eyes came to mind. The woman was looking down at a small wooden marker with a cross etched in the upper section of it.

The vision was so clear and distinct that Abby's knees nearly buckled.

Taking in a ragged breath, she closed her eyes as the couples walked by. When at last she opened them, she found the man with the Bible watching her with curious regard.

"Reverend Morley?" she stammered, her voice weak with fright.

He nodded, coming to a halt beside her.

"I'm Abigail Colton," she croaked. "By any chance has my brother Jon been to see you?"

Chapter Sixteen

Abigail waved as Jon looked up from his position atop the saw pit. His hand released the handle of the large whipsaw and sagged tiredly to his side. She watched him call down to Jimmy who stood below the nearly ten-foot-high platform working the bottom side of the saw. They'd been sawing a small fir, giving them the final few planks needed for the second boat while Abby had gone for supplies. Stepping close to the high platform, she raised her face as Jon peered down.

"Did you find more pitch?"

She shrugged. "Beauty and I found a little," she called back, "but not as much as you're going to need."

"Well," Jimmy said, "I think Carson plans to go after nails and oakum caulk soon. Maybe he can buy a little of it. A neighbor said a bunch of supplies came into Smithy's, so maybe we'll just have to fork out more cash."

"Seems like that's what we're always saying," she called back.

As Jon and Jimmy returned to their saw, Abby turned and walked to where Carson was pounding nails into several boards, the shape of their second boat coming to life beneath his hands. It was rather impressive, she decided. Though this boat was shaped like their first, with a flat bottom, somewhat flared sides, and a squared stern, its frame was longer and broader and would hold more supplies than their first creation.

As she moved alongside and glanced over his work, Carson looked up. He smiled as she reached out and touched the rough boards of a newly formed hull.

"Well, what's the verdict?" he asked. "Will it pass inspection?"

She smiled at him. "As long as it floats and keeps me dry."

Carson rose to his feet. "Without adequate caulk and pitch, I don't know if I can guarantee that, but with a few extra slab boards in her bottom, hopefully we can keep our goods above the leakage."

She looked back at the boat's long planks and felt hopeful. "Actually, it appears to be shaping up quite nicely, Carson."

"That's what I'm thinking," he said. "What with the overall length of twenty-two feet and a breadth of seven, we should be able to carry three tons or more."

She looked up. "A lot of weight to row if we don't have wind for the sail."

Carson leaned forward and pulled up a long rowing oar. "That's why I'm making you a really nice oar here." He grinned. "This one has your name on it."

She laughed. "If that one is mine, where's yours?"

"Oh, that. Well to be right truthful with you, I will have to make a steering oar for the stern yet." He paused and patted the tip of the bow with pride. "But I dare say she is a peer of all handmade boats on this lake."

"Not that you might be bragging?"

He smiled. "No, not that," he said. "So, what do you have there?" he pointed to her bucket.

"A little more pitch I found in the woods," she said. "It isn't enough, but I wasn't able to find any at the supply stores close by and didn't have much time to look in the woods, either." She shrugged. "Maybe Beauty and I can search again tomorrow morning. It's a bit sparse what with everyone in Bennett looking for it."

He nodded. "Heard there was some being brought in today, but the last time I checked it was three dollars a pound and going up." He shook his head. "Maybe I'll quit and go check out Smithy's place and see what supplies have come in."

"Better yet, why don't you take a turn with Jon and I'll go looking for supplies," Jimmy called out.

Abby turned to see Jimmy walking up to them. "You gotta' keep working and catch up for all that time sitting around and watching the ladies."

"Carson's been watching the ladies, has he?" Abigail gave Jimmy a curious look.

"Yup," Jimmy quipped. "I heard all about those ladies on the trail and you being invited and all."

She looked back at Carson with a raised eyebrow. "Now who could have told you that?"

"Don't worry, Abby," Jimmy whispered. "I'm keeping your little secret from the big brother over there. It's all hush-hush between the three of us."

Abby snorted. "Oh, wonderful. That gives me a lot of confidence."

Jimmy grinned. "Well, I'm thinking that as long as you cook for the two of us, you won't hear a peep about it from me. So now, what's for supper? I'm starved."

Abby shook her head at the tall man beside her. "James, I do believe I've never known anyone with an appetite quite like yours. The only way I could get adequate pay for cooking for you would be to charge by the pound."

Jimmy stepped back and raised a hand in defense. "Aw, you wouldn't do that, now would you? Besides, judging from your size, it would be well worth it."

"I'm not talking about *my* poundage, Jimmy."

"Hey, what are you three jabbering about?" Jon shouted.

With a leap down to the ground, Jon started walking toward them. "If you're talking weight issues for the boat, I've got to tell you that Beauty alone is going to weigh as much as a month of suppers."

Abby looked over her shoulder and scowled at her brother. "We already reached a compromise, Jon. You can't change your mind now. Besides, the man who took Handsome said that these dogs are a good breed of sled dog and can pull five times their weight in gold. So," she added sweetly, "when I finally find my cache, you'll be sorry you don't have your own dog to help get it home."

Jon walked up to the three of them with a smile. "Nope, never pays to argue with you, Abby. So like Jimmy said, when's supper?"

She shrugged. "I'm afraid I'll be making stew again, but it won't take much more than an hour. I thought to dig into our supplies and bake something special today, but then I decided to wait and do a bunch of baking just before we leave."

She turned back to Carson. "When do you think we'll be launching? I overheard some men say the breakup is coming on quite fast now.

They were talking about leaving in three or four days providing this warm May weather holds out. What do you think?"

Carson tapped the toe of his boot along the bottom edge of the boat. "Won't be long but we have to make sure these boards have some time to shrink and have plenty of caulking between them to boot. Wish we had better boards in her instead of this punky spruce." He looked up. "But she'll do. She should be ready in about five days."

"I thought you said she was a beauty?"

He smiled. "She is. Just a little young and inexperienced, that's all."

Abby cocked her head. "But a necessity and the best thing you could have right now, correct?"

"Right."

Jimmy laughed. "So who are we talking about, Abby or the boat?"

Abby turned on her heels and started for the hillside to where they had set up camp. "Come, Beauty. Let's be fixing some supper," she said loudly. "And you men had better get back to work. Five days will come fast and I'm holding you all to it. I don't know about you three, but when this lake breaks open, I'm packing my bags. I've had enough of this tent-city mud and muck to last me an eternity."

She heard Jimmy's roll of laughter and began to smile. It was a laugh that came from deep down in his chest and even the hearing of it made her want to giggle. Carson could be a handful, and Jon, though loving and honest, could be such a pain. But Jimmy? Jimmy was pure delight.

With the sound of cheers and gunshots echoing across the lake, Carson reached for the guide rope to open the sail and felt the breeze kick the boat into high gear. Once the wind caught, he looked back at Jon, Abby, and her dog and then circled his fist in the air, as if to say *we're off*. At that, Jon stood up in his smaller boat and unfurled the sail, and even as Carson watched, he saw that their boat was picking up speed quickly.

With the wind in his face and the smell of spring in the air, Carson smiled at Jimmy. "We're flying, Jimmy me boy, flying on to the Yukon and places shimmerin' with gold!"

Jimmy, who was seated near the mast, glanced over his shoulder and laughed. He raised his arm and pointed north. "Onward, ho," he shouted. "All that separates me from me riches is a mere five hundred miles of sailing delight!"

Still smiling, Carson turned back again to watch several other boats departing from the shores of Lake Bennett. It had been a spirited send-off this morning, but in his mind, the best bode of goodwill came when a light breeze arrived with the morning sun.

Turning his attention to their northbound passage, he considered the day ahead. It would take a fair time to cross this long lake before coming to the outlet where they would merge into Tagish and Marsh Lakes. Past that point, they'd quickly find themselves caught up in swift river currents, but he doubted they'd be that far until tomorrow. As Jimmy had said, hundreds of miles of rivers and lakes were ahead of them.

With his mind on the days to come, Carson knelt by the sail and adjusted their course. After he made certain that they were heading directly for the outlet at a rather nice clip, he motioned to Jimmy who was watching him carefully.

"Keep your eye on this sail and make sure we're headed straight on, would you? I'd like to jot down a few thoughts."

Jimmy nodded and moved to the stern while Carson found his journal and perched on a nearby crate. After finding his last entry, Carson began a new line.

> *May 30, 1898: Stretching before us for a distance of several miles is a glorious panorama of mountain and lake scenery. Behind, on the shores of lakes Lindeman and Bennett, one can see a considerable mass of white tents and small wooden buildings serving a population, if one includes Lindeman and Bennett, of over six thousand. The conditions of life in this remote place are in many respects foul with muddy sand, a variety of garbage, and manure such as has never occurred in this country before, but it is, as well, a scene filled with excitement. What with the thousands pouring over both the Chilkoot and the White Pass, in but a matter of days and weeks, they have all managed to converge to this area and now press forward into the headwaters of the*

Yukon River system. All this, with but little knowledge for what lies ahead and even less in the way of finances to maintain them.

Every camp has at least one central path known as Main Street. In Bennett, as with other up-start towns, businesses of all kinds line the way with shops, hotels, saloons, doctor and lawyer offices, and a host of entrepreneur tents for every kind of need. Hotels and saloons, of course, predominate and are occasionally lively places, but come Sunday morning, for the most part, the men rest and even a few attend church services. There are surprisingly few drunken brawls, what with the good order of the North-West Mounted Police and British Columbia officials, but what is most surprisingly commonplace is enthusiasm and a good spirit.

Still, each man must surely be contemplating what lies ahead, whether riches or poverty, new life or death, and if not doing so by tongue, then at least by mind.

In this regard, I have heard a few gloomy forebodings from the 'old-timers' who have taken the journey before, and perhaps it is worthwhile to note that some of these sinister predictions are not without foundation. To begin with, the great majority of the boats are being built by men who have never done so before. Added to that is the known fact that these waters, currently navigated by men who have never even been in a boat, are described as treacherous, and in some cases positively dangerous, on account of rapids and rocks. So it will be readily understood that when a mob of thousands take to their destiny, each struggling to get ahead of the other, there is likely to be trouble.

Strangely enough, though the dangers are admitted freely, no one seems to think that he or she, individually, is taking any risk. What one observes, instead, is the simple but strong disposition of the mining and business enthusiasts alike: gold and riches await any of them who will take it.

"Hey, Carson," Jimmy called out. "Wind's picking up. Better put away your papers."

Carson glanced up and saw that the choppy waves were growing in strength. He'd been so intent in his writing that he'd not noticed how white caps had formed all around them. He peered forward and seeing that the outlet of the lake was not far away, he turned to Jimmy.

"You suppose we can make it to end of this thing before we have to tuck the sail?"

Jimmy shrugged. "Guess we can try, but it might be a rough ride."

"It would be better than rowing," Carson retorted. He looked over his shoulder to find Jon and Abigail being tossed about in their smaller boat. He stood up and pointed to the outlet. Jon waved and nodded.

"All right, Jimmy. Let's keep going!"

Though they whipped out their oars just in case, Carson was pleased when they at last rounded the bend of the outlet and found a current carrying them forward. As they entered the narrow channel, Carson and Jimmy tied up their sail and sat back to let the water's movement do its work. The next several miles, they drifted slowly by an area called Caribou Crossing and then floated on to Lake Tagish. When they reached the smooth surface of Tagish, Carson started to move toward the mast to open its sail when he noticed a large amount of water in the bottom of the boat. They had sprung a leak, perhaps several.

"Jimmy, we're taking on too much water," he called out. At once, he stood and waved to Jon and Abby who were not more than a hundred yards behind them. After motioning them toward shore, Carson turned the stern paddle and then helped Jimmy row. When they reached a small sandy beach, Carson and Jimmy hopped out of the boat, and while Jimmy held the tow line, Carson went to help Jon and Abigail come alongside.

As Carson pulled them onto the sandy beach, he smiled. "What did you think of your first ride?"

Jon grinned. "A little wild at times, but at least we've made good ground." He looked around and then stepped out of the boat. Abby remained seated on a crate near the center with Beauty at her feet.

"I'm not certain if we should go any farther today before I try to fix some leaks," Carson said. "It appears our caulk needs a bit more help."

Jon nodded. "Actually, I was thinking the same thing and about to raise our red flag to let you know we needed to head for shore."

"Not such a grand start," Carson said with a shake of his head. "But maybe it's better to get all the bugs worked out now and not try to push on." He looked up at the midday sun and then at the area around them. "This looks like a fair place to camp for the night, and that would give us time for repairs."

Jon looked back to Abby. "It appears you have your wish for a quiet and peaceful camp. While we get started on these leaks, can you fix us some grub?"

Abby rose to her feet. "Who's making the campfire," she asked. "If someone will help me find kindling, I'll make you all some griddle bread."

"That'll be me," Jimmy said with a grin.

Abby slept poorly that night. Memories of the waves slamming against their boat seemed to haunt her dreams and were still on her mind even when she awoke and dressed. After restarting their small campfire, Abby boiled water for a breakfast of mush, coffee, and what remained of the griddle bread from the night before.

The sun was still behind the mountain when they pushed off from their Tagish Lake shore and began to row slowly through the smooth waters. By the time they'd reached a midpoint at Lake Marsh, the sun was high in the sky, and the decision was made to row to shore for rest and a lunch. While they ate, Abby found her mind turning to the rapids ahead. She was dreading the thoughts of a wild river pounding their boat and heaving them side to side. At the thought of it, she ran her hand across her stomach.

Jimmy walked up beside her and sat down. "You feeling all right?" he asked.

She sighed. "I'm not really looking forward to the rapids. Perhaps my imagination is getting the best of me, but from what I heard, they won't be easy. On my part, the waves at Lake Bennett were excitement enough."

"Do you swim, Abigail?"

At the sound of Carson's voice, Abby glanced sideways to where he sat eating his bread, his face more serious than usual. "A little," she replied. "But I have no inclination to test my ability."

Jon placed his tin plate on the ground and studied Abby a moment. "I was talking to an old-timer in Bennett. He said he'd been over this route two times before and he recommended that we stop ahead of Miles Canyon and hire a pilot to take us through both the canyon and the Whitehorse Rapids. They have a few men there who hire out for such things. It might be the safest thing for Abigail. Either that or she should walk around the rapids, but the old miner didn't recommend the hike either since it's a brushy and mosquito-infested area."

Jon hesitated and then looked at Carson.

"So, I'll be planning to stop and see if someone might be available," he said. "You two can maybe follow us through. I heard that a fella needs to take the right channel at Miles Canyon even though it appears you can go either way, but I'm thinking it's best to find some help since most river flows vary depending on the runoff and conditions changing year to year."

"Actually," Carson said, "I would agree. You take the lead, Jon. We'll pull over to the side when you do. A guide may be the best idea since my purpose is to arrive at Dawson in one piece, not to challenge my boating expertise." He smiled and rose to his feet. "So if we're done with lunch here, I say let's be on our way and Godspeed."

"Godspeed," Jon muttered.

They had traveled no more than a mile or two when Jon spotted a group of men and boats and rowed over to the side of the river. Jimmy and Carson followed close behind. After Jon spoke to several men, he signed on with one who called himself Captain Singleton. When at last the lanky, tough-looking man stepped into their boat, Abby felt the palms of her hands growing moist. Calling Beauty back from the bow, she commanded the dog to lie at her feet and began to pet her in an effort to calm her nerves.

Most of her life she'd been fearless in following after her brothers. Where they rode, she rode, even if her mother would have paled to know the truth. She prided herself with the fact that she could follow them anywhere. But now her heart and soul felt a weakness, an inward fear for the unknown. She thought of the vision she'd had when the tearful woman in Bennett passed by. Had that sudden scene in her mind's eye been a mere thought of compassion?

But what if, for some strange reason, she'd been able to see something ahead in her life?

Abby felt a shudder run through her completely.

When Jon and Captain Singleton began to row them into midstream, she gripped the crate beneath her even tighter. She hated the thought of what waited around the river's bend.

Chapter
Seventeen

With her heart pounding in her chest, Abby thought of the Popo Falls not far from the ranch. She had ridden to the overlook many times. The thunder of it had always given her the shivers, especially when she'd tried to imagine her parents climbing the walls of that canyon while escaping renegades years before. Her brothers had always made much of the story, shaking their heads in admiration while she and her mother had remained silent.

At the thought of her mother, Abby felt a strange longing deep inside. She'd not thought much of her parents recently, but at the moment, it would be wonderful to be the recipient of their embrace. She admired her mother. A product of an English mum and an Irish papa, Maggie Colton was an interesting mix of both heritages, the proper schoolteacher personality on the one hand, yet she also had an Irish love for words and adventure. Her father had thought her mum quite frail when they'd first met, but she'd proven to be anything but frail.

Abby surmised a part of that heritage flowed through her veins and wondered if she was becoming more like her mother every day. But in truth, she had always been quite partial to her father, whose calm and dark gaze seemed to reach inside her and understand her very motive for living. He had understood why she wanted to leave.

At eighteen and unable to afford any further schooling, she had been resigned to working in Mac's Mercantile and Post. And though others in Benton appeared content with life, especially her older brother Sam and his wife Sarah, she and Jon had been restless to find their own place in the world. Jon had moved to a Montana ranch, becoming the assistant foreman to Dundee's father, and when he'd brought Dundee a year later to their doorstep, she'd been certain that he was everything she'd been waiting for. He carried so much promise.

"We're about to it, Abby," Jon called out. He pointed to the growing swiftness of the water. As they entered the ever narrowing canyon, with the roar ahead like a freight train, she felt tears gathering.

Oh, Dundee ... why aren't you here!

She felt her body being pitched forward and clung to the ropes about the crate beneath her. Beside her, Beauty whined. As the captain shouted, Abby heard a great crack, like that of a pistol shot. The boat at once whirled, turning about in the current.

Abby watched in horror as Captain Singleton seized an oar and yelled out. "Never mind, boy! Let her go stern to!"

She gasped. A sheer wall of rock now leaned over them, its various sharp and angular projections speeding by her vision at an incredible rate. Abby glanced up. Beside them was a canyon wall so similar to the one at the Popo River near the ranch.

Gritting her teeth, she spread her legs and clung to the ropes. As if riding a bucking bronco, she readied her body to be tossed to and fro. The roar about her sounded incredible, something she might hear if she stood in Benson's sawmill with the machines going full bore.

Abby's heart pounded.

It would be certain death if anyone went overboard. She felt the boat whipping first up and then down, over and over again, and though she wondered it they would ever be done with it. At last Captain Singleton reared back on his oar and gave a command to Jon, and though she could not understand his words, when they came about, she saw how, for the most part, they had moved beyond the worst of the waves.

Abby released a long-held breath. She tried to breathe normally while for several more minutes they bounced along with the shore slipping by in amazing swiftness. Finally, with another loud command, the captain shouted at Jon and they edged the boat into another series of rapids that nearly took her breath away. She was near to numb when they began to row to shore.

When they landed, Jon jumped from their boat with Beauty at his side and quickly began to pull them to dry land. She sat momentarily stunned, hearing only the shouts of Carson and Jimmy as they rowed in beside them.

"Whoa! What a ride!" Jimmy yelled. Grinning from ear to ear, he leapt from his boat and helped drag its bow forward.

Captain Singleton stepped around her and jumped from their boat while Carson leaped to the rocky shore and moved to Jon's side.

"You boys hear that crack?" Jon shouted excitedly.

"No, but I saw you flip around," Carson said. "What happened?"

"Oar broke," Jon cried.

"Shoot," Jimmy laughed. "You had to have all the fun! Going through it backwards? Now that's what I'd call an adventure. Why couldn't *we* do that, Carson?"

"Want to try it again?" Carson taunted back. "We've the extra oar in our boat.

Abby jumped to her feet and stared at them. "Don't you men even think about it! Now would someone help me out of this death contraption? I need to find some privacy."

Carson's eyes were twinkling as he stepped to the bow of the boat and reached for her hand. When her feet touched the ground, she wordlessly turned away. Perhaps she may have overreacted, but someone needed to have some sense. As she marched off, Abby heard Carson's voice behind her, and though she didn't readily understand his words, Jon's laugh was clear enough.

"She's tough," her brother called out so that Abby could hear. "I've worked too many hours putting these boats together. Not going to spend time and money changing plans now. She'll be fine."

When Abby returned, the captain had already departed and so they all scrambled back into their boats. Once they'd moved into the Yukon's flow and she'd settled back on the crate, Jon immediately promised that the next few hours would be much calmer.

And indeed, they were—far too calm, in fact.

Though at first the winds were contrary at Lake LaBerge, within an hour, there was not even the slightest hint of a breeze and she was once again at the oar. Following a long and laborious row, they spotted an Indian village and decided to stop just north of it in a small clearing. After they unloaded some of their gear and set up camp, Abby began to prepare biscuits and supper. While she worked, Jimmy took Beauty off for a walk while Carson sat by his tent, writing. Jon walked up beside her, his fishing pole in hand.

"Won't be gone long," he said. "Maybe I can find us something fresh to eat."

Without looking up, she nodded. "Good idea."

She'd barely sat the iron skillet on some glowing coals for fried biscuits when four native men walked into their encampment and stepped up to where Abby was cooking by the fire. From the corner of her eyes, she saw Carson stiffen. When one of the men held up a medium-sized trout and nodded, pointing from the fish to Abby, Carson got to his feet and walked up beside her.

"How much?"

"Un dallar," the man said with a heavy accent.

Carson pointed to another fish the native held on his line. He held up two fingers and smiled. "Two for un dallar?"

At first the young man only stared at him, and then he nodded. As Carson reached for his coin purse in his pocket, another man, much older, walked up close to Abby and studied her carefully. Though she took a step backwards, Abby knew enough from her Shoshoni heritage to keep her face clear of any fear. Instead, she looked at the old man directly, as if to warn him away, but he merely smiled and spoke in an unfamiliar tongue to the man with the fish. The younger native handed both fish to Carson and nodded at Abby.

"How much," he said, pointing. "Nice squaw. We like her. Does she belong you? We give you many fish, even money. She stay here for us."

Abby felt the blood draining from her cheeks as Carson turned his gaze to her. His face held little emotion, his eyes no shock, and seeing it, Abby felt her heart move in her chest.

"Carson . . ."

Carson turned back to the young fellow, still poker-faced. "No," he said, shaking his head. He placed the fish on the ground and then stepped up close to her and put an arm around her shoulders. "She is mine. We need her very much. She is not for sale."

The older man's face fell as he stepped back. The younger man bowed his head lightly and then with no further words, the four of them walked away. As Carson's arm slid from her shoulder, she heard him chuckle.

"I wonder how many fish they would have given us."

Abby released a pent-up breath and sighed. "Carson. Don't make light of that. My heart nearly stopped beating when he pointed at me."

He nodded, his face turning somewhat somber. "In truth, so did mine." He looked at her for a long moment and then gave her a slow smile. "You seem to cause quite a stir wherever you go, Abigail. I'm thinking that you show some appreciation for me now and then. Maybe you should even consider an extra biscuit for me tonight?"

Abby shook her head then knelt to her warming skillet. "I believe you are the proud owner of two fish," she said. "You might want to clean them before they're cooked." She glanced up and met his eyes. "But don't be gone long. I shouldn't want to argue with those men all by myself."

He smiled. "Indeed." Fish in hand, he started for the river. "But you will remember the extra biscuit, won't you?"

Abby watched him walk away a moment and then called after him. "At least one, Carson. Maybe two."

Chapter Eighteen

The next morning, Carson noted the skies growing dark early on and was certain that the day would bring them rain. As they loaded their gear in the boats, he, Jon and Jimmy talked of the trouble spots that might be ahead. Captain Singleton had offered them advice for two more sections of the river, Thirty-Mile, just beyond Lake LaBerge, and Five Finger Rapids near Fort Selkirk, though from the fort on to Dawson, he said, they should have no problems.

They decided to stay as close to one another as possible, and especially be cautious when they left the lake and entered the area called Thirty-Mile. As an additional precaution, they placed ropes at the ready in both the bow and sterns of their boats. Better safe than sorry they assured Abigail, though he noticed that she offered no comment in return.

While Jimmy rowed, Carson stood in his boat and broke open the sail. He felt thankful for the light breeze at their backs. With luck, this part of the journey would have less rowing than anticipated. After securing his sail, he turned to watch the small boat beside them. He was impressed to see Abigail rowing with strong movements while Jon set their sail. He'd seen her rowing several times over the past few days, and considering how the oars were rough and heavy, he admired her pluck.

He looked back from where they'd come. With the lake being over thirty miles long, he imagined that they'd covered more than two-thirds of it, but they still had a few miles to go. Without the current breeze, it would take much longer to cover that distance. They were, once again, fortunate.

Plans were to reach Hootalinqua, a spot thirty miles beyond LaBerge before evening, and hopefully, find a more open place to camp. Last night, though they were in beautiful and lush surroundings, the moment the evening breeze dropped away, clouds of mosquitoes had immediately driven them into their tents.

Sitting back on the crate near the stern, Carson watched the shore drift by for several minutes before he leaned over the side and looked down. As before, he couldn't see more than a foot into the waters of the spring runoff. They'd been told that the greatest danger in the river ahead would be the unseen rocks, and knowing that the water remained cloudy, he figured it would be difficult to steer clear of them.

With a conscious effort, he turned his gaze to the low mountains on the northern horizon. He was pleased to see the increasing gentleness in the terrain beyond. Once they had Thirty-Mile behind them, he figured most of the danger would also be behind. Content with their prospects, he began to whistle.

Jimmy smiled at him. "You thinkin' all is well, I take it."

Carson nodded. "Seems like it, doesn't it? Although I hope we don't get rained on before we make camp."

Jimmy looked up. "I'll agree to that. I've been kind of enjoying the drier side of the mountains. Believe the coastal area's too wet for me."

Carson thought about the steep glacier-covered mountains and deep blue inlets. "Mm, I don't know, Jimmy. Think I prefer the coast area. Was incredibly beautiful."

For a long time, they sat in silence watching the shore go by. When they reached the river, they once more lowered their sails and secured their oars in place as the current swept them forward. But to Carson's relief, they floated on for several more minutes without the river growing any swifter. The float appeared to be quite manageable.

Jimmy stood up and looked toward a bend in the river. "There's some swirling water ahead," he cautioned. "Might want to be ready."

Carson glanced over the side and whistled sharply at the sight of a large rock not far from their boat. "Whoa," he called out, "we've got some big ones down there. Keep a sharp eye out, Jimmy."

He'd no more than spoken the words when he heard a terrible crack. When he glanced to one side, he felt a moment of complete disbelief when he saw Abigail and Jon go flying into the river. Behind them, their boat had come to a standstill, midstream. As it listed to one side, goods rolled into the river. Carson swallowed as he jumped to his feet.

"Jimmy! Row hard!"

Carson lunged for his oars and began cranking them back and forth as hard as he could. "Can you see them?" he yelled. Jimmy suddenly stopped rowing and stood. "She went under."

Carson jumped full to his feet. "Where?"

"There!" Jimmy pointed to where Jon and then Abby rose to the surface. Abigail was thrashing her arms about as if in a panic.

"Row, Jimmy!" And with that Carson jumped over the side, feet first into the river. Though the cold made him suck in a quick breath, he immediately began to swim as fast as his arms would take him. Abigail was floating just beyond him, with only her dark hair in sight. He lunged for her and rolled her chin into his hand.

"Carson!" she gasped.

"Hang on! Try to swim on your back. I see a crate." He kicked his legs, stretching out one arm as he tried to drag Abigail with him and reach for the crate. Suddenly, he spotted another box coming right at them and reached out.

"Abby, grab this!" He clung to the small crate of goods while she thrashed about and finally took hold of the other side.

"Don't let go!" he shouted. "Maybe we can ride this out to that sandbar ahead." He pointed downstream then kicked his legs and tried to guide them closer to shore.

He looked at the white tinge to her face and shouted at her. "Hang on, Abby, and don't let go! You got it?"

He saw her swallow a mouthful of water and cough, but she clung to the box as she gasped for air.

"All right," he yelled again. "We're getting closer. Keep that grip!" He kicked harder, paddling with a free arm with all his might. Suddenly, he felt a sharp stab of pain in his left leg. He groaned then kicked again. Rocks.

He felt the gravel. They were close to shore.

With every ounce of energy, Carson tried to find his footing. He reached for her arm and, standing now, pulled her from the box. While the crate bobbed away, he struggled until he found solid ground and pulled her close to him. Panting now, he half-carried her as she struggled for footing until they were in only a few inches of water.

By this time, Abigail was moving on her own feet, choking and gagging as they scrambled onto a sandy bar. As they reached dry ground, Abby fell to her knees, and though he dropped beside her, gasping for air himself, he knew by the way she sagged forward on the sand, that she was nearly unconscious. Sucking in a ragged breath, Carson pitched forward and wrapped his arm about her waist.

Abby felt his arms lifting her into his lap.

"You're freezing," he said.

She tried to control the shaking, but couldn't. Her lips and arms felt numb. She couldn't speak. Feeling her panic, she pushed against him and tried to struggle to her feet. She wanted away from the river. Carson held her tight while they stumbled to some willows. As they neared them, she turned to Carson in horror. "Jon?" she mumbled.

"He went . . . on," Carson stammered. "But I think Jimmy was right behind him." He sucked in a breath. "He'll get him."

Abby began to shake so hard, she once again fell to her knees. She was so cold.

Carson sank beside her and pulled her against him.

"Don't," she gasped, "you're freezing." She pushed away, clasping her arms around her body.

"Abigail!" he said firmly. "Come here." She felt him grab her arm once again as he crawled behind her. She felt his hands at her neck.

"Wha . . .?" She tried to talk, but her teeth were chattering.

"Where's the button?" he muttered. "Get this wet thing off." Carson's voice nearly sounded angry. She felt his hands struggling at the back of her neck, pulling, tearing.

"Carson . . ."

She felt a yank and heard the rip. She tried to pull away from him.

"Hold still," he commanded, the voice in her ear held a roughness that shocked her. Startled, she knew he was struggling out of his own shirt and undergarment. Then he reached for her, bare-chested.

"I'm going to hold you," he said. She felt his cold skin on her back, heard the ripping of more material and then felt his arms drawing her tight against him.

"In a few minutes," he mumbled, "I think we'll begin to get some warmth between us."

"Carson," she stammered between shudders, "whatever are you doing?"

"You're shaking Abby. You're too cold. I'm going to hold you close to me until we start to warm up. Then we can hike downriver and hopefully find Jon and Jimmy. We'll build a fire and get out of these wet clothes. But first, you have to stop shaking."

Wordless now, Abby leaned back, allowing him to snuggle her against his chest. As the skin between them began to warm, she felt his arms encircle her tighter. He leaned his cheek close to hers, and though numb with cold, she felt her heart racing as she pressed her head against his. Panting, she began to control the shivers that ran through her like flitting butterflies. At last, as the warmth between them grew and her shaking began to cease, Abby felt her breaths coming and going in even spaces.

"There," he whispered. "Better now?"

"I think so," she whispered back. "Thank you."

"A few minutes longer," he murmured. "I'm cold, too. The only warmth I feel is what's between us." He paused. "In fact, I'm dreading the thought of releasing you and putting that cold shirt back on."

She began to pull away. "Carson. I'll be all right now." But as she moved, she suddenly realized that her dress was torn from neck to waist at the back. Shocked, Abby reached for the shoulders of her dress and turned to him. "What did you do? How am I ever going to walk with my dress torn like *this*?"

"Where's your cape?"

"I don't know. It must have come off while I was struggling in the water."

"Well, maybe we can put that nice cold shirt of mine over you." He made a feeble attempt to smile as he reached for his shirt. "My undershirt will serve me good enough, I suppose. Hopefully, it won't be too long before we can find Jon and Jimmy."

"Abby!"

At the sound of Jon's shout, Abby looked up. "Jon! Jon!" she cried. "We're down here!"

When Jon's face came into view above them, his eyes were large with fright. "Are you all right?"

Behind her, Carson scrambled to his feet. "She's extremely cold, Jon. I was trying to warm her."

Jon bounded down the embankment then came to a halt with a puzzled look as Carson wrapped his shirt around Abby's shoulders and helped her to her feet.

"I wasn't sure how far away you might be," Carson offered. "She was shaking like a leaf, and so I used a technique my brother taught me. Basically, take off some of the wet clothes and hug."

As if uncertain what to say, Jon nodded. "We're not far," he said, waving a hand downstream. "About a quarter of a mile, I guess. I told Jimmy I'd come looking for you and he said he'd start a fire."

"Good," Carson said. "Let's go."

With Jon's arm protectively about her shoulders, the three of them struggled up the embankment and through the brush. Abby felt the wet cold of her dress and boots and wondered at her and Jon's circumstances. What would she do if there was nothing left of their goods? What if she had nothing else to wear?

As her thoughts plagued her mind, the distance seemed like miles before, at last, they stumbled toward a sandy embankment where Jimmy knelt by a smoky fire. When Jimmy looked up, he got to his feet and jogged forward.

"Abigail," he said breathlessly, "you gave us such a scare. Come over to the fire and let's get you warm." He took her hand and looked at Carson. "You all right?"

"Yes, I think so," Carson said. "Just downright cold."

"Here," Jimmy said, pulling her forward, "you stand by this fire and I'll find all three of you some warm duds to put on. The first thing we have to do is get you out of those wet clothes."

Abby, with Jon still at her side, knelt close to the fire while Jimmy ran to the boat which was pulled up on shore nearby. He grabbed two bags and then turned back, sitting one beside her.

"Listen, I brought Carson's for you. My clothes won't begin to fit, but maybe Jon can find something in my bag. We men will step away and let you change, and then while Carson and Jon get on some dry things, I'm going to set up our tent. We'll get you settled yet, Abby. All right?"

Abby looked at the concerned face above her and nodded. After the men headed for the boat and turned away, Abby struggled to remove her dress and petticoat then pulled on a pair of Carson's pants and one of his shirts. After finding some socks for her feet, she shuffled over to them.

"I left your bag by the fire, Carson. Hope I left you something warm to wear."

He nodded and started for the campfire.

Once the tent was up and a blanket freed from the gear bag, Abby stepped inside the tent and wrapped the blanket around her. Still shivering, she sat for several long minutes while Jon changed into some of Jimmy's clothes. When Jon came back to the tent and looked inside, she made every effort to smile at him. She was certain he had to be feeling as devastated as she was.

"Are you getting any warmer?" Jon asked.

"Yes, but has anyone seen Beauty?"

He shook his head. "The three of us are going to wander downstream and see if we can find anything. Maybe she'll find us."

Abby swallowed. "I'm sorry this happened. But we'll make it through."

He stared at her a moment. "I was going to say that to you," he said. "At least we have each other and another boat, and Carson said their supplies are ample enough to last us for a few days."

"Are all our bags gone?" she asked. Her voice was barely above a whisper.

"All in our boat, but we did stuff three crates into Jimmy and Carson's."

Abby stared at him, trying to remember. "I can't even think what was in them. Do you remember?" She thought about their bags of clothing, the crates of food, the small stove and cooking utensils. But where had they stored Jon's tools and the letter from Dan Fogherty and C. R. Thorne? They could buy some supplies, but without the letters, they'd have no papers regarding the Smythe claim on an inheritance.

"I think the crates in Jimmy and Carson's boat have some food supplies, extra blankets, and at least one canvas tarpaulin." He shrugged. "Plus a few mining tools."

Abby stared at him. "I was afraid of that. So we have no other clothes, or personals? No letters?"

"I don't believe so."

She felt a growing silence between them, a desperate sound.

"Listen," Jon said softly, "why don't you come out and sit by the fire while we go downstream and scout for some goods that might have washed up? It'll be warmer."

Slowly, Abby rose to her feet. She wrapped the blanket tight about her and stepped out of the tent and toward the fire. Wordless, she sat down near to it and began to stare into its bright flames as the three men walked away.

In the glow of the embers, she listened to the sound of rushing water nearby and envisioned her grandmother's Bible riding the waves of the Yukon. She pictured its dark, soft cover and gold-edged pages at last settling into a watery grave in muted silence. A gift the night of her wedding, it would be, like her marriage, gone now. In her mind's eye, she remembered the carefully penned words on the inside cover.

Draw nigh to God, and he will draw nigh to you.
Love, Mother

The Promise

Part Two

The Klondike
Dawson, Northwest Territory of Canada, 1898

Chapter Nineteen

Dawson - June 15, 1898

From Hootalinqua they moved into the dangerous but manageable Five Fingers Rapids. Abby and Jon decided to walk around it as Carson and Jimmy followed a larger boat through on the right of the largest rocky finger, but from there on, the float proceeded smoothly and they reached Fort Selkirk without incident. Over the days following the accident, however, Carson became aware of a quiet spirit settling on Jon and Abigail. It was disheartening. He hurt for them, for all the hopes that appeared to be derailed.

To their good fortune, Jon had at least carried most of their money in a money belt around his waist, and more importantly, both were alive and well. In addition, they did have a few supplies in his and Jimmy's boat, plus they'd recovered a bag of Jon's clothes and, most consoling to Abby, Beauty herself. But neither Abby's personal luggage nor the rest of their supplies, including the letters, had been found.

As Carson thought about Abby and Jon's situation, he glanced to where Abigail sat near Jimmy's feet. She was still clad in his pants and a muslin shirt, and though she wore her own boots, he found her looks quite appealing as she sat in that feminine manner curled up on a crate, her pant legs rolled halfway to the knees and his wide-brimmed hat pushed back on her head. In his mind, she looked like a young Huckleberry Finn. He smiled as he recalled the way she'd moved about camp earlier this morning, what with her youthful step and the outdoorsy look of men's clothing about her small frame.

He saw Jimmy reach over and pat Abigail's arm then point ahead.

"I think I see Dawson on the horizon," Jimmy said.

While Abby struggled to her feet, Carson looked up to search the low hills for any signs of town. At last it came into focus, appearing first as bundle of white dots then slowly emerging as a myriad of tents, cabins, boats, rafts, shops and warehouses. Finally, he spotted a landing stage directly ahead.

"Welcome to Dawson," he announced.

For several heartbeats, no one responded. Weeks ago, he was certain there would have been cheers, but today the four of them, along with Beauty, simply stared forward in silence. To his eyes, the place was busier than he had ever expected, and as they neared the area where many boats had been docked along the river, several waved.

"Hey, Mister," one man called out. "What do you have there? Got anythin' ye might be a sellin' a body?"

Jimmy waved and shook his head. "Afraid not, my friend."

As Jon stepped off the boat and pulled them in to tie up, several other bystanders crowded around. Many asked questions, anxious for news of the outside world while several more asked the same question about obtaining fresh food of any sort. In Carson's mind, it was not an encouraging sign. While he stepped up and helped Jon and Jimmy secure the boat, Abby sat on a crate, Beauty at her side. At last, Jon walked back and looked at her.

"You getting off?" he asked.

"I'll stay here until you find a dress for me," she said quietly.

Carson walked back to them. "Abigail. Come with us. No one here cares, and what would it matter if they did. Besides, I'd count it a privilege if you'd allow me to buy you a dress. It's my fault the other one is torn."

He glanced toward town and back to her. "Listen, we'll find some rooms and a bath, and then you'll feel better." He turned to Jon. "What say we take an evening to get cleaned up and eat, and then come back tomorrow, unload, and find a place to camp."

"That won't be easy," Jon said, nodding at the crowds. "I'd like Abby to get a bath and a bed, but maybe I should stay somewhere around the dock with Beauty and keep an eye on things."

Carson shrugged. "If you want," he said.

For a moment longer Abby simply sat with large, quiet eyes then at last she stood and moved forward. He reached for her hand. "Good. I'm glad you're coming. Now let's find a shop and you can pick out something to wear."

"Carson, you don't have to do this. You were only trying to help."

"Please, Abby."

She shrugged. "All right. I imagine I need something bigger to wear anyhow. Later, I can mend my old dress and wear it this coming winter."

As Abby stepped from the boat and started for shore, Carson followed along behind realizing that he'd nearly forgotten her situation. As far as he could tell, she looked the same, yet when he considered the woman draped in baggy garb a step ahead of him, he found his mind wondering about the changes taking place beneath his shirt.

When the four of them reached the top of the riverbank and looked toward town, they stood a moment in sheer wonder at the commotion around them.

"Well," Carson sighed. "Let's see what we can find."

Jimmy released a low whistle and shoved back his hat.

"I'm thinking that I'll stay right here with Jon and Beauty," he said. "I have no desire to get into that throng. Just come get me when you're ready to eat, Carson. In fact, I'd be plumb happy to spend the night here with our supplies and Beauty instead of you, Jon." He turned to Jon. "Maybe Carson can let me know about a bathhouse or something, but for this first night, I think you should be with Abby."

After they stood in an awkward silence a moment, Carson sighed. "Tell you what," he said. "Since I'm the one that's gainfully employed here, just as soon as we find Abby a dress and I secure a couple of rooms, I'll treat us all to supper." He shrugged. "For my part, I can't very well go about interviewing people like I am now," he removed his favorite fedora and scratched his head as he looked around. "Not that anyone would notice."

Jimmy laughed. "Come on, Jon. Let's take Beauty and stretch out our legs along the river while we wait for supper. You two go on and just come back to get us when you're ready. We'll go along with whatever you decide."

When Jon and Jimmy turned back, Carson and Abby crossed the street to a boardwalk heading for the center of town. As they walked, Carson began to read the myriad of signs and notices all around them selling food, mining supplies, and every other thing in between. One sign in particular caught his eye. *Charlie Brimstone, Undertaker,*

Bodies embalmed and shipped to the Outside—an optimistic note for the newcomer if ever he'd seen one.

Here and there, a few horse-drawn rigs pulled their loads on wooden sleds or wagons, but everywhere, both in the streets and on boardwalks, men of every height and manner seemed to be scurrying about at a near frenzied pace. Though he saw an occasional woman, most of the crowded streets were filled with men dressed in flannel shirts and baggy pants with suspenders, but he did note that some wore fine clothing, wearing dark suits and sporting fancier hats than any he'd seen in previous camps and towns.

The day was warmer than they'd had for awhile, and though the light of an afternoon sun still filled the northern sky, by the sounds coming from the dancehalls and saloons along the boardwalk, Carson decided that no one here appeared to care whether is was dark or light before they began celebrations. After he and Abby crossed another street and turned east, he saw a sign announcing *drinks, 50¢,* but though it sounded rather inviting, Carson kept walking.

After a few minutes, he spotted a hotel nearby and took Abby's arm. "I think I'll step inside and check for room rates. Maybe the desk clerk can also direct us to a dress shop."

Abby nodded. "I'll wait here," she said.

After Carson found the clerk and secured two rooms for the night, he then asked for shopping information, to which a rather stiff and stately man responded, "go to Miss Findley's, sir. Only two streets down on the left. If you find it too expensive, there are a few others nearby."

When they at last found the shop and stepped inside, a clerk with blonde hair piled high on her head gave them a swift perusal and then continued her work without comment. Slightly annoyed, Carson took Abby by the elbow and walked directly up to her.

"Good afternoon, Miss. I would appreciate your help to find my friend something suitable. She has endured the loss of all her goods and had to stoop to the lowly clothing of her brother, I'm afraid. Would you have a day dress for her? Something proper."

He saw the rather amused look in the clerk's hazel eyes before she turned to Abigail and gave her a careful appraisal.

"I believe I have several," she smiled serenely. "Follow me, my dear."

Abby followed and a short while later reentered the room with a pinched look about her face, although for his part, the way the royal blue dress flowed over Abby's frame, it made his heart leap. Straightening from his slouch at the wall, he gave her close regard and smiled.

She stared at him a moment and then walked closer. "It's too expensive," she whispered.

He took a step backward and appraised her. She looked positively wonderful in the dress. "It appears to fit fine enough," he offered. "Won't it serve you well for finding that lawyer and speaking to Miss Mulroy like we talked about yesterday?"

She edged nearer to him, placing her body between the clerk and Carson. "Yes, but it's priced at twenty-five dollars," she declared in a rather hushed tone. "I should be able to find one for far less."

He smiled. "I doubt if you could here. Besides, you look lovely in it."

She stared back at him. When he saw the edge of tears in her eyes, it jolted him to his very core. For a moment, neither of them spoke.

"Someday, you can pay me back with your own kindness," he said gently. "In fact, I think you already did in Sheep Camp. I believe I owe you something for the beautiful and timely writing not to mention the nursing care."

She sighed. "All right, if you put it that way, perhaps I can accept your very generous offer."

Carson grinned. It would cost him dearly, but the way she looked was worth every penny.

Though it was past seven in the evening before they reached the Golden Nugget Restaurant, the sun was still bright in the horizon when he and Jimmy walked inside and looked for Jon and Abby. It was crowded in the room, but once they stepped deeper into the darkened interior, he saw them at a table on the far wall. When Jon spotted him, he waved and Abby looked up. Noting her relaxed demeanor, Carson felt his heart move within him. As he took a seat next to Jon, Jimmy slid into a chair next to Abby and grinned at her from ear to ear.

"Abby, you look fine in that dress, mighty fine."

She gave him a gentle smile. "Thank you, James."

"Well, here we are," Carson quipped, "in Dawson, with good company, and safe and sound." He gave Abby a long look. "You're looking quite refreshed, madam. Feeling anything like the old self again?"

"I suppose I haven't been myself for the past few days," she said. She glanced at Jon before turning back to him. "Before you and Jimmy came in the room, Jon and I were talking. Maybe this whole thing in Dawson could be a wild goose chase, but we've decided to look for some work, establish ourselves, and start inquiring about the claim as we've planned all along."

Carson was curious. "Had you been thinking of returning to Seattle?" he asked.

She nodded. "For the past few days, Jon's been after me to reconsider. And I have." She paused, as if searching for the right words. "Something changed for me that afternoon I was tossed into the river," she said. She turned her gaze to Jimmy and then back to Carson. "When I realized my life had been spared, I started drawing inside, listening at a deeper level than I ever have for that still small voice of God. I realized that I felt anxious about the future, but then I slowly began to sense that a greater good will come out of our trials." She shrugged. "So, I told Jon that he has to be patient and give us—or at least me—more time. I still believe it best to stay and help him."

Carson shifted in his chair as he considered her words. Both Abby and Jon were younger than he, and yet they often demonstrated a strength and wisdom that surpassed his expectations. "So what's next?" he said with a smile.

"We're not certain," Jon said. "Not yet, anyhow. We think the first order of business is to talk to Miss Mulroy, as we discussed yesterday. We're hoping that she might direct us to someone who knows many of the miners, and perhaps even to an honest lawyer in town. If we can find C. R. Thorne, Dan Fogherty's friend, and he could personally testify to the will being signed in front of him, we may have a case to take to the commissioner."

Carson was about to question them further, when a man came to their table to serve them, and the subject of Jon and Abby's plans turned instead to discussions about food.

After the food arrived, all four of them fell to eating without much conversation at all, but when Carson sensed that his stomach was beginning to be satisfied, he looked at Jon and found his thoughts returning to their plans.

"Not to prod," he said, swallowing, "but in regard to your earlier comment about the claims, what are you planning to do next?"

Abby spoke up. "I saw a post office not far from this hotel, so I'm planning to write Mrs. Smythe and ask her to send me whatever proof she still has to Mr. Fogherty's claims. Hopefully, she can send us another letter stating that we are hired on her behalf."

Abby looked at Jon a moment before turning her eyes back to Carson. He saw a hint of sadness in them. "She might wonder why *I'm* inquiring and not Dundee, but for now, I will simply say our letters were lost in the river. Hopefully, she can send us a response before too many weeks go by. Meanwhile, my friend," she said with a soft smile, "you can get your writing mailed off, while Jon and Jimmy look for a place to camp."

"Hey, what's this *friend* business?" Jimmy said as he jerked his head toward Carson. "What about me? I'm the one spending the night with your dog, you know."

Abby's smile broadened. "Yes, and for doing so, you are the dearest, for certain, although I might envy you sleeping under the stars with that deep fur coat beside you keeping you warm."

Jimmy snorted. "Yeah, but like me before I found the bathhouse, she smells." He chuckled. "I think your four-legged friend needs another tossing in the river."

"In that murky water? I'm not certain it would do much good," Abby retorted, "but I tell you what. After I try to meet with Miss Mulroy tomorrow, I'll stay with Beauty at the boat and see what I can do. I can at least brush her."

"Abby," Carson said quickly, "would you mind if I joined you when you call on Miss Mulroy?"

Abby shrugged. "No, I wouldn't mind at all. I suppose she might even be more receptive to seeing me if you were along."

"Are we ready for some dessert?"

A young, fair-skinned woman smiled as she stepped up beside Jimmy and looked at them expectantly. Jimmy promptly grinned and then ordered some bread pudding, but when she walked away, Carson saw Jimmy's eyes linger on the young woman's disappearing form for several seconds.

"I do believe Jimmy is acting like one of these lovelorn miners I see standing around," he said with an easy smile.

Jimmy turned a light shade of pink and laughed. "Who me? Naw." He looked at Jon. "But I sure wouldn't mind doing a little claim work with you. Listen, if I help you build a cabin and we stake out a small claim, how much do you think we could pull out of it?"

Abby reached across the table and patted his partner's hand. "Jimmy, haven't you heard the saying, all that glitters is not gold?"

Jimmy shrugged. "I suppose," he said. "But finding a few nuggets to pack in my pockets before we leave Dawson might not be so bad, now would it?"

Chapter Twenty

"Good morning, Miss Mulroy, it's kind of you to meet with us today," Carson said.

"Mr. Stuart, Miss Abigail, how nice to see you again. How was your journey into Dawson?"

Abby smiled. "It was quite adventuresome. We fared well most of the time, although my brother Jon and I did go on the rocks at Thirty-Mile. I'm afraid I experienced some turmoil at losing a fair portion of our goods."

"My goodness! Well, I'm glad to see you standing here. That's a treacherous place. I've heard of some lost lives there as well as supplies." She studied Abby carefully. "I assume everyone is safe then?"

"Yes, Miss Mulroy. Jon is fine. Carson and his friend Jimmy were travel partners from Skagway on, and they came to our rescue. All in all, we were fortunate, except for the loss of some important papers."

Georgia gave them a curious look. "I see. Is there something amiss?"

Carson smiled. "Somewhat, but other than a few words of advice from you, Miss Mulroy, Abigail and I did not come to be a bother but wanted to see your wonderful new establishment. Are you eager to open soon?"

Georgia clapped her hands together with excitement. "I am indeed. Do you have the time for a tour?"

"We do," he said brightly. "I would find it interesting to add a description of your hotel to my Dawson story. I'm thinking readers will be quite surprised by the grandeur of it."

"That's very kind of you, Mr. Carson. Well, then," she smiled, "let's be about it."

With Georgia leading the way, Abby and Carson followed her through a narrow room that held a long wooden bar to one side. Behind its highly-polished wood surface, workers busily added supplies beneath the counter and along the shelves nearby. When they reached the dining hall, Georgia proudly showed them her ceiling chandeliers and announced that the dining tables would be set with crystal, fine china and good linen.

Carson pointed to a chandelier above him. "You mean, when we saw you on the steamer, you were just then bringing all these things to Dawson?"

She smiled. "Indeed, this and more, including a few brass bedsteads."

He looked at her with curiosity. "How did you get everything here in one piece?"

"Well," she laughed, "that in itself is quite a story."

Carson pulled his pen and paper from his jacket pocket. "Miss Mulroy, I would love to record your tale, if you wouldn't mind sharing it with others."

"Actually," she said, "I wouldn't mind at all. You know how it's reported that Soapy Smith in Skagway is quite the rogue? Well, to me, he is a dear, and he came to my rescue. You see, all these things wouldn't have made it to Dawson in a timely manner, if not for him. I told Soapy that I consider him a friend."

While Carson wrote, Georgia told of hiring a packer to take her things over the White Pass into Bennett just as soon as they arrived in Skagway. But they'd barely made it two miles out of town, when someone else offered him much more money to take whiskey instead.

As Carson looked up over his papers to Abby, Georgia took in a light breath.

"Well," she said, "you cannot imagine how angry I was. I had previously talked to this Mr. Tulley when we came out through Bennett a few months before. In fact, I'd paid him a down of four thousand dollars, and then he dumps my goods along the trail!"

"It wouldn't happen to be a Mr. Joe Tulley, now would it?" Carson asked.

Georgia looked surprised. "Why, yes. You know him?"

Carson winked at Abby. "Not really, let's just say Abby and I had a run-in with his brother, but please, don't let me interrupt. Go on with your story."

Georgia glanced to Abby and back to Carson and shook her head. "I certainly hope you fared better than I did with that man, for Mr. Tulley would pay me no heed. And so I hightailed back to Skagway and was I boiling mad!" Georgia's eyes sparkled, but then she began to smile.

"When I went to Mr. Smith, about the only decently dressed man in Skagway I might add, he offered to take care of the problem, and he certainly did. He marched right out there, took control of the pack train, unloaded the whisky and packed my freight directly to Bennett." She smiled. "And that's what Soapy did for me and I like him for it."

Carson wrote furiously for another minute while Abigail and Georgia walked about the dining hall and kitchen, each sharing more of their own experiences in Skagway and on the trail. When Carson caught up to them, Georgia was embellishing on her newly hired chef and telling Abby about all the extras purchased for her kitchen as well as the latest fashions for lace curtains in all the rooms.

After that, Georgia led them up the stairwell to both the second and third floors, where bedrooms were currently being furnished. Though most rooms held a simple bed and only an occasional dressing table, Abby was amazed at the beautiful rugs located in a few of the finer rooms. The only discouraging news concerned a few windows.

Carson pointed to one window opening covered by cheesecloth. "Were your windows broken en route?"

Georgia sighed. "Yes, although that was separate incident. So, I've ordered them again, but they will most likely be late. And who knows when or which steamer will deliver."

"What happens if it rains?" Abby asked.

Georgia turned to her with a smile. "My, you haven't been here long." She chuckled. "There will be a time, Miss Abigail, when you will be hoping for a little moisture, but you will discover that a rainy day is a rare day in Dawson."

Abby smiled. "Sounds like summer in my home town."

While they spoke of the weather and continued to share their traveling adventures, Georgia led them back down the staircase to first floor, but as they reached the dining hall, Abby decided to be direct.

"Miss Mulroy, if I may be candid, I'm hoping that you might have information that would help us find a miner by the name of C. R. Thorne. On the steamship, you mentioned that you may be able to suggest someone to help us?"

"Oh, yes. I do remember that you were looking for someone. If I recall, you said this Mr. Thorne was an old-timer, is that correct?"

"Yes. It's my understanding that he mined first at Circle and then Forty Mile before coming here early on."

"I see. Well, there is a spunky lady in town by the name of Madge Cafferty. Many of the prospectors believe her to be practically an angel unaware. Having been a miner herself years ago, she now tends to these men at her cafe and social hall near the middle of Dawson. I've heard it said that she leaves her door open day and night and has a wonderful listening ear and provides food and help as she can. Many of the older miners go there, so I would suggest that you begin your search with Miss Cafferty."

Georgia waved a hand and pointed. "Go two blocks east and one south. Then you will see her small sign that says *Madge's Eatery and Lodging Hall*. I think she is almost always at her establishment every night, so if this Mr. Thorne is in the area, she would be the one to know of him."

"I sincerely thank you," Abby said. She hesitated. "Might you also be able to recommend a lawyer who would be honest and reliable?"

"Hm . . . honest and reliable? Well, you may be asking for a pot-full on that one, but I do know of one man who is highly regarded. His name is John Young. You will find him on Queen Street, I believe." She gave Abby a long, thoughtful look.

"Now, is there anything else I can do for you? It sounds as if you had a bit of misfortune on your arrival."

Abby offered Georgia a smile. "We've had misfortune, yes, but Jon and I will manage, unless, of course, you happen to know someone who might need a willing soul to put to work?"

"And would that soul happen to be you?"

"Yes," Abby nodded. "It is."

"What do you have in mind?"

"I would leave that to your discretion," Abby said quietly. "I want honest work, but I do have my schooling diploma and am able to deal with figures and read well. I believe I also meet easily with people, and I can even cook."

"Well," Georgia said, "you wouldn't by chance be interested in helping at my lodge in Grand Forks would you? The place is in need of a day clerk. Someone who greets people, arranges for lodging and food, watches over the dining hall, and enters daily figures in the account books." She paused, giving Abby a thoughtful inspection.

"I do believe you could fill the bill nicely, Miss Colton, for I need someone I can trust to work with the Grand's manager now that I have my hands full here. I have given a man by the name of Mr. Daniel Hanover the general rein of things, but for the most part, he comes in late in the afternoon and works at night when most of the miners fill the place."

Georgia turned. "Follow me," she said.

After Carson promised to wait for her in the dining hall, Abby followed Miss Mulroy to a small room off to one side. There, Georgia walked up to a large desk and opened a drawer. "I will pay you one hundred dollars a month," she said, "including room and board. In addition, you will be allowed to keep any personal tips that you might receive, but we have a policy with our clerks that they do not actively seek special tips as do some entertainers."

Georgia put on her glasses and looked at her over the top of them. "Do you understand what I'm saying, Abigail? Though I'm quite certain, I will not have an issue with you."

Abby nodded. "I believe I do, Miss Mulroy. Though I must be honest, I have little knowledge about gold towns. I'm from a ranch in Wyoming, far from such things, though I saw entertainers in Skagway and Sheep Camp."

"Yes, well, one finds good people in all sorts of circumstances," Georgia said simply. "Don't judge the girls too harshly, dear. Though some take entertainment a bit farther than singing and dancing, others do not. But you see, the men that are coming to our establishments are lonely, especially these new arrivals who are young and fit and unaccustomed to the long winters. They are more than willing to share their nuggets with the beauties that will show them attention. They are such *boys*," she said with a small chuckle in her throat. "And all seem to have the need for the soft touch of a woman, even though some go crazy and lose their whole diggings over such likes."

She shook her head. "If you stay here long, you will see it." Georgia reached for a paper, pen and ink and then hesitated. "Now you do realize, don't you, that the Grand Forks Hotel is a little more than ten miles outside Dawson, near the original claims at Eldorado and Bonanza Creeks. Is that distance from Dawson a concern to you?"

Near the original creek claims? Abby couldn't believe her ears.

"No," she said quickly, "not at all. In fact, that might be a very good area for Jon to look for a claim and build a cabin."

"Then you must see what's available as soon as possible," she said. "Most claims there have been taken. For now, let me write a note of introduction to Arthur Hanover, my general manager. You may present this note of employment to him whenever you're ready. Meanwhile, I'll send word through my men as well." She quickly scribbled out a letter, then folded it and handed it to Abby.

Elated, Abby gave her a small nod and placed the note deep in her pocket. She then thanked Georgia again and returned to the dining hall to find Carson. As they stepped from Miss Mulroy's grand three-story building, Abby was still excited when Carson announced that he wanted to find the local newspaper editor. Though deciding to part company for the moment, they agreed to meet back at the boat for lunch.

No sooner had Carson walked away, when Abby felt her lungs release a big sigh. With an inward prayer of thanks, she glanced up to the blue sky and closed her eyes. She nearly had to pinch herself to be sure she wasn't dreaming. How was it that in this congested town full of mud and thaw, hardship and clamor, she'd found such generosity?

With a swift intake of air, Abby opened her eyes and started off for those small shops in the heart of Dawson, knowing that now she could afford a few more basics. After ignoring the shop where Carson had taken her, she moved straightway to the other merchants down the street. With care, she purchased a dress of medium-weight, navy voile with a loosely fitted jacket to cover her waist. She then bought a sensible but attractive pair of work shoes, a light wool cape, and a few larger undergarments.

After returning to her hotel room, well–pleased with the day, Abby folded away her new purchases and gloated on the fact that she'd spent only a little more than what Carson had paid for the blue dress, and yet she had a practical set of garments for employment, and most importantly, ones that could be worn loosely about the waist.

She would be able to get by with these clothes for a few months, though at the onset of fall, undoubtedly she would need a coat and perhaps a warmer and larger day dress. Thinking of her poor tattered dress and the days ahead when she would need to let out her garments, Abby decided that the next purchase would have to be a needle and thread.

After changing into her newest dress, Abby strolled down the waterfront street until she came to their boat and found the faithful Beauty.

"Hello, my Beauty," Abby said cheerfully. "You've been so patiently waiting, haven't you, while all your friends are out and about."

Abby smiled at the sight of Beauty's wagging tail, and calling her to the dock, she brushed her with an old comb for several minutes before washing her hands and turning back to the boat. Thinking Carson would be along soon, she dug into their food crate. After finding a sack of dried apples, she opened a can of tinned meat and then began to slice the fresh bread she'd purchased on her walk about town.

She had barely finished layering the meat on the bread when she looked up and noted that Carson was strolling briskly down the street toward them. With a warm feeling inside, Abby paused from her work to watch him walk up to the dock, his steps somewhat jaunty in manner.

After a moment, she turned back to place the sandwiches on a plate and considered the emotions that Carson was beginning to tap. For weeks, she'd been certain that he was drawn to her, but it was disconcerting to discover that he was becoming dearer to her as well. Was it wrong of her to even consider him?

Abby swallowed. "Look, Beauty," she said. She reached for the soft spot behind the golden ears. "I think we have a friend coming."

Beauty moved to the edge of the boat and placed her front paws at the bow, offering a deep whine and light bark as Carson approached.

"Well, hello there, Miss Beauty, Miss Colton," Carson called out cheerily. He walked up beside them and looked down. "You're both looking mighty pretty sitting there in the sunshine. Say, is that a new dress?"

Abby smiled. "It is. I thought perhaps I should find a more practical one for working." She wiped her hands on a nearby damp rag as he stepped inside the boat.

Abby pointed to the bread, meat, and dried apples on a plate. "Might not be much, but I've made us lunch."

"Looks good," he said. He picked up a slice of bread and then took a seat on a crate nearby. "So, I assume things went well in Miss Mulroy's office?"

"Yes, I can't believe such good fortune," Abby declared. "I've employment!"

"And employment that came rather painlessly," Carson said swallowing. "That's wonderful. We should be celebrating with something more special than tinned meat I have a feeling." He smiled and took another bite.

"If I had my stove," she said with a shrug, "I could offer us something better and perhaps even brew you a cup of coffee, but for now, we'll have to wait." Her gaze moved to the river nearby. "Besides, I don't like the look of the water around here."

He nodded. "Polluted."

"Indeed."

She looked off to the town's busy thoroughfare before she spoke. "I feel as if my prayers have been answered."

He studied her a moment. "I like it when your eyes look happy, Abby. They radiate so much color."

"Carson . . . you must stop. I'm not resisting as well these days."

He hesitated. "All right," he said, "tell me more about your happiness. I was in the other room when you made your arrangements."

"Miss Mulroy hired me to be her day clerk at the Grand Fork Lodge near the old mining claims. It will be perfect if Jon can find a spot to build a cabin nearby. I will earn one hundred dollars a month, plus room and board *and* any tips. That should go a long way in helping Jon with our expenses."

"Good for you," he said. "I may have added a bit to my salary today as well."

Abby was curious. "So, now we're both rich?"

He laughed. "Oh yes, you with your big salary and me with mine. I was told today by the editor of the Dawson's newspaper that it costs about six dollars a day to live in Dawson. In fact, after he hired me to give him a story or two for his weekly, he offered a whole host of comforting information."

"Goodness!" Abby gaped at him. "So what more good news did you learn?"

Carson took a small notebook from his pocket before he met her gaze. "You certain you want to hear this?"

She nodded. "A well-known rhyme says that words can never hurt me."

Smiling, Carson looked down at his notes. "Well, according to my source, a common laborer, male that is, can earn about eight dollars a day, providing he can find any work, what with the tremendous influx of new miners. A cook's income is about the same as your offer, while a laundry worker can bring in the big sum of five dollars a day with room and board." He offered her a wry smile. "Sorry, don't mean to bring a negative note to your happiness."

Abby shook her head. "A laundry worker slaves over hot water and a stove day and night, Carson. I'd rather have my employment, even though it is less money. Besides, I might earn sufficient tips to take up the slack."

"Be careful about the tips, pretty lady. A face like yours is going to earn a few, but someone might have an error in his understanding."

"I'll be careful enough," she said slowly, "but do you think when I start getting big with child that anyone is going to give me a second look?"

He smiled. "Maybe they'll feel sorry for you."

Abby sighed. "Carson, do you always have a comeback?"

"Well," he said, "at least you won't be too interested in knowing who really earns the big money."

"The gold miners and their belles?"

"So, how did you know? Have you been peeking at my notes?"

"How much do they earn?"

"That," he said with a slow smile, "depends on the favors. Actresses, even bad ones, earn around $150 a week. And those that promise a good deal more can almost name their price, what with some of the desperate miners around here with a cache of gold and nowhere to spend it."

"That's disgusting," Abby snapped.

"Is it? Why so?"

"Because to be wanted for your flesh and nothing more is hardly biblical and it's not very satisfactory in the end anyhow," she said with a low voice. "I should know."

Carson stuffed his notebook in his pocket and took another bite of bread. After a moment, he swallowed then looked back at her. "Do you think that's all you meant to him, Abby?"

She studied his eyes for a long moment. "Carson, do you realize that since you saved my life, you've been calling me Abby?"

"I have?"

"Yes."

He lowered his sandwich and gave her a lingering smile. "I would want you for far more than your flesh, Abigail."

She snickered. "You can be so contrary, Mr. Stuart. What makes you think I would even give you my flesh, let alone more than it?" Though Abby was shocked to hear the frankness of her words, she kept her gaze steady. She was curious to see his reaction, to hear his response.

"Because you know I care," he said. He looked away. "Are you going to someday seek an official divorce, in case he never shows up?"

Abby blinked. Her only thought had been to simply go on, to someday return to Wyoming, but nothing more. "I don't know, Carson. Though I still feel hurt and angry at times, I haven't taken my thoughts that far. In truth, I doubt I could do something like that for a long time. It wouldn't seem right."

"He may have abandoned you, and with child to boot."

She sighed. "Can we talk about something else?"

After a long, silent pause, Carson wiped the crumbs from his jacket and offered a piece of his crust to Beauty, who had been begging at his feet for several minutes. "I can't look her in the eyes and eat in front of her," he said.

"You're too soft," she countered.

"I suppose."

Abby released a long, slow breath. "So," she said, "are you going to write about these flamboyant women and all?"

"Some. But there should be a few other events to pursue as well."

She nodded. "When will you send in your last story to the *Post*?"

"Within a month."

"Then will you go home?" she asked carefully.

"I'm not certain of my plans at the moment."

She stared at him. "You would stay here, Carson?"

"Not for long, but I'm itching to follow the scent of these golden opportunities, Abby. It seems like this whole country is ripe with history in the making. I can't help but wonder if I should take more time, write more about it." He gave her a wry smile. "Maybe some historian will one day read me."

She smiled back.

Carson rose to his feet and stood looking out across the river. "Well, I suppose one never knows." He turned back and held out his hand. "By any chance would the Madam Abigail Colton care to join the wanderlust adventurer Carson Stuart on a jaunt through Dawson? That is, of course, until her brother should properly arrive this evening."

Abby stood, and though deep inside she heard a voice of warning, she instead made a small curtsy. "I believe I would, sir."

As Beauty rose to her feet, whining and wagging her tail in anticipation, Abby bent to rub her neck. She looked up. "And the Beauty, too?"

He looked down with a hint of amusement in his eyes. "I suppose we must. It appears the Beauty does not wish to be left behind."

Chapter Twenty-One

"Come in, my boy!"

Dundee smiled as the butler led him through the open door and into the most luxurious library that he'd ever seen. A broad mahogany desk stood in the corner near a large window, and rich, gold drapery hung along the window's tall frame, its deep folds tied back with long velvet cords. Filtered light from the morning sun exposed rich hues in a deep burgundy and gold rug, and on every wall stood bookcases filled with a mix of books and gadgets, all of which looked expensive as far as Dundee's quick perusal could determine.

"Jackson tells me that you have been excellent help in designing the new field pipelines, and I wanted you to drop by and let me offer my sincere appreciation."

Mr. Conrad Appleton leaned forward in his chair and then rose laboriously to his feet as Dundee approached. When the rather rotund man extended his hand, Dundee grasped it and shook it firmly.

"That's not really necessary, Mr. Appleton," Dundee said quickly. "Jackson is quite a capable engineer and I am honored to be his helper."

"Well, I have heard good things and wanted to let you know." Mr. Appleton motioned to a chair. "Sit down, sit down, son. I don't have but a few minutes then I must be off with the missus, but please have a seat." He smiled. "I know you're new here, so perhaps you haven't heard. Each June, my wife Katherine plans a rather gala event in our home for our staff and several of our neighbors. In fact, I'm sure you will be hearing more about it. It's a rather traditional thing for us, I'm afraid."

"Knock, knock, am I disturbing you?"

Dundee turned to see a most striking woman standing in the doorway.

"No, no," Conrad Appleton called out. "Come in, my dear. I would like you to meet Jackson's new assistant, Dundee Andrews. Dundee, this is my wife, Katherine."

Dundee stood. He gave a slight bow with his head and smiled. "It's very nice to meet you, Mrs. Appleton."

Dundee allowed his smile to linger while the tall, slender woman, who looked to be half Mr. Appleton's age, stepped forward and extended her gloved hand. He took it lightly in his own a moment, and then watched her as she offered a rather sweet, coy smile before she stepped to her husband and kissed him on the cheek.

"Are you certain I'm not interrupting," she said lightly. "I can very well keep myself busy with my secretary for a few minutes. We are still readying the invitations, of course."

Katherine Appleton swept behind her husband's chair then turned her hazel-green eyes toward him. "I hope you will be able to join us at our dinner and dance, Mr. Andrews. It's the highlight of our year on the island."

Dundee offered a quick nod. "I'd be delighted to come," he said. "Sounds like an event no one should miss."

"Indeed," she said, smiling.

"Well, I shall go back to my library, Conrad. When you've completed your business, do come and rescue me. We have an appointment at two this afternoon, but we have plenty of time."

With a nod, she looked at her husband then gave him a gentle smile before she once again swept toward the door, her long lavender skirt trailing behind. At the door she paused and glanced over her shoulder, her blonde hair glimmered in the filtered sunshine that streamed in from the window.

"Now you won't forget to come, will you, Mr. Andrews?"

Dundee smiled. "No, ma'am. I will look forward to it."

No indeed, Dundee thought decisively. He wouldn't forget to attend, nor would he forget the charming woman who extended the invitation. Sobering his expression, Dundee turned back to Mr. Appleton. And though he listened patiently to the man while he explained the processes that had first set him to bringing down the water from the mountains above them, Dundee knew that deep in the recesses of his mind he was still reeling from the beauty who had so graciously swept in and out of the room.

It seemed unnatural to see a young lovely woman like her married to someone as old and portly as Mr. Appleton, but then of course, Conrad owned this plantation and the mill, and Dundee couldn't even begin to imagine how much the man would be worth.

No. He would not fail to attend the upcoming gala event.

Chapter
Twenty-Two

Abby listened with interest while Jon and Jimmy explained how they'd gone to the Mining Commissioner's office, and once they'd confirmed that both Dan Fogherty and C. R. Thorne had filed claims, they jumped a ride on a delivery wagon and headed for Grand Forks. For several hours, they then meandered along Eldorado Creek until they found the claims numbered nine and eleven, where Dan Fogherty had once mined, and number ten, which belonged to Dan's friend, C. R. Thorne.

"But," Jon grumbled, "just like I figured, there were men working the claims, and when I spoke to one worker, he pointed out two big and burly men who were supposedly the owners."

"The moment I laid eyes on those two fellers," Jimmy declared, "I had a hunch about them. They looked like scraggly criminals to me. Even from where we stood, I could see that the one gave us a downright mean gaze."

"Rather than confront them," Jon added, "we ended up talking to another man farther down the creek, and from what we could gather, these two men just appeared one morning about two weeks after C. R. up and left without talking to anybody."

"Seems mighty strange," Jimmy muttered. "I told Jon that we should go talk to those two, but he thought we should wait and watch them awhile."

Abby sighed as she stood and reached for her dress jacket. "Well, at least Miss Mulroy gave us a name and a place where we can inquire about C. R. Why don't we go have something to eat at Madge's Eatery," she said. "Maybe Miss Cafferty can give us some information about locating Mr. Thorne. Besides," she said, "I'm hungry."

After a quick agreement, the four of them headed for downtown Dawson. While they walked, Jon talked about making an all-out effort to find C. R., but at the same time, they needed to find a place to set up a camp. After discussing the matter, Jon and Jimmy decided to look for work and find a place to camp near Eldorado and Bonanza Creeks, and Carson, being eager to talk to the miners in that area, said he would be glad to join them.

Though now evening, the sun was high in the sky when they entered Madge's small eatery. The establishment was plain and simple compared to Miss Mulroy's, but the aroma in the room smelled fine enough for Abby. After they sat down at a rough-hewn table, she looked around. There were only a few men in the room and, true to Miss Georgia's comment, most of them appeared to be older.

They had barely made themselves comfortable when a stocky woman with salt and pepper tones to her braided knot of hair ambled over to their table. "You folks here for supper?" she said with a smile.

"Yes, we are," Jon nodded. "Are you the owner?"

"I am. What can I get you? I have a few things ready as listed there." She pointed to the sign above her counter. "Would recommend my special dinner tonight of roasted moose meat, macaroni, beans, and fresh pie."

"Sounds good to me," Jon said. He smiled. "We're new into Dawson, and in addition to eating, we also have a few questions. Are you Madge Cafferty?"

"That I am," she said. Her full voice held a jovial tone to it, Abby noted, and while the woman looked from face to face, her deep brown eyes seemed to sparkle. "So you're new here, eh? Like all the others filling the town to the brim." She shook her head. "Almost more than a place can bear."

Carson nodded. "I couldn't agree more," he said. "It's even difficult to walk the streets, but Miss Abigail," he waved a hand toward Abby, "had the opportunity to speak to Miss Mulroy and she recommended we talk to you about a man we're looking for."

Madge raised an eyebrow. "Indeed. From that fancy place, you came here? You must be hurting for funds, I take it."

Abby smiled. "Well, you might not be far from the truth, but we've plenty enough for our meal tonight." She smiled. "For my part, I would enjoy a bowl of soup and, hopefully, like my brother said, maybe a moment of your time. Would you have a few minutes this evening to talk, or should we come back tomorrow?"

Madge gave her a curious look and then nodded. "Well, don't know that I'd have anything of interest for you, but the place isn't busy, as you can see. I'll bring you all some food and then sit a spell and you can ask away."

After serving soup to Abby and the moose meat dinner to all three men, Madge sat heavily beside Jon. She gave him a curious look.

"So, you're looking for someone?" She frowned. "Are they in trouble with the law?"

"No," Jon said quickly, "not at all." He stuck out his hand. "Miss Cafferty, my name is Jon Colton and this is Abigail, my sister, and our two friends, Carson Stuart and Jimmy Patten."

Carson extended his hand in greeting, as did Jimmy, before Jon continued.

"Abigail and I came to Dawson to represent some friends from Kansas City. Last September, our friends received word from their brother that he'd struck it rich in Dawson and that he was coming out to share some of his funds with them before returning to his claim. The next letter they received said their brother, Dan Fogherty, had died."

Jon paused. Beside him, Madge's eyes grew thoughtful. "Dan Fogherty you say? The name's sort of familiar, but I can't quite place the face." She puckered her lips briefly as she rubbed her chin. "But then again, I haven't been in Dawson too long. You see, I just got myself back in the mining business only a year ago."

"That so?" Carson said. "You were involved in mining before?"

Madge chuckled. "Oh, yes, from California and on to several points north. Then I took a breather and stayed in Arizona until I felt the need to come north again." She smiled. "In fact, only a few days ago I bought myself a claim. Though I couldn't find one available down on Eldorado Creek, I did buy one above it along a small stream called Little Chance. Now, I'll just need to find me a good man to work it and see what happens after that." She chuckled and patted her stomach fondly. "As you can see, I'm not in much shape to work it myself like I used to."

"Sound's like mining is in your blood," Carson said, giving her a warm smile.

"That it is, young man."

"I have a feeling that you may have an interesting story or two." He nodded toward Jon. "Jimmy and I started our journey from Seattle with Jon and Abigail. We've been working our way into Dawson since March and floated into Dawson only a day ago. Along the way, I've been trying to record a few interesting stories for the *Seattle Post-Intelligencer*. I'm a writer for them."

"That so!" she exclaimed. "They're havin' a real heyday what with all their glorious announcements, aren't they? I have a feeling that it must have brought *them* a poke of gold by spreadin' the news to all those eager bodies in the lower forty-eight."

Carson grinned. "Can't keep the news from happening. We just report it."

She laughed, her dark eyes gleaming merrily.

"If you don't remember Dan Fogherty," Abby said, "have you by chance heard of his friend, C. R. Thorne? We saw a letter that said he was a witness to Dan's will, but the family never heard from any lawyer and Mr. Thorne doesn't appear to be at his claim."

"C. R. you say? Now I do know a man who is partners with a C. R. up at Forty Mile. Name's Nels Goodwin. He was in just the other day and was down on his luck. Not sure if he'll be back here anytime soon, but if he comes again, I can see if his partner might be that man." She glanced from face to face. "Where you staying?"

Jon leaned forward. "By any chance, Miss Cafferty, do you have anyone working that claim on Little Chance yet?"

She gave him a thoughtful look. "Madge, son. Call me Madge. And no, I can't say that I do have anyone definite in place yet, though there's a plenty out there for the hiring."

Jon nodded. "So I noticed." He sat up straighter and looked directly into Madge's eyes. "I'm a hard worker, Madge, straight from a ranch in Montana. We started out with Abby's husband to find this gold, but truth is, we don't know if her husband is alive or dead. And though Abby's been hired by Georgia Mulroy to work at her Grand Forks Hotel," he shrugged, "she's due to have a baby and it's primary that I find us a place to live." He leaned forward. "I was wondering, if you'd allow me to build a small cabin on the land while we seek to do our business. I'll work your claim for dirt cheap."

"Well, now," she said slowly. "That would take a heap of work, young man."

"I could help him," Jimmy spoke up. "I'm strong."

Carson eyes turned to Jimmy. They had a curious look in them.

"My, my," she said. "Two men for the price of one, have we?"

Carson leaned forward. "Well," he said, "maybe if everyone is heading that direction, perhaps Madge knows if there is any more property in that area."

Madge frowned. "A reporter like you interested in a claim?"

"It was just a thought," he said.

Carson turned to Jon. "Did you see any other land up there that wasn't staked?"

Jon shook his head. "Guess I wasn't looking for that. Was mostly wondering why someone was working Dan and C. R.'s claims when they were never sold, not legally anyhow."

"Claim jumpers," Madge said with a low voice. "Happens."

She shifted in her chair and looked at the men then she leaned forward and rested her strong arms against the table. "I have to tell you that I've felt it my Christian duty to watch out for these miners, especially the old breed. You should hear some of the stories they sing to me late at night." She shook her head. "Some are plumb sorrowful. I do what I can, but I hate it in particular when I think that someone might be stealing away the property of a man who's worked long hours and endured the most cold and dark of nights."

She gave Abby a long, lingering look. "Got some work at The Grand, did you? Miss Georgia must have been impressed with you, girly. Imagine that she trusts you, and as a matter of fact, so do I." She smiled.

"I reckon I could hire you boys to help me with the claim and build a cabin on it. In fact, if you're a mind to supply the labor for it, I'd be willing to supply the goods. I'll see if I can buy up some of those boats coming in. That along with a few logs might do it. Make a good place for whoever works there."

For a brief moment, Madge drummed the fingers of one hand on the table as if taking her thoughts into more detail. "I'll make a deal with you, Jon," she said carefully. "I don't have much in the way of funds to pay you, but in addition to buying the cabin materials, I'll hire both you and your friend for six dollars an hour apiece. The going wage around here is eight, but if you happen to find me some gold, I'll add ten percent of the take for any man who works the claim as well."

A strand of silver-tinged hair fell loose as Madge's head bobbed thoughtfully. "Yup, this might work out right good," she said. "Come back in a night or so and we'll see what I can scrounge up for supplies. Meanwhile," she said, "you keep me posted on what's happening with those claims. I'd be interested in helping you with that problem."

Jon nearly jumped out of his chair. He reached across the table and shook Madge's hand. "Madge Cafferty, you are a saint just like I've heard people say. Be assured, ma'am, you have a deal!"

Late that night, as Abby slipped into her bed, she felt wide awake from the excitement of their new prospects. Although the four of them agreed that they were still a long way from solving the case of the lost claims and the missing inheritance, the opportunity for work and a place to build a cabin in such a short time was nearly beyond belief.

For three nights after their boating accident and again last night, she had prayed, nearly begging for God's merciful hand, but in her heart, she knew doubts assailed her by day. She felt humbled by the gracious way things were working out. All her life, she'd been full of pride and self-assurance. She'd been ready to take on the world. And then came anger, fear, frustration, and many an anxious night.

Abby sighed.

It felt wonderful to lie in this bed and for the first time in a very long time, have a sense of hope and peace. Jon had been right. That night in their Seattle hotel, she'd never imagined how arduous the journey would be.

As Abby recalled their conversations earlier, she thought of Madge's concern for the miners. She was even working to raise funds for a hospital for them. It surprised Abby. Without a doubt, Madge Cafferty was far more than an old miner struggling in a boom town. She was a compassionate and strong woman with God's purposes at heart, and when Madge had mentioned that she could use help to canvass the town for the funds, Abby had quickly offered to help.

Tucked soundly between her sheets now, Abby tried to imagine walking the claims with this bold woman. *They would make certain,*

Madge had promised, *that everybody had a chance to show their community spirit.*

Abby smiled at the woman's pluck. And with the image of Madge's broad, wrinkled face lingering in her mind, Abby at last felt the soft edge of sleep.

The next morning, Abby woke early, washed, and then quickly dressed in the fine blue dress Carson had given her. She combed her hair into a wrap, adjusted her small combs, and then gave her appearance a thorough consideration. The dress was a bit big but she had purposefully opted for the largest dress the proprietress had handed her, knowing that she could tie the waist straps tighter for now and still give herself space to grow in the months ahead.

September would come quickly.

With a long sigh, Abby wondered if she should have mentioned that she was with child to Miss Mulroy. If asked, she would have told the truth, and yet she hadn't been completely forthright either. The need for money had sealed her lips, but she knew she wouldn't be able to hide it for long.

Abby placed her brush on the dressing table and stared at her image in the oval mirror. No matter what her condition, she would do her very best to be a good employee. And whether they would still be in Dawson when she had this baby or on their way home, she would simply have to remain strong. She had no choice.

At the sound of a knock on the door, Abby turned.

"I'll be right there, Jon," she called, but when she opened the door, she was surprised to see Carson instead of Jon waiting outside.

"Good morning," he said cheerfully. His eyes moved down over the dress she wore. "I see we're wearing the blue dress again. You look very nice."

"Thank you. Hopefully, I'll be able to manage with my grandiose wardrobe of two outfits, at least until I receive my first pay." She smiled.

"So are you ready for your appointment with your new boss, Mr. Hanover?"

"I am. But where's Jon?"

"I told him I would bring you downstairs for breakfast. He's finding someone with a wagon to take a portion of our supplies out to Madge's claim. If we can set up a camp there with our tents, what with the warm days, we should do fine until we get the cabin built."

"We?" she said lightly. Abby stepped into the hallway and closed the door. As they started down the hall, she smiled at him. "So, you're planning to help?"

"Actually, all three of us will be staying and working at Madge's claim. I'll help build the cabin by day and write by night, so to speak. A couple days a week, I plan to go into Dawson, but by staying near the infamous claim area, I can interview the miners more easily. Once the cabin's built, I imagine I'll head back to a hotel in Dawson."

"You and Jimmy are being extra kind to us, Carson."

He merely smiled.

After a breakfast of sourdough flapjacks, something the mining establishments were known for serving, Abby felt full and content as the four of them piled into a wagon. She and Jon sat on a narrow board seat with the driver while Carson, Jimmy, and Beauty found a place on the supplies loaded behind.

As they jostled down the road to Grand Forks, Mr. Joseph, their driver, and Jon spoke in length about their mutual experiences with horses. The rest of them, on the other hand, simply listened. When they at last pulled up in front of The Grand, Abby stared at the building in complete surprise. It was much bigger than she ever imagined.

In awe, she stepped down from the wagon and looked around. Situated at the narrow junction of Bonanza and Eldorado Creeks, the establishment held an imposing position, being seen from all directions for miles. The name of the place, she decided, was an apt description. Three times as long as it was deep, the huge building stood two floors high with a large sign on its roof announcing: *The Grand Forks Hotel.*

Several smaller buildings were located a stone's throw from The Grand, and here and there along the creek's rocky banks, were a myriad of tents, large and small. Temporary homes, she imagined, for those hundreds of miners working the claims.

Carson climbed down beside her and handed Abby her satchel. He looked at her with curiosity. "Would you like me to accompany you inside and make sure that we have a Mr. Hanover about?"

"That would be nice, but it's not necessary."

"Actually," he said, "I'd rather like to have a peek inside." He looked back at Jon. "If you wouldn't mind, I'd enjoy nosing around the area before I join you. Would that be a problem?"

"Not a bit," Jon said. "I'd feel better knowing that Abby was situated before I spend a day at the claim anyhow."

"Good, then it's settled," Carson said. He reached into the wagon for his small writing satchel. "All I need is some directions to this Little Chance Creek."

After Mr. Joseph pointed out the way, she and Carson turned for The Grand's large door. Once inside, they took in the smell of breakfast that wafted across a nicely decorated entry and looked around. To the right of them stood a fair-sized clerk's desk, but at the moment, no one was stationed behind it. Not far from the desk was a small window looking back to the entry porch and the road outside, while on the far wall beyond, two small overstuffed chairs sat directly in front of a rock-lined fireplace. Above the fireplace mantle, the head of a large moose seemed to eye them suspiciously. Abby quickly decided that she would not enjoy being in the same room with it.

Directly across from them, from the sound of things, an open doorway led to the dining hall. To the right of that entry, a staircase climbed to the upper floors, while to the left, a long cloth, dark and heavy, hung over yet another doorway.

Wordless, Carson sat her luggage near the counter and then followed her into the dining hall. For a moment, they both gazed at the commotion of men and waiters milling about. Abby was uncertain what to do when a short and slight-built man turned from a conversation at a table nearby. Following a brief nod to the man beside him, he rose and started their direction in quick, short steps.

"Good morning," he called out, his nasal tone nearly lost in the din around them. "Might you be Miss Colton?"

Abby nodded. "Yes, I'm Abigail Colton, and this is an acquaintance of mine, Mr. Carson Stuart. He's a writer for the *Seattle Post-Intelligencer* and thought he might have a look at The Grand while I spoke to you."

"Yes. Well, welcome. I'm Mr. Hanover," he said simply. He waved his hand back to the entrance of The Grand. "Please, let's go into my office to talk. It's a bit noisy here."

Abby and Carson followed him, stepping through the cloth-covered doorway and into a small room filled with a large desk and several book shelves. Mr. Hanover paused at his desk.

"I was only told a day ago that you would be coming, Miss Colton." He gave her a curt nod. "It will be a delight to have someone working with me." He offered a polite smile as well to Carson.

"Would you care for a cup of tea, Miss Colton, Mr. Stuart?"

"No, thank you," Carson said. "I don't wish to be a bother, and I'm sure you have things to discuss with Miss Abigail. I merely came with her because I wanted to take some notes on The Grand and the creek area today. It's always good to include descriptions of establishments as well as the landscape." He smiled. "Would it be a problem if I walked around the hotel a bit?"

"Be my guest," Arthur Hanover said with a hint of pleasure in his gray blue eyes. "Please, any good review, of course, will be most appreciated. We may be far to the north of Seattle, but I've heard tell that Dawson is rapidly becoming the Paris of the North."

"Yes," Carson nodded. "I've heard that as well. Remarkable, isn't it?"

"This is an area of much wealth, Mr. Stuart. Much. And I do believe that in time, it will become an even grander city. I've recently been told by Dawson authorities that the population is close to thirty thousand and climbing." His pale face held a broad smile as he adjusted his small rimless spectacles on his nose. Still smiling, he turned to Abby.

"Well," he said carefully, "shall we be about our paper work or would you like to look around first?"

"Whatever you say, Mr. Hanover."

"Well, then, let's get right down to business and we'll let Mr. Stuart be free to wander about." He smiled again at Carson. "If you've any questions, please, you've only to ask."

"Thank you," Carson said. He looked at Abby. "I imagine Jon or I will be back around five, if that's a good time."

She turned back to Mr. Hanover. "I'm assuming you plan for me to work today. Is that correct?"

The narrow-shouldered man tapped his pant leg a moment before he spoke. "Perhaps for starters, we might want to make a half day of it. Why don't you allow me to show you around then we'll talk about your responsibilities, and after that you can settle into your room." He looked around. "I would assume you have some luggage?"

"A little," she said. "I've a valise in the entry."

"Very well, then. Let me show you the room you'll be sharing with two of our employees, Miss Anna Toppley and Miss Sara O'Toole. The room is small, I'm afraid, but it's all we have available at the moment."

"It will be fine, Mr. Hanover. Hopefully, before long my brother Jon will have a cabin finished not far from here, so I might have other lodging anyway."

"Is that so? Where are you locating?"

"On a claim at Little Chance Creek."

"I see," he said. "That will be a walk for you. I imagine it's well past a mile from here. You will manage fine in the summer, but winter will be a challenge."

"Yes, well, perhaps we will have to make adjustments," she said simply.

The graying man with the spectacles gave her a penetrating look as Carson fished for his pocket watch.

"Perhaps her brother and I might come back for Abigail around two-thirty in the afternoon? Would that be considered a half day, Mr. Hanover?"

"Yes. That will be fine."

"Good," Carson said. "I will see you then, Abigail." And with that, Carson made his exit from the room.

Abby took in a light breath to steady her nerves as the small man beside her stabbed a bony finger toward the same doorway.

"Shall I show you where you will be staying?"

Chapter
Twenty-Three

For several minutes, Carson wandered about the hotel. After venturing up the stairs, he peered into a room whose door was ajar and looked around. It appeared to be decorated in a plain but adequate manner. Afterward, he descended the staircase and walked to the large dining hall that held a dozen or so tables. He jotted down a few notes in his notebook, and then strolled back to the kitchen area to where a large man stood by a stove. Two ladies were working nearby.

"Excuse me," Carson called out. "But Mr. Hanover said that I might look around and give an accounting of The Grand's appearance to my newspaper." He hesitated at the way the man at the stove looked at him. "Might I ask a few questions?"

The man stared at him. "You say Mr. Hanover sent you?"

"Well, yes, in a manner of speaking," Carson replied. "Are you the chef?"

He shrugged. "Of sorts. I'm the breakfast cook. Name's Cal."

Carson stepped through an open doorway and looked around. "Appears to be a well-kept kitchen. Have you worked here long?"

Without looking up, Cal shook his head. "About a year, I guess."

Carson smiled. "Cal." He repeated the name. "Sounds like a short name for my home state of California."

The cook nodded. "Yup, came up here from California. Been following the rushes."

"Gold rushes?"

The large man nodded and turned to grab a basket of eggs. Wordless, he began cracking them into a bowl. Carson, getting the general drift of the man's unfriendly body language, took quick note of the kitchen's general appearances and then waved to him. "Well, thanks for allowing me to see the kitchen."

"No problem," the man grunted.

Carson stepped back into the dining area and, seeing a side door, headed outside. As he strolled to the front of the building, he thought about the cook named Cal. The man seemed rather unfriendly, unlike most folks who, once they know you are a reporter, begin a rather long and detailed description of their adventures. Instead, the man had made a vague comment about *following the rushes*, whatever that meant. As far as he knew, the last big gold strike in California was in the early sixties with the Comstock of Virginia City.

After Carson walked around the building to the front of the hotel, he paused to survey the sprawling tents nearby and the low hills beyond that held the occasional stand of scrub fir on the north and aspen and birch on the south. He took a minute or so to commit the sights to memory then headed down the trail. When he came to the junction where the Eldorado merged with Bonanza Creek, he hesitated and looked back at The Grand.

Spending a few nights at the hotel as well as staying in camp with Jon and Jimmy might work nicely for a while, he decided, for though he wanted to eventually return to Dawson to interview a variety of people for the *Post* and the local *Klondike*, the thought of staying at The Grand to bathe now and then, as well to have a decent place to write, sounded appealing. Besides, it wouldn't hurt to know how Abby was managing.

Carson sucked in a light breath and released it slowly. He hoped the hotel wasn't too expensive. His finances were getting tight, and though he'd been able to mail his Chilkoot Pass and Lake Bennett stories as soon as they'd arrived in Dawson, he figured it would be several weeks before he'd receive any compensation. Hopefully, he could make do.

Buying Abigail a pretty dress hadn't helped, but he didn't regret it. He even wondered if it had given Abby a sense of well-being, for she appeared to be considerably more confident when speaking to Miss Mulroy than she'd been those last days on the river. Perhaps the dress had even helped her secure the clerk's position. But no matter if it did or not, he knew purchasing the dress had abrogated some of his own guilt. Tearing the back of it like that seemed a fool thing to do in hindsight, even though she had been dangerously cold.

As he thought about her, freezing wet, and yet still determined to stay the course, he realized that most of the stampeders he'd met had that kind of resiliency. He was amazed that more of the thousands pouring into this harsh land hadn't died or turned back somewhere along the way. It would have been disappointing had Abby done so.

Carson sighed. He would enjoy staying longer in the north country and writing a great deal more about the many characters both in Alaska and the Klondike, but he doubted the *Post-Intelligencer* wanted more than two or three articles to publish. Unless he could find that *stocking full of gold*, extending his time here would be near to impossible.

For a moment, he studied the mounds of rocks strewn along the creek beds ahead. He could see several miners here and there working as if in rhythm to the earth and water around them. Maybe, somewhere along those mounds, a story was waiting to be told. Maybe even, he'd discover it while on his way to Little Chance Creek.

With long strides, Carson set off along the trail that ran parallel to the Eldorado, all the while keeping an eye open for what might be a good opportunity. He'd hiked less than half a mile when he spotted a woman sitting at the edge of the creek. Dressed in gray attire with a rather up-to-date hat atop her head, she peered down into a pan that she was rotating from side to side.

Carson felt his curiosity rising.

As he walked toward the woman, he studied the two men just beyond her working at a large sluice box. To his surprise, they wore white shirts, and though they had rolled their sleeves to their elbows and appeared to be busy, they looked far less like the typical miner than another group of men just beyond them. He walked to within fifty yards then hesitated as the woman looked up.

"Hello," he called out. "I hope I'm not a bother to you, but I'd like to introduce myself. I'm Carson Stuart." As all heads turned, he took a few steps closer. "I'm a reporter for the *Seattle Post-Intelligencer*," he continued, "and I'm hoping to get an accurate sense of what the Klondike is all about. The lady here really captured my curiosity. May I ask a few questions?"

The elder of the two well-dressed men stepped out from his box and walked forward. Behind him, the woman smiled. A strong, husky arm reached out as Carson extended his hand. "I'm Earl Cummings," the man said, "and this is my wife Clara. My brother, John, is there behind her."

John nodded but kept to his work.

"Quite a crew you have," Carson quipped. "Some better looking than the average miners I've come across."

The woman by the rock pile laughed. "I keep telling Earl that I'm worth my weight in gold," she said.

Carson nodded. "By the looks of your production here, maybe even more," he called back. He turned to Earl. "Have you been in the creek area long?"

"Our second year," the man said, beaming. "It's been a good one."

"Earl Cummings?" Carson rolled the name over his tongue, trying to remember. "You aren't *the* Earl Cummings, one of the few that came to San Francisco last year with all the gold?"

Earl nodded. "In the flesh."

Carson raised his eyebrows in surprise. "Well, I never dreamed I'd meet the man that ended up creating a job opportunity for me."

Earl chuckled with a deep, hardy sound coming from his chest. "Glad I could be of service."

Carson was curious. "Are you planning to make this a yearly procedure by returning to San Francisco for the winter then coming back to Dawson for summer?"

"Well, maybe not every year," Earl drawled, "but most times Clara wants to go out at least three weeks before the Yukon freezes."

"And what time of the year would that be?"

Clara smiled. "If I can get Earl to quit and leave it to the boys, the first part of September is the usual time, though even that's cutting it a bit close some years."

"You take a steamer to the mouth of the Yukon and then go south?" Carson asked.

"We do," Earl confirmed. He hesitated and then waved his hand behind him to where water was being drawn from the river. "Would you like to take a look at our operation?"

Carson brightened. "I would at that. Appears to be quite a pile of gravel you're going through." He nodded to the mound of rocks nearby.

"Yup, sometimes we dig through almost thirty feet to get to the good stuff," brother John called out. He continued to talk as Earl and Carson moved closer. "Since the ground is frozen deep around here, we often build wood fires to thaw the soil before picking and hoisting it to the surface. Then warmer days, when the creek's flowing, we sluice it."

Carson stepped up beside John and studied the string of sluice boxes, one after another, which contained a smattering of small rocks and gravel still lying along the bottom after the water had passed over it. Beside him, John worked at scooping a shovel full of pay dirt into Clara's pan. As he watched, he thought about the amount of work that would be ahead for Jimmy and Jon.

"Have some acquaintances that are planning to help Madge Cafferty mine a claim not far from here," Carson said, "and though I imagine she'll be directing how they set it up, it's interesting to see the process at work."

"Madge bought a claim up here?" Earl said with surprise.

"Well, not here at Eldorado, but on a tributary called the Little Chance."

Earl nodded, as if he knew the place. "Up beyond us then."

"Do you mind if you could point the way. I haven't been to the claim yet, but was planning on helping my friends for awhile today."

"Sure, just follow the trail that leads up that small creek beyond. It's probably on the bench higher up the hill." He looked at Carson with curiosity. "You say they're friends?"

"Yes. Jon and Abigail Colton and a big fellow named Jimmy Patten, plus myself, will be working up there. Jon and Abigail actually came here in order to help a family recover some claims, but it appears that someone else is working them."

"That right?" Earl, who had leaned over his sluice box, looked back over his shoulder. "It wouldn't happen to be the Eldorado numbers nine, ten, and eleven would it?"

"Yes," Carson said. "I believe those are the right ones."

Earl stole a glance back to the woman working her pan. "I told you, Clara. It just didn't look right to me. Never heard why old Dan and C. R. left. Cabin and all their equipment still there, but haven't seen hide nor hair of them since we returned."

"Well, I don't know if I should be saying this, but Abigail and Jon were told that Dan died late last fall, but they're not certain where C. R. has gone." He hesitated. "So," he said, "you're positive that none one of the men working those claims is Mr. Thorne?"

"Nope, definitely not. Old Dan and C. R. were great talkers," Earl quipped. "Some of the good ol' boys that go way back to Forty Mile, where we all got started in ninety-six."

Carson nodded. "If you don't mind, I'll pass your words along since Jon is investigating what happened to the claims. If by chance you hear of anything more, or happen to see C. R., please tell him that Jon is building a cabin up the hill and he'd like to talk to him. Over the next few weeks, my friend Jimmy and I plan to help Jon while Abigail works at The Grand during the day."

"That right? Well, Clara," he said boldly, "looks like we might have to pay a call."

Clara nodded with a smile. "It will be right nice to have another woman about the area. Are they a young couple?"

Carson nodded. "Yes. Brother and sister. They were coming north from Seattle with Abigail's husband when her husband disappeared. They're good people. I think you'd like them."

"Well, now," Clara said with a soft voice. "Tell them we will definitely come by sometime. You say you'll be building the cabin soon?"

"Yes, ma'am. This week."

Clara, he noticed, gave him a broad warm smile as he came alongside and began to question the way she was moving her pan.

Chapter Twenty-Four

Abby's stomach tensed at the feel of his breath near her ear.

"No, Miss Colton," Mr. Hanover said in a whispery voice. "From now on, you will not need to bother totaling these columns." He turned the page to a clean journal sheet and pointed.

"Simply make your entries for each day in the proper column under food or lodging and, of course," he said, as if speaking to a child, "continue to note the date at the top before listing the income below. Always keep the receipt book and the ledger on the shelf across the room where I can find it, and after that I will take care of everything."

"You don't want me to total my day's receipts?" she asked.

He gave her a rather crooked smile. "No. It will be much easier if you simply list the amounts, and then when I enter the other numbers later in the day, I will calculate the totals."

He patted her arm lightly. "Now," he said, "other than the account books, is everything else going well?"

Abby shifted in her chair so that she could face him. "Yes. I believe so. I have made certain that the housekeepers are changing the linens and taking them to the laundry next door, and every afternoon I check all the rooms. The help appear to be maintaining the rooms in good order. In addition," she said carefully, "the business in the dining hall seems to be doing well every morning, although the afternoon is slower."

As a serious frown worked its way across his brow, he stepped back and considered her. "Which reminds me," he said, "wouldn't it be better if you started work earlier than seven-thirty in the morning? What with the light of summer, the men are coming in at all hours now."

Abby smiled, wondering if more time to her day meant an increase in pay or simply an earlier morning. "Of course," she nodded dutifully. "When would you like me to begin?"

"Would an hour earlier be all right for you?"

Abby hesitated at the thought of rising before six, especially when she considered how every evening she walked to the cabin site in order to cook the men supper. It was always late before she began the long walk back to The Grand. This new schedule would make for very long days.

Abby forced a smile. "Yes, of course, Mr. Hanover. I'll be in the lobby at six-thirty sharp." Disheartened, Abby rose to her feet. "Will I be leaving at the same time then?"

She saw the gleam in his eyes as he leaned closer to her, much too close. "Well, we'll see how the days work out," he said carefully. "Perhaps I might come a little earlier in the afternoon myself, that way we could talk about the business transactions before you leave for . . . well, wherever you go." He gave a small shrug. "I believe it will make our transition a bit smoother."

Abby nodded and stepped back, trying to keep her mind free of the growing dislike in her heart.

"Good afternoon, Abigail, Mr. Hanover."

Abby looked up to see Carson standing in the doorway. For the past few weeks, Mr. Hanover had tied back the curtain at the doorway into the room, telling her that she needed to be able to see into the entryway for customers.

"Might you be finished for the day, Abigail?" he asked.

Mr. Hanover jerked to full height then reached into his pocket for his watch. He glanced down as he spoke. "My, how time flies. I see that it's past your time to leave, Miss Colton. I apologize for the lateness, but I guess five in the evening comes quick, especially when there's hardly a difference between day and night in the northern summer."

"May I suggest that there be a clock somewhere in the entry area," Carson said. "I think it would help keep her hours more timely, and perhaps it would be helpful for customers, like me, as well.

"Why, yes," Mr. Hanover said. "Thank you for that idea. Perhaps we can look for one later this week when I visit with Miss Mulroy in Dawson."

"Mentioning Dawson," Carson said, turning to Abby. "Jon is waiting outside. We're all heading into town for more supplies and a little fun. It's the Fourth, you know, and though we're in a foreign country, we've heard there will be celebrations. You want to come along?"

Abby perked to the news. "That sounds interesting," she said. She turned to Mr. Hanover. "I assume we're finished for the day?"

"Oh, yes. I think we've covered my concerns. You have a nice evening, Miss Colton."

As Abby reached for her jacket, she thought about the way Mr. Hanover lingered on the word *Miss*. Something in the way he spoke it made her wonder if he could tell that she was growing thicker about the middle every day. Would he make an issue of her being with child, especially since she listed her name on Mr. Hanover's ledger as a Miss, not a Mrs.? Perhaps it was time to speak to Georgia Mulroy.

Still deep in thought about talking with Miss Mulroy, Abby walked down the hotel steps unaware that Carson was talking to her. Realizing that he was muttering in low tones beside her, she glanced at him.

"Did you say something?"

"No. Well, more or less, I did." He looked at her. "Abby, is Mr. Hanover behaving himself around you. I mean, is he making any advances toward you?"

"Mr. Hanover?" she asked with surprise. "No, I don't think so. He just seems to be leaning over my shoulder and nervous about my every move, that's all. That and adding an hour to my day."

Carson frowned. "An hour? That means you'll have a long day if you keep wandering off to the creek to cook supper every night. So now he wants you up with the birds, as if you aren't already," he said crossly.

"How would you know, now that you're staying at The Grand and writing all night?"

"Exactly. I know that it's late when we walk back from camp, and then I find you've been up for hours when I come down for breakfast, so that *is* my point."

She sighed. "Well, another hour doesn't concern me as much as Mr. Hanover's general lack of eagerness about my presence. I thought Georgia said he was looking for a helper, but as far as I can tell, he's making sure that I don't become too comfortable, or that I don't have much to do with his precious records."

Carson looked at her with a hint of concern. "That sounds somewhat suspicious."

She nodded. "I rather thought so. I've a notion to total my daily entries, whether he wants me to or not. Maybe I'll make notes on a separate paper and keep them with me, out of sight, of course."

"Are you sure you aren't shouldering more responsibility than necessary for a hundred dollars a month?"

She shrugged. "Miss Mulroy trusts me and I appreciate the employment. At least this work is in a clean and warm environment. Besides, I find it interesting to talk with the miners."

Carson snorted as they walked up to the wagon where Jimmy and Jon sat talking to Mr. Joseph. Reaching for her hand, he helped her climb up to the seat beside the driver. "Good tips?" he whispered as she moved past him.

Abby sat down and nodded pleasantly to the driver. "Evening, Mr. Joseph."

"Evening, Miss Colton."

"What's this about finding a pleasure in talking to the miners," Jimmy said from the back of the wagon. "Don't you have enough fellas around to be plumb sick of men by now?"

Gathering a look of mock concern about her face, she turned and gave Jimmy a narrow-eyed glare. "What? Grow tired of you men, what with the cooking, the washing, and the mending? Now, why would I ever do that?"

With a distinct smirk on her face, she shifted forward as the driver slapped the reins and the wagon lumbered off. "Though I imagine," she added firmly, "I could offer to let one of you make supper now and then. Why don't you learn to cook, Jimmy? I'll bet you'd be darn good at it, don't you think so, Carson?"

When she glanced back and saw three somber faces staring back at her, Abby wondered if she had teased a bit too much. "You can relax, boys, you couldn't keep me away from making sure that cabin got properly built."

Carson spoke up behind her. "All right," he said. "You've made your point, and now I want you to remember mine. I think," he said with equal candor, "that you ought to be careful around this Mr. Hanover."

Abby shook her head. "I was complaining about the cooking, Carson, not the books."

"Listen, Abby," Jimmy called out, "you don't need to come to the claim every evening for us." She heard a long pause behind her and then the distinct sound of his voice once again. "Although I'm thinkin' Beauty would be pretty depressed if you didn't show up. Besides, I'm afraid the rest of us would get sick if we ate my griddles for breakfast, lunch, *and* supper."

Abby tossed him a gentle smile. "Not to worry, Jimmy. You know how I love coming out there and petting Beauty." She looked at Jon. "Mentioning Beauty, why didn't you bring her?"

"Thought there would be some loud celebrations," Jon said. "Listen, we men are planning to attend a local fight in town, so if our paths don't cross at suppertime, just wait for us at Madge's. We'll eventually be along," he said, "though it might be late."

"A fight?"

Jon nodded. "Frank Slavin, heavyweight champion of Australia is here with a mate to demonstrate his sport at the theatre tonight."

"You're serious?"

Carson laughed. "I told you she wouldn't like it." He smiled. "Now with all the talent here from Paris and the world around, why wouldn't we want to take a peek at it?"

She shook her head. "Why would someone come this far to *fight* for heaven's sake."

"Same old answer, Abby, adventure and the dollar. Especially if there's enough gold dust waiting, and apparently there is."

"Money," she sighed. "The root of all evil."

Carson, who was sitting directly behind her, leaned closer. "I thought the Good Book said it was the *love* of money that was the problem. Besides, if it's such evil, why are you here?"

Abby sat quietly, debating whether to give him a response, when he spoke again. "Hey, Jon," he said. "Overheard that pleasant little Mr. Hanover instructing Abigail that she has to start work an hour sooner tomorrow."

"An hour earlier?" Jon said. "Is that right, Abby? Didn't Miss Mulroy tell you what your hours would be?"

"Yes, but I'm not going to fuss," she said firmly. "I need the work and Mr. Hanover knows it."

"Bloody creep," Jimmy declared.

"Well, somebody has to work around here," she retorted.

"Jimmy and I are going to earn a little on the side hauling freight," Jon spoke up, "right after we get the cabin built. Mr. Joseph said he could use the help."

She smiled at Mr. Joseph. "He convinced you he's a good horseman, did he?" She looked over her shoulder with a serene smile. "Just find me a stocking full of gold, Jonathan David. That will solve it all."

Carson chuckled. "Jonathan David?" He looked at Jon. "Been keeping that a secret have you, Jon boy?"

"Yes siree, just keep laughing, Carson," Jimmy chided. "Especially since the *J* in your middle name stands for Josiah. Carson Josiah Venturi Stuart. How's that for a mouthful?"

Abby laughed. "Josiah," she said. She repeated the word carefully, then turned to look at him. "I like it, Carson."

After Mr. Joseph drove the wagon into the downtown area of Dawson, the four of them made final plans then climbed down from the wagon and went their separate directions. Jon and Jimmy started for the boat dock to bargain for more planks, while Carson headed for the *Klondike Nugget.* After reminding the men to meet her at Madge's, Abby set off to find a local seamstress.

As she made her way down the disheveled boardwalk, Abby heard shouts of laughter in a nearby saloon, and just as she approached a set of swinging doors, a young woman came staggering out into the street, nearly bumping into her. Clad in a short skirt and a sheer, silky blouse, the woman waved her hands and bemoaned her trials while a man at the swinging doors begged her to come back inside.

Startled, Abby watched them a moment, then in dismay, crossed the street and continued on her way, but as she moved on, she couldn't help but wonder what kind of life the woman endured. It wasn't the first time she had encountered women of this nature. Earlier this week, several young women had come strolling into the dining area just as she was leaving for the evening. Dressed in low-cut tops and very short skirts, she was told that they were singers and dancers, but she had wondered.

For the most part, these entertainers were about her age, although they certainly carried a rounder and more endowed bust line. Abby thought about the changes taking place in her own body these days. She had always been a bony scamp of a woman, near to the figure of a young boy instead of a nicely shaped woman, but of late, she had been growing a bit plump, and not only in her middle, but in her face and arms as well. There was even a different glow to her skin, especially about her cheeks.

Abby sighed. She had experienced so much change within the year.

Only a summer ago, she'd been working at the Post and Mercantile in Benton and riding with her father and brothers to help round up cattle from the nearby hills. She recalled how thin she'd been. Even her own grandmother had quipped that she looked like a little *tough* on the streets of St. Louis.

She doubted Grammy Mary would think so now.

With a sense of longing, Abby looked around and tried to remember the instructions Madge had given her. Surely, she had to be close to the shop. Turning her eyes from sign to sign, she at last spotted the small handwriting above a door. *Miss Matsen's Laundry*, it read. She quickly crossed the street and entered the shop, but as she closed the door and looked about, Abby's heart nearly jumped from her chest.

Ingrid?

Abby couldn't believe her eyes. Filled with excitement, she rushed forward.

"Abby!" Ingrid squealed as they hugged.

"Ingrid Johansen, I was beginning to believe I would never see you again! When did you arrive? Where are you staying?"

"Oh, Abby, not so quick with the questions," her friend sputtered. "I arrive only this week. But already Hansen is working for a man building a home and I am here, helping Miss Matsen. She washes, irons, sews and mends for so many. And I help."

"So then, you are safe and well, and you still see Hansen?"

Ingrid smiled as she nodded. "Ya. It is very nice, I think."

"This sounds serious. Have you news?"

Ingrid's smile broadened as she ducked her head. "If we can save up the money, we will marry before the year is out."

Abby grabbed her friend's shoulders and gave her a warm embrace. "Ingrid, I am so pleased for you. Our adventure was difficult, but not so overly hard on us it seems."

"And look at you!" Ingrid said, stepping back. "You are looking very goot these days. The little one, she is growing. Ya?"

"She?" Abby laughed. "With all these men about, you think I would have a girl?"

"Aye, why not?" Ingrid grinned. "So where are you and Jon staying? Do you still see Carson and Jimmy?"

"Yes, in fact, Jimmy and Carson are helping Jon build a cabin on a woman's claim. It's out on Little Chance Creek near the Eldorado south of town. She's even paying Jon and Jimmy to work it. And, I've found employment as a clerk at The Grand Hotel, a lodge near the claim."

"Goot, goot!" Ingrid said brightly. "We are blessed, are we not?"

"Yes, we are, although Jon and I lost almost everything at Thirty-Mile Rapids. Did you come through everything fine enough?"

Ingrid nodded. "But I have been wondering about you. I am so glad to see you. Will you be coming to services Sunday?"

"Here?"

"Ya! A small group of us are meeting on Church Street. Plans are made for building the church right now, so we meet there at the site until it's complete."

"I don't know, Ingrid. We live more than ten miles away, but I will hope to come in sometime." She smiled and looked around. "Well, I suppose it best to let you go back to your work, Ingrid, but before you do, I must tell you that I came here for a needle and some thread, and hopefully, some material as well. I need fabric for our cabin and for a few baby clothes. Can you help me?"

"Of course!" Ingrid beamed. "First, let me introduce you to our seamstress, and then we must make plans to get together again, all of us. Would that not be vonderful?"

Abby just stared at her. She still couldn't believe her eyes.

The hotel lobby was empty as Carson stepped inside and looked around. He'd hoped to cancel his breakfast order for the next morning. It was late when they returned from Dawson, but seeing the amount of food sacks and wood Jimmy and Jon had to carry to their camp, he decided to help them and then spend the night at the claim instead of the hotel.

After placing a brief note on the counter, he stepped out into the dining hall full of smoke and men in hopes of finding Mr. Hanover before he left. At the far end of the room where the spirits flowed freely, several men were sitting at a large table, talking and laughing. Carson noted two women among them, encouraging them on for more drinks, he imagined.

After a quick glance about for the manager, he started to turn back to the lobby, when he spotted Mr. Hanover coming inside the dining hall through the side door not far from the kitchen. For a brief moment, Carson studied the round-shouldered man whose drawn face held a distinct frown. Something had soured the man's countenance.

Carson started toward him. "Thought I might find you at the counter," he said. "But since you weren't around, I decided to leave you a note. I wanted to make certain that you had a clear understanding of the adjustments I'm making in regard to breakfast and my length of stay. I'm leaving for the night, helping some friends, but I plan to return tomorrow evening for my last night here."

Arthur Hanover nodded. "As you wish, Mr. Stuart."

"I've left most of my clothes in my room and tomorrow I will give you my payment in full."

"That would be good," he said.

"Well, then, I'll see you tomorrow." Carson turned and started for the front door.

"Good night, sir."

As Carson walked along the trail to where Jon and Jimmy waited, he noticed two shadowed shapes at the side of The Grand. He hesitated, wondering at the two men walking away from the side door. When he reached Jon and Jimmy, he nodded toward the building.

"Look over by the side door of The Grand," he said quietly. "You see those men?"

"Nice looking gents," Jimmy said.

Jon threw a sack of goods over his shoulder then started to turn away when Carson touched his arm. "Wait," he said. "Do those men in the shadows look a little familiar to you?"

"They're big fellas all right," Jimmy murmured thoughtfully. "I only remember seeing a few men that big around here, except for me, that is. Are you thinking about those burly men on Dan and C. R.'s claims? You think they're them?"

"Might be," Carson said. "Wonder what they're doing at The Grand?"

"I don't know," Jon said. "But I'm tired. Let's get these things to camp."

With Jon leading the way, they walked in silence for several minutes before Jon broached the subject again. "Have you ever seen those men at The Grand in the morning, Carson?"

"No," he said. "I was just thinking about that myself. Wonder why they'd be hanging around outside like that in the dark?"

"Well, everyone needs to eat and have a little entertainment now and then," Jimmy offered, "though it seems a little strange that they're at the side door, not the front."

"Exactly," Carson said.

"Maybe they have some friends there," Jimmy continued. "While waiting for you, another man talked with them for awhile. A short guy who looked to be agitated by the way he waved his hands all around."

Carson stopped in his tracks. "Wait a minute. That had to be Mr. Hanover. I spoke to him in the dining hall, and he'd just stepped in through that very side door with a mighty sour look on his face."

Jon paused and turned back. "Mr. Hanover, Abby's boss?" he said with surprise.

"The same. I have to tell you," Carson mused, "I rarely go on gut feelings about people because they can often mislead a man, but I don't particularly like Abigail's boss. I wonder if he has any connections to those men on your claims. Maybe you should stop by the Constable's office and complain with a little more fervor about the investigation."

Jon shook his head as he started forward once again. "Maybe. But the last time I spoke with the Constable and the claim commissioner, they said their hands were tied unless I can give them proof that those men didn't get permission to work the claims. I told them that a letter would be arriving soon from the Smythe family, but I didn't check the Post today. It was late and we had our plans."

Carson grunted. "Well, it might be worth checking soon."

"Listen," Jimmy said. "We've got enough planking that Carson and I can finish the table and at least a stool or two, so why don't you go back to Dawson tomorrow and follow up on things."

"And while you're at it," Carson said. "Maybe it would be well to ask about something else. Last night, while writing an article, I found a note in my journal about the Cummings. They used to mine at a place called Forty Mile. Earl Cummings said C. R. had been there with them, and if I remember correctly, Madge Cafferty also mentioned a man who partnered with a C. R. at Forty Mile. Maybe the Constable should try to locate Mr. Thorne in that area."

"Good idea," Jon said.

As they turned and started up the hill, Carson felt a cool breeze descending the hillside. "Chilly out here tonight," he mumbled. "I hate for Abigail to be walking back to The Grand late in the evening."

"I agree," Jimmy said. "And the more I think about what we've said, the more I don't like the idea of Abigail being around that Hanover guy. She's probably all right at work, but I'd feel better if she were sleeping out here."

Jon stopped in his tracks and looked at them. "Good grief," he said. "Abigail, Abigail, Abigail. Sometimes I wonder what this trip would have been like without her."

"Not nearly as good," Jimmy said with a slow grin. "Not even close."

Chapter Twenty-Five

Abigail rose early and bathed, and as she readied for the day, thoughts of Ingrid's happy face kept coming to mind, so it was with a light step that she entered the dining hall and began to greet the workers and customers alike. After eating a bit of breakfast and checking to make sure all was going well, she'd barely walked back to the entry desk, when Jon opened the front door and stepped inside.

"Well, good morning," she said. "What are you doing here?"

"Did you forget? I told you that I left most of the planking for our beds in Dawson, so I'm going after them today."

"Oh, yes, you did say that. Guess my mind's been on my chance meeting with Ingrid. I'm still so happy, Jon, finding her like that and all, and then to have her give me some beautiful fabric for the baby. I feel completely renewed this morning."

When he said nothing, she gave him a curious look. "Is everything all right?"

"Good enough, I reckon." He moved up to the desk and touched her hand briefly before he gave her a small smile. "I'm happy for you, Abby, and extra thankful for Jimmy and Carson's help as well. They're at the cabin as we speak, building a table and some stools while I go into town. We owe them, Abby."

"I know. I've been praying a blessing for both of them each and every day. Perhaps we repay our debt a little by offering good company and good food." She smiled.

"Doesn't hurt."

Jon looked at her. "Listen, Abby, I'm going into Dawson today for more than the boards. I also plan to speak to the mining commissioner and the Constable," he said. Jon lowered his voice to a near whisper. "The three of us were talking last night and we decided that we should ask the Constable to check to see if C. R. is at Forty Mile. I'm also going to stop at the Post. Maybe the Smythe family has sent us a letter."

He hesitated. "Meanwhile, I think you should be observant and careful around here."

She cocked her head and stared at the seriousness in her brother's eyes. It was unlike him. "All right, but . . ."

"No buts, Abby. I know I'm speaking in riddles because there's nothing definite to tell you other than a few suspicious men were out back of The Grand last night. Just keep an eye out for things that don't look right, and watch your backside as you do."

Abby's heart began to thump inside her chest. She nodded. "All right," she said slowly. "When will you come back from Dawson?"

"Not certain, although I'm planning to be home for supper anyhow. Jon and Jimmy will be waiting for you at the cabin. I'm going to see if I can get Mr. Joseph to take the planks as far as the bottom of the hill at Little Chance."

When two men came in the front door, Jon stepped back and gave her a simple nod. "I'll see you later for supper?"

"Yes, see you then."

After he walked out the front door, Abby turned for the dining hall sensing that all the joy she'd felt earlier had been replaced with a light edge of fear. With his warning still heavy in her heart, she helped serve breakfast and pour coffee, and then, seeing how the girls were busy with many customers, she began to carry some dirty dishes to the kitchen. Afterward, she returned to the front desk and began to make a list of necessary items to give to Mr. Joseph. Mr. Joseph with his supply wagons was a lifesaver for the outlying areas of Dawson.

As the day wore on, Abby climbed the stairs to check on the cleaning processes, and after helping Miss Toppley straighten a few rooms, she tiredly traipsed back down the stairs to enter some receipts for the day. She found the books on the shelf in Mr. Hanover's small office and sat to make her entries.

But as she began to write, she noted a light penciled scribble beneath the previous day's entries and paused to look at it more carefully. She checked each column and realized that, if the pencil figures were supposed to be totals, they did not add up. She glanced up, making sure no one was about, and then reached for a clean sheet of stationery.

Abby penned yesterday's date at the top and then began to list all the entries for that day. Finally, when she'd finished, she made a few calculations and entered the totals. Hurrying now, Abby found yet another clean sheet of paper and repeated the process, recording the entries of two more days within the past four weeks. Following a few calculations, she began to list the totals by date on the bottom of one paper before quickly folding the papers and sliding them into her pocket.

She wasn't sure what Jon meant about being observant, but something about Mr. Hanover's instructions made her wary of his journals. When she'd worked for Mac McGruder at Benton's Post and Mercantile, she'd been very careful to always total the day's sales. If there were any errors in these ledgers being reported to Miss Mulroy, she did not want Georgia to think they were from her hand!

After finishing her entries, Abby rose, returned the ledger to the shelf, and then went back to her work in the dining hall. But as she moved about the hotel, she felt uneasy and was more than grateful when Mr. Hanover at last appeared and she was able to leave for their camp.

The sun was still high in the horizon when Abby started for Madge's claim. It was warm. And the longer she walked, the more the weight beneath her ribs seemed to be growing by the minute. Deciding to rest a bit, Abby sat down on a nearby stump.

She released a deep sigh as she thought about the days ahead. She was healthy and strong, but into her seventh month now, if her calculations were correct. Soon, she would need to make more effort to have things ready for the birth of her child. For a few minutes, she gazed out across the creek to where several men were at work. Earlier in the week, Clara Cummings and her husband, who had a claim in this area, had come to call at the cabin. She'd not been there, but was pleased to know that there was another woman in the area.

After watching the men below her for several minutes, Abby rose slowly to her feet and started up the hill, her thoughts turning to the myriad of things yet to be done in the cabin. As she stepped into a stand of scrub pine, she heard a loud snap in the forest behind her and hesitated. She looked around, wondering if Jimmy or Carson were nearby.

As she stood quietly, Abby suddenly felt a strong sense of foreboding flow over her. With a sudden urge to move, she turned and hurried on up the path, relieved when she at last spotted Carson standing outside the cabin with Beauty lying nearby.

"Hello," she shouted. Beauty jumped to her feet and started running for her. After stroking her great shaggy friend, she walked close to where Carson was pounding a nail into the leg of a stool.

"Not the best," he said, shaking his head. "But it should get you by for the short haul." He tossed her a quick smile then straightened and studied her face. "Are you all right? You look a little pale?"

She shook her head. "I'm all right."

"You're certain?"

She smiled. "As certain as one can be in this world of unknowns." She turned. "Where's Jimmy?"

We finished making the table and two chairs a couple hours ago, so he went down the hill to the old sluice boxes on the place. Think he's trying figure a way to improve them as Madge indicated."

"We'll be able to eat on the table tonight?"

"That we will," he said proudly.

"Well," she quipped, "I guess I won't have any good excuses not to cook you a good supper tonight."

He grinned. "No, I'm afraid not. No excuse at all."

Seeing the evening shadows long about them, Carson rose from his stool. "Was mighty good food, Abby, but I'm thinking I'd like to get back to The Grand. I'll walk you back. Are you about ready to leave?"

Abby glanced up, pan in hand. "As soon as I wipe the inside of this, I will be."

Carson turned to Jimmy. "In case you don't remember, I'm returning to Dawson in the morning. I assume you're staying here as planned?

Jimmy nodded. "Yup, tomorrow Jon and I will start sluicing some of the piles of gravel that are already on the claim." He looked at Abby. "When do you think you'll want to move into the cabin?"

"In about five weeks," she said with a sigh. "In some ways I will miss everyone at the hotel, but I think its best to quit and stay here as my time nears." She glanced at Jon. "Will it be possible to pipe that spring water into the cabin as you'd hoped?"

"I could, but within a couple months it'll freeze up, Abby. This is mighty cold country. Through the coldest months, we'll have to thaw ice on the stove for water." He rose from his chair and crossed the room. He washed his plate in a pot of sudsy water and then watched Abby while she wiped it.

"I'm thinking that you'd be better off staying at The Grand," he said.

"I don't want to stay there, Jon. With the baby and all, I couldn't stay where I am, and it's too expensive for an upstairs room. Besides, I would prefer more privacy for the baby. Those walls are paper thin." She shrugged. "You know what Gram Mary said when we left Benton, *don't forget to boil the water*." So that's what I plan to do, and it won't matter if it's ice first.

"All right," Jon shrugged. "I guess it's your choice."

She gave Jon a studied look. "I know it will be extra work for you and Jimmy, but before you start working the gravel, I'd still like you to pipe some spring water to the cabin. It might not be flowing for long, but it could be very helpful for those first days."

Carson smiled. "Sounds like you're losing again, Jon."

Jon nodded. "Have a feeling this winter could get to be a long one."

"Well," Carson said, "maybe you won't have to be here that long. If the letter comes and C. R. is found, things could change quickly." He turned to Abby. "Are you about ready to go back to The Grand?"

She nodded then wiped her hands before reaching for her jacket. As the two of them started down the hill, Carson noted Abby's quiet and somewhat weary demeanor. When they reached the open space midway down the hill, he reached out and took her arm.

"Come on, Abigail, you look tired. Before we go any farther, let me show you a nice spot out in the meadow. With the evening shadows, it should be pretty there and relaxing."

She studied him moment, as if to consider, then nodded. "All right."

Carson led her through a meadow to where Little Chance Creek tumbled over a small rocky outcropping. Near to it was a stake marking the edge of Madge's claim. Earlier today, while exploring the length and breadth of her claim, he'd noticed that the area had a good view.

After adjusting their hips on a log, Abby raised her feet and placed them on a small rock in front of her. She leaned forward, resting her arms against her knees as she stretched her back like a cat rising from sleep.

"You're tired, aren't you."

"A little," she said quietly.

Wordless, he reached over and began to rub her back with his hands. At first he felt her hesitation, but as he ran his fingers along her spine and pushed his palms gently against her ribs, she began to relax.

"Umm, that feels so good," she moaned.

"My father was an unusual man for his day," Carson said. "Though he's gruff-voiced and rather takes the role of the dominant male quite nicely, if one of his own ever becomes ill, it's Papa who comes to their bedside and massages their backs. I saw him massage my mother's many times, not that she didn't deserve it since she maintained a house with a pack of children and then helped him at the mill."

"They work in a mill?"

"Did. It was their pride and joy. Papa started their flour mill nearly thirty some years ago, and it functioned as a centerpiece for the town, until they closed it a few years back."

She sighed, as if his words had touched a nerve. "I'm sorry to hear that, Carson. It's been hard times for many of late." She sighed again and sat up straight, looking at him. "What's your family like, Carson?"

He smiled and turned his gaze to the meadow as he recalled them. "My mother is a stout Italian with a no-nonsense approach to work. She has a compelling way of living life to the fullest. With energy and great gusto, Maria doesn't wait for life to happen, she makes it happen." He looked at her. "You would like her, I'm certain of it."

Abby smiled. "I would guess you rather take after her, the gusto part anyhow."

"Maybe," he said with a shrug, "but everyone says I look more like my father, and whether I do or not, I know I admire him. Until the latter years, he was strong, industrious and full of adventure, and each summer, when the mill would be idle before the wheat came in, he'd take us older kids on pilgrimages into the Sierra backcountry." He smiled. "He isn't Italian, like my momma, but is a true Californian, his father being an early pioneer who fought to bring California into the American frontier. Being a mix of German, English and Scotch, Grandpa had a history, I was told, going back to the American colonies."

Abby smiled. "That's like my family," she said. "My mother comes from English and Irish blood who first located in Boston and then St. Louis. My father's father was an original mountain man in the Wyoming Territory, and he married a half-French, half-Shoshoni woman. You can't get any more rooted in American soil than that, I suppose."

He studied her face a moment noting her dark lashes and steady gaze. "As I look at you, Abby, I can see all of them in you." He smiled. "And above all else, you've always had that certain look, as if you're peering into my mind to read what's inside. Perhaps that's a part of your heritage, I don't know, but it's a rather penetrating gaze, Miss Colton. Has anyone ever told you that?"

She chuckled. "Yes, actually, they have. My mother says it's a gift from my father. It always seemed like his dark eyes could look right through to your heart."

Carson thought about the feel of her small back, warm against his fingers, and removed his hand. He knew he'd been sincere that morning in Deep Creek, the morning he'd promised to give her only his friendship, but he also knew his need for her was growing. In part, it was a man's pure attraction to a comely woman, but deep inside, he knew there was more.

"Abby, I want to be truthful with you. I've begun to care about you in a whole new way of late. At first, I was attracted to your beauty, and you rightfully nailed me on that one. But then, I became aware of you as an intelligent and capable woman, a hard worker, sensitive and yet bright. And now, it's even more." He released his breath and looked down, searching his mind for the right words.

"Maybe this is an oversimplification, Abigail, but I want to be in your presence." He looked at her. "And I can't imagine not having you around."

As she gazed down to her hands in her lap, he reached for her chin and turned her face to him. Her eyes were laced with emotion as he began to draw his thumb gently along the length of her jaw. He recalled the way she could move her chin with a hint of determination.

Carson slid his fingers lightly down her neck and then paused and held them still. He stared at her lips, soft and full, knowing his desire was strong to taste them. He began to draw her toward him.

"No, please," Abby whimpered. She dropped her head.

"Why, Abby?"

She met his eyes. "Carson. I can't. We can't. I once made a choice to marry a man for the way he touched me, for the security he represented, a man I did not know even as well as you. But I'm having his baby and he may very well be alive." She shook her head. "I can't let this happen."

He sighed and dropped his hand to his knee. Wordless, he stared out across the meadow to where a pile of logs created a shadowed backdrop to the golden hues of summer grass.

Light and dark. Good and bad. Joy and sadness. Just like the scene before him, the counterpoint of opposites always seemed to live side by side in odd contrast. Why would God have made it so?

"So, what do I do with my feelings for you, Abby? Just go on ignoring them?" He looked to her. "Would you ever think to return them someday?"

"I don't know," she murmured. "I have no answers, Carson. I wish I did."

Seeing the light quiver on her lips, he reached for her knee and held it firm in his grasp a moment. "I have none, either."

In silence, Carson wondered how long he could be around her and be put off. Taking in a light breath, he stood and offered her his hand. "Have you rested enough to go on?"

"Yes," she said. She placed her small hand in his and rose to her feet beside him.

"I'm sorry, Carson. I truly am."

Chapter
Twenty-Six

With Beauty at her side, Abby hiked into the meadow where Carson had talked to her nearly four weeks ago. As she moved to the same log and sat down, she recalled the way he had touched her. His hands had been tender, loving. The look on his face as they'd returned to the trail still haunted her.

As Abby sat staring at the creek bubbling along nearby, she once again felt the desperate longing inside. More often, these days, she awoke in the mornings with a deep sense of sorrow and uncertainty hanging over her like a dark curtain.

It was Sunday, a day of rest from The Grand but also quieter than normal at the cabin, and so she had decided to go for a walk. Closing her eyes, Abby listened to the light sound of voices coming from the claims below. She thought about Jimmy and Jon back in the cabin talking about their gathering flakes of gold and how they should take their poke to Madge sometime this week.

Abby thought about Reverend Garner's sermon long ago in Sheep Camp, about making plans to *go here and do this and that.* Looking back, she knew this had been her mindset, especially after they left Bennett. But where in all these plans had she put her trust in God? True, she had a clear reminder of her vulnerability the day Carson had saved her, and she'd even prayed and listened for God's voice with much desperation for a few days afterward, but what had been in her thoughts since then? Had it not been their plans, gold, and returning home? Other than the coming baby, so much of her life revolved around those things.

Abby sighed.

It had been three weeks since she'd been to services in Dawson with Ingrid, and even longer since she'd read his Word. At the thought of her grandmother's Bible being swallowed up by the river, Abby felt the disquiet in her heart increasing.

"Lord," she whispered. "I am in need of your counsel and have but your spirit only. Father, what do I do now?"

Abby sat in silence, feeling confused and abandoned. The very thought of Carson sitting here weeks before made her heart ache.

"God, please forgive me. I have placed myself in such a quagmire." For the first time in a long while, thoughts of Dundee came to her with a new sense of guilt and inner turmoil. "Lord," she moaned, "if he's alive, where is he?" What would she do if he appeared now?

Dear Lord in Heaven. I can't love two men, but I do.

With a heavy heart, Abby slipped to her knees and fell forward to her fists. *Show me, Father. Give me clarity. Please, help Dundee if he is alive, and Carson . . . Oh, Father, how I ache for him, for the goodness both he and Jimmy have shown. Bless them Father and help them find their peace in you.*

In the silence that followed, Abby listened with her whole heart to the calming sounds of the breeze in the trees, a bird, of laughter from men down the hill. When she opened her eyes and sat back, she gazed at the meadow to where a small bird flit from one bush to another. In the forest beyond, she heard the chatter of a small squirrel.

Life was all around her. Ongoing. A promise.

Live life, the earth seemed to say. *Go on. Be in my will, but go on.* Raising her voice to the air around her, Abby began to sing.

> *"There's a land that is fairer than day, and by faith we can see it afar; For the Father waits over the way, to prepare us a dwelling place there.*
>
> *In the sweet by and by, we shall meet on that beautiful shore. In the sweet by and by, we shall meet on that beautiful shore."*

As her voice once again sought the words of the chorus, Beauty suddenly rose up on her feet and pointed her nose to the sky. In a long low voice, she began to howl. Abby smiled as she sang on, peace filling her as Beauty's high, sliding notes rolled to a pitch and then fell away. As they finished, Abby stared at her. Tears sprung into her eyes as she watched Beauty hesitate and then turn to face her, as if to say, "Hey, we're singing here, keep up with me!"

Seeing the happy look on Beauty's face, a slow chuckle rose in Abby's throat then turned into a full laugh. Beauty nearly leaped up as she ran to her side. Wrapping an arm about the giant shoulders beside her, Abby began to smooth Beauty's fur with her hand.

"You're a gift," she whispered. "Do you know that?"

Beauty lunged forward licking Abby's face. Laughing again, Abby pulled away. "You slobbering old pup, so you think I need a bath now, do you?" After scratching Beauty's ears and rubbing her shoulders and haunches, Abby slowly rose to her feet. She looked down to her shaggy friend for a moment. "Maybe we do make good music to our Maker, eh?"

"Abbyyy . . .!"

Abby turned at the sound of Jon's long shout and saw him standing by the trail waving at her. She waved back. "Over here," she called out.

"You have company," Jon yelled and pointed down to where Madge's short frame came into view.

"Madge!" she cried. "I'll be right there!" Abby at once started for the trail in the trees where they waited patiently.

"Dear lady," she said as she approached, "what brings your good company so far out this way?"

"Well," Madge said with a plaintive voice, "I reckon I took you for your word and came to see if you would help me secure those hospital donations. I've been several places in Dawson over the past few Sundays, but since I was in the area today, I thought I'd seek out your companionship. Couldn't find you at The Grand," she said. "Was told you'd be here."

Abby smiled. "I'm so glad you found me. I'd love to go with you. Would you like some tea first?"

"No, my dear, I think we'd best be on our way. It will be a long walk to even cover a part of Eldorado and Bonanza. You certain you're up to it?"

"Of course. A walk would be the very best medicine for me today. That and your company," she said.

Madge stepped back and eyed Abby a moment. "Well, by the looks of you, girly, I'd say we might shorten it a bit, but let's be off, and then we can have something good to eat when we return. You can put the soup on while we're gone, Jon."

He smiled. "You ladies have a nice walk."

Abby frowned. "Jon, you should be coming with us, but never mind. Maybe we'll bring Beauty instead." She looked at Madge. "If you don't mind."

"Oh, my," Madge laughed. "When those miners see an old lady, a woman big with child, and a dog with a mighty handsome set of teeth, they certainly won't be able to turn *us* down! Who could say no to the likes of us?"

For several long hours that afternoon, the two of them walked from claim to claim. For the most part, Abby just listened as Madge gave her spiel, and often as not, Madge would receive a promise from each miner that they would bring something by her eatery later in the week.

Abby was surprised that though many of the men Madge approached looked to be poor and barely making their way, most made generous offers in support of the hospital. It took only about five stops to realize that Madge truly had an unusual relationship with the men of the creeks, and as they turned back for their cabin, Abby began to question her.

For some distance, the older woman shared how she had worked her diggings from dawn to dusk, year after year, following along with those earlier miners in California and points north.

"But," she added with a flare, "I rarely had a moment of trouble with the boys back in those days," she said. "They helped you when you needed it, and you helped them, but it's a harsh place in the wilderness, and not much better livin' in the boom towns. So, I had to take leave of it for awhile and went to help my family. Still, I missed the old codgers," she said with a grin, "missed the feel of God's great outdoors and a life of true livin' as I call it. Couldn't stand all that city nonsense, the females with all their silliness. Was more than a body could take. So, I came back to the fields."

She hesitated and took a deep breath. "Though I must say, it's a piece harder, I believe, to survive up here."

When at last the three of them started up the familiar hill toward the cabin, Madge stopped halfway to the top of the hill and looked back, gazing over Eldorado Creek below.

"So what are you planning to do?" Madge turned, fastening her eyes to Abby's face. "What if you don't find your gold? Are you staying into winter, even with the baby coming and all?"

"Would that be so impossible?" Abby asked quietly.

Madge shrugged. "No, I reckon not. But it will be frightfully cold."

"We had cold in Wyoming."

"I doubt if anything like here," Madge mumbled.

"Maybe not," Abby said, "but I'd hate to go home defeated, and I don't feel called to do so. Even more, I would feel terrible leaving Jon here alone."

"He might have Jimmy."

"Yes, I know."

"What about your husband? You plan to go looking for him?"

Abby shrugged. "Maybe, although Jon tried to find him while we were in Seattle, and it was all to no avail. We even stayed an extra three weeks after Dundee disappeared, but there was not a hint as to what happened, not even from the authorities. Everyone just seemed to shake their heads."

Abby sighed. "Besides, he knew where we were going. He knew which steamer we had secured for passage to Skagway and that we were coming to Dawson." She looked away. "It's been months, Madge. If Dundee was alive and wanted to find us, I think he could have."

Madge frowned. "What about remarrying, Abby. Have you thought about it?"

"Some."

Madge stood in silence a moment then took a deep breath. "Been a long walk today, but I'm glad you and the dog came with me," she said. She gave Abby a quizzical look. "I reckon it's none of my business, but I've noticed that there seems to be something between you and Carson. You care for him?"

Abby gazed off to the creek below. "Yes. I suppose I do, but I've been trying very hard to not let it happen." She looked back to Madge. "I can't. Not until I'm more certain about Dundee's fate." She momentarily bit her bottom lip before continuing. "But if I don't hear soon, I will need to send a letter to his father explaining our situation." She shrugged. "I don't know what else to do."

"And a year from now, if no one hears from your husband, what then?"

"I'll just have to cross that bridge as it comes," she said.

With a sigh, Madge took a lumbering step up the hill. "I suppose you're right, Abby. Just seems a dang shame that with the baby and all you don't have a husband by your side."

"You managed without one."

Madge snorted. "Got me there, girly. Sure enough, you got me there." She looked at Abby with a sharp eye. "Maybe you'll be fine after all. But I have to tell you, I'm likin' that Carson fellow, so you think on it. All right?"

"You got me there, my friend. Sure enough, you got me there."

Abby and Madge laughed out loud together.

Chapter
Twenty-Seven

Carson stood ruminating about his situation as he waited in the long line in front of the Post. A large log building in the center of town, the Post was where one could always find a crowd, but today the bodies around him seemed to be moving at an even more frenzied pace. The summer days were passing. It was already mid-August and the sea of men around him appeared to be frantic to find their fortune before the artic blasts fell upon them.

It had been a while since he'd spoken with Abby. And even then their chance meeting had been quite coincidental. A few weeks after he'd left Grand Forks, he'd been seated at Madge's dining room one Sunday taking notes over a conversation with two old sourdoughs when Jon, Abby, and Jimmy had walked into the room with Ingrid and Hansen not far behind. They'd been to church together and were about to partake in a bit of lunch before parting.

He'd been both astounded by the off-chance of seeing them again and yet depressed by knowing that he'd been out of the loop of friendship recently. Even Jimmy had carried a sense of belonging about him that for a moment made him jealous. He had wondered, even then, if Jimmy would stay behind with Jon and Abby rather than go out with him.

Did James have more interest in Abby than he'd known? Was Jimmy perhaps staying in the tent at the cabin and merely waiting for the news of her husband's death—while he, about to run out of money, had no choice but to leave before winter?

Sensing that his thoughts were taking him down a poor path, Carson sighed and tried to take stock of his options. Riches came to some in Dawson, it seemed, but it did not appear to be coming his way. Just to stay afloat, he had written and sold a few articles on the side to the *Klondike Nugget*, but most of his earnings fell far short of carrying him through a winter in Dawson. Besides, if he wanted to keep his job with the *Post*, he'd have to return to the States soon. In truth, unless some sort of miracle happened, he had just enough money set aside to pay for his room and board and still purchase a passage on a steamship bound for Seattle.

If only the *Post* would give him the nod on his newest proposal. If that could happen, then everything would change for him. He'd worked hard getting these latest stories, from walking claims to again pursuing Miss Mulroy and several other theatre performers in Dawson.

He thought about his interview a few weeks ago with the singer, Miss Marinda. She had round and lustrous dark eyes, and even now he found it hard to shake his mind from them. After the interview, he'd written his final chapter for his Klondike series and sent it off. And now, after weeks of watching and waiting, he was once more standing in the Post's long line.

"Long wait there, Mister?"

Carson stepped up to the counter and nodded. "Carson Stuart," he said tiredly. "Do you have anything for me?"

The man shuffled through a large box and pulled out an envelope. "Here you go, Mr. Stuart."

Filled with renewed hope, Carson grabbed his mail and walked out of the dingy room. In nervous anticipation, he tapped the envelope against his hand then looked up the street and headed for the dock area along the Yukon River. For some reason, he felt a need to connect to the watery place that had brought him into Dawson.

After finding some logs lying alongside the muddy bank, he sat and stared once more at the slightly crinkled parchment in his hand. As he held it, his mind pictured Abigail eating beside him not far from here. With worry niggling at the edge of his mind, Carson took a deep breath and looked up.

He couldn't open it. Not yet. First he had to decide what was important and what was not. For a minute, he studied the area around him with a fresh eye.

Dawson was not a handsome city nor was it located within a particularly appealing landscape. With its strip of beach and swampy ground here and there, its total length and breadth, he figured, had to be no more than a mile and a half long and a half mile wide. Beyond the town's northernmost border, the Midnight Dome rose to about two thousand feet above the river valley. It was a cold country with much smaller trees than the coastal area, but rivers were in abundance from the turbulent Klondike River on the south to the mighty Yukon on the western flank. He stared off to the east, where the low Klondike hills lay, and then shifted his gaze to the southeast, to Grand Forks, where his mind, he knew, often lingered.

Was it important to stay in the area? Or was it more important to do everything humanly possible to stay in touch with the people the area had brought into his life?

Releasing a long, pent-up breath, Carson looked down to the envelope and began to open it. With relief, he immediately saw that a bank draft was enclosed, but when he opened the letter behind the draft and started to read it, he had to stop, back up, and read the first words again.

> *Much to my regret, I must inform you that along with a bank note paying you for your interesting and colorful stories, we have to inform you that we will no longer be in need for more articles, however interesting they may be. It has been an unfavorable year for the "Post-Intelligencer" I fear, and indeed, regrets are even greater in that we must terminate your employment with us.*
> *Best of luck for your writing future,*
> *Herman Grapples, Editor-in-Chief*
> *P.S. If you would happen to request a recommendation for future employment, we shall be happy to grant it.*

Stunned, Carson dropped the letter in his lap and stared down the street. He couldn't think. His mind seemed blank. For several long minutes, he stared at Georgia Mulroy's now infamous hotel and restaurant high on the Yukon's embankment.

It was the talk of the town.

Only a week ago he'd interviewed her again for the *Klondike Nugget*. Still had plans, in fact, to return and do a feature on the singer, Miss Marinda.

Near to anger, Carson stuck the letter and bank draft back in the envelope and stuffed it in his pocket. He was sick of all the work, of the effort and hardship in Dawson, and all for what?

Had he not given it his all?

Interesting stories . . . we must terminate . . .

Now what?

Carson felt the sudden need to celebrate, to find a companion. He was tired of being alone. He did not want to give another moment of his day to anxious thoughts about Abigail or the changes that were ahead for all of them.

He looked down the street once more and thought of the lovely Miss Marinda. Would she be available?

Celebrate. Go on. Maybe this newfound freedom wouldn't be so bad after all.

With a strong determination, Carson jumped to his feet and started off down the walkway blind to any thought but one. Tonight, he would do any fool thing he wanted!

Abby was certain that the time had come.

After talking Jon into taking her with him into Dawson, she had visited Madge and a nurse, Miss Kathleen, who Madge had befriended, and then started out for Georgia's new hotel while Jon picked up a few mining supplies.

As she pushed through the throng, Abby kept a fast pace until she spotted the Grandview in the distance, its design appearing stately in the evening sun. Slowing her step, Abby wondered what exactly she would say to Miss Mulroy. Would her simple few pages and concerns over receipt totals be sufficient indication that Mr. Hanover wasn't trustworthy?

One more time, Abby slipped her hand into her pocket to make sure the papers were secure. At the feel of them, she heaved a sigh. No matter the outcome, she would be glad to quit The Grand soon, what with the effort to walk to the cabin and knowing that Mr. Hanover's hostility, as well, had not abated. Further, the burden of worry about his honesty was wearing on her nerves.

Abby hesitated at the porch steps, moving aside as two men and one woman walked past her and sashayed up the stairs to the main door. Was she making a fool of herself? Could she be in error about Mr. Hanover?

For a moment, she reconsidered, but as the pull on her heart grew stronger, Abby wiped her hands along her skirts and stepped forward.

When she entered the lobby, Abby's confidence slipped even lower, if anything, when she realized that all of the women around her were attired in gowns of satins, lace and broad sweeping chiffons, and had hair arranged in splendid coiffures along with fancy hats to match.

Sensing her shabbiness, Abby hovered near the door until everyone in the lobby had been escorted into the dining hall to be seated. Her navy voile dress was clean and pleasant enough, she imagined, but it hung about her in great folds making her feel plain, overly large, and quite common. Somehow, she had managed to come here at the dinner hour, the proper time for food and entertainment for the elite in town.

With the sound of a woman singing in the dining hall and gay laughter in the background, Abby swallowed back her nervousness and stepped up to the entry desk. She met the gaze of a large man with dark hair and smiled.

"May I help you, Madame?"

"Yes. I'm Miss Abigail Colton, an employee for Miss Mulroy at The Grand. It is very important that I speak to her. If possible, I need to do so now since I'm in town for only a short time. Is she here?"

"I believe so, Madame, but I never interrupt her over the dinner hour, unless of course, she happens to be about her work."

"This is important," Abby said with urgency. "Would it be possible if I at least look in the dining area and see if she's available?"

"Well, I . . ."

"Please, sir. You will be doing her a great favor, I can assure you. If she is with someone, I promise, I will return here and wait, or come another time. Might that be a possibility?"

He considered her a long moment, then looked around, and seeing no one about, leaned forward. "I'll be busy here with my books for a moment. If you need to pursue your actions, I might not notice. But be prompt."

Thanking him, Abby stepped around the desk and into the dining hall where she began to slowly work her way around the edge of the hall. As she thread between the outlying tables and looked about for Miss Mulroy's face, she heard the sound of an unusual, near whinny of a laugh, and hesitated. But when another laugh joined in with the first, Abby felt her heart nearly drop into her stomach. In disbelief, she turned to the table behind her.

"Mr. Carson, you are such a delight," the woman said with wave of her hand.

Abby's mouth gaped open when she spotted Carson leaning close to the shoulder of a brunette. She was a beautiful woman, with glossy hair and rich creamy skin, her dark eyes held a sparkle that nearly matched the glitter of her green silk gown. With a long, delicate feather dancing from her hat, she leaned close to him as he reached for his glass of wine. His lips held a sensuous smile and though his cheeks were reddened, his eyes were narrow with merriment and a something more. It was a look she well knew.

Abby swallowed. Stunned and speechless, as if frozen to the floor, she merely stood there until she saw his eyes turn from his glass and, equally stunned, look up at her. Abby struggled with the tightness in her throat. "Hello, Carson."

"Abigail . . ."

In the awkwardness of the moment, Abby could think of nothing to say. She sucked in air, as if forcing herself to breathe.

"I . . . I came to find Miss Mulroy," she sputtered mindlessly. "Don't mind me," she said, waving her hand. "Carry on, as I'm certain you will."

In sudden anger, Abby spun on her heels. She moved swiftly, near to a dead run as she headed for the lobby. Her eyes filled with tears. She desperately wanted to be out of this place.

What was she doing here anyway?

She did not belong in such a fancy establishment. What did it matter if Georgia knew her concerns or not? Her small sheets of information would be of little importance in the grand scheme of their lives. Georgia could well take care of herself, just like Carson. Without a doubt, they knew all the tricks. *How blind could she be!*

"Abigail!"

Though she heard his voice, Abby marched on, passing swiftly by the startled receptionist and out the door. As she reached for the banister and started down the steps, she heard him behind her.

"Abigail, please wait. Listen to me."

Gripping the rail, she halted at the bottom of the steps and looked at up at him.

Carson hesitated and then hurried down the steps beside her. "It's not what you think," he said quietly.

"Oh, is that so? Then what is it, Carson? I know I have no right to make any demands on you whatsoever, but I saw your eyes. Remember what you said about me reading your mind?"

She felt her tears. "Somehow, I thought you were different, that wine, song and the flesh of a woman might not be so primary on your mind, that instead the attributes of love, patience, and prudence would prevail." She shook her head. "How foolish of me."

Abby turned.

"Abby, listen. Yes, I'm no different from any man, but I came here only to assuage some deep hurts, she's just a singer that I've interviewed. Besides, what do you want of me? You, for all the world, have just been leaving me hanging. What am I suppose to do with that!"

Hanging?

She stopped in her tracks and glared at him. "My, but isn't *hanging* an appropriate word coming from the wonderful imagery of a writing man. Well, that's just where I'd like to leave you, Carson Josiah Stuart. Hanging right on a tree next to Dundee J. Andrews!"

Chapter
Twenty-Eight

Abigail found it difficult to talk to Jon on their ride back to Grand Forks that night. With few words, she simply stated that she'd not been successful finding Miss Mulroy and that, instead, she ran into Carson. She didn't speak of her disappointment or about the way she'd confronted him, only that the evening had not proved to go well.

The following two days had been hard for her, and even this morning, as she began to ready for her last day at The Grand, Abby knew that her mood was swiftly souring. After doing her usual routine for the morning, she went into her small room and packed the few things that remained. At Mr. Hanover's suggestion, she had not told any of their customers about her departure. Only Miss Anna and Miss Sarah knew of it.

By afternoon, though Abby felt a terrible sense of discontentment moving into her heart, she finished all her normal tasks and then, as usual, went into Mr. Hanover's office to enter the receipts in the journal.

After placing the receipts on his desk, she started for the ledger on the shelf when she noticed Mr. Hanover's satchel was sprawled open on the floor at the inside corner of his desk. She leaned down to prop it up and saw, to her surprise, the black ledger tucked among some papers inside his satchel.

Though curious as to why it would be there, she pulled it free and placed in on the desk then sat to find her place. But as she flipped through the pages, Abby began to notice something different and stopped to examine one page. She peered closely at the numbers.

Her instructions had always been to simply put the date at the top of the page and then list all income and expenditures below. But as she looked carefully at the dollar amounts listed, she was certain that the numbers looked slightly different from the way she penned them.

Had she made these entries? Abby looked at the front sheet of the ledger and saw a brief notation of the date. She stared at it, thinking it familiar, and then realized that this was the day she had arrived at The

Grand. Could that be? All this time, she was certain that she'd written in a ledger that had been used long before she started working for Mr. Hanover. Puzzled, Abby turned to yesterday's receipts and looked at them carefully. As she did, she began to feel uneasy.

Remembering the entries that she had copied to show Miss Mulroy, she quickly flipped back several pages. July fourth. The day they had gone into Dawson for celebration. That had been the first page she'd copied. If she remembered correctly, the other dates had been June twenty-fifth and twenty-seventh.

As she ran her finger down July fourth's first column, Abby suddenly realized that one receipt in particular was not there. She distinctly recalled that one man had made a rather substantial payment for his room, around three hundred dollars. She did not see it.

Glancing down the food receipts listed for the day, Abby suddenly felt a knot forming in her stomach. She was certain that there were fewer receipts listed here than she had copied on her separate sheet. The copy she'd made weeks ago showed errors in calculations, and that had been concern enough to her, but this was something entirely different.

But how . . .?

Abby closed the book and jumped to her feet. She spun around and walked up to the shelf where the ledger was normally kept. To her dismay, a black ledger sat there, exactly where it was stored from day to day.

Abby looked back to the one lying on the desk, and knowing that she had pulled it from Mr. Hanover's satchel, suddenly felt a tingling up her spine.

She returned to the desk, touched the ledger and then looked up. No one was around. Mr. Hanover would not be here for at least two hours. If she hurried, she could copy at least one of the pages she had copied before and still have time to finish her regular entries. She then could take the two conflicting copies to Miss Mulroy and the authorities. It would be proof of his dishonesty, proof without Mr. Hanover discovering her.

Abby sat heavily in the chair. Taking a deep breath, she opened the desk drawer and found a sheet of stationery. Returning to the July fourth entries, she swiftly copied the receipts listed in this bogus ledger then slipped the book back into Mr. Hanover's satchel and stood it up against the desk's inside wall. Most likely, he'd left the satchel there last night, never dreaming that it would fall over and Abby would see his duplicate ledger by mistake.

Hurrying now, Abby folded her sheet of copied figures and placed it in her pocket. With a quick intake of air, she stood to find the real ledger, when, with her hand still in her pocket, she looked up to see the morning cook pass by the doorway.

For a brief instant, Cal's gaze lingered on her before he moved on. Abby's heart began to beat wildly in her chest as she removed her hand and stood listening to his footsteps cross the entry and move out on the porch.

Had she looked suspicious?

Only an hour more, she breathed. *And then she would be finished with this place!*

Abby released a shaky breath and tried to steady her nerves. She still had the day's receipts to enter, and though every fiber of her wanted to flee Mr. Hanover's office and never return, she would be found out directly if she behaved in such a manner. She had to act as if nothing unusual had just happened.

Swallowing back her fears, Abby reached for the black journal still on the shelf and sat back at the desk. She worked quickly entering the day's receipts, and then put everything away and returned to the front entry. Seeing that all was quiet, she slipped into her room, found her satchel, and then took it to the lobby and set it by the front door. She would make her escape as soon as possible.

"Miss Abby?"

Abby looked up to see Sarah O'Toole standing on the stairwell.

"I've finished me work, Miss Abby, will you be leavin' soon?"

"Yes, Sarah. As soon as Mr. Hanover returns."

"Well," Sarah said softly, "Miss Anna has already left for town, and we know you was working, so she didn't interrupt, but, well, we want to say that we shall miss you."

Abby smiled. Both Sarah and Anna were shy girls who cleaned and tended to the bedrooms and laundry. Anna came to Dawson with her family and though she stayed in Abby's small room at night to sleep, many days she returned to an area near Dawson where her family kept a small boardinghouse for a livelihood. Sarah, on the other hand, said she was an orphan, someone who had taken a long journey to a hard place for opportunity.

Abby walked closer to the banister and reached up to take the young girl's hand. "You've been such a good worker, Sarah, always reliable and a kind roommate. I know my comings and goings as well my moving into your room has not been easy for you and Anna." She smiled. "So, I want to thank you. And please tell Miss Anna a thank-you for me, would you?"

Smiling, Abby released her hand and stepped back while Sarah made a small curtsy. "You've been so kind, too, Miss Abby," she said. "Please come back after the baby is born. We want to see you again."

"If I'm here, I certainly will, Sarah." Abby took in the look of the young woman's large sage green eyes. She hoped the girl would find a good life. "You take care of yourself, now. All right?"

"Yes, Miss Abby. I'll do my best. I must be off now, but I do hope to see you soon."

"Goodbye, Sarah. I will plan to come by if I can."

As Sarah walked into the dining hall and disappeared from sight, Abby sighed.

So many unknowns in so many lives.

Turning, Abby began to consider what she should do to keep her mind occupied until Mr. Hanover arrived. With a burst of nervous energy, she grabbed the duster lying on the small entry desk and began to dust the room. When at last Mr. Hanover appeared in the doorway, Abby was surprised to see a pleasant smile on his face.

"Well, Miss Abigail," he said brightly. "Are you ready for your newfound freedom this evening?"

Abby placed the duster under the desk and turned, mustering as pleasant a smile as possible. "I am, Mr. Hanover. I'm afraid it's becoming quite awkward to get about these days."

He gave her a thin smile. "Would you like someone to help you carry your luggage to your cabin?"

"Actually, no," she said quickly. "My brother Jon took everything home yesterday except for a few simple items I have in my small satchel. I should be fine."

He nodded. "Have you said your goodbyes to Miss Anna and Miss Sarah?"

"I have."

"Well, then, I do wish you the best on the upcoming birth of your baby. Has your husband arrived yet as you'd hoped?"

She shook her head. "No, not as yet." Abby moved toward the door and picked up her satchel then turned back, smiling. "If there is nothing more that I need to do, Mr. Hanover, I will be off."

"Certainly, Miss Abigail," he said with a slight nod. "Good luck on your days ahead."

"Thank you, Mr. Hanover." Abby stepped outside, praying that her last words had held a note of confidence. And though feeling anything but confident, she started for the trail and for Little Chance, happy to be free of The Grand.

As she walked along with the bright sun overhead and the familiar sight of miners at work, Abby at last began to feel her fears dissipating and thought of the days to come. It was mid-August now, and though she was still near a month from her due time, it felt as if there was precious little time to prepare for a baby.

She was resigned to it now—they would have to stay in Dawson. She would not chance having her child in some steamer or along a trail. To her and Jon's disappointment, nothing had come of the Constable's investigation in trying to find C. R, and as the sun shifted ever lower in the sky, it seemed their hopes for a speedy departure from Dawson looked near to impossible.

With a deep sigh, Abby halted along the road to watch the hard-working Cummings family busy at their claim. She wondered how much longer Clara and Earl would be staying. But she was certain, what with the many hands to dig and shovel, they would leave successfully. She thought about Jon and Jimmy.

They worked so hard from dawn to dusk, returning from the creek bed with but a pittance, and yet they appeared to be hopeful, especially Jimmy. She smiled at the thought of his jovial yet determined attitude.

Catching Clara's eye in the distance, Abby smiled and waved as she often did, and then she slowly turned and started up the hillside. Feeling her tiredness from the day's work, she took laborious strides up the narrow trail that ran along the meadow and into a small grove of birch and aspen. She wondered if the ache in her back was a normal thing for being large with child, or if the nervous tension she'd felt earlier was more her problem. Either way, she knew she would have to endure another long wagon ride to Dawson tomorrow, and though she wanted to see Miss Mulroy as soon as possible, she dreaded the bumpy excursion.

At the crack of a twig not far from her, Abby looked up. At first, she thought perhaps Beauty was about, but then a deep silence flowed over her.

She turned and just then Cal stepped out from behind a tree.

"I'll take that now, Miss Abigail."

A cold sensation rose along Abby's arms at the sight of his dark and brooding eyes. "Take what, Cal?" she said calmly, "I have no idea what you're talking about."

"I'm thinkin' you do, Miss Abigail. I want what's in your pocket."

Almost instinctively, Abby brought her fingers to her lips. As her shrill high-pitched whistle rang out, Cal started for her.

With a cry, Abby turned to run. At the sudden realization that her short legs and awkward movements would never keep someone like Cal from catching her, she quickly darted behind one tree and then another, veering first one way and then the next as she tried desperately to dodge the man behind her.

Abby heard the panic sounds coming from her throat as Cal groaned behind her. He was close, so close. Suddenly she felt his grasp on her shoulder. She stumbled, twisted her body, and tore free. Gasping, she scrambled around a tree, found her balance, and ran with all her might for the trail.

She managed few steps when she felt cold, hard hands at her neck.

Abby felt herself reeling backward, and as her head smacked against the ground, she flailed her arms above her and screamed.

"Leave me alone!" she screeched.

As a smothering hand covered her mouth, she heard his snarl above her. "Shut up! Just shut up and give me what's in your pocket," he snarled.

Abby struggled against him. But his arms were strong, too strong. She could barely breathe. She tried to wriggle away, when suddenly, his arm smacked her in the chest—a searing pain tore across her cheek. He leaned into her, tearing open her dress pocket as she cried out.

With a fury rising inside her, Abby reached for his arm and bit down with all her might.

He yelped. Then cursed. "You bitch," he shouted. "You'll pay for that one!"

There was a horrible tightness of strong hands at her neck. Abby struggled. Tried to breathe. So much pain . . .

Abby felt a new fury . . . weight . . . movement.

Cal screamed.

As the force about her throat suddenly diminished, she saw a flurry of gold fur. *Beauty!* Abby groaned as the force of two bodies struggled over her.

"Get him off her! Beauty! Beauty move!"

Carson?

A loud thud sounded as Cal groaned and fell away.

"Can I kill him, Carson? Would they hang me for it?" It was Jimmy's voice.

She reached out, struggling for air, as hands took hold of her. Abby tried to suck in a breath but couldn't. *Lord! Don't let me die!*

She gasped, struggling, and finally inhaled a deep gulp of air. She felt arms and Beauty's body heavy against her.

"Beauty . . ." She reached for the warmth of fur, and as a tongue caressed her cheek, she breathed deep again and looked up at two worried faces. Carson leaned over her.

"Be careful, Abby. Easy, go easy." She felt Carson's fingers running down her cheek and across her chin.

"Did he break it?" Jimmy said. "I'm going to kill him."

"No, I don't think so," Carson said, his voice husky beside her, "but we need to tie him up before he comes to."

"I'll get some rope," Jimmy said quickly. "Here, Beauty, here girl, don't let this man move!" he called out, and with that he ran off.

As Beauty stood over Cal, whining and growling in an odd mix of tones, Abby rolled to her side and leaned on Carson's arm. Slowly, he lifted her up and then snuggled her against his chest. She closed her eyes and leaned into him, her mind seemed unclear. Her cheek and tongue burned, as if she had bitten it, not once, but several times.

She felt Carson running his hands down her shoulder, wrapping her tightly against him as his voice rumbled in her ear. "Lord, Abigail. Will this ever stop? I never want to rescue you again. You are going to break my heart, Abby . . . Abby, can you hear me?"

"Yes," she whispered. "Carson. Just hold me. Hold me, please."

For a long time, she felt him rock her in gentle motion, rubbing her gently while she breathed deep. A shudder ran through her as she clung to him.

"We heard your whistle," he said gently, "and you know how Beauty mopes around in the latter part of the afternoon. She knows when you should come home. She was lying there, calm as could be, when suddenly she jumped to her feet with a low and intense growl and started off down the trail." He paused. "For a second, we just looked at her streak out into the forest, and then without a word, Jimmy and I dropped everything and ran after her." He paused pulling her up straight.

"Here, can you sit up? Do you have any bad pains other than your jaw?"

"I don't think so," she whimpered.

"Abby . . ."

"I've got some rope," Jimmy shouted as he bounded back toward them. "That blackheart still out?"

"Yes," Carson said. "Tie him up against a tree so he can't possibly get free and then help me get Abby to the cabin. We might need some medical help."

As Carson held her, she groaned. "He was after my paper," she said weakly.

"Your what?"

"Do you remember the bookkeeping journals I told you about at The Grand?" she whispered. "I made duplicate copies. . ." she breathed deep. "Then I found another ledger, Carson . . . I made another copy. It's . . . it's in my pocket."

She struggled to reach for her pocket, but instead she found a gaping tear in her dress. She looked around feeling her panic. *Had she lost it?*

"Carson, it's important," she groaned. She struggled to sit straighter and looked at her torn pocket.

"I don't see anything," Carson said.

"A simple folded paper," she gasped. "I need it."

"You looking for this?" Jimmy, who had been tying up the man named Cal stood up with a small sheet of paper in his hands. "It was lying beneath the brute's arm."

"Yes . . . yes, he was after that," she stammered. "We need to get it to Miss Mulroy." She looked at Carson and swallowed. "Mr. Hanover's been cheating her."

"Abby, listen," Carson said. "Don't worry about this now, we'll take care of it later. Let's get you to the cabin."

As Jimmy squatted down beside her, she looked up. "Mr. Hanover must know I have proof that he's stealing from her." She looked to Carson. "The first copies I made of his records are in a small wooden box in the cabin," she mumbled. "Please, take them and this second copy to the authorities and explain it to Georgia." She looked at him intently. "I don't want to have suffered this in vain. I don't want Mr. Hanover to get away. He's been keeping two ledgers."

"All right. All right, Abby, I will. Now do as I say and let Jimmy and I get an arm around you and we'll carry you to the cabin."

"I . . . I think I'll be fine. I can walk." With their arms tight about her, Abby stood. After a light breath, she took a step forward, but as she moved, another deep and hot pain seared across her middle. She heard her own cry as she bent forward.

"What? Abby?" Carson cried. "Do you have pain?"

Abby nodded. When the second one rolled over her, she moaned aloud. "Carson . . . the baby."

Without further words, Jimmy swooped her into his arms and carried her almost at a dead run. All the while, Abby simply clung to his neck and tried to breathe deeply. When at last they entered the cabin, Carson flung back the quilt on Jon's bed while Jimmy propped her up on a pillow. When the third pain ripped through her, Abby curled up in a ball and gripped the quilt. Trying to keep from crying out, she held her breath and moaned.

For a moment, she wondered if it would ever stop.

"Carson," she breathed between clenched teeth. "Send Jimmy for help. The baby's coming."

"Good Lord," he mumbled.

"I'll go find Jon down at the diggings!" Jimmy exclaimed. "Maybe he can find Clara Cummings, and then I'll head for Madge's. She knows a nurse that Abby plans to have."

"Good, good," Carson said. "Send Madge and the nurse, and then bring the Constable up here. And before you go," Carson said quickly, "make sure that Cal isn't going anywhere!" Abby felt Carson's fingers on her shoulders tighten. "Abigail," he said, gently. "Just tell me what to do."

Chapter
Twenty-Nine

For a several long minutes, Carson held the small bundle against his chest as he stared down into the tiny crinkled face with wild dark hair. She was small, so small.

Across the room, Clara Cummings straightened the sheets and pulled the blanket up to Abby's chest. "There now, Abigail, you just rest a bit. For having a firstborn and being a little early to boot, you've done well . . . very well."

"Are you certain she's all right?" Abby mumbled.

"Yes, she's fine," Clara replied. "Remember, we counted all her fingers and toes and they're all there." Clara gave her a pat on the arm. "Carson has her now. She's all bundled up and resting, like you should."

Abby mumbled her thanks then turned her head to the side and fell quiet.

Clara lightly brushed a strand of hair back from Abby's damp forehead then tucked the covers up tighter about Abby's shoulders. Her gaze lingered a moment before she walked over to Carson. Smiling, she looked down at the baby in his arms.

"She's a tiny one all right, but she has good color. Still, I don't know much about the care of such little ones. My babies, I'm afraid, were much larger." Clara clucked her tongue as she straightened. "Is Earl still outside?"

"Yes," Jon said. "Keeping a watch on Cal."

"Good," she said.

Jon stood and walked over to Abby. He stared at her.

Carson watched Jon a moment, recalling how Clara had cut the baby's cord and then wrapped her tiny wriggling form in a blanket and handed her first to Abby and then to Jon.

It was silent as stone in the cabin now. He imagined that the screaming, the groaning, and the sight of Abby fighting her pains had completely unnerved Jon as much as it had him. He was thankful that

Clara had arrived in time to help at the end. It had been all he could do to ready the bed, help her out of her dress and then hold her gripping hands until Clara had arrived.

"Is she going to be all right?" Jon asked to no one in particular.

Clara turned. "Abigail?"

Jon nodded.

She shrugged. "I think so, provided she doesn't bleed too much. But I'll be happier when Jimmy gets here with that nurse." She sighed. "One good thing about the gold in Dawson is that it's brought a whole host of people here now. It wasn't like that last year. No nurses then, in fact I doubt if there would have been one anywhere within five hundred miles, though I imagine Abigail would still have made it fine."

Jon looked back. "We can't thank you enough, Clara."

"Think nothing of it," she said. "Well, I believe I'll go outside and let Earl know how things are. I'll be back in a while. For now, we'll just let Abigail rest."

After Clara slipped outside, Jon released his grip from Abby's pillow and moved to Carson's side. He bent forward, peering down into the child's face.

"Wild looking little thing, isn't she?"

Carson nodded. "You want to hold her?"

"After a while. You're doing fine, I'm thinking." He studied Carson's face. "I'm mighty glad you were here. If you and Jimmy hadn't gone up to the cabin, I doubt if the two of us working at the creek would have known what was happening. I'll forever be thankful."

"Being there is thanks enough, Jon." He glanced at Abby a moment then turned his gaze once more to the baby. "She's beautiful in a way," he said. "So tiny and fragile, yet already a person of her very own." He looked up at Jon with a smile. "I've never been around a newborn like this before."

Jon reached for the stool and sat close to Carson. He leaned forward, his arms resting against his legs as he looked at the baby. "I have a faint recollection of my younger brother being born," he said. "But mostly," he chuckled, "I only recall feeling that the whole thing was unworthy of all the commotion." He smiled a moment before turning his eyes to Carson.

"You care a great deal for Abby, don't you?"

Carson's shrugged. "I suppose I can't deny it."

"Not after today. I thought her delivery was going to break your heart."

"It seemed pretty rough to me."

Jon glanced at Abby. "Yeah."

Jon dropped his gaze to his hands. "We still don't know what's happening with our plans, Carson. But I wish Abby wouldn't try to go through the winter here." He looked up. "I talked to the Constable today after I got Mrs. Smythe's letter, but he still felt there wasn't enough evidence to do anything. Now if C. R. would show up and testify that those men don't belong there, that would be another thing, but . . ." He shrugged.

"Maybe we can get some issues resolved and we can leave," Jon continued, "but the way things go, I'm not counting on it. The Yukon River will start freezing up right soon. We don't have much time." He sighed. "To be truthful with you, Carson, it would be my hope that she'd go out with you and go back home."

"I agree." Carson said. "In a few days, I'll come back and talk to her. Maybe she'll consider it now."

"Dundee wasn't near the man you are, Carson," Jon said somberly. "To tell you the truth, I hope he is gone. Right now he's hanging over her like a dark cloud."

Carson studied the small baby in his arms. "She's going to need a daddy."

Jon nodded. "And Abby, as strong willed as she is, is going to need a real husband." He paused. "Do you love her enough to take the both of them on?"

Carson looked at Jon. He saw the edge of worry in his dark eyes. "I'm afraid that love might not be the issue for Abby." He sighed. "I don't know if she trusts me, Jon, and there are many unresolved issues, not only her husband, dead or alive, but my current lack of employment doesn't help."

Jon nodded. "I know, but don't you have some possibilities in Juneau?"

Carson shrugged. "Well, that's my hope. Mr. Russell of the *Klondike* said that the town has long-term potential and that a newspaper man there is looking for someone." He looked up. "It's worth a try."

Jon stood as he heard a noise outside. "That might be Jimmy," he said.

He crossed to the door and opened it, revealing the large bulk of their friend behind Madge and another young woman. Carson felt his heart leap with encouragement.

"This here is the nurse with Madge," Jimmy said quickly. "Constable will be along soon."

As all three slipped inside the cabin, Jimmy's eyes turned first to the bed and then to the bundle in Carson's arms. "How's Abby?" he said.

"She's good," Jon said with a grin. "And we now have a baby girl who appears to be fine as well."

Jimmy stood by, silently watching while Madge and the nurse Kathleen peered down into the baby's face.

"Well, now," Madge crooned, "another wonder for this small family. For all the world, Carson, you look just like a proud papa."

He smiled and looked down to where the small face began to pucker her lips, almost frowning at the suggestion. He chuckled. "I'm not so sure this little one likes to hear you say that. Now look what you've done, Madge, she's waking up. And if she starts crying, I'll give her to you and be on my way."

Madge laughed and reached out for the child. "Would guess the little thing's just hungry, but you will come back later, won't you?"

"I imagine."

"Give her a few days, Carson." She said as he handed her the baby. "And then come and talk to her." Madge started to croon to the child while Carson stood and momentarily watched the nurse checking Abigail's chin.

He started for his jacket and then hesitated, looking back at Abby's long dark hair and pale face. He felt the sickening feeling come over him again. Why hadn't he stopped at The Grand to walk her home? Why had he decided to first talk with Jimmy and Jon and then wait for her at the cabin? He could have prevented this.

He saw the younger woman smile up at him. "She's sleeping," she whispered, "but her color looks fine."

Carson slipped on his jacket and moved to the door. As he grabbed the handle, he paused and turned to Madge. "I'll be on my way soon," he said. "Take care of her, won't you?"

Abby awoke with a start at the sound of a small cry. Startled, she looked about then relaxed when she saw Madge's face beside her.

"Madge? When did you come?"

"Jimmy came for us and we just arrived," Madge said. "He came charging into town with quite a story and we headed for Miss Kathleen's, the nurse you met. Glad to see you and the baby are doing fine. We've been prayin' the whole way here, and I can't tell you how pleased we are to see you and the babe." Madge handed the baby to her as she continued. "Appears that Clara, Jon and Carson did a right fine job by you."

Abby snuggled her baby tight against her before she looked up. "Where are they?"

"Clara and her husband went home. The men are outside with the Constable. Carson said he'd be going back to Dawson soon."

Abby peered down to the tiny, reddened face with a deep wonderment in her heart, but when the child began to whimper and utter a light cry, she felt a desperate sense of heaviness coming over her.

She came too soon. Abby felt tears gathering in her eyes. Was the child strong enough? Abby could barely breathe from the tension inside her heart.

"Do you think she'll be all right?" she whispered.

"I checked her over, Miss Abby," Kathleen said. "She looks to be small but otherwise fine. She has a healthy enough cry, and right now, I believe she's just hungry. We'll need to work on that problem."

Abby tried to sit up and then groaned. "Umm, I hurt all over."

Kathleen and Madge reached for her, helping her to sit up straighter as Kathleen continued to speak in a low and soft voice. "It's my plan to stay here with you until we can get this little one nursing and on her way. We'll have to watch her, keep her warm and well fed, but I believe she has a good chance."

Kathleen reached out and touched Abby's shoulder, examining her cheek and chin once again. "We heard about the attack," she said. "I think we should wash you up a little and then I want to check you over thoroughly, Abigail."

Abby nodded quietly and then looked back to the baby who was beginning to utter a weak and sorrowful cry. As she peered down into her baby's dark eyes, hot tears began to roll down her cheeks.

"Oh, dear God in heaven," she whispered, choking back a sob. "Please let her live."

Chapter Thirty

Carson walked up to the tent where Jimmy slept but seeing that both he and Beauty were gone, he turned and headed down the hill to the creek. In the distance, he spotted his friends working side by side on the sluice box. As he walked closer, Jimmy paused from his work and turned to face him.

"Coming to see Abby?"

"And you," Carson called back. "The steamship will be leaving in five days. Thought I'd stop by and see if you were still planning to stay here in Dawson."

"Yup, afraid I am. Got an itch for some gold, I reckon. Hopefully, I can have a small poke of my own someday." Jimmy grinned.

Carson walked up to the two of them. "Won't be long, Jimmy, before the darkness will set in and it'll be colder than you might be anticipating." He shook his head. "It would be my hope that the three of you can get out of here before the Yukon freezes up."

Jimmy smiled. "Well, friend, I'm thinking this could be a good thing here for me. Even if Abby and Jon go out, I'm not sure I will. Wouldn't mind helping that sweet old gal Madge find some glittering stuff or maybe even getting my own claim." He shrugged. "It's as much a potential as I have anywhere."

"Constable came out today," Jon said. He tossed a shovel full of gravel into a pile and then leaned into his shovel. "Said that somehow Mr. Hanover got word about the attack and he and those two claim jumpers lit out of town in the dark of night. Appears Cal and those three were all tied in together, as we suspected."

Jimmy shook his head. "I don't know about you, Carson. But I really could have killed that guy Cal. Tore me up to see Abby there beneath him."

"At least he's in custody," Jon declared.

Carson nodded then turned to face his broad-shouldered friend. "Listen, Jimmy, if I thought I could stay here, I would. But I'm not sensing that the gold-digging life is for me, unless . . ."

Jimmy shrugged toward the cabin. "Abby?"

"Yes." Carson studied Jimmy's eyes. They'd been friends since childhood. He wanted the best for him, but he wanted to be honest. "I'd like to convince her to go with me, but I'm doubtful she will. Until now, I wondered if Abby was the reason you were staying."

Jimmy looked over Carson's shoulder to the cabin. "She's a right nice lady, Carson. And I'd take her in a minute if she wanted me," he said, "but she doesn't." He shrugged. "I have an inkling that those feelings are being saved for you."

"Maybe. Maybe not," Carson said quietly. "As far as I can tell, she's still conflicted about her husband and that keeps me in an awkward position." He shuffled his stance then walked over to their sluice box and looked down. "A lot of work here, boys."

Carson gave them a brief smile before letting it fall away. "Listen, I don't know if I'll be back again, unless it's to come get Abby. So, this might be my farewell for now. I plan to talk to her, but if she won't go with me, take good care of those two ladies, won't you?"

Jimmy grinned. "You know we will."

"I'll write and keep you posted on what happens in Juneau. Hopefully, I can find work and you can stop by on your way out. But letters will be few once the rivers freeze shut.

"Yeah," Jimmy drawled. "Like you said. Might be a long winter."

Carson reached for Jimmy's hand, but as they shook hands, they embraced, patting each other on the back in an emotional silence. He then turned to Jon and held out his hand. "I will miss you, Jon, and I'm hoping we will see each other again."

Jon nodded, his face somber. "Abby and I couldn't have made it without you and Jimmy. Thank you, Carson. For everything."

Carson slapped Jon on the shoulder and smiled. "Come see me in Juneau when you can."

"We both will," Jimmy said brightly. "Just as soon as we get that stocking full of gold."

"Well," Carson said, "I think I'll talk to Abby now, and if she listens to me, I'll come back in a couple days. If not, you boys take care."

Jimmy nodded. "See you soon, friend."

Carson glanced up the hill, smiled, and then set off, but though the cabin wasn't much more than a hundred yards away, he felt as if he were hiking a long, steeply pitched trail.

At the cabin, he knocked lightly, and when she opened the door, it was all he could do to keep from wrapping his arms around her and insisting that she put all aside and come with him. But instead, he simply removed his fedora and smiled. It was dark and quiet when he stepped inside.

"Is the baby sleeping?" he asked.

"Yes. She seems to be sleeping a lot."

He walked a few steps deeper into the room, and spying the small, crudely made cradle, he motioned with his hat. "May I take a peek at her?"

Abby nodded. "You might want to call her by her name," she said. "It's Josie Faith Andrews."

"Josie?"

"It's as close as I could get to Josiah and keep it feminine."

He stared at her, speechless for several long moments. "I'm not deserving of it."

"I think you are." She gave him a tender smile. "No matter what happens, I want you to know that I believe you are."

Carson felt a deep ache in his chest as he turned to the cradle.

"Hello, Miss Josie," he said gently. He studied her, surprised to see how her skin looked much lighter now and held the texture of fine silk. "It's only been a few days and here she is a pretty little thing already."

They stood in an awkward silence before Carson turned back and studied the face of the woman he loved. "Can we sit and talk a bit?"

"Of course."

Abby moved to the table and sat quietly as Carson pulled a stool close by. After situating himself so he could face her, he paused to gather his thoughts.

"I'm getting ready to go to Juneau, Alaska," he said. "I've heard that I might find work there, so I want to try. Did Jon or Jimmy tell you that the *Post* let me go?"

He saw the sorrow in her eyes as she nodded. "I'm sorry, Carson. I know it was important to you."

"Well, it's not all bad. They paid me a fair sum for my stories and said they'd give me a good recommendation." He looked down at the hat in his hand. "Appears I came along at the wrong time for finding a position that would last."

"Something else will come, I'm sure of it."

He nodded. "I believe so, but for your sake, I wish I were in a better situation." Carson placed his hat on the table and took her hand. "Abby, please listen to me. I have enough funds to get us to Juneau, and once we're there, I can later help you secure another steamer to Seattle. After that, you can take the rail to Wyoming. Or if you want, I'll take the journey with you to Wyoming." He paused. "Abby, I want you to come with me."

She sighed deeply and looked away. When she turned back, tears glistened at the edge of her eyes. "Carson, in my heart, I want to go with you, but you know my predicament. Besides, I believe this child needs to stay right here."

"Through a long, cold winter?"

"Winter will be long and cold anywhere I go."

"But there isn't a doctor here and disease is still taking men. During the winter, it might get worse."

She nodded. "I know. But it's a chance either way, and she's not very strong. There's disease on the steamers and in Juneau, too. I think for the next few weeks, she'll be safer right here." She looked down. "Carson, I'm afraid to leave now. Afraid to take that chance."

"Afraid?"

Abby shifted her gaze to the cradle. "Yes."

"You think she'll not . . . ?" Stunned, he stopped talking as Abby's eyes took on a faraway look.

"Did the nurse say she's sick?"

Abby shook her head. "No, not sick, just small and weak." She scrunched her lips together as if to hold back a deep sorrow within. "Perhaps I shouldn't even tell you, but that first day in Bennett while looking for the minister, I saw a grieving couple near a graveyard above the hotel. When they passed by me . . ." Abby's voice quivered. "I . . . I had a clear vision of a grave marker and a woman filled with grief."

As tears streamed down Abby's cheeks, Carson stood and pulled her into his arms.

"Abby, don't." Carson pulled her tight against him. "Surely you couldn't see your baby's death. You must have been feeling compassion for that couple."

He could feel her fighting the sobs against him. After a minute, she pulled from him and wiped her face with her sleeve.

"Carson, I don't have strong visions like that often, but when I do, they usually come true. There's nothing I can do. Nothing but keep her warm and fed and not take any chances."

He swallowed. "Abby, you've told me that you have faith in God. Shouldn't you trust and believe for the best, not the worst."

She nodded. "I'm trying, but you and I both know life has problems. And though I know God cares about us, the more I endure, the more I sense that I cannot depend on everything working out the way I want it. Not on this earth." Abby sniffed and wiped her eyes again. "All I know is that my final hope lies on a cross, no more."

Wordless, Carson stepped up beside her and reached for her hand. He held it tight.

"Pray for us, Carson," she whispered. "Pray for Josie. Can you do that?"

With a knot tight in his gut, he nodded. He rubbed the back of her hand with his thumb, trying to rationalize their circumstances. "So, then," he whispered coarsely, "you won't come with me?"

She looked at him. "No."

Pulling Abby's hand up to his lips, he kissed her knuckles tenderly. "Perhaps I should go now, but I want you to know that you both will be in my thoughts every day." Still holding her hand, he kissed her on the top of her head then released her and turned for the door.

"Take care," he said. He didn't look back.

Chapter Thirty-One

Dundee rolled to his back and swatted away something flying about his head. In the dark warmth of the room, he couldn't sleep. For a long time, he simply lay on his back and listened to the sounds outside his veranda. Wooden slats covered the windows, nothing to keep out sounds, just something to allow the trade winds into the interior of a room to cool it by night.

It was a different land for him. Somehow, he felt trapped by it. Knowing he was on an island, with miles of ocean between places, made him uneasy.

He'd been a rover for the past ten years. A little schooling here, a little there. A job in Kansas City, gambling in Chicago, riding in Montana. It had seemed the best of all worlds.

So how did he get here?

Dundee sighed.

Once again, he thought about that night in Seattle. Lately, it had come back to haunt him many times, and along with it came thoughts of Abigail. She was a beauty, that one. He recalled the first time he'd seen her. Jon and he had ridden to the ranch that day, but though he'd met her parents, she'd been out with her older brother checking some cattle. When they saw riders coming, Jon ran to the corral fence, removed his hat, and then waved it full bore.

Abigail must have recognized her twin, because he never saw anyone ride quite so crazy. Like a banshee riding on the wind, she had leaned forward, her face to her pony's neck, her hips high and fluid in the saddle as she galloped around the corral post. Bringing her horse to a skidding stop, she dismounted in a bound and then raced to the fence and leaped into Jon's arms, hugging him tight.

He'd never forget the look of her as a big hat had fallen back and her long, dark hair spilled down her shoulders. And when she'd turned to him with those penetrating blue eyes . . .

Dundee sighed again.

He thought about their last night together. She'd been sick and was mad that he was leaving. Frustrated, he'd grabbed his hat and started out the door when she'd yelled at him.

Good, just go then and never come back, she'd shouted.

He breathed deep at the memory of her voice. He didn't mean to never come back. It had just happened. But nothing really was stopping him for doing so. Not now. So why hadn't he?

He wondered how she and Jon would be faring in the northland. He was certain that they would have gone on. They wouldn't quit the opportunity, if he was any judge of their natures.

Feeling hot and clammy, Dundee threw off the sheet and rolled to his side. He needed to get some sleep. It had been mighty late when he'd closed up from the table and meandered back to his room.

Life on the island wasn't a bad life. The weather was mild, he had all the freedom he wanted, and even plenty of action at a table. It was just confining. And something more.

Would Abigail ever take him back?

She might not, and maybe he wouldn't blame her. His life probably wouldn't be what she had exactly expected, but then, she did have spirit. She was adventuresome, and he missed the way she felt against him, the smell of her, the sweet thrill of her.

Was he lonely? *Was Dundee Andrews actually lying here lonely?*

Maybe.

So if that was true, what was next?

Sleep, he thought. Think on it tomorrow when you have some good sense. But without a doubt, he knew that he needed to think on it some more.

The Promise

Part Three

A Journey Home

Dawson to Skagway, November 1898 – June 1899

Chapter
Thirty-Two

"What happened with the claims?" Ingrid asked. "Why don't you have the gold?"

Abby shrugged as she thought over the events of the last two and a half months. Where to begin?

"To our good fortune," she said slowly, "the claims were quickly made a legal inheritance for the Smythe family, and so we can now have a share of any gold that we mine or find, but we are still uncertain what happened to Dan's stash. The Constable said that right after Cal's arrest a higher authority sent some Mounted Police to Forty Mile and at last found C. R. Thorne. Mr. Thorne told the investigating Mounties that late one night, during early winter of eighty-seven, some men came to him with Mr. Hanover and said old Dan had been stabbed and that the Constable was coming after him. It was a lie, of course, but fearing the worst, C. R. took off for the Forty Mile area. Mr. Thorne still doesn't want to come back to Dawson, but at least he confirmed that he had witnessed the signing of Dan's will and knew the claims were to go to Dan's sister.

Abby sighed as she picked up Josie and held her to her shoulder, burping the sleepy child against her. Ingrid smiled and leaned forward making a face at the baby.

"She is getting so plump that little one. Abby, you are blessed to have her making such improvements by the day."

"Yes, I know, but I feel that I must continue to be very careful, as you should be."

"Aw, Abby. What can one do but eat well and hope for the best? Sickness is sickness. It comes. It goes."

Abby looked at her. "Maybe for us, but someday as a mother, you may feel differently."

"Ya," she said. "Maybe so. Maybe Hansen and I shouldn't have come."

"Oh, no, Ingrid, I don't mean for you to think that. Without company now and then, I do believe I would go mad. I am so happy to have you here. Other than Madge coming by a time or two, it has been quite lonely since Clara and Earl left."

Ingrid nodded. "I'm sorry I have not been here more, but I have to insist that Hansen take the time from his building work and hitch up the sleigh." She shook her head. "He is trying so hard to be done soon with our home."

"I understand completely. You must be ready for the cold as well."

"Will you be staying in this cabin all winter?" Ingrid asked. "It's so far from everything."

"I imagine so. With Jon's help, I'm doing fine, for though he's working at The Grand, he stays with me each night and helps to chop wood and brings me supplies." She nodded. "He's been a saint."

"Ya. Hansen says he works the jobs of two men." Ingrid looked at her curiously. "But, Abby, I am still puzzled about the main gold. Do you think Mr. Hanover took old Dan's stash?"

"We're not certain," Abby said. "But we don't think so. If Mr. Hanover had it, why wouldn't he and his thugs have left long ago? I think they were biding their time, taking what gold they could from the claims and Miss Mulroy's business, and all the while looking for Dan's cache. Jon and I think that they were never able to find it, and it was my discovery of the second ledger that sent them running."

Ingrid leaned forward and drummed her fingers across the tablecloth, her eyes narrowed. "I wonder how Mr. Hanover knew of this stash in the first place."

Abby shrugged. "Well, perhaps old Dan told him one night at the Grand, or maybe the lawyer who made out Dan's will told him. Either way, the lawyer C. R. named claims that he hadn't heard of Mr. Fogherty's death. It appears that only Mr. Hanover and his cohorts knew about Dan's final demise, other than C. R., of course."

"Sounds like the truth will never be known," Ingrid sighed.

"Could be," Abby agreed. "Although when the authorities found Dan's body buried beneath a gravel pile not far from his cabin, they said it didn't appear there was any foul play, and that he looked as natural as could be expected after near to a year in cold gravel."

"And no gold was found anywhere?"

"No, none whatsoever, even though remarkably enough, most of Dan's private things were still inside his cabin, even down to his Bible and a small note tucked inside referring to his will. To an outsider, it appeared that C. R. and Dan had simply gone back to the states for awhile, leaving town and paying these men to work their claims like the Cummings do. The scoundrels, of course, kept every ounce they could get their hands on, but I'd be willing to bet that they were mighty unhappy to leave before they found Dan's big stash."

"The leeches," Ingrid said, shaking her head. "So, do you think the gold is still about?"

"Actually, I do, but where is another matter. C. R. is certain that his friend Dan didn't keep his cache in the cabin, but he also said he didn't know where Mr. Fogherty kept it. Jon and the authorities believed him, especially since he wrote the Smythe family to tell them about Dan's death and the will."

Abby sighed. "For all practical purposes, though the claims have been returned, all of Dan's savings is lost. It's not in a bank or anywhere that we can find. It just disappeared."

"Forever you think?"

"Perhaps."

Abby nodded toward the Bible lying on the table beside them. "Poor man. He didn't even have much in his cabin that one would want, but when Jon saw this, he brought it to me. I lost mine, which was my grandmother's, in the Yukon River." She shook her head, wondering at the hard years Dan had spent mining, and then to lose his labor's profit, like her Bible, in a brief moment. "It's too bad about Mr. Fogherty, Ingrid, though from the wear on this Bible, I do think he was a believer."

"So, maybe you have found much more than gold, ya?"

"You're right, Ingrid. It's been good for me to read it these past long days, giving me hope while I watch and worry over my little one." She looked from her baby's sleeping face to her friend and smiled.

"So tell me now, what is the news about you and Hansen? When is this marriage you talked about?"

Ingrid's face grew brighter as she smiled at Abby. "Yust as soon as he's done with our cabin. He's making it big enough that we can live there and also rent two rooms. I will cook and make breakfast and suppers for as many as we can fit in our place, that way we may have goot enough income so that I can work less hours at the laundry."

"Goodness, aren't you the industrious ones," Abby declared. "And here I sit while Jon and Jimmy try to keep us going."

Ingrid frowned. "Abigail, do you need help?"

"No," she said, shaking her head. "We are doing fine, but you are kind to ask. When Jon and Jimmy found that we had two more claims, they hired help and recovered a fair sum before the cold started. And then, as you know, Jon was asked to manage The Grand and Jimmy is now staying at Dan's cabin and working for Mr. Joseph. So," she smiled, "I'd say that God has more than provided."

At the sound of footsteps and a knock on the door, Ingrid stood. "Let me get that, Abby. I be thinkin' it's Hansen returning for me."

When the broad-shouldered man stepped inside, his large body nearly filling the room, he removed his hat and nodded with a smile.

"Greetings, Miss Abby. How are you and the baby?"

"Hello, Hansen, we're doing well, thank you."

Hansen nodded again and then looked at Ingrid. "I think we best go now. The days are growing short and the sun is already low. It wouldn't be good to wait much longer."

"Ya, I get my coat and hat." Ingrid said.

As Ingrid reached for her outer garments, Abby rose to her feet and quickly moved to her friend's side. "Josie and I want to thank you for coming and especially for the wonderful bunting you knitted for her."

"You most velcome," Ingrid murmured. She reached out and patted the baby's shoulder with a gentle touch. "Josie. That is such a nice name, though I've not heard it before."

Abby smiled as she looked into her baby's face. "I thought it a good strong name, but actually, it comes from Carson's middle name, Josiah. If it wouldn't have been for Carson, Jimmy and Beauty, I doubt little Josie would be here."

Ingrid nodded, her eyes growing serious. "We will continue to pray, won't we."

"Yes, Ingrid. We will."

Ingrid glanced at Hansen and then back. "It may be a while before I can come again, Abby. Please, you must plan to come to Dawson the Sunday before Christmas." She smiled brightly. "We are planning to have a celebration if our home is complete and make it the day of our wedding." Ingrid beamed as Hansen walked up close and placed a hand on her shoulder.

"My, how wonderful," Abby cried. She reached for Ingrid and hugged her while Hansen looked on proudly.

When they parted, Ingrid tugged at her large furry hat and nodded. "We must go, but we will see you soon." Ingrid smiled broadly. "When our plans are made, Hansen can always send a message through Mr. Joseph or Jimmy to The Grand. You will come?"

Abby hesitated, and then nodded. "If Josie continues to do well, you know I wouldn't miss it."

"Then goodbye, Abby. God bless."

"And to you," Abby murmured.

After a final parting wave, Abby closed the door and listened to the sound of their voices disappearing down the trail. In the silence, Josie wriggled and began to whimper. For a few minutes, she patted Josie's small form, and then she placed her in the cradle and stooped to rub her tiny back until the baby settled into a peaceful sleep. When at last Abby straightened, she gazed across the darkening room and thought about her conversation with Ingrid.

She was happy for her friend. And though the winter might be a long and dark obstacle looming ahead, she was certain that they'd been blessed with many good resolutions. Most importantly, Josie appeared to be growing fat and content.

Abby released a long breath. Though fear had lingered at the edge of her mind over the past several weeks, she would need to remember her blessings and continue to be thankful, no matter what came.

Still, it was useless to deny the deep longing inside, and in the silence of the room, Abby's thoughts once again turned to Carson and how, after he'd walked out of the cabin that last day, there seemed to be a great emptiness remaining in her heart.

Chapter
Thirty-Three

"Carson, my boy, I do believe you spend more hours at this machine than I did when I started this whole printing business. You need to take some time off."

Carson looked up from where he was bent over the press and wiped his hands. "I should be finished in a few minutes," he said, "and then I suppose I'll head for home."

"Well, instead of doing that, how would you like to come with me and a friend of mine for dinner? It will be my treat, sort of a bonus you might say. My wife is hosting a group of women this evening who are putting the finishing touches on this Christmas Charity Ball." Burton Russell raised his grayed, bushy eyebrows and frowned. "I've no desire to be about the house tonight for that," he said, shaking his head, "so Judge Morgan is dropping by in a few minutes. Come with us."

Carson tossed the towel aside and held up both hands, ink-stained and dirty. "Sounds good enough, but are you certain you want someone looking like this to tag along?"

Burton laughed, giving Carson a rather jarring slap on the back as he moved by him for his desk. "There's water in the basin. Wash up and that'll be good enough for me. I rather like the look of ink on my employee's hands," he called out cheerfully. "Looks like money to me."

Carson chuckled then began to straighten up the area and wash as told. The printing was complete, the press cleaned, and the morning edition ready for the boys early in the morning. As he thought about it, the newspaper business was backbreaking work, and yet being able to produce a daily press for the small town of Juneau, as well as Douglas on the island across the channel, was more than satisfying.

Carson figured that as long as the A. J. Mine south of Juneau maintained its share of employees, while the Treadwell kept Douglas going, Mr. Russell's *Northern Star* would be successful, quite unlike the other gold seeker presses that had gone the boom-and-bust cycle. He'd heard that, of late, Dawson was even losing thousands to Nome's gold stampede, and though a few thousand less men would be good relief for the town's headaches, still it wouldn't be much help to the businesses there.

Carson recalled his first image of Dawson as the four of them had rowed toward the dock. It had been a far cry from Juneau's harbor the day he'd steamed down the Lynn Canal and into port. For some reason, the touch of rust tones coloring Juneau's soaring mountains, the lush countryside, as well the harbor's deep blue waters had made him feel as if he'd come home. Even the opportunity to work for the renowned Burton Russell had felt right to him. Indeed, every turn over the past few months felt more positive than he had imagined possible.

Everything, that is, except for matters of the heart. How he missed his friends, and especially Abigail.

As Carson scrubbed his hands, he thought of his recent letter and the small crate of oranges and lemons he'd sent to Dawson. Through his California sources, he'd arranged for a gift to be sent in time for Christmas, although the clerk for the California steamship had seemed incredulous when Carson explained that the crate would be then taken by horse and sled freighters from Skagway to Dawson.

"That's gonna' cost you a pretty penny," the man had declared. And he was correct in the assumption, but knowing that the fruit would be about the dearest item of purchase come winter, he'd paid the price and been happy to do it. Frozen or not, it wouldn't matter, he had explained. The goodness of the fruit wouldn't be spoiled, unless it thawed before arrival.

At the sound of the bells jangling at their front door, Carson turned to see a wiry man sporting a black fedora step inside. While the newcomer shook a few snowflakes from the shoulders of his heavy wool coat, Mr. Russell swept across the room.

"Judge Morgan," Burton said with eagerness. "So glad you were able to drop by and have dinner with us."

Mr. Russell motioned to Carson. "I would like you to meet my right-hand man, Judge. Carson was a reporter for the *Seattle Post-Intelligencer* and spent near to a year traveling from Seattle to Dawson and back to our fair city. He reported on the Klondike."

Dark eyes shifted to him. Judge Morgan gave Carson a thorough once-over and then offered a slow smile. "Quite an adventure, I imagine?"

"Yes, sir." Carson said. "At times, I miss some of that action, not to mention the friends I made along the way, but I rather like it here in Juneau."

"You spent a fair amount of ink putting the experience to paper I take it?"

"Yes," Carson nodded, "although some events can only be written on the heart."

Mr. Russell reached for his coat. "Carson left friends in Dawson just so he could work for me. Guess my reputation's more renown that I realized."

The judge smiled as Carson slipped into his jacket. "I would imagine, Mr. Stuart, that you've already discovered how Mr. Russell has little aptitude for humbleness or indecision."

"Ha!" Burton snorted. "Tell me one decent newspaper man out there who does!"

Judge Morgan laughed.

As the three of them stepped outside, Carson buttoned his coat and waited for the others to take the lead. "Shall we head up to Vogmann's?" Burton said. "Hear they had some mighty nice steaks brought in yesterday. I've been hankering for something other than fish for some time now. How about you, Carson? Does a good steak sound like a bonus to you?"

Carson smiled. "I'll take whatever I can get, Mr. Russell, and considering what I've been eating lately, it sounds mighty fine."

"I heard Burton say that you left friends in Dawson," Judge Morgan said. "Can I deduce that you don't have a wife cooking for you then?"

"That's right, sir. Left behind two good friends and a mighty comely woman that I wouldn't mind seeing again, but who knows what will happen."

"A woman?" The judge raised an eyebrow.

"Yes, my close friend and I met a man and his sister on the steamer out of Seattle. By the time we reached Skagway, we decided to partner with them for the journey. But, like I said, they're all three still in Dawson."

Mr. Russell snorted. "Fool thing to leave a single woman in that part of the country, Carson. Except for the beauties for hire, she'd be one in a thousand I'm guessing."

"Maybe so," he grunted, "and Abby's pretty enough to turn heads, but she and her brother seem to hold their own." He shrugged. "But I didn't blame them for staying longer. They had some gold claims that they hoped to sequester for a patron. It was an inheritance issue and a rather messy set of circumstances, but it might be worth up to four hundred thousand dollars for them."

Mr. Russell looked at him with sudden interest. "You don't say!" He clucked his tongue and nodded. "Yes, indeed. I've heard of tales like this. I've even interviewed several of the female persuasion that's been following the glitter. Ask the judge. He's always marrying some lonely gold miner to some *gold digger*."

"You're too harsh on them, Burton. As far as I can determine, the couples I've been marrying seem young and exuberant and might do as well as most."

Mr. Russell shook his head. "A fool way to get life started as far as I'm concerned. The female is always a struggle to understand, and one that has been used to roving around wouldn't appear to be a good choice to my way of thinking."

Carson thought about the lovely Miss Marinda and the night Abby had caught him entertaining her. He could well understand how the loneliness of a miner could influence his thoughts. And yet, for some reason, the loneliness here in Juneau felt far different to him. The long nights didn't appear as deeply stressful. Instead, it was as if he was simply biding his time, waiting.

The attributes of love, patience, and prudence, Abby had shouted at him that night in Dawson, attributes that she'd thought he possessed, attributes she wanted different from her husband.

Returning to the moment, Carson listened to the two men talking beside him. Times were changing, Judge Morgan declared. Alaska was being noticed. And as he and Mr. Russell talked on about new government policies and the men jostling for political gain, he found his mind turning to a tiny form held tight in his arms, to that small head with wild dark hair and a sweet, innocent face.

Carson breathed in steady, matching the rhythm of his steps in order to keep abreast of his companions, but as they trudged up a Juneau street covered with a thin blanket of wet snow, he knew his mind had drifted to a far-off, much colder land. He recalled the cabin on the hill and hoped that the small life he'd helped bring into the world would by now be thriving—right along with the woman who held her.

Chapter
Thirty-Four

"Here, Miss Abby, let me have the baby while you get in the sleigh," Jimmy said.

He reached out and took Josie, holding her stiffly as Abby climbed in. After Abby settled her bag alongside her feet, she tucked Josie under a blanket in her arms and secured her tight against her. With a smile, she looked around. The ground and trees were gleaming white in the dim light of a midday sun, the air cold and still about them.

Jimmy smiled broadly. "You ready for your first outing?"

"I am," she smiled.

James muttered his command and the team began to turn slowly in the meadow. As the sleigh picked up speed, Abby felt the cold air on her cheeks and tucked Josie even closer against her. If covered properly, she decided, the temperatures shouldn't hurt the baby. It certainly hadn't been an issue for her and her brothers growing up in Wyoming, but Carson and Jon had been right. The air here held an extra edge of bitterness to it.

Abby turned her thoughts to the days ahead. Christmas was a mere week away, and tomorrow Ingrid and Hansen would be married. It didn't seem possible that the end of the year was fast approaching, but the more she considered the amount of wood it took to stay warm and the frosty feel in the cabin before Jon stoked the fire, the more she realized that the deep of winter had at last arrived. Even now, she often had to bring wood for the stove inside the cabin and finish chopping it with her hatchet as it thawed. In many ways, she dreaded the thought of the months ahead, but at least Josie was growing stronger and more vigorous every day.

Before spring returned, she would have months of cold to endure, and she would have a hard time keeping up. If Josie wanted to crawl and move about, she would need to make warmer clothes for her. She might even have to put blankets and their fur robe on the floor. She had already draped blankets about the walls to keep out the draft, but beyond the cold, her greatest concern was the need for water.

"How are you doing with the baby in all this cold?" Jimmy asked. "She's sure looking right healthy with those rosebud cheeks."

"Actually, I was just thinking about the winter ahead. I'm faring well enough, I suppose, but like everyone warned, it keeps a body busy just to stay warm." Abby glanced down to adjust both Josie's heavy quilted blanket as well as the fur throw over them. They would soon be at The Grand where Jon waited for her.

"Are you doing all right in Dan's cabin, Jimmy? Or has the cold become a bit much for you as well?"

"Can get right nippy now and then, can't it?" He smiled at her. "But like you, I'm surviving. I have Jon and you to visit and, weather permitting, the fires to keep going so we can pick away at those infernal rocks."

Abby thought about Jimmy's inclination to stay at work on the claims. "It will get colder in January. You won't be able to continue digging under the fires then, will you?"

He shook his head. "It's doubtful. And in truth, we're not doing much even now, but it's something to keep me busy when I'm not driving for Mr. Joseph."

"Are you glad you stayed, Jimmy, or do you wish you'd gone out with Carson?"

He looked at her with a thin smile. "Right now, I reckon I can't answer you that. Maybe in a few months I'll know. When I strike it rich, then we'll know for certain, eh?"

She shook her head. "You and Carson, the eternal optimists."

"You gotta' stay hopeful, Miss Abby. Life would be plumb awful if you didn't."

She smiled at him. "You're a dear, James Patten. You always seem to know what to say to cheer me."

"Had my instructions from Carson before he left, you know."

"Did you now?"

"I did." He nodded. "I got a letter from him the other day, and a package, too. Actually, it's for all of us and it's waiting at the Grand."

She stared at him. "Really? A package?"

"Well, more of a crate, you might say. A gift for Christmas."

Abby studied Jimmy's face to see if he was serious. "You aren't teasing me, are you? It takes forever to get a package into Dawson these days."

"No, ma'am. Would I do such a thing?"

She laughed. "Well, then," she said brightly, "maybe this will be more of a nice outing than I thought—a night in a warm lodge, a gift, tomorrow's Sunday services and then a wedding. Truthfully, Jimmy, I feel like a kid in a candy shop!"

He nodded. "We'll have a good time, Abigail," he said. "I'm thinking you are right about that."

Abby smiled and then shifted her attention to the mounds of snow-enshrouded gravel and the crisscrossing sluice boxes all about the valley. Although most areas were silent and still along the Eldorado, she noted activity at the Cummings' claims.

"What are those men doing, Jimmy?"

"They've been burning their fires in that area for awhile, and now they're using a hand windlass to bring gravel up from the holes. They're getting quite a pile of rocks for sluicing next summer, like the rest of us are attempting to do. I just reckon they have a little nicer equipment to work with."

Abby nodded. "Why does it always take money to make money?"

"It's the way of it," Jimmy laughed.

As they approached The Grand, Abby glanced at the rolling hills on the west. Though it was the middle of the day, the sun hung low in a hazy sky, barely visible as it skimmed over the southern portion of the hills. By three in the afternoon, its light would be gone altogether.

"Here we are," Jimmy said. He smiled as he pulled the team to a halt in front of the hotel.

Abby studied the large, plain structure, remembering all that had happened when she had worked for Mr. Hanover. Just then Jon stepped outside and waved.

"Hello there, if it isn't my two favorite ladies," he called out.

Abby waved and returned his smile then pulled the sleigh robe back. Jon reached for Josie. "Here, let me have that little rosebud," he said.

"I have a bag in the back," she nodded. "If you'll unload it, I can carry it inside."

"No, you keep Miss Rosebud and I'll grab it." He looked back to Jimmy as he reached for her luggage. "Hurry along to the stables, James. Warm food is waiting inside."

"Don't need a second invitation for that," Jimmy laughed, and as soon as Abby stepped away, he at once started off to where Mr. Joseph kept his wagons, sleighs, and a few lean ponies.

As they walked along, their footsteps crunching in the snow, Jon smiled. "I'm glad you accepted the invitation to spend the night here," he said. "We can get an early start that way in the morning. Ingrid will be so pleased to have you at her and Hansen's wedding."

"I hope so. I still worry about exposing Josie to people, but she seems to be very healthy, and I imagine I'm a bit more comfortable in this role of being a mother, though it's not easy."

"No, it isn't. I've never said this before, Abby, but during those times when you were up at all hours, I wondered how you managed. Somewhere in the middle of one night, before I rolled over and went to sleep, I remember thinking that we never gave our mother much credit for things that were far more critical than we knew."

She laughed. "Well, maybe *you* didn't give her credit, but I could see the toil and trouble we all gave her and Gram Mary."

"Oh, of course, the perfect darling, you were."

Abby smiled, but when Jon opened the door and she stepped inside, she felt her smile fade as she stopped in her tracks and looked around. Decorations of pine boughs and red bows were everywhere.

"Goodness, Jon. This is beautiful!"

He grinned at her from ear to ear as he stepped inside and closed the door. "Perhaps more than you know. Come on, I want to show you around."

"Good afternoon, Miss Abigail."

Abby turned. "Sarah! I'm so glad to see that you're still working here. Has Jon been good to you?"

"Ah, yes, Miss Abby. He's a much more pleasant man to work for than old Mr. Hanover."

Abby laughed. "Well, there you go, Jon."

"Come," he said. "Please excuse us, Miss Sarah. I'm going to show my sister where she and little Rosebud will be staying."

"Yes," Sarah nodded quickly, her eyes sparkling as she gave him a knowing smile.

Abby looked from her face to Jon, sensing some sort of secret, then dutifully followed as Jon led the way down the hallway beyond the room where she had bunked with Sarah and Anna. As they moved along, she realized that he was taking them to the room where Mr. Hanover had stayed, and though she felt a growing tenseness, she kept walking.

When Jon pulled the long, heavy curtain aside and they at last stepped into the room, Abby's jaw dropped in amazement. On the far wall a fire blazed warmly within a large rock fireplace and before it sat two rocking chairs. To one side, a table and four chairs held a bright red tablecloth and plates were arranged on it for three. A large floral rug adorned the center of the room and off to her far left was a chair and bed.

"Here," Jon said, "come inside a little more. Look to your right, behind that curtain."

As Abby stepped closer, she drew in a quick breath. "Jon. What a beautiful cradle!" she exclaimed. "Oh, my!"

"That's a bit of a small bedroom, Abby, but on the other side of the bed and the cradle is a sideboard table plus a deep lavatory, and it's all for you."

"For me?" She looked puzzled. "But . . ."

"Please hear me out," Jon interrupted, "maybe this wasn't right of me to make this decision without you, but I talked with Georgia and she insisted that she help me create a better place for you to winter with little Josie. Between her and the staff here at The Grand, we set up a private place where you and the baby could stay in comfort. I will be sleeping in the bed on the left, so we'll be sharing this as our quarters, but I thought overall it would be much better for Josie and you." He shrugged. "Actually, even for me, since I didn't figure it was good to be gone nights from The Grand, and yet I couldn't leave you out there in the cabin by yourself."

Jon placed an arm around her shoulders and gave her a light squeeze before stepping back.

"Well," he said proudly, "what do you think? Do you like your Christmas present or not?"

Chapter
Thirty-Five

With the crunch of his footsteps loud in his ears, Carson made his way past the corner lamplight and started up the darkened street to where he rented a small room in the lower level of a rooming house. The woman who owned the place was pleasant enough, but he found it amusing that she daily asked him about his work and how he was managing as a newcomer. And each time she asked, he would almost always give the same answer, "I'm doing fine, Mrs. Knudsen. Doing fine."

But was he?

It was Christmas Eve, and other than a letter of greeting from Jimmy and regards from Jon, nothing was written in Abigail's own hand. He had tried to keep it from grating on him, but somehow, tonight that fact bothered him more than ever. Why he continued to have hope about her, he didn't know, but at least word had come that the baby was doing much better than expected, and he was heartened by the news.

Still and all, tomorrow was Christmas Day, and he didn't especially relish the idea of spending it alone. So to keep his mind from it all, he had worked later than normal this evening, making extra certain that their special holiday edition was filled with every detail about the Christmas Charity Ball and listing all the activities in town during the holidays. It seemed that everyone around him was feeling up for the season—everyone perhaps but him and those few he saw lingering about the saloons down on Front Street tonight.

On the positive side, his mother and sister had written, telling him about life in his home-town, about those who had passed on while others moved in, or out, still searching for work. And as he'd read their words, he pictured them all, recalling fondly the usual commotion in his parents' home. When he considered the distance between them, it felt as if he had moved off to the moon.

As Carson stepped closer to the rooming house, he suddenly had the urge to keep walking. The last thing he wanted to do was stay inside his small room and stare at four walls. Besides, the night was clear and the sky filled with stars. Off in the horizon, he could even see a rosy glow and figured the aurora borealis might offer a spectacular Christmas Eve show, if he kept his eye on it.

Taking a left turn, Carson stretched out his legs and started up a long hill. When he at last came to a flat area near the top, he swerved again and made his way along the ridgeline that overlooked the harbor along the Juneau side of Gastineau Channel. For several minutes, he stood looking across the water to the lights glimmering within homes on Douglas Island.

He took in a deep breath and filled his lungs with the cool, crisp air. To his relief, he found renewal from it. Then spotting a path that led down the hill on the opposite side, he started off toward the water. There was a sense of excitement building as the urge to explore became strong. After reaching the bottom of the hill, he began to wander among several small homes and businesses, until, at the sound of voices singing Christmas carols, he came to a stop and listened.

The music was coming from a nearby house. He stepped closer and gazed at the home's bright light flickering in a window while he listened to the few warbling sopranos and a bass or two. In the darkness, he saw movement and then the lithe figure of a woman appeared at the doorway. Feeling somewhat embarrassed to be standing there looking at her home, Carson started to turn away, but she was too fast for him. She swiftly raised her small lantern and called out.

"Hello? Are you looking for someone?"

Carson stared at her, trying to place her voice and face, and then it came to him.

Maria Riley? Was that really her?

Maria stepped down the porch steps, and still holding her lantern high, she moved toward him. In somewhat of a daze, he simply stood there a moment watching her.

"Hello," she said again. "Are you looking for the Riley gathering?"

"I . . . well, I really didn't think I was, but are you Maria Riley?"

"Yes," she said. She stepped a few feet closer and peered out from behind the light with dark, luminous eyes. "My goodness! Is that you, Mr. Stuart?"

"Yes, it is. But I must tell you, I was just walking about and am so surprised to find you here. I thought you were living in Dyea."

Maria held the light forward and offered an appealing smile. "Dear heaven, it really is you," she said. "Yes, we were living in Dyea until this fall and then my father decided to come here. Some of my mother's people live in Juneau and Dyea was quickly beginning to change. I think Father decided that the time had come to take his business elsewhere, and so he moved us to this home and started a small grocery and bake shop not far from here."

Speechless, Carson nodded. It seemed as if fate had almost guided him.

"And you, Mr. Stuart. What brings you to Juneau? Is Abigail here?"

"Well, actually, she's living in Dawson with her brother and my friend, Jimmy, but due to certain circumstances, I came out to Juneau and am working for Mr. Russell at the *Northern Star*."

"Still in the newspaper business I take it?"

"Yes, guess I am."

There was a slight pause then Maria waved her hand. "Goodness, I can't believe this. Please, Mr. Stuart, if you aren't on your way somewhere, come in and say hello to my family. They will be delighted to see you. I was watching out the window, expecting a few more friends to come and share the Christmas spirit with us. Would you have the time?"

He hesitated. "I don't want to interrupt. I was just walking about when I heard your singing."

"No, no. You won't be. It's only a simple gathering. Please, come in."

Carson smiled. "Well, actually, I would enjoy that very much, Miss Maria. Seeing you brings back good memories of our Chilkoot adventure. I would enjoy meeting your family."

Feeling somewhat awkward, Carson stepped inside the warm living room with Maria. As several heads turned, he realized that he only recognized two people, Mr. Riley and Arlie. In addition, except for one other couple, the rest appeared to be Tlingit or like Maria, partially so. Mr. Riley at first gave him a curious look, and then with sudden recognition, he stood, smiling broadly.

"Father, do you remember Mr. Stuart, the reporter who stayed to recover with us in Sheep Camp last year?"

"Well, my word. That I do. Welcome, Mr. Stuart. Are you just passing through town?"

"Actually, no, I've started working at the *Northern Star*, and for now, I've taken Juneau as my residence."

Mr. Riley quickly crossed the room to offer him a warm handshake. "Well, what a coincidence. It's good to see you. Please have a seat, won't you join us for a cup of wassail and visit awhile?"

Maria chimed in. "Father, you won't believe it, but he said he was just out for a walk when I happened to see him from the porch. Isn't that . . ." she paused and looked at him, "isn't that such a wonder?"

George Riley nodded and pointed across the room. "Mr. Stuart, I'd like you to meet my wife, Ruth. And there beside her is the Reverend William Mackay and his wife Helen, and this is my brother by marriage, Charlie, his wife Edna, their son Frank and, of course, Arlie, whom you already know, and his new wife, Annie."

Carson nodded, greeting their calm and wide-eyed stares with a smile. He felt a mixture of warmth and quiet reserve in their greeting and wasn't quite certain how to respond.

The Reverend stood and reached for his hand. "I'm quite eager to hear more about this story of you at Sheep Camp, Mr. Stuart. By chance, did you happen to meet Ira Garner, a friend of mine, while you were there?"

"Ah, yes. I believe he spoke at services we attended one Sunday. On second thought, I met him yet another time when Abigail, my partner's sister, insisted I give a rather broken-down pony to him named Patches."

"Patches? Now that's quite a name for a pony. Poor things. So many of them, you know, never live more than a year up there. Terrible waste of horseflesh."

"Yes, well, I've no idea how Patches fared, but she certainly had it better for awhile once a Miss Abigail got hold of her."

Maria smiled at him then nodded to the Reverend. "I doubt that Carson would have fared so well either if it hadn't been for Miss Abby," she said lightly. "Carson was quite sick while he stayed with us." She turned to him. "You're looking very healthy now, I must say. The rest of the trip must have been good for you."

"Somehow we managed, I guess."

George Riley waved his hand toward a chair as his wife brought him a cup of steaming wassail. "Please, Mr. Stuart. Have a seat." As Carson uttered his thanks to Ruth Riley, he took the cup and sat down. Across from him, Maria perched beside her brother on the edge of the sofa.

"And how is Abby, Mr. Stuart? Have you heard from her?" Maria's eyes were bright with curiosity. Carson wondered where to start, so much had happened.

"Not directly," he said, "but from her brother. She now has a baby daughter, Josie, and I'm hoping they are doing well. They're still trying to recover some gold for a client, but at least some progress has been made."

"Oh, I'm so glad to hear it. She is staying with her brother then?"

"Yes, I believe so. I just received a letter from Jon stating that he hoped she'd stay in Grand Forks for the winter, at a fine lodge run by Miss Georgia Mulroy called The Grand."

"Ah, yes," George Riley said quickly. "The celebrated Miss Mulroy. She has quite an ability to make money it seems. I heard from a friend that she is reportedly setting up another establishment in Nome, what with the gold rush moving ever northward."

"That so?" Carson found this bit of information quite interesting. "It appears the news gets around quickly in these parts, even if there are thousands of miles between point A and point B." Carson smiled, and as he did, he noted several others in the room smiling back.

"I think you've gained a fair amount of insight within your short stay here in the North Country," Reverend Mackay declared. "Are you content to stay in Juneau for long?"

Carson looked into the man's large gray eyes and wondered. Would he stay here very long? "To tell you the truth, Reverend Mackay, I'm not certain of it. But I believe I'm learning considerably more about what it takes to be content." He nodded. "Considerably more."

"Mr. Stuart," Maria said carefully, "might you be able to come over tomorrow? We would love to have you join us for Christmas dinner, wouldn't we, Father?"

As Maria gave him a warm smile, Mr. Riley smiled as well.

Chapter
Thirty-Six

Abby watched Josie reach for a small cup lying on the rug and paused, pen in hand. Josie was growing rapidly these days, her chubby arms and legs now in constant motion, struggling at every waking moment to learn something new, to reach, to scoot, to roll, and this morning, to crawl. In between her constant movement, Josie ate with enthusiasm, smiled often, and talked in her very own language with the best of them. In general, she kept Abby on the run to meet her needs for food, clothing, and cleanliness, and the more she thought about Josie's nature, the more she couldn't imagine trying to raise her in that tiny cabin tucked away from all civilization.

She had been foolish to even consider it. But at least the cabin had given her a place to be tucked away from everyone while Josie grew stronger, for even now, people were coming down with the fever. Abby was still certain that she needed to be very cautious about Josie's exposure and what she ate and drank. Her fear of the fever, in fact, had nearly paralyzed her at Ingrid's wedding, for it seemed as if everyone wanted to greet her bright-eyed little daughter.

Abby smiled as she watched Josie bang the cup on the floor. That day her daughter had nearly been the center of attention.

"What are you smiling about?" Jon asked as he looked up from his book.

"Me?" Abby started, "Oh, I guess how Josie captured so much attention at the wedding. Even though she can drive me to distraction, she can also be quite the charmer."

He chuckled. "I wonder how she comes by that? Just look at her," he continued. "I think little Miss is trying to crawl. Next she will be running about and then what will you do to confine her?"

Abby scrunched her lips. "Life has a way of pushing along our plans, does it not?"

"Always."

She looked at the journal in front of her and sighed. "Well, since Carson sent me this journal for writing my thoughts, I think I'll record at least a portion of her antics and changes. It may be interesting to read these comments in my old age, providing I live to an old age."

"Somehow, Abby, I think you will." Jon set his book aside and looked at her. "Have you heard from Carson or written him since Christmas? It's almost been a month now."

"Last week, I sent a thank-you note for the wonderful oranges and lemons and for my journal, but I imagine the note was shorter than it could have been."

"Why do you put him off, Abby? I know that marriage is sacred to the faithful, but don't you think that Dundee may not be living or never return? After all, he knew where we were, and now that we've received a letter from his father, we also know he's not contacted his family."

Abby looked down to where she had been writing about Josie's progress. "I know, Jon. But something inside me tells me to wait. Pray and wait. Perhaps when we return to the states, I will be more certain what to do."

Jon rose to his feet and stretched. "I suppose you're being wise, but I have to tell you I like Carson. He and Jimmy have been true friends, and that means something."

She watched him cross the room and reach for his boots. "Are you going out to check on things for the evening?"

"Yes, thought I would. It's getting late. Although in this darkness, I feel as if it's much later than it actually is."

"I agree. It's wonderful to have the extra hours of sunlight in the summer, but this darkness makes one tired early."

"Yup, everyone but little Rosebud there. Right now, she looks as if the night has just begun." He tied off his last boot lace and looked up. "I do believe she has your level of energy."

Abby laughed. "You look so worried," she said. "Was I that bad?"

Jon simply smiled, grabbed his coat and hat, and then reached for the long curtain that separated their room from the hallway. Abby stared thoughtfully at the curtain as it fell forward. No matter who came in and out of her life, Jon would always hold a special place in her heart, and thinking again of her journal, she once more picked up her pen.

> *January 31· the year of our Lord, 1899:*
>
> *Darkness is about us, but the warmth of love and light dwells inside this small room where Jon and I stay. I am slowly healing from my despair of you, Dundee. More often now, I am releasing you and letting you slip from my mind. Instead, other faces come to dwell in my thoughts each time I consider the past year. Faces who grow dearer with each day. I pray that my heart is not ruling my thoughts in this, praying that your will be done, Lord. But as I consider the lives of Carson, Jon, and Jimmy, I hope that you will bless them—for they are dear to my heart.*

She gazed at her frank admission and wondered how she would feel when reading these words years from now. How would this adventure into this far North Country all resolve?

With a sigh, Abby closed her journal and placed it on the shelf where she and Jon kept old Dan's Bible and several other books and papers. It was a simple life here at The Grand, much different from life in Dawson. It amazed her to think of the glamorous actresses and entertainers, the fine dining and luxurious theatres and hotels, and all that in a frozen land amid the simple creek men trying to survive.

Sadly, many men were sick and dying this year Madge had said recently, but at least through the Jesuits, Madge had made some inroads towards building a small hospital. Abby was certain it would bring welcomed relief. It was just a shame to be taking so long.

Turning back to her daughter, Abby knelt to pick up Josie, hushing her as she complained loudly.

"Hey, little lady," she crooned softly. "You have had a full day, my little pumpkin. And now it's time for you to consider your beauty rest, or at least mine."

And with that, Abby headed for the shelf where the baby's sleeping gowns were carefully piled.

After seeing that all was quiet in the dining area, Jon ambled over to the door, buttoned his coat, and then slipped on his warm hat and gloves. It wasn't much beyond eight o'clock at night, but since it had been a cold day, few men were about this evening. Still, it was his routine to always check the hotel and then the stables and doors about the various buildings, making certain all was well before he went to bed.

As he stepped outside, he immediately felt the air stinging his nose and lips, but he shook it off and looked up. The sky above him was radiant with glowing ribbons of greenish light. For a moment, he watched them dance across the sky, gyrating from north to south. He was amazed at their broad expanse in the northern heavens, and though he'd seen them more than a dozen times, he doubted that he would ever look at them with anything less than profound awe.

With his thoughts on the heavens, Jon started across the expanse of ground between the lodge and the barns. When he reached the clearing where the roadway from the creeks angled toward the lodge, he stopped again and looked around. From there he would have a glorious view of the sky in all directions. But when he turned to look up, he hesitated. Was there something on the roadway? He focused on a dark lump in the middle of the trail to Eldorado Creek.

What was it?

Stepping forward, Jon felt the beat of his heart increase more rapidly. The closer he came, the more the shape appeared to resemble that of a man curled up in the snow. With a start, Jon moved forward, his legs stretching out in long, swift steps.

When he reached the crumpled form, he stared down at the sight of a man's back. From all appearances, the poor soul had curled up there on the roadside, face down, and passed out. Seeing that the man looked stiff and bent awkwardly, Jon doubted if the fella was still alive.

Going to his knees, Jon started to roll the large frame on his back, but even as he reached out, he felt his breath leaving him.

No!

"Oh, God," he breathed. *It couldn't be.*

Jon hesitated as a deep pit of cold ran straight through his middle. Then in anguish, he leaned over the body and peered into the face, but before he even saw it, he knew.

"Jimmy," he moaned. How could this be? Why would Jimmy be curled up here on the road? Jon wrapped his arms around him and heaved, trying to pull Jimmy over.

"Come on, Jimmy. Don't give me this. Get up! Get up!"

But the more he attempted to rouse the stiff form within his grasp, the more he realized that Jimmy was no longer living inside that cold body.

After rubbing Josie's back to calm her, Abby stepped to the far wall and reached for her coat. She was satisfied that her baby was content enough. She would make her way outside, though she dreaded the icy visit to the outhouse. As she rounded the counter in the lobby and shuffled to the door, Jon suddenly opened it, wide-eyed and pale. He looked as if he'd seen a ghost.

"Jon," Abby gasped. "What's wrong?"

"I need some help," he said quickly, then without further explanation, she saw him run up the stairs. For a moment, she stood there stunned, wondering what had happened and if she should follow him. She heard Jon's voice and his pounding on a door. With her heart racing, she watched two men come flying down the stairs behind Jon, one still struggling into his coat as he moved.

"Sorry, Abby," Jon shouted as he ran passed her and all three headed for the door. "I'll be back. Wait here."

Speechless, Abby followed them outside and saw the men running for the trail.

"Over here," Jon cried. "He's over here."

Abby felt a shiver run through her as she moved across the porch. She could barely make out the forms of the three men kneeling now on the roadway. While broad bands of northern lights danced eerily overhead, the men struggled to pick up and carry a dark form. As she watched them, she knew they were carrying a man.

Abby swallowed. Her chest felt heavy.

"Jon!" she cried out. "Who is it?"

When the men reached the edge of the porch steps and lay the man before them, Abby felt her head grow light. Speechless, she watched

Jon remove his glove and run his hand across Jimmy's face and down his neck. Another man leaned close and felt his chest and then his wrist.

"He's dead, Jon. I don't believe there's a hint of life here."

Abby rushed to where Jimmy lay on the snow and dropped to her knees beside him.

"Oh, no! Jimmy! Oh, dear God!"

Abby sat dazed in her chair as Jon stepped into the room. She brushed away the tears when he knelt beside her. For a long moment, neither of them spoke. When he placed his hand on her knee, she reached out and covered it with her own.

"Have you finished?" she sniffed.

"Yes. We have him in a coffin of sorts and we placed him inside the shed by the sleigh. We'll have to find a safe place for him until the ground is thawed enough for official burial."

He shook his head. "It's hard to believe he's gone. He was so full of life only days ago."

"What could have happened, Jon? He must have had the fever or something like that," Abby whispered.

Jon nodded. "We'll probably never know, but I'm certain he wasn't in his right mind and was trying to get help. His coat wasn't even buttoned."

"Oh, Jon," she groaned. "He meant so much to both of us. We will miss him terribly. He was such a comfort and a great companion for you, and just a delight to me."

Jon sighed. "Tomorrow, we'll have to contact Ingrid, Hansen, and Madge as well as Mr. Joseph and the men who worked with Jimmy at the claim. Hopefully, we can have some sort of service for him the next day."

"Carson will be crushed," she said simply.

Jon nodded. "I would like you to write him, Abby. I don't believe anyone else can handle it as well as you. I don't even know where Jimmy's parents are, but I know he and Carson lived in the same small community. Carson will have to contact them, so I think we must send a letter tomorrow."

"Do we need to contact the authorities here?"

"I don't know, but it wouldn't hurt."

Abby gazed into the fire as Jon rose to his feet. She felt the burning around her eyes from all the tears she'd shed.

While she stared forward, Jon knelt by the stacked wood near the fireplace. He reached for a small hatchet and a long slender piece of wood. For several minutes, he trimmed away the edges of the wood until he'd made a long thin board. Then he placed the hatchet on the floor and reached in his pocket for his knife. When he began to carve a cross at the top of the wooden slab, Abby rose to her feet and stared at the marker taking shape in Jon's hand.

It was small and plain.

With tears streaming down her cheeks, Abby recognized it.

She had envisioned its form with a tiny cross carved at the top months ago. She'd been on a hill overlooking Bennett.

Chapter Thirty-Seven

Carson's legs wobbled as he jogged down the trail. Nearing the bottom of the hill, he sucked in a deep breath and leaned forward, his hands to his knees. For a minute, he wondered if he would be sick. At last, he found his heart beginning to calm, and with every ounce of effort, he stood erect and tried to breathe.

But the words in his head wouldn't stop.

It grieves me to tell you, but Jimmy is dead.

Carson looked down the street, wondering why he had come looking for Mr. Riley. What could he do anyway? There was nothing to do now. He had brought Jimmy to the Klondike. He had left him behind, asking him to care for Abigail. He should have been there. Not Jimmy. Jimmy should be in California.

James . . . I never thought it, James.

I am so sorry.

As tears stung his eyes, Carson stepped forward, hurrying now down the street to the familiar house. Since Christmas Eve, he had accepted several invitations to Sunday dinner, even attending services with them occasionally beforehand. There was a sense of love and comfort in the Riley home. He needed it now, and with the rain pelting his head, he stumbled up the walkway and across their small porch. Then he hesitated.

He hated to arrive unannounced in such a state of mind. Still, the more he'd read Abby's letter, the more he'd felt compelled to speak with George. At every turn within his mind, his guilt was overwhelming. And Abigail was right. He needed to be the one to contact Jimmy's parents. But what would he tell them? That he'd invited their only son into the wilderness and then left him behind to die?

Sucking in a swift breath, Carson raised his hand and knocked on the door. When the surprised expression on Ruth Riley's face came into view, Carson felt a damp chill running up his spine.

"Why, Mr. Stuart," she said. "What an unexpected pleasure. Please come in."

"I'm sorry to simply arrive on your doorstep like this," he mumbled, "but would your husband happen to be home?"

"Yes, we were about ready for supper. Come in, please. Join us."

"No, thank you, Mrs. Riley. I can't stay long, but I'm afraid I need a little advice."

"Carson," George exclaimed. Mr. Riley looked at him curiously and then moved across the room, "and what brings you out in such a storm?"

Carson swallowed, not once but twice as he struggled against his emotions. His chest felt as if a great weight pressed in on him. "I'm afraid," he stammered, "that, well, that terrible news arrived today from Abigail and Jon Colton. My good friend Jimmy Patten, who stayed behind to help Jon, was found frozen on a trail."

"Glory, Carson! What a horrible shock this must be for you." George stepped up beside him and touched him lightly on the arm. "Please, Carson. Have a seat, won't you?"

Carson nodded weakly. "Yes. Yes. I don't want to bother you, but I'm struggling with this." As Carson sat on their sofa, George Riley pulled a chair close by and sat down while Ruth quietly slipped from the room.

"Tell me," George said. "What happened?"

Carson pulled the letter from his jacket pocket and held it out to George. "It appears he was trying to get help. Jon found him slumped down on the trail that leads to the creeks. And, since it was near to zero degrees, Jimmy was gone. He hadn't even buttoned his coat." Carson paused. "It doesn't seem possible. He was such a strong and healthy man," he mumbled.

George glanced through the letter and then looked up, his eyes soft with sorrow. "I assume you were close friends?"

Carson nodded. "Yes. Good friends since childhood. We played together, worked in my father's mill together, and when I came home from college, we even made plans to strike out together. He was like a brother, George, maybe more."

"I'm terribly sorry, Carson. Times like these can be difficult." He paused and then leaned forward. "Can we get you some supper, or at least some coffee or tea?"

"No. I'm fine, thank you. I guess I simply felt the need to talk to you. You see, I'm going to have to contact his parents, but I'm not sure what to tell them. Out of four children, Jimmy was their only son."

"Was he this strapping young man Arlie spoke of, the one who went from Sheep Camp to Bennett with Abigail's brother?"

"Yes."

In the quiet of the room, Mr. Riley nodded. "Why didn't he come to Juneau with you?"

"Before I left California, I asked him to come with me to Dawson. He was to help me shoulder the journey and I would pay the costs since I was on contract by the *Post*, but he got swept up in the effort to reclaim the gold with Jon and didn't want to come out with me. He wanted to see if he could find some golden nuggets and gain a new life."

With a deep heaviness inside, Carson took a breath and released it slowly. "Maybe he got his wish, just not the one he expected."

"Was he a Christian, Carson?"

"I suppose so. Abigail reminded me in the last part of her letter that he'd attended occasional services with them, and only recently had commented about his desire for eternal life. Abigail believes he understood God's grace."

"I see," Mr. Riley said. "But you'd never talked with him about such things?"

Carson shrugged. In younger days, he recalled them talking about being baptized in the river, but the conversation, as he recalled it, was more about the girls that would be going in the river with them.

"I guess we never talked much about religion." Carson managed a thin smile. "But he was a good man, George. Big physically and even bigger in heart, a man that did his best for his friends and was kind and friendly to all. Although I doubt if he was ready to go."

George nodded. "Well, it's hard to judge such things, Carson. One never knows really. Only God is the hearer of all hearts." George sighed. "And yet, when the finality of life touches us, we often see how we've failed to acknowledge that which is most important of all. Why is it we can easily speak about worldly issues and yet let those words about faith and the next life go by the wayside?" He looked at Carson with a gentle expression then leaned forward.

"Sometimes we can be so blind, not knowing that time is short. I know. For years I ignored what God wanted to say to me. Then when I came within an inch of my life, I realized that I'd put the good Lord off for far too long."

Carson nodded, unsure what to say.

"So what about you, Carson? I sense that you are carrying a burden."

Carson looked down. "I feel as if I have a gaping hole inside of me, George. And that, for the most part, I'm responsible for his death."

"In what way?"

"Not only did I take James to Dawson in the first place," Carson said, "but I didn't really encourage him to come out with me, to reconsider his idea about staying behind." He looked up at George, wondering if he could have made a difference.

"Instead," he muttered, "I encouraged him to stay, to watch over Abigail who it pained me to leave behind." He paused. "I know I told you all about her situation and that she had a baby just before I left, but what I didn't tell you is that I love her. And since she wouldn't come with me, I . . . I was glad that Jimmy stayed behind to help." He swallowed. "I encouraged him to seal his fate."

Carson stared at his hands. "I'm not sure I can ever face Jimmy's mother."

"It's not your fault, Carson."

"Maybe not, but it feels like it."

"This life is full of issues that make us feel guilty," George said gently. "Some of our words and actions should, since they're selfish and at times downright destructive, but all of us are guilty of something. It's why God sent his son to offer us something we can't do for ourselves. Each and every one of us needs the grace of God that Jesus offered on a cross."

George hesitated. "Carson, if Jimmy believed in eternal life through that sacrifice, then it is his. The apostle John wrote something that has stuck in my mind since that day I saw my own need. It goes something like this, *Verily I say unto you, he that heareth my word and believeth on him that sent me hath everlasting life.*"

George Riley stood and gently laid a hand on Carson's shoulder. "Would you like me to pray for you, for what you must say when you write his mother?"

Carson's chest ached. His eyes burned. "Yes," he said simply. "I would like that."

A hot pain rose up inside him as George's baritone voice filled the room, and as a few of the words resonated strongly in his mind, Carson prayed along.

We trust you Father . . . forgive and lead us . . . hear your voice. Give grace and wisdom for Carson, and Jimmy's parents . . .

So be it Lord. Amen.

Chapter Thirty-Eight

Jon stood in the doorway, pale and somewhat withdrawn as he shrugged his coat from his shoulders and hung it on the coat pegs just inside their curtained entry.

"Glad you're home," Abby said quietly. "I was getting a little worried. I know the sun is considerably higher in the sky these days, but I thought you'd be home sooner."

"Sorry. Guess I wanted to spend a little extra time at the claims today. Hired a few more men and we've got the fires burning in several areas. Want to be ready when the thaw comes."

Abby nodded then stepped over one of Josie's toys while her daughter began to crawl toward Jon with a bright smile. After finding her potholder, she pulled back the heavy cast-iron kettle from the fireplace and lifted the lid to peek inside. Most days, they ate what the cook in The Grand prepared, but on occasion, she would prepare a stew as she'd done today, keeping it warm by the fire until Jon returned.

"Fixed your favorite soup today," she said. "It tastes fair, considering I had to use the usual moose meat. Would be wonderful to have a slab of beef flank now and then," she added wistfully. She grabbed the pot's handle securely and then carried the stew to the table, and while she filled Jon's bowl, Jon began to tickle Josie lightly under the chin with his fingers. It was always heartwarming to see her daughter bubble over Jon with a mix of welcoming jargon.

"Think this one's going to be a talker," Jon said.

Abby smiled. "Quite unlike her uncle."

"Yup." He reached for a spoon.

"Josie and I have eaten," she said, "but I'll bring a cup of tea and join you." Seeing his simple nod, she moved to the steaming kettle of water hanging over the fire and silently made a cup of tea while he ate. Afterwards she returned to the table and reached for the whimpering Josie.

"She misses you," Abby declared.

"Always good to have someone miss you, I guess." Without pausing to look up, Jon took another bite.

"You seem tired tonight, Jon. Do you feel well?"

He shrugged. "Good enough."

Abby took a sip of tea and considered his sullen demeanor. After a moment, she turned to play patty-cake with Josie then carried her daughter back to the toys on the floor. As she moved back to the table, she gazed down at him.

"Jon, I can tell by the way you look, walk and talk that you're either worried, discouraged or still feeling the pain of Jimmy's death. Do you think we should go on with our effort here to find a little gold, or just simply say it's over and go home?"

He looked up from his bowl with a scowl. "I already told you that I don't want to go back empty handed. For my part, I thought *you* should have gone out last summer, although as I recall, you wouldn't listen to me."

"I know," she said quietly. "And I understand how you want to see this through. I felt that way last year as well, but we've settled the claim issue, and there doesn't appear to be any gold stashed away, so other than a few ounces you might gain from a summer's hard work, I wonder if there's any real reason to stay." She hesitated. "I'm beginning to fear for your health as well as your heart."

He shrugged, turning back to his food. "I don't need you to lecture me."

She sighed. "A year ago I would have argued with you, Jon. But, you're right. You don't need me to push you. It's just that I'm beginning to wonder if we've lost sight of what's best. I always thought of you as the practical one. Have you continued to pray for wisdom about our circumstances?"

"More or less."

With a grunt, Jon pushed back from the table and rose to his feet. "I forgot to bring you some mail from the post today, something for us personally."

Abby watched with interest as Jon ambled over to his jacket and began to dig through his pockets. He looked gaunt to her. There wasn't the same spark inside him, and though they'd had several discussions as well as an uplifting memorial service for Jimmy, she knew her brother's demeanor had changed. That robust face now held a pinched look. She had hoped the arrival of spring would help, but if anything, his countenance seemed only to sour over the last three months.

Certainly, her own sorrow lingered as well, but they'd received an encouraging letter recently from her mother and grandmother. And though little was said about the ranch's circumstances, she'd found their words comforting.

Jon tossed the new letter on the table beside her. "It's from Carson," he said. "It's addressed to both of us, but why don't you read it out loud while I finish another bowl of soup."

As Abby picked it up, her heart began to race. She stared at the slanted strokes of his handwriting on the worn and tattered envelope. Mail was precious to those in Dawson, and for good reason when one considered the distance it had to come by dogsled over a frozen, wintry landscape. Even in summer, when the steamers were able to make their way up the Yukon in fewer days, it still took weeks to receive mail. Not counting the precious shipment of oranges and lemons from Carson, she'd received but three letters since Josie's birth.

Recalling the pain in writing to Carson, Abby slowly removed the paper from the envelope. She'd been praying for him, hoping that his sorrow would not be too heavy. For a moment, she glanced over the page and then she began to read aloud.

>*Dear Abigail, Jon and little Josie,*
>
>*Even though I write to you filled with such misgivings and sorrow, I am hoping that this letter will find you all in good health and peace of mind. When I first saw your handwriting on the envelope, Abigail, I was thrilled to see it, but of course, I found the content of your kind note devastating.*

Abby swallowed, trying to keep her voice free from the emotion that nearly overwhelmed her before she read on.

>*It has taken me several days to come to grips with Jimmy's death, and in some ways, it will be a lifetime of grief. I believe that it's been only by the grace of God that I am able to respond to you now.*
>
>*I wanted you to know that with the kind help, again, of Mr. George Riley I was at last up for the task of*

contacting Jimmy's parents. I can only hope that what I said will be of some small comfort to his family. In truth, I have never found any words more difficult to write.

I know I bear the guilt for much of what happened to my friend. There is no denying it. And yet what has been done cannot be changed, what paths are started can never be taken back. And I would hope and pray that your understanding is the same, that you bear no sense of guilt for Jimmy's passing. He loved you both. He will be greatly missed by all of us.

On the publishing front, I have been enjoying my work here in Juneau, pleased to be busy gathering news for the community and gaining confidence as Mr. Russell's assistant. As well, I have become reacquainted with the Riley family who has practically adopted me, much to my surprise and appreciation. You will be delighted to hear, Abigail, that they are diligent in keeping me on track, even including me in their small home church and regularly filling me with their wonderful Sunday dinners.

I hope with all my heart that the three of you are managing well. I think of you often, and especially feel the need to pray, as you requested Abby, for little Josie. May her days be full of joy and rich with blessings, as is my wish for her momma and uncle as well.

In closing, I must mention that the Riley family sends their greetings, Maria in particular to you, Abigail. If the opportunity ever comes for you to sail into Juneau, I think you would find this to be a welcoming place. It would be my greatest pleasure to hear from you, and most certainly to see you again.

    Best regards,
      Carson

Abby slowly lowered the letter to the table, her heart full of wonder at his words.

Maria! Carson was spending time with the Riley family, and more importantly, he was praying for Josie. She looked up to see Jon sitting by the fireplace with his bowl. He stared into the fire as if lost in thought.

"It's so good to hear his news," she sighed. "How amazing that the Riley family is in Juneau and that Carson has found them. I must tell Ingrid about this."

"Yes," Jon said simply. He looked at her a moment, his eyes filled with thoughtful reflection. At last he stood and placed his bowl in the dishpan. He shifted his shoulders about, as if to free them from their soreness, and turned back.

"Maybe you should write Carson. It wouldn't hurt to encourage him. Jimmy meant a lot to him." Jon hesitated. "And, while you're at it, send greetings to the Riley family from both of us. I'm sure Carson can pass that on."

He puckered his lips briefly, as if trying to find the right words to say. "I'm thinking that before I leave this North Country for Wyoming, I would like to stop in Juneau and see them."

"See who? Carson or Maria?"

He gave her a thin smile. "Does it matter?"

Abby laughed. "No, Jon. It does not."

It was late that night when Abby found a piece of stationery and sat to compose her thoughts, but for some reason, she was unable to start writing. Abby wondered at her fear.

Was she afraid to open the door of her heart when she still didn't know what the future held? Or was it something more?

With a sigh, Abby rose from the table and found her Bible. For a brief moment, she held it tight in her hands and prayed for guidance. Afterward, she sat back in her rocker and tried to resist the temptation to once again revisit the on-going debate in her head. What she needed was a simple word of encouragement, encouragement that the loss of Dundee and Jimmy, the pain of loving without being able to claim it, all this she could lay at God's feet and trust that he would work it out.

She looked at her Bible and wondered where to begin. In the Psalms of David? The suffering of Job? The hope in Romans? Uncertain, Abby opened Daniel and began to read. It was late when she at last placed a marker in her Bible and moved to her bed. She was far too weary to compose a letter to Carson now.

Perhaps tomorrow.

Chapter Thirty-Nine

With a sigh, Abby fell into her rocker and tried to relax. Josie was asleep, Jon was in the lobby talking to one of the miners that worked for them, and now tired and worn from the days work, she leaned back and closed her eyes.

She had spent the entire day helping to prepare the hotel for incoming customers since word was out that the mighty Yukon, heaving and grinding its way northward, was breaking up. It wouldn't be long before the steamers would once again return to Dawson, and today, The Grand had been bustling with the news.

With light now long in a June sky, summer was at last here, and though she welcomed it, Abby knew well that the restlessness that had plagued her heart all winter, if anything, was increasing with the length of each day. As she rocked back and forth in the silence of the room, Abby noticed old Dan's Bible lying on the shelf nearby. She reached for it and gently fingered its cover. During the winter months, she'd read it often, but since the activity at the hotel had picked up pace, she'd left it lying on the shelf since the night she'd tried to write Carson.

Abby sighed as she noted the beginnings of her letter still tucked inside her Bible. She had not finished it, much to her shame. She was still waiting for the right words, the right thoughts. Would they ever come?

She wanted to write him, knew she needed to do so, and yet each time she had sat to finish it, the turmoil in her heart would not let her continue.

Nothing had changed.

In frustration, Abby opened the Bible to the book of Daniel where she had left off her readings. As she flipped the pages, she paused to read a few hand-written words scribbled in a rather wobbly fashion at the top corner of one page.

Unlike the man who'd studied these words earlier, she had never thought to write on the pages of her Bible, though she could understand why Dan would do so. Lonely, discouraged and without a journal, she imagined that he'd found an outlet for the long, dark days of winter. She peered closely to the words he'd written. *Glory and praise, for I'm forgiven.*

For a moment, she considered the image of the miner in her mind. Of late, she had begun to think of him as a departed old friend, much like her dear Uncle Samuel. Abby lowered the Bible into her lap, and thought about the old gent. Would she and Jon someday look back to their days in Dawson with regret? Or was there still purpose for them to be here?

In truth, she was beginning to fear for her brother, especially for the emptiness she sensed inside him, for now that the days were growing longer, he appeared even more feverish in his attempts to make the journey worth their while.

Turning back to the Bible in hand, she began to read Daniel, chapter twelve, when she noticed another handwritten notation above the eighth verse. The words of that verse seemed extra poignant to her as she read them aloud.

"And I heard, but I understood not: then said I, O my Lord, what shall be the end of these things?"

Above the word *things*, Abby saw the notation, *see verse 13*. Curious, she turned to verse thirteen. *But go thou thy way till the end be: for thou shalt rest, and stand in thy lot at the end of the days.* Holding the Bible closer, she saw that there was yet another small scribbled note written above that last word of verse thirteen. It simply said, *he suffers, C.J. 17:15-16.*

For a brief moment, she drew her hand over his scribbled notation and wondered at its meaning. This last comment seemed far different from any other notes she'd found in his Bible. The others had reflected his heart's condition or his insights, which to Abby's surprise, had been far wiser than she had ever expected from someone of his circumstances. Abby studied the notation again.

C.J.? Was this someone's initials? If so, why would he write the numbers 17:15-16 alongside? The numbers looked to be references to verses, but *C J.?*

"Is our Rosebud sleeping?"

Startled, Abby looked up. "Oh, Jon, you frightened me. I didn't hear you coming."

"Sorry. It appears that you're fairly intent in your reading."

"Yes, in fact, come look at this. Old Dan made a strange note alongside some verses. I usually look up any scripture references that he makes, but this looks different. Have you any idea what it might mean?"

Jon looked over her shoulder as she held up the Bible. "C. J. 17:15-16. Looks like he's noting another scripture."

"Yes, but why didn't he make the reference clear, as he has in other places? There are no books that begin with both a C and a J. It's as if he didn't want anyone to readily understand this reference."

Jon walked away with a shrug. "I have some news," he said carefully. "I was talking to a miner in the lobby earlier. He's the new one that Madge hired to help me. She sent him to tell us that the mining commissioner wants her to stop working the property. Guess the owner of a neighboring claim has filed for a formal survey, believing that the boundaries are inaccurate. There's some dispute over the borders of three different claims in the area, and so until it can be settled, we're not allowed to work her claim."

Abby sighed. "Well, I'm sorry for Madge, but perhaps this will make it easier for you. You have your hands full enough with Dan Fogherty's claims."

Jon slumped into a chair and scratched his head. "There is always something to confound things, isn't there? In truth, Abby, I haven't much heart for this mining business any longer. I simply want to find enough to make it worth our while."

He sighed and turned to face her. "You and Josie deserve it. I've led you into such a mess. Once I feel we can recover enough funds to afford to be on our way, I intend to put someone in charge of the Smythe claims and be off, either to Juneau or to Wyoming, whatever you choose. We'll leave as soon as possible."

"All right," she said gently. "I'm glad that we are in agreement, Jon. I've been praying for you, for both our hearts. I have been so touched by Jimmy's death. In a way, nothing seems worthwhile now."

Jon took a deep breath and nodded. "Is that paper in your Bible the letter you were writing to Carson?"

She looked down to the folded stationery. "Yes, I was looking for something appropriate to say to him."

"Do you intend to finish it?"

She shrugged. "I imagine so, but I can't seem to feel entirely right about it."

Abby opened the Bible to where she had stuck Carson's letter and looked down. She'd been tired that night, and after reading Daniel, she'd simply tucked the letter inside the Bible, closed it, and gone to bed.

Job. She looked at the title at the top of the page and thought how Job had suffered far more, and yet did not blame God but instead drew even closer to his heavenly Father.

Job?

Abby looked at the heading on the page once again.

J? Was this not a book of the Bible that began with J?

Abby turned to Daniel and looked at old Dan's notation. "C. J. seventeen, fifteen and sixteen," she whispered.

See Job chapter seventeen, verse fifteen and sixteen? Could J. refer to Job, and C. to *see*?

At once, Abby flipped back to Job and read the verse. *And where is now my hope? As for my hope, who shall see it? They shall go down to the bars of the pit, when our rest together is in the dust.* And there, at the end of the verse, another hand-written notation: *C.J. 38:22-23.*

Abby then read chapter thirty eight, verses twenty-two and twenty-three. With a sense of wonder, she glanced up and saw Jon slipping into his jacket. "Jon, wait. Before you go outside, come give me your opinion about this."

While her brother paused and looked back, she read aloud. *"Hast thou entered into the treasures of the snow? Or hast thou seen the treasures of the hail, which I have reserved against the time of trouble, against the day of battle and war?"*

"So what's unusual about speaking of treasure?" he said. "I need to go back to work, Abby, not fuss with your interpretations."

Abby's heart moved within her as she looked at him. "Jon. I don't believe I'm looking at interpretations. I have a feeling this is something else, maybe even that Dan Fogherty was leaving a message in his Bible for someone and it's concerning a treasure in the snow!"

Though Jon had moved near the doorway, he hesitated and looked back. "A treasure in the snow, that's what it says?"

"Yes, the verses say that, but he also keeps making notations that lead from one verse to another. Come look at this."

Wordless, he started for her, moving quickly to her side.

She pointed out the scribbled notes at the end of the verses and then looked up. "Before I go on, find my journal and pen. Maybe you should write down these different notations and verses."

"I don't suppose it would hurt," he said carefully. He turned for the shelf where they kept her journal and a pen and then turned back to the table and sat down. "All right, what now?"

"The next reference is Job: 23:8-9: *Behold, I go forward*." Suddenly, Abby leaned in close to the page. "Above the word *forward*," she exclaimed, "he's written the words, *twenty-one paces*, and then where the next verse says *on the left hand*, he wrote another note, and it says, *ten paces*."

Abby stared at her brother, startled at her potential discovery. "Jon, this truly does appear to be some sort of direction, doesn't it?"

Jon stared at her. "I don't know, Abby, but I plan to write it all down and then see what we have. Job twenty-three, eight and nine. All right, is there anything else?"

"Yes," she said, "the ninth verse continues, *where he doth work, but I cannot behold him: he hideth himself on the right hand, that I cannot see him: But he knoweth the way that I take: when he hath tried me, I shall come forth as gold.*"

Abby swallowed. "By the word *gold*, Jon, he made a notation to see Job fourteen, seven." Seeing Jon nod, Abby turned the pages and read on. "*For there is hope of a tree, if it be cut down, that it will sprout again, and that the tender branch thereof will not cease. Though the root thereof wax old in the earth and the stock thereof die in the ground.*"

For several minutes, Abby read on from one reference to another, reading first the verse and then the notation as a clear picture of a certain place began to unfold. "Job 8:17, *His roots are wrapped about the heap and seeth the place of stones.* Job 18:16, *His roots shall be dried up beneath, and above shall his branch be cut off.* Job 24:8, *they are wet with the showers of the mountains, and embrace the rock for want of a shelter,* and Job 14:17-18, *my transgression is sealed up in a bag, and thou sewest up mine iniquity. And surely the mountain falling cometh to nought, and the rock is removed out of his place."*

Stunned, Abby looked up. "He's giving us a place to look, Jon. A tree with a branch cut off, in a wet place, a rock . . ." Abby shook her head. "Could it be?"

"Is that the last notation?" Jon asked.

Still dismayed at the discovery, Abby shook her head. "No," she said, "there's more. Here, he notes we should see Job twelve, twenty-two." Turning again, she read on. *"He discovereth deep things out of darkness, and bringeth out to light the shadow of death."*

Abby hesitated. "He's scribbled a note at the edge of the page." She struggled to read his writing. "It looks as if his words say, *take heed and be not deceived*: *Job 33:28-30."*

Without hesitance, Abby turned the pages and looked over the scripture before she spoke, her voice now full of wonder. "This is his final message, Jon. There are no more notations. Listen to this. *He will deliver his soul from going into the pit, and his life shall see the light. Lo, all these things worketh God oftentimes with man, to bring back his soul from the pit, to be enlightened with the light of the living."*

Dundee awoke with a start. He rolled from the bed, slipped on his pants and grabbed his shirt as he stepped to the window. He took in a breath of air and rubbed his chin as he gazed out to the swaying palm beside the patio. It was dark now, but a full moon lighted the shape of trees and the slope of the lawn that led to the ocean beyond.

He didn't feel good about the night. It hadn't been his idea, but his loneliness had been stronger than his wisdom, he guessed. And thinking about his considerations over the past few weeks, he knew he was ready to make a change.

Maybe it was the lack of a challenge. Maybe it was missing Abigail. Or maybe it was even the fact that a whole lot of gold was still out there possibly for the taking.

Was he missing out?

Dundee buttoned the last button on his shirt and tucked it in his pants then reached for his shoes. As he sat to put them on, Katherine rolled over and looked up.

"Dundee, are you leaving?"

"Yes. I think it's time."

She slipped close to the edge of the bed and watched him tie his shoes. "Will I see you tomorrow?"

"Not certain. Maybe."

"Too busy are we now?" she chuckled. "Come back as soon as you can."

"I'm not certain what will be ahead for me, Katherine."

She sat up and looked at him in the shadows of their darkened room. "What do you mean? You're talking in riddles, Dundee. Are you trying to tell me that you don't *want* to see me any longer?"

He finished lacing his shoe and then sat straight, giving her a long look. "No, not necessarily. You're a beautiful woman, Katherine. But I've unfinished business in other places, and it keeps calling me, that's all."

The room was silent a moment before she spoke, her voice sounded cool to his ears. "Dundee, you have a good job, a pleasant atmosphere, and you are welcome to my room anytime we can arrange it. Now what would be so important that it couldn't wait awhile?"

Dundee smiled. "Well, you might have a point there. But even you must realize, Katherine, that this can't go on. Secrets aren't kept forever, and I don't want to be running off at the last minute."

He sighed. "I feel that it's simply time for me to go. I'm afraid I'm in need of a change."

"A change?" she asked tartly.

"I deeply regret it," he said. "You are a special woman, and you won't be easy to leave. But I need to make a change in my life, and soon." He hesitated. "Who knows? I may be back. I can't say." Dundee rose to his feet and looked down at her. "I hope this won't be the last time I see you."

She sighed and fell back on her pillow. "Just go, Dundee."

"I'm sorry," he said. He stepped to her outside entry and started to move through the doorway when he heard her voice calling him.

"If you decide to come back to this island, things might be different."

"I know. I'll just have to take that chance, I guess." He paused. "Goodbye, Katherine. Stay well." And with that, Dundee stepped out on the darkened veranda and moved to the steps that led down to the shore.

When he reached the beach and heard the pounding surf boom across nearby rocks, he paused to look back to the stately Appleton mansion behind him. He sucked in a breath of air. Deep down, he knew he needed to make some adjustments in his life, but he wondered if he would live to regret leaving Katherine and all the potential she represented.

Chapter Forty

"Abigail, you and that little darlin' Josie will be sorely missed, even if I haven't seen you often these past few months."

Madge smiled as she jostled Josie on her knee much to the delight of the child. "Would you look at those curly locks around those rosy cheeks and a button nose? She is changing. Looking more like her momma every day."

Abby watched the two across the table from her, hoping always to remember the sight of Madge and Josie. The evening with friends was drawing to a close and their goodbyes would be final soon. Ingrid walked up and patted Josie on the head as she joined in on the child's fine entertainment.

"Ya, Abby. You will write to us as soon as possible?"

"I will," she said, smiling. "I promise."

"So has Jon convinced you?" Ingrid continued, her blue eyes turning to hers. "Hansen tells me he you are going to Juneau first."

Abby nodded. "Yes, although I've mixed emotions about it. If you want my opinion, I think he actually wants to visit with Miss Maria Riley before we go on to Seattle."

"Will you then go to Wyoming?"

"That's our plan. I want my family to see Josie, but we may have to stay in Seattle for a while." She shrugged. "Some of our plans depend on whether we find Dundee or not. If he is still missing, I'll have to contact a lawyer and see what can be done."

"Have you heard any more from his father?" Madge asked.

"Yes, as you know, he wrote after I told him of the baby and Dundee's disappearance, but this spring, he sent another letter to me. Although in both letters, he said that they've not heard from Dundee and that they fear the worst."

"Well, young lady. I am truly sorry to hear it, though I believe you will know soon enough," Madge said firmly. "I can feel it in my bones.

And listen, when you're in Juneau, you give a big hug to Carson for me, all right?"

Ingrid grinned. "She is beating about the bush, da?"

"Da," Abby chuckled. She looked from Madge's grinning face to that of her younger friend and felt a deep sadness in her heart. "I will miss you both so very much. You have been at my side for friendship and advice, and kept me in your prayers. You have helped little Josie to be healthy and safe and encouraged me. I cannot thank you enough."

"Aw, go on," Madge waved her hand. "Friendship is always two-way or it isn't a freindship a'tol."

"Ya, so," Ingrid nodded, "I agree."

"Did ya' say your goodbyes to Miss Mulroy, Abby?"

"Yes," she nodded. "Only yesterday, she came by The Grand to give her best wishes. And now she's off in search of new opportunity in Nome."

Madge shook her head. "She's one ambitious gal."

"Jon and I were glad to see her and to thank her in person. She's been kind, and I don't know what we would have done without her employment."

"True, I suppose. But her fortune was rewarded, too, ya?"

Madge handed Josie to Abby and nodded. "You're right on, Ingrid girl. 'Cause if you ask me, Abby, you and Jon did your share, especially when you darn near staked your life on revealing that scoundrel."

Ingrid sat beside Abby and reached for Josie's hand. "Has anyone ever heard if the authorities caught up with ol' Mr. Hanover?"

At that moment, Jon walked up and smiled down on them. "Sorry, ladies, I'm afraid time is getting on and I imagine we best be going to the hotel. By the time we gather everything into our rooms and settle in, it will be way past little Rosebud's bedtime."

Abby looked at Madge and Ingrid with a sly smile. "See, what did I tell you? Jon has such a wonderful relationship with Josie that I don't think I need a husband, not as long as I can keep my brother single."

Madge laughed with a deep, chesty chuckle while Ingrid giggled behind an upraised hand.

Jon frowned. "As a matter of fact, my dear sister, I've been thinking about this very thing myself, and I've decided that I've lived with you long enough. It's high time that you find someone else to take a turn at this worrisome chore."

Offering a cocky grin, he raised his eyebrows at Madge and Ingrid. "I'm not certain if she's ever listened to my advice, however. But I can always try."

"Do that," Madge said simply.

"Well," he said slowly, "I really am sorry that I have to pull you ladies apart, but I think it's time. We've a mighty fine room waiting for us, but an early morning out on the sternwheeler."

"Oh, Abby. Is that not wonderful of Miss Mulroy, to let you stay free at the Grandview as a parting gift? You must feel like a queen, ya?"

"Yes," Abby agreed, "although I'm sorry we have to leave now. A part of me doesn't want to say goodbye, even if it is to retire to such a grand place."

As Abby rose to her feet, Madge stood and encircled her arms about her and Josie. "I'm thinking we'll meet again," she muttered. "If not in this life, then in the next. So hang onto that thought."

Abby felt her eyes tearing as she nodded. "I will."

Ingrid reached for her and gave her a long embrace. "Come back sometime or let us plan to meet again, somewhere in the future."

"That will be my hope, Ingrid."

After their final goodbyes to Hansen, Mr. Joseph, and the many others they had enjoyed knowing in Dawson, Abby handed Jon the now wiggling Josie and they started off for the Grandview Hotel along Dawson's riverbank. As they walked in silence, the sights and sounds of Dawson began to fill her senses as if they were determined to make a long and final impression before they left. Abby was certain that she would carry the memories made here for as long as life allowed.

The more she thought of friends, of dear Jimmy, and even of the loyal Beauty who would remain behind with Ingrid and Hansen, the more her heart ached. She would miss them all, including Beauty, for though she'd been busy with the baby and her world within The Grand, Beauty had always remained at Jon's side at the claims. Sometimes, she'd hauled supplies back and forth on a sled, a delight to the dog's natural inclination, but whenever Abby had ventured outside, it was Beauty who would come running at her beck and call.

She would never completely understand how and why everything happened as it did, except that more and more, she saw how God had a guiding hand in things. It had been such a strange set of circumstances that day Jon and several miners set out with her, Bible in hand, and found the old tree stump halfway up a hillside of Eldorado number nine.

Twenty-one paces from the north end of the cabin, and ten paces to the left, they had found the tree. The stump had a branch, which was still struggling to live, and its roots were wrapped about a large rock at its base. And when they'd dug into a pit below and found a well-hidden cache, Abby and Jon had been shocked.

They were still amazed at the miracle of it. By the grace of God's Word and the careful messages of a determined man, Jon and a few miners had found Dan's cache, and it had assayed out at over five hundred thousand dollars, not quite the amount stated to the Smythe family, but an amazing amount nonetheless.

"You're awfully quiet," Jon commented. "Thinking about all the things that have happened to us?"

"That I am, Jon. It's amazing."

He nodded. "Listen, before we set off to our rooms," he said, "I want to confirm that Mr. Joseph, Hansen and I delivered the gold while you ladies were visiting. We secured it in Georgia's safe at the hotel for the night. Tomorrow, before we board the steamer *Flora* and head to Whitehorse, it will be crated in special gold boxes and I've listed both our names plus Carson's name and residence on them, just in case something happens to either you or me."

"Have you heard anything more about the railroad?"

"Yes. Hansen and Mr. Joseph both said they heard the rail is finished from Skagway to Log Cabin and that there's a good chance it will be complete to Bennett by the time we arrive."

Abby shook her head in wonder. "Can you imagine? A railroad already into such high country. How can they do that?"

"On the backs of some very brave men and animals," Jon grunted.

"What time do you want me waiting in the hotel lobby?"

"I believe we should start out by six in the morning," Jon said. "It will be early, but I want to make certain all our cargo is aboard and secure before departure at seven-thirty."

Abby sighed. "With as much light as there is in the sky and the restlessness of my soul, I will be ready."

"Just in case," he said, "I've asked for someone to knock on our doors at five o'clock."

In silence, they made their way up the Grandview's broad steps. At the lobby, Jon spoke to a clerk while Abby walked into the dining hall where she had once ran from Carson, brokenhearted. In spite of her and Josie's new dresses and a complete new set of circumstances, Abigail felt uneasy, as if she still did not fit well with the crowd that moseyed about. With a sigh, she decided that the feeling would serve her well in the future. No matter her financial state, she would never want to make another soul feel out of place.

When they at last made their way up the stairs, Abby held her breath as the young man leading them opened the door and she stepped inside. The plush velvet curtains and bedding, the bedside vanity, the colorful wallpaper and carpet, all of it breathtakingly luxurious compared to their previous simple surroundings.

Like Ingrid had said, she felt like a queen.

The next day, as well as the day after, Abby settled into the rhythm of walking about the sternwheeler and taking in the sunshine and the green hills around them. And as they plowed their way upriver, sudden memories often returned, remembrances of their small boats, the feeling of fear and anticipation, the rapids and swift waters. They had swept into this land of wind-whipped lakes and deep river passages with but a few crates filled with food and supplies, and at times, only the simple clothes on their backs.

Her heart ached at the memory of it all, of Carson's slow smile and quick wit, of his eyes and how they looked at her, and of his arms wrapped tight about her giving warmth to her shaking body. And mingled within, came fresh memories of Jimmy, of his bright smile and broad shoulders, of how he winked at her and called out loudly across the waters of Lake LaBerge. She recalled the dearness of his kind heart at every step of the way.

It was Jimmy who had wanted to join with her and Jon. Jimmy who had said it was good that she came with them.

It was Jimmy who she thought would never falter.

And when they at last rounded a bend in a broad, wide valley and Jon pointed out the buildings of Whitehorse ahead, it was only then that Abby could turn toward Dawson and silently wave her last goodbye to friends, both in this world and the next, a goodbye to a place that had been etched deeply into the secret places of her heart.

Chapter Forty-One

"Here she comes, Abby. Are you ready?"

Jon winked at her while the crowd around them cheered and a few men nearby threw their caps high into the air. With the hoopla growing noisier, the small narrow-gage train puffed and steamed its way to the station's platform then squealed to a halt while the men continued to roar their approval.

Abby clung to Jon's arm as they pushed forward and moved up the shiny steps into a car. It seemed to take but little time before the whistle sounded and "All aboard!" was shouted for a final time. Not far from where they found seats together, a young man, thin in his tattered coat, shouted to an older man across the aisle.

"How long since you been in one of these things, Jack?"

"Way too long for this sorry soul to remember," the companion whose eyes held a teary look called back.

Beaming now, the younger man laughed and then started to sing out loud as the train blew its whistle and started off. Soon, the whole car full of miners and a few ladies began to sing their slightly off-key rendition of *Home Sweet Home*, and as she and Jon joined in, Abby noted one primly dressed older couple who simply stared at the men in disapproval.

Abigail found it odd that in such circumstances some stiff and stately folks would find the plight of the poor miner returning to civilization to be unworthy of celebration. When the gentleman who began the song turned his gaze to her and the baby, Abby smiled, and suddenly raised her voice as loudly as she could muster.

Her voice rang out at the chorus. "*Home, home, sweet, sweet home; there's no place like home, oh, there's no place like home.*"

Indeed, the words sounded wonderful to her ears.

After the bravado of a few more loud comments, and some slightly ribald song concerning a miner, Abby began to wonder about the time they would spend in the infamous town of Skagway. Yet though the music was a bit suggestive, she couldn't help but smile at the way the men around them beamed at little Josie, especially when she began to clap her hands and rock her head to the music about her.

Fortunately enough, by the time they reached the small valley where the little village called Log Cabin rose out of the wilderness, most of the men had settled into light conversations and, to her relief, Josie had fallen asleep in Jon's arms. As they loaded and unloaded freight, Abigail studied the faces of her sleeping daughter and that of her twin, now leaning back in his seat with closed eyes as well.

He was right about Josie. She would fare better with a father, and though Jon had borne the weight of them on his shoulders, it was time for him to be free of her and Josie.

She wondered if their paths would part in Juneau, as they had in Benton. She had felt terribly lonely when he'd left for the Montana ranch. Then, as now, it would feel strange if Jon wasn't around. She and her twin had a near-silent language between them, and though there had been the usual conflicts as siblings, she realized that they both loved one another.

Abby turned to look out the window as the locomotive once again picked up speed. For several minutes, she gazed at the passing trees and the high distant mountains piercing a deep blue sky. As they steamed upward toward an approaching mountain pass, she once again thought of the Chilkoot Trail and of Sheep Camp, who many said was near to empty now.

Her mind drifted to the Riley family and Maria.

As far as she could tell, Maria Riley was a lovely woman, inside and out, but Jon was young and still full of the adventuring spirit. He would make a good husband and father someday, she was certain of it, but she also knew he had an unsettled heart. He had skills for ranching and riding. Could he fare well in a seacoast town? She hoped that Maria, if she ever began to care for Jon, would be able to see that his heart might not be able to survive a place like that.

Abby sighed.

Jon was capable. She wondered why she was worrying over him. Perhaps a woman always concerned herself about the members of her family, even if she had all she could handle with her own life. And certainly, there were enough unknowns in her future without having to worry about Jon's.

Carson.

At the thought of him, Abby felt a tight sensation about her heart. She had never admitted it to another soul, but deep inside she longed to be with him. The way he talked, honest and open, the way he smiled and held a positive approach toward life. All of those things she loved, and especially the integrity she saw in Carson's character. She knew that it would be easy to love him deeply, to walk her whole life alongside him, and though she wasn't certain that he would ever want her as his wife, she knew the innuendos had been there.

She needed to talk to him.

Before any future plans could be started, she wanted to hear what was in his heart, what had transpired in his faith. She wanted to understand his hopes for the future, or more to the point, if he would ever want her and Josie in his future, providing Dundee was indeed gone as she imagined he was.

It had been encouraging to hear of Carson's work and his contact with the Riley family in Juneau, but was this North Country the place where he wanted to be? If so, did she? It was so far away from their respective homes. It was a different world here, and yet there was opportunity and more than enough adventure if one had the heart for it.

"You look as if your thoughts are in a faraway place," Jon said quietly.

She turned. "I thought you were sleeping."

He smiled. "Probably was for awhile. The warmth of little Miss Rosebud here made me a little drowsy."

"You'll make a good husband and father someday, Jon."

He blinked and looked away. "Maybe, someday."

"Seems impossible that we're all grown up and that I have a little child of my own." Abby frowned. "Do you realize that in a mere twenty years, she will be my age?"

"Are you looking forward to going back to Benton and family?"

Abby nodded. "To see our family, yes." She looked outside her window for a moment to where the train appeared to huddle close to the deep forests and a rocky hillside. "But for some reason, I still have a strong pull in my heart for this place as well."

"Because Carson is here?"

"In part," she said. "You probably already know how I feel about him, Jon, but I find this still a difficult situation. I need to keep my mind on my real circumstances, not on what I would wish them to be." She sighed.

"I never told you this before, but as you may know, our parents were most unhappy about me marrying Dundee. Mother told me the night before our wedding that if I married him, it would be a decision I had to live with for the rest of my life." She looked at Jon. "And here I am, wondering what to do. If he's alive, it will be difficult. But I did make a promise, and I should at least try to keep it."

Jon's eyes met hers for a long moment before he turned his gaze out the window.

"Dundee wasn't at his father's ranch much before we met," Jon said. "He seemed intelligent, he'd been around, and I liked the way he could talk to almost anyone, but even then I never figured him to be the marrying kind." He looked at her. "So, I was surprised when he fell for you and wanted to marry you so quickly, and even more surprised when you felt the same."

"He had a certain magic about him," she said, looking away. "Back then, I thought his thrilling touch was all that mattered. We seemed to be mutually attracted in some sort of magnetic way." She sighed. "That, and the fact that I knew he came from a well-to-do family. I imagined that he would take care of me in good fashion." She shook her head. "I never even suspected the other side of him, the part that couldn't leave money on the table. I was shocked when we arrived in Seattle and he started gambling."

The silence between them lasted for several heartbeats before Jon spoke again. "Listen, as long as we're confessing some things here, I need to tell you that I felt quite responsible when we arrived in Seattle and I saw what he was doing." He hesitated. "I should have known, should have been able to warn you and encourage you to stay behind in Benton."

"What? Leave me behind?" she intoned in mock disgust. "In all honesty, Jon, I might not have wished for some of my circumstances, but I've learned a lot struggling through each thing—how to pray and wait, how to keep going, how to love deeper. I don't believe that would have happened by staying home. And then there's Josie to love." She leaned close to him.

"Shame on you for thinking to leave me behind, Jonathan David. Shame on you."

Chapter
Forty-Two

"Will this be kept on deposit for the entire two days?" the clerk asked.

Jon nodded. "Yes," he said simply.

"Very well," the clerk responded. He looked down to the papers Jon had filled out. "Let me see, these crates are to be listed in the names of Mrs. Abigail Andrews and Mr. Jon Colton. Is that right?"

"On second thought," Jon said carefully. "I would like to list four of our crates as belonging to Mrs. Abigail Andrews and four of them to be set up in my name. Would that be an inconvenience to you?"

"No, sir. Not at all. You will just need to fill out new bank deposit cards and then sign the appropriate ones."

"All right," Jon said. He took the new forms and made the adjustments. After he and Abby finished and handed them back, the clerk waved to a well dressed man who came directly over to where they stood.

"I believe we've signed all the papers, sir, and so the freight can be unloaded now."

The manager of the bank read over the signature cards and smiled. "Indeed, everything looks to be in order." He looked up and shook Jon's hand then nodded to Abby. "It's very good to be doing business with you, Mr. Colton, Mrs. Andrews. We will have your crates kept in a well-sealed vault and have them at the ready."

"Thank you," Jon mumbled.

With Abby alongside, Jon turned and walked from the building, and after they stepped from the doorway, Abby heard Jon release a long sigh.

She imagined that once they had their heavy crates of gold sealed inside the bank vault, he would feel much better. While she watched, Jon walked up to the four men lingering by the wagon and spoke to them, waving to the bank clerk who stood near a back door. After the men began to unload the wagon, he walked back to where Abby stood waiting.

She smiled at him. "I do believe you are nervous about carrying all this with us."

"Shouldn't I be?"

She bent to pick up Josie as Jon stepped up closer.

"Listen," he said, "I want to stay here and make certain it's all unloaded and put in the vault as discussed."

Abby sighed. "Wealth is as much a burden as poverty, I have a feeling."

"Wealth is all a matter of perspective," he retorted. "Around Dawson, this didn't seem to be anything to worry about. Gold nuggets and dust traveled from hand to hand as if it was nothing sometimes. Earl Cummings said he took out over ten thousand dollars worth of gold one day last year."

Jon shifted his body in order to watch the men and scratched his neck thoughtfully. "Although, as I think on his words, I imagine that was a mighty big day even for him. Jimmy and I were lucky to find fifteen dollars worth a day on Madge's claim, and after paying for the workers, we didn't clear much more than that off each Smythe claim."

"Maybe most of the gold had already been taken out before we arrived in Dawson."

"That's what a lot of folks said," he muttered. "Guess knowing that we had meager pickings made it even more remarkable when we pulled up all those sacks from Dan's cache." He started to move back to the wagon. "Go on to the hotel, Abby. I'll catch you there later."

"All right," she called out. "But remember, since you're so rich, I'm expecting you to take me out to dinner." She smiled. "Josie and I are hungry."

Jon laughed. "Indeed. We've starved ourselves through enough months. Maybe it is time to have a little celebration."

And with that Jon walked on to the wagon while Abby turned for the hotel, her daughter tucked neatly on her hip. She would look forward to a bath and a wonderful meal. They'd held out only a few sacks of gold for their travels, but it would certainly be enough to pay for a good dinner, and probably much more, if she knew Jon.

She looked forward to the two days they'd planned to stay in Skagway. Although the trip back to Skagway was much easier than the trip into the Yukon, she and little Josie were weary from all the commotion.

A bath, dinner, and sleep, and in that order, sounded most welcome!

"There goes a mighty attractive woman if ever I've seen one," Rube said. He stuck his cigar back in his mouth and reached for his card.

Dundee glanced up to see a brief flash of dark hair piled at the back of a woman's head before the lady slipped beyond sight of the swinging doors. He hesitated.

Could it have been Abby?

As he thought about it, he decided that he'd also caught sight of a smaller head. The woman was carrying a child. It wouldn't be Abby.

"Are you in, or not?"

Dundee smiled. "I'm in and I'll raise you ten."

Rube and his friend Mack tossed in their hands with a groan. "Well, that's enough for me," Rube growled. "Think I'll take a break and head into the dining room and have some dinner. You and Mack want to join me?"

"Sounds good to me," Mack said.

Dundee shrugged. "Thanks, but I'm not hungry."

Rube nodded upstairs. "You joining us later?"

Dundee slowly raked in the chips as he thought it over. "Not sure about tonight. I made some plans earlier, though maybe I could put them off."

"So, the pretty Miss Belinda is singing tonight, is that it?" Mack smiled. "Don't know if I've known anyone with a better knack for finding pretty women than you, my friend."

"Well," Rube said, "we won't be starting until late in the evening. If you can find the time, you know where we are. See ya' around."

Dundee nodded then leaned back in his chair and watched his companions stroll across the room and out the swinging doors. He rubbed his eyes a moment, then gathered in his chips and waved to the barkeep.

"You ready for a count, Mr. Andrews?"

"That I am, Gus, and then I'll call it a day. Quit while you're ahead, I always say."

"Good plan, Mr. Andrews."

"You want a menu now for a little food or can I get you another drink?"

"Nope," Dundee said as he untangled his legs and rose to his feet. He smiled. "Can we put the tab I've accrued this afternoon on the books and let me catch you later?"

"Sure, Mr. Andrews," Gus drawled.

After a polite nod and a smile at the man behind the counter and the young woman beside him, Dundee stepped forward and pushed back the swinging doors that led to the lobby. He noted that the place was filling up since it was the dinner hour.

He imagined he'd bring Belinda back here and they would eat after her shows, so maybe for now he'd find his room and take a nap. Pushing his hat back on his head, he began to move to the stairway when he heard a small child's voice around the corner of the wall.

At the sound of the woman's voice hushing the child, Dundee came to a halt. Slowly he turned and walked to the far wall where he could stand by a coat rack and still have a partial view of the dining hall. Keeping himself well hidden, he made a quick sweep of the dining area until he found the familiar faces of Abigail and Jon.

At first he was startled to see them, and then he took in a deep breath and wondered at his surprise. After all, waiting and watching for Jon and Abigail had been one of the reasons he'd come to Skagway—that, and the fact that the gambling and entertainment was almost nonstop. Though he wasn't certain if they'd come out of Dawson by the same route they went in, he knew for certain, through ship and hotel records, that they had indeed gone through Skagway early last spring.

With growing curiosity, he studied them while they sat eating. They looked relaxed and healthy enough, he decided. Jon's hair was longer and his chin now held a short, well-trimmed beard, and Abby, if anything seemed to hold even more of a glow. She was an attractive woman, though it appeared that she'd put on a little weight.

He studied the child that sat in her lap. The little girl had dark curly ringlets about her small face, and above her round rosy cheeks, big dark eyes looked about the room with grave curiosity. He stared at her long and hard, and as he did, a lump grew in his throat.

Had Abby been sick because she was going to have a baby?

That had been mere weeks after their marriage. He'd been careful, hadn't he? How could it be? And yet, he didn't see any other man with her except for Jon.

Dundee stepped back and slowly moved to the staircase with his heart thumping in his chest. *A child?*

How in the world would he ever handle that?

The sun was high in the sky the following morning as Dundee adjusted his hat and stepped into the bank. It shouldn't be an issue since he had recently become acquainted with Mr. Jackson, the bank's owner. Rube had given him enough information at last night's table that he figured if he dropped a few names, it would speed things up a bit as well.

All he needed was to place his signature on his wife's account. He wasn't certain what that would mean in terms of finance, but by the look of Jon and Abigail, he knew they hadn't come out of the Yukon penniless. Then his next stop would be the steamship office.

He sighed. After that it was all up to Abby and Jon.

But either way, he'd have an option.

Chapter
Forty-Three

Abby felt the rhythm of her steps in concert with the happiness in her heart. It had been a good day so far. She and Josie had slept into the late hours of morning, eaten breakfast, shopped for clothes as well as a gift to take to Maria, and then rested again following a simple lunch.

It was a little past two in the afternoon. Jon would be coming soon. They had decided to take a carriage ride and explore Skagway and all its changes before the dinner hour, and though it was a bit early to dress for dinner, Abby quickly changed into her newest purchases she'd draped over the bed. For the next two days, she would wear her new skirt and blouse and save Carson's cheerful blue dress for their time in Juneau.

Juneau.

It didn't seem possible that they were but a few hours north of Carson. Though she and Jon had no way of knowing the exact date they would arrive, she had finally written Carson to tell him that she and Jon would take a sternwheeler up the Yukon River and the White Pass Rail to Skagway, and after that, they would book passage to Juneau before traveling on to Wyoming. At the thought of seeing him and Maria soon, Abby felt her pulse rising.

Abby reached for Josie and pulled a white embroidered cotton dress over her head. She was about to tie its small red sash about her daughter's waist when a knock sounded at the door. Finishing quickly, she hurried to the door, curious about the travel information Jon would have.

But when Abby opened the door, instead of seeing Jon, a man with soft brown eyes and sandy-colored hair smiled back at her.

Abby felt the air in her lungs escape with a loud whoosh.

"Dundee? Oh . . . Oh, Lord." Abby's mouth dropped open and her knees nearly buckled beneath her as she stepped back in complete dismay.

"Abby," he said gently, "I know this must be a shock to you." He slowly stepped inside as she backed up to the bed and stood gaping at him.

He reached for her arm to steady her. "I'm sorry to surprise you this way, but I didn't know how else to talk to you, except to simply come to your room."

Pressing her fingers to her lips, Abby pulled free from his hand and scooted sideways, moving away from him as if he was a snake slithering into their room.

Dundee stood quietly, watching her as she tried to catch her breath. She struggled to find words, but instead of wanting to talk, she suddenly felt the strongest need to scream at him. She wanted to hit him, to pound her fists against his chest.

Taking another deep breath, she whirled around and crossed the room to where Josie stood on wobbly legs by the dressing table, whimpering now in scared tones. As Abby bent to pick her up, Josie fell to her bottom and wailed, holding up her hands for comfort. It was as if she understood the distress inside Abby's heart.

Abby picked up her child and spun on her heels to face him. She swallowed.

"Well, don't just stand there, Dundee," she said with a steely voice. "Shut the door."

The moment Abby opened her door Jon knew something was terribly wrong. But when he stepped inside and saw Dundee standing across the room, he felt as if someone had hit him square in the solar plexus.

"Dundee?"

"In the flesh. How are you, Jon?"

Jon stood in shocked silence. Somewhere between deep disappointment and outrage, he moved to the bed, threw his hat on it, and then stood staring at Dundee for a long moment.

Dundee shrugged. "I know it's a shock to see me, Jon. But I'm all right, and I finally found you."

"What happened to you? Where have you been?" Jon found the level of his voice rising with each word.

Dundee offered a slow smile. "Well, I was just explaining all that to Abigail," he said carefully. "I came very close to not getting out of Seattle in time. Had some pretty sore losers on my tail." He paused and nodded, as if to emphasize his woe.

"Took awhile to shake them and then I came to Skagway. I searched through some ship records and several hotel registries and finally confirmed that you had indeed been in town, but," he shrugged, "not knowing for sure which way you'd gone, I decided to wait here."

"Which way we'd gone? How many trails are there to Dawson?" Jon snapped. "Only two, and one of those is near to shut down. Besides, we've been in Dawson for a year, Dundee. You had plenty of time."

"Well, I really wasn't able to come here until just a few months ago, and I was advised it would be better to simply wait." Dundee nodded toward Josie who was pulling herself to her feet with the curtain. "I had no idea about this little one. Honest."

Jon shook his head. He didn't know what to say. The man was an incredible liar as far as he was concerned, but how could he say anything with Abby here, knowing how she felt about being loyal to her husband.

"So," Jon snorted. "Now what? What do you want from us?"

"What do I want?"

"Well, if you had wanted to help your wife and partner," Jon growled, "you would have. But you didn't, and you waited here. I imagine this looked like a fairly good place, what with the women and the gambling. Kept those few months from keeping your sorry . . ."

"Jonathan!"

Jon swallowed back his words and turned to his sister who stood near the window with Josie.

"It will do no good to be angry," she said. "I felt the same way, Jon. I understand. But Dundee and I have been talking and perhaps you should hear what he has to say."

Jon drew in a sharp breath and released it quickly. "All right. I'm listening."

Dundee made a small gesture with his hands. "We can talk here, or we could go to the dining room for a late lunch. Perhaps we could discuss things better on full stomachs rather than standing here."

"Abby and I aren't hungry," Jon said. "Just tell us what you want and let's deal with it, and then you can make dinner plans later. Whatever else you do with your life is your business. How much of the gold were you figuring to get since Abby and I did all the work?"

Dundee shrugged. "Never a man to mince words, are you, Jon. Well, since it was my deal, my friends that made the arrangements, I would imagine I should have a portion of that eight hundred thousand."

"It wasn't that much. Five at the most, and half that belongs to the Smythe family."

Dundee crossed the room and stood by the window, gazing out toward the gathering storm clouds darkening the sky. "What do you think my bringing you here and financing this adventure is worth to you, Jon?"

"Fifty thousand."

Dundee turned with a raised eyebrow. "Fifty? And for Abby?"

"She paid her way with more effort than you know. Seventy-five thousand. But it will be in her name and only her name."

"And that completes our share?" Dundee intoned.

"If that's how you choose to look at it."

Dundee nodded thoughtfully. "All right. I guess that's fair enough. You have the gold here in Skagway?"

"Yes. In the bank under my name."

"All of it?"

"Enough."

"We'll need to make arrangements to take it to the Smythes," Dundee said slowly. "I've checked with the steamship desk and know that we can sail from here to San Francisco two nights from now. If you would want to come with me, that would be my choice of departure and then we can take a train across country. I'd prefer to avoid Seattle."

"Jon," Abby asked quietly, "were you able to make reservations on the steamer for Juneau tomorrow?"

"Yes."

She nodded. "I would imagine those could be transferred for later arrangements to include Dundee?" Abigail looked at him without any emotion in her eyes, but he could tell from the way she said the word Juneau what she was thinking.

"Doesn't appear I have any choice. What about you, Dundee? You certain you want me along?"

Dundee looked up from where he stood studying the street below. "I know we have several things to settle, Jon. But I would hope we could come to some agreeable conclusion. Perhaps we can meet for dinner or afterward to talk?"

Jon swallowed. How he would manage to avoid Dundee over the next month, he didn't know. But he would. And he might as well be honest.

"I haven't the slightest inclination to talk with you, Dundee. I imagine you and Abby should do so, but leave me out of it." He looked at Abby directly. "Let me know if there's anything you want me to do, otherwise I'll check back with you at suppertime."

"Jon and I were about to take a carriage ride about town," she said, turning to Dundee. "Maybe you should join me instead of Jon and we can discuss things a little more."

Dundee nodded. "I should be able to do that in an hour or so."

"Good," Abby said. She looked at Jon. "You certain you don't want to come along?"

"Certain," he said quickly.

Abby bent to pick up the baby and then after a small hesitation, she handed her to Dundee, who looked as if she'd handed him a dirty puppy. Jon watched as Abigail began to place a shoe on Josie's foot. When the child wiggled and complained, Dundee looked quite uncomfortable.

"Since you have such strong feelings, Jon," Abby continued, "maybe it will be best if we meet for breakfast tomorrow, and then directly after, we can change our steamship reservations. Would that meet with your approval?"

Jon's hand was already on the doorknob as she spoke. He swung the door open and nodded. "See you tomorrow," he said simply. Still hot beneath his collar, he stomped out.

That night Abby ran Dundee's proposal over and over in her mind as if in the repetition, it would sit better on her stomach. But no matter how she played the words in her head, they only seemed to deepen her frustration. He wanted to take the gold to the Smythe family, and after that they would split up their monies and, if she chose, their lives. He would go to Kansas City and she would be free to return to Benton or stay with him.

You've changed, he'd said, *and though I thought I could change when I married you, I'm not sure I can. This is it, Abby. This is who I am. So for the next few months, we need to consider if our marriage is workable.* He finished by saying he wanted to give her time to think.

Time to think?

His words had hurt her to the core. She wasn't certain why she'd begged him to reconsider his lifestyle, but in spite of the bitterness in her heart, she asked him to try, for Josie's sake if nothing else. He'd only given her that alluring, warm smile that was uniquely his.

Oh, God, would he ever change?

He had such potential. But he was blind.

Or did he know intuitively that she would not want to seek a divorce, and thus by default, he could go on with his games while she would forever live alone, separated from the need for someone's arms, for comfort, for a partner in raising a child and securing a home.

He'd seemed sincere enough, telling her with downcast eyes that he would provide. Either way she chose, he would give her money, he said, even if they separated. But did she believe him?

No. Not really. He would give her money if he *had* it, and in the long run, she wasn't certain if he would. Still, what choice did she have?

Abby began to weep silently in her bed.

Somehow, she had known all along that it was wrong of her to begin to care for another. How would she ever tell Carson? If they left for San Francisco in a few days, she would never see Carson again. She couldn't bear writing him another letter.

She couldn't.

And Jon?

Abby could still see the look of anger on her brother's face. He would never trust Dundee, and if she stayed with him, she would rarely see Jon as well.

Sobbing, Abby rolled to her side. She was too brokenhearted to even pray.

Chapter Forty-Four

Jon strode up to the door in the driving rain and quickly stepped inside the musty building where men and women were jammed inside, full and tight. He looked around, incredulous at the number of people in the room. He turned to a man beside him who appeared fairly calm.

"Excuse me, can you tell me what's going on here?"

"Not sure," the man said. "I came down to book passage this morning and found that the ship that left last evening had posted a distress call, and now the steamer I planned to take has been cancelled entirely."

"Cancelled due to weather?"

"That and the fact that they are planning some kind of rescue attempt, although no one seems to know what's happening with the effort."

"What time did the ship leave last night?"

"I believe it was around seven or eight o'clock. It was a full one. Heard they went aground on some rock in the Lynn Canal."

Jon looked back to the young man, startled. "Not far from here?"

"Was told about halfway to Juneau."

Thinking about the reservation he'd made yesterday, Jon was shocked that the ship in trouble had sailed off within a day of their departure. The thought of them sinking in the cold Pacific with small Josie along gave his heart a jolt. Maybe they were fortunate after all.

"Where was the ship headed?"

"My understanding, all ports south and ending in San Francisco."

"San Francisco?"

"It's what I heard. Lots of folks heading out of the gold country with their stashes, I heard say. One was seen to take on board a couple crates of it."

With a cold sensation growing deep in his gut, Jon turned his gaze out the small window then started for the door. "Thanks, mister. I appreciate it."

"Certainly. Oh, by the way. They said earlier if you need to know who's on board the ship and what's happened, they should have an update with a list of passengers by late this afternoon."

"Thanks," Jon called out, but his mind wasn't on the steamer any longer. It was on the young clerk and the deposit cards at the bank.

Abby felt listless that morning as the wind and the rain pelted her window. She and Josie had breakfast early and then waited around in the dining room hoping to spot Jon, but he hadn't come. She wondered what she would do all day. It would be nerve-racking to sit and wait for either Dundee or Jon to contact her.

As she leaned down to change Josie's top, she wondered at the journey ahead. Her little daughter seemed to take things in stride much better than she had ever imagined a ten-month-old baby could handle, but another long week in a steamship and more travel by train would frazzle the both of them, without a doubt.

Filled with anxious thoughts, Abby had just finished changing Josie when a knock sounded at the door. With a sense of dread, she stood looking across the room, still recalling the shock of seeing Dundee only yesterday. Did she want to talk to him again? Abby could feel the blood pounding in her temples as she walked forward.

"You alone?" Jon said quickly.

"Jon," she sighed with relief. "I'm glad it's you. Yes, I'm alone. Why?"

Jon stepped inside and closed the door. He looked at her with wide eyes. "I went down to the steamship office to see if I could adjust the reservations," he said.

"And did you?"

"No."

"No?" She studied her brother's guarded demeanor. "Is something wrong?"

"I think we need to see if we can find Dundee."

"Find him? What's that suppose to mean?"

"Two things, I'm afraid. And neither one is very good."

Abigail sat back on the bed and stared at him. "What? You're not making sense to me, Jon. What are you trying to say?"

"First of all, all four crates of gold that were in your name at the bank are gone."

Abby felt her jaw slacken. "They're gone? But how?"

"You're husband, being the head of the household, of course, said he was in charge of them. He removed them from the bank."

Abby rose slowly to her feet. "What? But . . . but we aren't leaving for a couple of days, are we?"

"Maybe *we* aren't, but I have a feeling that Dundee might have left already."

"Left?"

"Abby, we have to see if we can find him. Did he tell you where he was staying?"

"Yes. Strangely enough, he's staying right here in this hotel."

"I guess that doesn't surprise me," he muttered. "Come on, let's go talk to the hotel clerk and see what we can find out."

Abby gathered up Josie and followed Jon out the door. As they walked down the hall and toward the stairs, she could tell by Jon's quick footsteps and somber expression that he didn't want to talk, but she was certain that he was keeping something from her.

"What is it, Jon? You're not telling me everything."

"Nothing to tell yet, Abby. I will when we know more."

As they stepped up to the desk, Jon spoke to the clerk. "Pardon me," he said, "Abigail Andrews and her baby were planning to meet her husband Mr. Andrews in the lobby, but we haven't heard from him. We haven't a key. Might you show us to his room or leave a message?"

"A Mr. Andrews, you say?"

"Yes."

"Let me see, when I arrived early this morning, I saw a letter addressed to Mrs. Abigail Andrews at the desk. Oh, yes, here it is. I believe it was left for you last night."

Abby's eyes shifted to her brother's face before she reached for the sealed gray envelope. With Jon at her elbow, they moved to the chairs near the lobby windows. She handed Josie to Jon and then sat to open the letter.

> *My dearest Abigail,*
>
> *I know you must think me the world's biggest cad, and I believe you would be entirely correct. You are a beautiful young woman, inside and out, and my inability to care for you as a man has little to do with you, Abby, and a great deal more to do with me.*
>
> *I would ask you to forgive me, but that would appear to be presumptuous of me. Instead I am doing what I believe will be the fairest and best thing for you. I am taking what I feel is my share of this adventure and leaving for San Francisco. I plan to give half of what I've taken to the Smythe family, as promised, and let you and Jon do likewise. But instead of traveling together and putting you through more torture than you need, I am simply freeing you to find a new life.*
>
> *I will contact a lawyer when I return to Kansas City. You will be hearing from him as to the proceedings for a divorce. Last night, I told you it was your choice, but I never should have placed you in that position. In all honesty, I don't see myself settling into the kind of relationship you need, especially with a baby at hand. Abby, I am freeing you to go on.*
>
> *Forgive me for my weakness, Dundee*

Abby took in a shaky breath. Wordless, she handed Jon the letter. He read it silently then looked up. "I'm sorry, Abby."

Was she sorry? How did she feel? Her soul grieved for what could have been. But as she studied her brother's eyes and saw the moisture within them, she was surprised. "You're sad that he left?"

"No, Abby," he said carefully. "I'm sorry to tell you that there may be worse news."

Abby stared at him as he reached for her hand. "The steamship that left last evening went down in the waters near Juneau. Reports are not good for any rescue. Dundee may have been aboard."

Abby started. As a cold sensation swept up her arms, she shrank back from his hand.

"It can't be," she whispered. "Is that what you were keeping from me? Do you think Dundee was on that ship?"

"They will be posting a list of passengers soon. Until then, we can't be certain, but it was a ship whose final port was San Francisco. Dundee took your gold boxes out of the bank late yesterday, and the letter was left last night."

Abby closed her eyes as a low moan escaped her throat. "Oh, Dundee . . ."

Chapter Forty-Five

Carson slipped into his jacket, closed his door and started down the steps.

"Good morning, Mr. Stuart. And how are you this lovely day?" Mrs. Knudsen stood beside her desk in her housedress not far from the front door.

"I'm doing very well, Mrs. Knudsen. Very well." He gave the broad-hipped woman a knowing smile as she raised her brows.

"Indeed!" she said brightly. "Not *fine* this time, but *very well*? Has this anything to do with the widow Mrs. Andrews being in town?"

"It might at that. Time will tell, Mrs. Knudsen." He smiled.

"Are you on your way to work then, so late today?"

He hesitated, his hand at the door. "Actually, I'm taking some time off this morning. My friend Jon along with his sister Mrs. Andrews and her child are leaving today for Seattle and then Wyoming, and so I want to spend some time with them before they go."

"Wyoming? My, so far."

He nodded. "Yes, but hopefully not too far, if you know what I mean." He grinned. "I must be off. Don't wait up for me, Mrs. Knudsen."

"Go on, Mr. Stuart! You can be such a flirt." She smiled at him then waved her hand. "I will hope that the day be good for you, Mr. Stuart. The Mrs. Andrews looks to be a kind soul."

"She is, Mrs. Knudsen. I do believe she is. Well, you have a good day!"

"You also, Mr. Stuart."

Carson wasn't quite certain why his countenance felt full to overflowing and his step a bit brisker than normal. It wasn't as if all had been settled. What's more, he and Abby had been unable to spend much alone time together since she and Jon arrived three days ago. And yet, he held a sense of things that bode well in his heart.

Abby, he knew, was still in shock and carried a certain guilt with her husband's loss, that he well understood. For even though Dundee may have pressed his luck a few more times than prudent, she had loved him and grieved for his soul. He could see it in her eyes.

As he walked along in the morning sun, Carson thought about that first glimpse of her and Josie at the hotel. Abby had changed over the last few months. She looked stronger somehow. And not only rounder in form, but her eyes held a deeper level of peace than he'd remembered. And Josie, healthy and beautiful, had much to do with it, he was certain. They had all experienced so much change since that day on a dock in Seattle.

Carson's mind turned to Jimmy, and once more, he felt the deep hurt whenever he thought of his friend. He sighed. It would take a long time, maybe never to overcome the loss of him.

Taking a deep breath, Carson looked around as he stepped past dockside buildings and moved toward the foot of the hill, toward the several homes tucked into the shadows of his favorite knoll. For a minute, he allowed his eyes to rest at the upper edge of the knoll, a place where he often sat to dream.

It would be good to have Abby go with him up there, to see his *place of peace* as he called it. The idea had come to him last night, and the more he thought about it, the more certain he was that this would be the appropriate spot to tell her what was on his heart.

"Look, dear, here comes Carson. I see him walking up to the house."

Hearing Mrs. Riley's words, Abigail moved swiftly to the door and stepped out on the porch. The six of them, Maria, Jon, the Rileys and she and Carson, had made plans to gather for lunch and then to ride a coach on a tour of town before they said their goodbyes. The steamer bound for Seattle, with she, Jon and Josie aboard, would leave at two in the afternoon.

Smiling broadly, Carson walked up to the porch and reached for her hands. She briefly studied the way his eyes sparkled under the dark brows that tilted downward just enough to give his face a boyish, mischievous grin.

"Before we have lunch," he said gently, "I'd like you to come with me for a walk. It's been a whirlwind since you've been here, Abby, but I feel I must talk with you privately before we part." He smiled. "I already spoke with Mrs. Riley last night. She said she would watch Josie."

Abby chuckled. "You've thought of everything, haven't you, a place to stay, dinners, a buggy ride about town, even a jaunt to the incredible glacier in the valley. What more could you possibly say or do?" She raised an eyebrow lightly as he continued to smile.

"You still read my mind all too well, Miss Abigail. But you will come, won't you? I want to show you my favorite place in all of Juneau."

She smiled. "Yes," she said. "I wouldn't miss it."

After they spoke to Mrs. Riley and slipped quietly out the front door, Carson again took her by the hand and led her toward the hill above the Riley home. They hiked along a narrow winding path rising from the street below to the trees above. Though talking earlier, as the climb grew steeper, they remained silent while they trekked the upper reaches of the narrow footpath and came to the crest of the hill. Winded, Abby paused for a breath.

"There," Carson said. He motioned to the town of Juneau nestled against the foot of a mountain and the narrow ocean channel separating it from the rugged island across the way. "So, what do you think of the view from here?"

Abby took his hand and leaned into him as she looked around. "It's breathless, Carson, as am I. Do you lead your lady friends off to such places often?"

He grinned at her. "I wish. Will you come back, Abby, and be my lady friend?"

She looked into his dark gray eyes that held such hope and gave him a soft smile. "Perhaps so. Have you decided that this area will be home for you?"

He turned, looking out over the channel to where several smaller boats bobbed not far from a dock and a larger ship. It was one of those days that held a sparkling freshness to it following a storm.

"Yes, I think so. I like it here, Abby. I feel there is a future awaiting me, and I love the lush forests, the fresh clear sky when the rain blows on, the way the clouds hang low on the snowcapped mountains surrounding this place. I've hiked about extensively and find the area incredible. There is plentiful water all summer and all manner of creatures about."

He took in a light breath and turned back to her. "Mr. Russell has made innuendos recently that he may expand and set up another press in Fairbanks, farther north. He believes, with the gold discoveries and increased businesses there, that the potential is threefold of Juneau. But he wants to keep his business here as well and is considering me for managing it."

Carson slipped his arms around her and pulled her against him, tucking her against his chest. She snuggled her face into his shoulder and felt the warmth of him. In the silence, her heart began to flood with emotion.

When he leaned back and touched her chin, lifting her face to him, she saw the concern in his eyes.

"What's this?" he said. "Tears? For me or for Dundee?"

She swallowed. "I'm not certain, Carson. I know my emotions are on an edge, but you must know how wonderful it feels to have your arms about me and to know you care."

Carson ran his fingers across her cheeks, wiping away the moisture. "Am I going to have to let go of you and fish for a handkerchief?"

She chuckled and wiped her eyes. "No, don't let go. Don't ever let go." As she spoke, Abby felt his arms tighten about her shoulders.

"I don't intend to, Abigail. Not ever."

She looked into his eyes as he bent to kiss her. His lips were cool from the breeze about them but full and firm, and as he pressed against her, she felt the warmth growing between them as she had on the banks of the mighty Yukon. She relaxed into him, feeling the heat of their passion and something beyond. After a few long moments, she pulled back.

"Do you always kiss your lady friends on a hill in broad daylight like this?"

"If they'll let me," he whispered. "Abby, I love you. I want you for my own. Is this a possibility for you?"

She gave him a gentle smile. "Yes. I need to spend some time with my family, and someday, I would like you to meet them. That may have to occur first."

He nodded. "And I want you to meet mine. When you're ready, you write and set the date. If it be your wish, we can marry in your home and then travel to mine. Afterward, I would like to bring my bride back to Juneau. Is that also a possibility?"

"It is, Carson. Oh, yes," she smiled. "It truly is."

Epilogue

Abby breathed deep and stared at the wooden framing of a large two-story house. There were four men working about the area, the sound of hammers against nail and wood rang in her ears as she studied the sight in the evening twilight. Beyond the framework of what she someday would call home, rose a steep and rugged slope, the ridge that Carson so loved was but a small footstool to the high snowcapped mountain beyond. Abby studied one small waterfall streaking down its rocky face.

They would hike up there someday, Carson said, though he cautioned that they would have to be careful. It was no place for sissies, he'd joked.

Smiling, Abby turned and watched Carson as he led her small toddler up the street. He was bent over talking to her as Josie frowned and shook her head. Abigail smiled.

Poor Carson. Now he had two stubborn and willful women in his life.

With a deep breath, she shifted her gaze to the magnificent view toward the mountains across the channel on the island that was called Douglas. They would have an incredible view of the island's tall gray peak from the back of their home. As her eyes swept from west to east, she saw two eagles soaring high on the breeze that swirled about Mt. Roberts, the mountain to the eastern edge of Juneau that rose green and round above town.

The area held a lush environment, so different from her Wyoming home. And yet the same love she'd felt for the Wind River Mountains seemed to find an equal attachment to this rugged land as well. She would be content here.

She smiled. In truth, she would be content anywhere Carson wanted to be.

Carson, with Josie now tucked securely in his arms, stepped up close to her, released a deep breath, and smiled. "So what do you think, Mrs. Stuart?"

"I think we've found a place to stay awhile, Mr. Stuart."

Abigail kissed him on the cheek and smiled. "We're home, Carson."

Printed in the United States
202553BV00003B/22-72/A